NIGHTTIME VOWS

His Lordship walked closer and closer to the door of Cassandra's quarters, where, by all that was right, he should leave her. "Will Dora come to help you undress?" he asked.

"I dismissed her for the night," Cassandra answered, feeling embarrassed at her ineptitude. Again, she asked herself if she would ever learn to be a lady of quality.

Words came against Lord Ranleigh's will. "Then I shall help you. The buttons—"

"Oh, how could I have forgotten?"

This was true; she could not have thought that she would need help in unbuttoning those tiny buttons which reached from her neck past her waist. In truth, she had not given the buttons a thought. She spoke quickly. "I shall sleep in my frock. I've done it before."

"That won't be necessary. If you do not wish to disturb Dora, and it is quite late, then I shall assist you. After all, I am your husband."

"In name only," Cassandra reminded him.

"And I shall honor that. I assure you that I will not be tempted beyond endurance. Our agreement will hold fast."

"That is your agreement, not mine," she answered. . . .

ELEGANT LOVE STILL FLOURISHES –
Wrap yourself in a Zebra Regency Romance.

A MATCHMAKER'S MATCH　　　　　　　(3783, $3.50/$4.50)
by Nina Porter
To save herself from a loveless marriage, Lady Psyche Veringham pretends to be a bluestocking. Resigned to spinsterhood at twenty-three, Psyche sets her keen mind to snaring a husband for her young charge, Amanda. She sets her cap for long-time bachelor, Justin St. James. This man of the world has had his fill of frothy-headed debutantes and turns the tables on Psyche. Can a bluestocking and a man about town find true love?

FIRES IN THE SNOW　　　　　　　　　(3809, $3.99/$4.99)
by Janis Laden
Because of an unhappy occurrence, Diana Ruskin knew that a secure marriage was not in her future. She was content to assist her physician father and follow in his footsteps . . . until now. After meeting Adam, Duke of Marchmaine, Diana's precise world is shattered. She would simply have to avoid the temptation of his gentle touch and stunning physique – and by doing so break her own heart!

FIRST SEASON　　　　　　　　　　　(3810, $3.50/$4.50)
by Anne Baldwin
When country heiress Laetitia Biddle arrives in London for the Season, she harbors dreams of triumph and applause. Instead, she becomes the laughingstock of drawing rooms and ballrooms, alike. This headstrong miss blames the rakish Lord Wakeford for her miserable debut, and she vows to rise above her many faux pas. Vowing to become an Original, Letty proves that she's more than a match for this eligible, seasoned Lord.

AN UNCOMMON INTRIGUE　　　　　　(3701, $3.99/$4.99)
by Georgina Devon
Miss Mary Elizabeth Sinclair was rather startled when the British Home Office employed her as a spy. Posing as "Tasha," an exotic fortune-teller, she expected to encounter unforeseen dangers. However, nothing could have prepared her for Lord Eric Stewart, her dashing and infuriating partner. Giving her heart to this haughty rogue would be the most reckless hazard of all.

A MADDENING MINX　　　　　　　　(3702, $3.50/$4.50)
by Mary Kingsley
After a curricle accident, Miss Sarah Chadwick is literally thrust into the arms of Philip Thornton. While other women shy away from Thornton's eyepatch and aloof exterior, Sarah finds herself drawn to discover why this man is physically and emotionally scarred.

My Sweet Valentine

Irene Loyd Black

ZEBRA BOOKS
KENSINGTON PUBLISHING CORP.

To Jim
With Love

ZEBRA BOOKS are published by

Kensington Publishing Corp.
475 Park Avenue South
New York, NY 10016

First Printing: January, 1994

Printed in the United States of America

One

With a pad of cheap paper in hand, Cassandra Edwards sat on a small hillock above Ranleigh Hall. Her eyes glanced first at the sprawling house, and then at the paper, as carefully she drew the many peaked roofs, and placed the long narrow windows in their proper places.

Huge double doors graced the front, and at each end were round towers with crenellated roofs, used years ago, so she had been told, to guard against invaders from the sea.

She had worked on the sketch since Valentine's Day, long past in February. It had been too cold then to come to the hillock, but now it was early May, and the sun warmed her.

She stretched and sighed deeply. Then, meticulously, she drew a heart around the beautiful house and added lines that resembled lace. Although she had never owned a valentine with white lace, she remembered well when, years ago, a friend had received one from her parents. She remembered, too, how pretty she had thought the valentine, and how much she had wanted one of her own.

Time passed swiftly as she labored. There was no hurry, and every line must needs be just right. Finally, satisfied, she held her masterpiece out in front of her and smiled. It would be next year's valentine to herself.

Moving her gaze from the drawing to the valley below, she stared at the awesome, stately house that towered majestically skyward, to overpower, she was sure, everything that surrounded it, the tree-covered hillock on which she sat, and the blue-black sea that stretched as far eastward as the eye could see. High waves beat rhythmically against the sharp outcropping of huge rocks that constituted the Suffolk coast, while, inland, to the west, undulating, daisy-sprinkled meadows and fields of new crops flourished under the quiet sun.

Her gaze came back to the manor, where splendidly kept gardens and wide, spacious lawns had replaced what used to be a moat. Cold chills traversed her spine; Ranleigh Hall was the most beautiful place she had ever seen.

Lichen climbed up the dark walls to form an archway over massive front doors that shut out the likes of Cassandra, an orphan from Sister Martha's orphanage.

Cassandra was well aware of the great chasm that separated the polite world of Ranleigh Hall and the world of the lower orders in which she lived. But one could dream, she told herself, and this she did, every day, even at night when sleep lingered in the twilight of her mind. Visions of upstairs maids and finely dressed butlers bowing before her danced through her head. *As mistress of Ranleigh Hall, a lady's maid will be subject to my every desire.*

She laughed softly. Why should one's dreams be small? After all, 'twere only dreams.

And, of course, Lord Ranleigh would be there, wanting to please. And she would no longer have to go barefoot.

This day, the new grass felt cool beneath her feet. At the orphanage she was allowed only one pair of shoes each year. During the spring and summer she wore shoes on the Sabbath, and then only to church.

As she watched, a tall man sitting a handsome spotted horse cantered to the stables. A groom rushed to take the reins, and the man slid gracefully to the ground. With a determined, masculine stride, he made his way across the parklike grounds and disappeared behind the huge house. As her heart pounded against her rib cage, she wondered if this could be Lord Ranleigh. She had heard that his beautiful wife had recently died, and on-dits had it that he was worldly and hard-crusted, that he ruled over Ranleigh Hall with an iron fist.

But the Lord Ranleigh of Cassandra's dreams was soft and loving, considerate beyond bearing. He held her close and covered her face with the most delicious kisses. Even though she had seen twenty summers, she had never been kissed, and when she fantasized about the Lord of Ranleigh Hall kissing her—and sometimes he even touched her throbbing bosom—the strangest feelings came over her, making her want to do it.

It meant what her Mama had said a woman did with a man because it was her duty, and it had something to do with begetting babies.

That was all Cassandra knew. Surely her Mama was different from her, she thought, feeling flushed all over. She would gladly welcome his lordship's kisses.

Other fantasies entertained Cassandra. As Countess of Ranleigh, she would wear beautiful gowns when receiving morning callers, as she understood the upper orders did. She would go to London to enjoy the Season, her handsome earl by her side, and she would be the envy of all the chits who were looking for husbands. They would flirt with his lordship outrageously, to no avail, for he would have eyes only for her.

Lord Ranleigh loved her as no one had ever loved her. . . .

Two thick braids of sun-streaked blond hair hung

down Cassandra's back, the ends tied with white rags torn from a worn-out sheet she kept hidden in her room at the orphanage. A yank on one of the braids jerked her from her wonderful, fanciful dream. She swore under her breath and, jumping to her feet, squealed and whipped around, dropping her glasses and her precious valentine in her fright.

A slim-hipped man wearing skintight breeches and highly polished Wellington boots stood toe to toe with her. When her startled gaze moved to his face she saw that he was laughing.

His eyes were laughing, too, but they were like shards of blue ice, and an instant chill engulfed Cassandra. He was extremely handsome, but there was something terribly wrong about him.

Seldom did Cassandra judge so quickly, but as she stared into those cold eyes, she was overwhelmed with a feeling that something sinister lurked behind the laughter.

This could not be *her* Lord Ranleigh.

Lifting her chin, she asked, "What's so demme funny?"

"You. Who are you spying on?"

"I wasn't spying. I'm a bird-watcher."

His sensuous lips curled into a smile. "I don't believe you." He inclined his head to the valley below and asked, "What's so fascinating about that mountain of stone?"

He reached down and retrieved her glasses and handed them to her. Then, without looking, the valentine. She did not thank him, for, after all, he had startled her into dropping them.

"Don't call Ranleigh Hall a mountain of stone," she said with firmness. "It's a wonderful place."

"I shall tell my brother. Mayhap he will invite you to supper."

Cassandra felt his gaze move over her, her faded

dress, her bare feet. Even though she did not like the man, she was embarrassed. "I must needs go," she said, quickly turning away.

He grabbed her arm, and not gently. "You haven't told me who you are. How old are you? Four and ten, I would guess."

"You guess wrong. I've seen twenty summers—"

"And much too pretty for my brother." With his free hand he reached to touch her chin. "The mighty Lord of Ranleigh Hall would not know what to do with a gel with big gray eyes such as yours. I think I shall keep you for myself. Do you come here to spy often? I'll meet you . . ."

She slapped his hand away. "I think not. Now unhand me, or you shall feel the sting of my hand on your face."

"Oh, I like chits with fire—"

Cassandra's face burned with anger; unbidden tears stung her eyes. This . . . this jackanapes had ruined everything. Should she return to the hillock, he would think she had come to meet him. She jerked her arm free from his biting fingers and started running, swearing with every step.

The tall trees, with their wide, sweeping branches, swallowed her up, but raucous laughter followed her, and the leaves rustled with the sound. She looked back once to see if he was following her.

He wasn't, and soon she was on the narrow trail that led over the hillock and back to the orphanage, two kilometers away. Slowing her pace, she folded the valentine and slipped it inside the bosom of her faded dress.

In her small office, which once had been a receiving room in the ancient house, Sister Martha sat behind a scarred desk and stared at the missive. What was she to do? Raising her lorgnette, which hung from a ribbon attached to her right shoulder, she read the missive again, this time aloud:

Dear Sister Martha:

I come to you for a favor. I am aware that you place your orphans in fine homes as maids and grooms. I am in need of a wife. She must needs be loving, kind, and above all chaste. I have no interest in a gel for wifely duties, but my son and heir is in need of a loving governess. He is not a healthy child, and it is imperative that he be treated with love and tenderness. I've tried professional governesses, but they do not stay, and this seems to upset his condition. So I have concluded to remedy that by marrying someone you would recommend. I should hope that she would be a comely gel, as beauty is always pleasant to look upon, but that is not entirely necessary.

He had signed simply, "Ranleigh."

"The cold bastard," Sister Mary said, and then she crossed herself for forgiveness. Even though she was known as Sister Martha, and the orphanage went by that name, there was no affiliation with a church. Therefore, its support depended entirely on patronage. Lord Ranleigh was its most liberal patron. Many times she had gone to him for help for her children, and he had never turned her away empty-handed.

Now he was calling her debt.

She immediately thought of Cassandra Edwards, who should never have, at fifteen, come to the orphanage at all had she had another place to go when her parents were killed in a carriage accident. Out of pity, she had taken the young gel in, letting her help with the younger children for her keep.

It was true that at the orphanage the gels were trained to serve as maids to the Quality. That was the best she could do. The boys were taught to be grooms and coach-men and footmen, with the hope that someday they would become butlers. She wished she could be more sophisticated in her endeavor, but all her children were taught to read and write, and to cipher.

Sister Martha mused worriedly: *Cassandra has a sharp mind, is well read, and is much too beautiful to be a lady's maid.*

Leaning back in her chair, she tapped the palm of her hand with the now folded missive. Her mind went back to the day she had found two starving children alongside the road, abandoned to the elements. She had brought them home with her, home being this big old house, which was much too large to hold one spinster lady.

An only child, she had inherited the house from her parents, who had inherited it from an uncle of unknown wealth.

From the two children the household had grown with abandoned waifs, sometimes as many as thirty at a time, until it was called Sister Martha's Orphanage by the townspeople of Wickham Market, located near the Suffolk coast. To live up to the sisterly image, she began wearing simple white day dresses, high-top black shoes, and a white muslin headdress that fell to her shoulders. A black riband around her forehead held it in place.

Her once dark hair was now gray, and she could not remember the time passing. Her life had been full, she thought, as she sat there smiling happily. But when her thoughts returned to Cassandra Edwards, the smile vanished and a frown formed on her already wrinkled brow. Cassie was somehow special, very like the daughter she had never had.

And there was another problem. The gcl should have already been placed, but she was much too beautiful for any woman of the upper orders to hire for house-hold help, not even as a lady's maid.

11

Cassie deserves to be loved.

Shaking her head, Sister Martha read again Lord Ranleigh's words, "I have no interest in a gel for wifely duties."

A long time passed while her thoughts ran rampant. She knew of no one else who would love and nurture His Lordship's heir, and she knew of nowhere else for her Cassie to go.

There's nothing to it, she decided at last; *Cassandra it shall be.* But she would not tell her that she was going to Ranleigh Hall to become a governess for a five-year-old, *not* to be Lord Ranleigh's wife in the biblical sense. That would not do, for Cassandra Edwards, with her ready smile, was filled with pride, and she desired to live life to its fullest, in every sense.

She deserved to be a wife.

Not in any manner was she the subservient type.

If approached in the proper manner by His Lordship, mayhap she would take the position of nursemaid at Ranleigh Hall, but marrying the earl to be something other than his wife?

Never.

Should she know.

Taking a piece of parchment from her desk, Sister Martha lifted a feathered quill from the ink pot and wrote in flowing script:

My dear Lord Ranleigh:

After much contemplation and prayer, I have concluded that Cassandra Edwards will be the perfect mate for you. For five years, since she was fifteen, she has helped with the younger children at the orphanage, and her love for them is boundless. You could not find a kinder person to care for your heir.

Cassandra is subservient, rather pretty in an undeveloped way., and I am sure will expect no more from Your Lordship than that which you are willing to give. As far

as being chaste, she fills this requirement without ques-
tion. I am positive the innocent gel has never had an
unchaste thought in her life. Her father, before he was
killed in a carriage accident, along with Cassandra's
mother, was vicar at St. Martin's in Wickham Market.

Your Lordship, your future wife's upbringing was poor
in nature, but rich with love, and discipline was not
spared . . .

The pen stopped writing and stayed suspended above
the paper, for what Sister Martha had just written was
not true at all, except about the strict discipline. There
had been no love in the vicar's home, just hell-fire and
brimstone. She remembered too well Cassandra's terrible nightmares when she came to the orphanage to live.

She had cried out in the night against the beatings
for some alleged sin, promising that she would sin no
more, and many times, she, Sister Martha, had held
Cassie and comforted her until she could sleep again.

Mayhap that is why she is so special.

The front door of the old house slammed, and immediately Sister Martha placed the unfinished missive
in a drawer and closed it sharply. Cassie's bare feet
against the wood floor had a distinctive sound.

Pushing back from the desk, Sister Martha rose and
went to the door, calling out, "Cassie, come here,
please."

On the second step of the stairway, Cassandra turned.
"Yes, Sister?"

The pained look on her face startled Sister Martha.
"What is wrong, Cassie? You look as if you've seen a
ghost."

"I haven't seen a ghost, Sister. I'm just very, very
angry."

"At whom?"

"At a man who claimed to be Lord Ranleigh's
brother. But I am not sure he told the truth. There was

13

something frightening about him. I felt it. I'm certain he was putting me on. Nothing evil could come from Ranleigh Hall."

"Lord Ranleigh has a brother," Sister Martha said pensively. "I hear he's a rakehell of the first water. Still, this man could have been an imposter." She studied Cassandra's face for a moment. "Did he get out of line with you, try to ravish you?"

"No, except he asked that I meet him."

Sister Martha laughed. "Dear, that is no reason to become upset. It is perfectly understandable that a man would want to know you better. You are quite beautiful."

She looked at Cassandra's pointed breasts, pushing against the simple dress she wore, and sighed deeply.

"You don't understand," Cassandra said. "When I have time away from home"—she called the orphanage *home*—"I go to the hillock overlooking Ranleigh Hall and dream about living there. 'Tis wonderful fun. Now I can't go—"

"Do you dream about being married to Lord Ranleigh?"

"Oh, yes. And he's the most kind, gentle man. Even before Lady Ranleigh died, I dreamed of him. I know 'tis sinful—"

"Stuff! Every gel dreams. I did. But now I have wonderful news for you." Sister Martha stepped back and went to regain her chair behind the desk, saying to Cassandra, "Mayhap you should sit first."

Cassandra lowered herself into a straight-backed chair just inside the door. Her bare feet protruding from under her skirt, two years too short, she demurely clasped her hands together in her lap, as she had been taught to do.

But Sister Martha did not see an urchin to whom life had been most unkind. She saw a lady of quality wearing a fashionable gown that hugged her tiny waist and

14

showed to advantage her wonderfully shaped, youthful bosom.

And her feet were not bare. Shoes with roses on the toes covered them, and her blond hair lay in layers of sunshine and burnished gold around her shoulders.

High cheekbones stood out wide and fine beneath her almond-shaped, smoky gray eyes.

Dark eyebrows and long curling lashes framed those eyes, which, in Sister Martha's vision, were laughing with happiness.

Tears fell warm on her cheeks.

That's what I want for my Cassie, the happiness she deserves.

"I'm glad to know that you used to daydream," Cassandra said. "I thought I was the only one. 'Tis quite foolish."

"Not at all. Youth is full of dreams and desires, which take one from the real world. I had them all. Now I dream for my children."

Sister Martha was stalling; she simply did not know how to tell Cassandra that soon she would be living at Ranleigh Hall, as the Countess of Ranleigh. If only she could tell her the whole of it, she thought prayerfully.

Time passed, and the silence grew heavy.

Then, as if she were standing on a ledge about to jump into deep water—and she could not swim—Sister Martha drew a deep breath and began. "I have wonderful news for you, Cassie. Lord Ranleigh has asked permission to pay his addresses to you."

Cassandra sat forward in her chair so fast that she almost plunged out onto the floor. "Don't flummery me. Why would Lord Ranleigh want to court a chit from an orphanage when all of London is at his feet? I hear gels drool when he enters a room, not to mention their Mamas."

Sister Martha gave a false smile. "But none as beau-

15

tiful as you." A pause, and then: "Your chastity attracts him."

"How would he know I'm innocent?" She glared at Sister Martha accusingly. "You are funning me. Just because I told you that I daydream of being married to Lord Ranleigh, whom I've never seen. Dreams are stupid—"

"Sometimes dreams come true, Cassie. In truth, Lord Ranleigh wishes to marry you."

Sister Martha silently thanked God that she had finally told at least half of the bizarre story, and then she watched in dismay the color drain totally from Cassandra Edwards's face as she, moving in slow motion, toppled to the floor.

Sister Martha yanked hard on a drawer, grabbed a vial of vinaigrette from inside it, and rushed to bend over her Cassandra, waving the vial under her nose.

"Wake up, you silly gel. You're the last one I would expect to have a fit of the vapors."

She slapped her face gently, then a little harder.

Still, Cassandra lay there, pale as a ghost and as lifeless as a dead hen.

The thought entered Sister Martha's mind that mayhap the news had killed the gel. She gave her face another hard whack. If she were dead she would not feel it.

Cassandra moaned and turned her head from side to side.

"That's it, dear, wake up," Sister Martha pleaded worriedly as she continued to wave the vinaigrette in front of the swooning gel's face.

At last Cassandra's gray eyes flew open. She pushed herself up and slapped at the vinaigrette. "Why do you jest me?"

"I'm not jesting you, Cassie. His Lordship has asked that I recommend a wife to him, and I believe with all my heart that you will be the perfect mate—"

16

"Why so? His Lordship and I live in two different worlds. His rich, mine poor . . . no offense intended. I'm of the lower orders. 'Tis simple as that."

"But, my dear, you can learn how to go on in polite society. I've trained you as best I could, and His Lordship will teach you, I am sure."

Sister Martha was sure of no such thing. He had made it perfectly plain that he only wanted a nursemaid for his heir, and she had called him a bastard for his words.

She went on: "I know for a fact that Lord Ranleigh's a kind man. Many times he has helped me with the orphanage, giving great sums when I explained our need."

"Most likely he bought this dress," Cassandra said sarcastically. "Well, I shall ask him for a new one."

"Cassie, you must needs not do that! I believe His Lordship is looking for a more subservient type. In due time he will furnish a wonderful wardrobe without your asking. Just think, you will be traveling to London for the Season, buying new gowns and walking on Bond Street, with your abigail trailing two steps behind you."

Cassandra jumped to her feet.

Sister Martha went back to sit behind her desk. She looked at Cassandra, who, by now, had walked the length of the small room and back again. Sister Martha felt pity, and the uncertainty of what she had done rose in a new wave of anxiety.

For a long moment she waited in pensive silence, then, with the toss of her head, she set her small chin in a characteristic stubborn line and told herself that if she had been a doubting vacillator she would never have brought those two starving children home with her all those years ago. But she had done it without thinking, and that was what she must needs do now. Where else was there for her Cassie to go?

"Is it really true?" Cassandra asked in a wavering voice.

Tears again clouded Sister Martha's eyes. " 'Tis really true, Cassie. God has smiled on you."

"If so, my heart will burst."

"That's how it should be when a gel is to be married. Now go to your room and get down on your knees and thank *Him*, and while you are at it, ask for guidance. I shall answer His Lordship's missive and request for a week in which to prepare you for the marriage. Surely, by squeezing the coffers, one new gown can be managed . . ."

Two

A cold dampness permeated the old house. In a small room on the second floor, Cassandra, after hiding her precious valentine in the bottom of a drawer, poked at the fire and felt its warmth. Soon the children would gather to hear her read a story before being tucked into bed, and then Sister Martha, though her aging legs would hardly allow it, would climb the stairs and kiss each child good night, staying for a moment and visiting with them individually about their day.

Besides Cassandra and Ellen Terry, a fifteen-year-old who also helped with the younger ones, there were ten children. Each year the number was smaller, for Sister Martha no longer could care for the large number that once occupied the house.

For a very small wage and her room and board, a housekeeper, Mrs. Daly, ran the house; there was Cook, a cheerful woman with a protruding stomach, and Lacewell, the groom, who worked the stables and trained the younger boys. A gardener lived in the gate-keeper's cottage and grew vegetables and fruit for the table.

The children helped with the chores, even the gardening, and Cassandra gladly did her share. She was adept at everything there was to do, but mostly she helped with the children, and she loved reading to them. This night, her mind was not on the story she would read. Nonetheless, she went to the shelf on which the books were stacked and pulled down Shakespeare's *Romeo and Juliet*.

Having read the tragic love story many times, she knew it by heart. The children did, too, so if her mind strayed, she reasoned, they could pick up where she left off and improvise.

Often they acted out the parts, and this was great fun for them, and for Cassandra, most especially when Ellen Terry could be coaxed to play the part of Juliet.

As she waited, sitting in one of the chairs that flanked the fireplace, Cassandra thought about Ranleigh Hall and Lord Ranleigh. Shock still held her in its grip, and she found it very difficult to believe what was happening to her. Surely it was an incredible dream. Any moment now she would awaken in her narrow cot, plucked back to reality, and she would once again be Cassandra Edwards, an orphan who belonged nowhere. And she would dress hurriedly and go help Cook prepare porridge and fresh bread for the children's breakfast, and Sister Martha would suddenly appear and tell her that she had only been funning about Lord Ranleigh's marriage proposal.

"Of course Lord Ranleigh did not send a missive asking to pay his addresses to you," she would say. "And marriage! What a preposterous idea!"

Ellen was the first to come. She was stunningly beautiful, Cassandra thought, as she let her gaze move over the child/woman with shining ebony hair and startling, deep blue eyes, which seemed as deep as the sea, and as restless.

"What does that faraway look in your eyes mean, Cassandra Edwards?" Ellen asked, giving a rare smile. "Have you been dreaming about the wonderful Lord Ranleigh again?"

Cassandra and Ellen shared the same attic space, and Cassandra often confided in Ellen about her trips to the hillock, and her fantasies of being mistress of Ranleigh Hall. Now, she felt herself blushing as she said defensively, "It costs nothing to dream."

She wanted to tell Ellen about her good fortune so badly that she could hardly breathe, but she would not. Not until she, herself, was convinced that it was true. What if it were not so? How foolish she would feel. Away from Sister Martha, insurmountable doubts gnawed at her mind. Dreams were so much easier to manage, she mused to herself, and remained mum to Ellen.

"Well, I have something to tell you," Ellen said, her blue eyes dancing in the semidarkness. "Something wonderful."

Cassandra, rising from her chair, went to light another candle, placing it on the mantelpiece.

She gave Ellen a kind smile. "What good news, Ellen? Did the post bring you a missive?"

Many times Ellen had written a message to herself, then pretended that the post had brought it from her mother.

"You know that Mama has never written to me, that I only pretend. But this day I do have some news. When Lacewell went for supplies I rode with him into Wickham Market, where a circus is performing, and the man there, the owner and seemingly a very intelligent man, told me he knew Mama, and he also said that she spoke of me often."

Cassandra, sure that the "seemingly intelligent man" knew nothing of Ellen's Mama, sighed deeply. Ellen drew attention wherever she went, and she would believe anything, so hungry was she for news of the woman who had left her at the orphanage when she was but a child of three, promising to come back for her but never coming, not even for a visit.

The news, true or false, had put Ellen in a gay mood, and when the children gathered around the warm fire she performed brilliantly for them. Afterwards she helped Cassandra tuck them into their beds, humming softly to herself.

"Ellen," Cassandra said when they had repaired to the attic, tiredly seeking their own beds, "promise me that you will not do anything foolish."

"Like what?"

"Like believing a man who claims to know your mother. Or going into London looking for her. Wait until you are older. I've heard that London can gobble up a young gel—"

"What are you, a mind reader?" Pain, almost anger, dripped from Ellen's words.

"No, I'm not a mind reader," Cassandra answered. She reached to pat Ellen's shoulder consolingly. "I'm older than you, Ellen, and I love you very much. For five years now you have been like a little sister to me, so I want you to promise that you will not do anything foolish before talking it over with me, or with Sister Martha."

Ellen scoffed. "She would forbid me to leave the orphanage. The most she has to offer is a position as a lady's maid."

"Then come to me." When silence met Cassandra's plea she implored again, "Pray, promise me, Ellen."

Ellen did not promise. Instead, she turned her face to the wall, and only an occasional smothered sob broke the heavy silence that hovered over the tiny space—it could hardly be called a room—in which they slept.

Nonetheless, Cassandra was forever thankful for what she had. The attic afforded some privacy, and she had the necessities. In the semidarkness, her eyes perused the room. This night, the attic seemed almost a mansion to her. She supposed it was because she would soon be leaving it.

A cracked looking glass hung over a makeshift stack of drawers where she and Ellen kept their meager clothes. A tin urn held cold water, and there was a tin washbasin in which to wash one's face and to soak one's feet.

Once each week, she would bring hot water from the kitchen and pour it into a round tub at the dark end of the attic. Sitting in the warm water, using homemade soap and a rag with which to scrub, to Cassandra it was pure luxury.

A homemade, hand-hooked rug covered the wood floor around hers and Ellen's cots; it felt warm to Cassandra's feet when, restless and unable to sleep, she quietly slipped from her bed and lit a candle. There was something she must needs do. Taking from the drawer her much neglected diary, which she only wrote in when something monumental had happened, she wrote down the day's happenings, even stating her disbelief.

And then she took the valentine she had this day drawn and gazed at it longingly, while wonderful, fanciful dreams once again invaded her mind.

As she sat thus, time passed without notice. Outside the narrow window the moon sent its silver light down onto the trees. Shadows danced on the ground and fireflies pierced the darkness with bits of orange fire.

At last Cassandra rose and hid her diary and her drawing of Ranleigh Hall in the bottom of the quilted satchel she had carried when she had arrived at the orphanage. Then, after stealing a glance at Ellen to make sure she was not watching, she went to stand before the looking glass.

After loosening her hair from the thick braids, she brushed it one hundred times. Suddenly a terrible quietness was upon her, and on the whole of the attic. Again she looked over at Ellen.

The sobs had stopped, but an inaudible word escaped

the gel's lips. Cassandra stood for a moment, waiting, but when silence again fell, she snuffed the candle and returned to her cot.

With a ragged quilt pulled up over her shoulders, she finally slept, though a troubled sleep, with wild, passionate dreams tumbling through her mind.

But there were dark moments when things were not quite as she had imagined: Lord Ranleigh was oddly cold and unrelenting.

The man she'd only this day met, who said he was Lord Ranleigh's brother, trampled the periphery of her mind. In the dream, as had been so in reality, something evil hid behind his cold blue eyes.

The dream made her unhappy, she thought to herself when she was awakened by the clanging of the bell over her head. The rope had been pulled by Cook, telling her, Cassandra, that it was five o'clock and time to come belowstairs to begin the day's work.

Cassandra sat up. Across from her, Ellen's cot was empty.

Cassandra scampered across the floor, splashed cold water on her face, and quickly braided her hair into the usual thick, plaits. Taking advantage of being alone, she took time to peer into the looking glass.

Her face scrunched in disapproval. She looked like a young gel, too young to be getting married. Little wonder Lord Ranleigh's brother thought she had seen only four and ten summers. The bell clapped again, louder this time.

Quickly, she wound the braids around her head, forming a crown, and pinned them with the few hairpins she treasured as if they were gold. She decided that with her hair pulled back, she looked much older, and her neck appeared longer, more swanlike. She had heard that that was the thing with the *ton,* and if it were the thing with the snobbish *ton,* then it must be the thing with Lord Ranleigh. She wished so much to please her future husband.

Her future husband! She could not believe it, but now there was no more time to flit away bemoaning her looks, for she must needs report to Cook.

So, before the bell could clatter one more time, or worse yet, have Cook come looking for her, she descended the stairs, taking the steps two at a time, rushing onward into the cobble-floored kitchen.

After breakfast had been dispensed with, Sister Martha said to Cassandra, "We must needs go into town to purchase cloth for your wedding gown." She had not slept much, for guilt rode her conscience. She added, "You may wear your shoes, and last night I lengthened a dress for you to wear."

"Thank you, but why? 'Tis not Sunday."

Sister Martha smiled. "We just might see Lord Ranleigh, though I doubt that we will. I understand he does not frequent Wickham Market overly much. His overseer, or a servant of the household, goes for supplies."

"Then you were not jesting about His Lordship wanting to marry me?"

Sister Martha felt her gaze, her questioning look. "I would not jest about a thing so important."

She then left the parlor, returning almost immediately with a piece of parchment, on which the waxed seal had been broken. She handed it to Cassandra. "This was delivered this morning. Read for yourself."

Which Cassandra did: *"Sister Martha, this is to inform you that I shall call for Cassandra Edwards on twelve May, before noon."*

It was signed *Ranleigh."*

Cassandra stared at the missive, and at last let herself fully believe that Lord Ranleigh would come for her. A lump the size of an egg formed in her throat, and her thoughts ran wild with plans: They would have a beautiful church wedding, or better yet, they would marry in the chapel at Ranleigh Hall, with all the servants in attendance. In this way her husband would be telling them they had a new mistress, Cassandra, Countess of Ranleigh.

From far off she heard Sister Martha's voice. "Cassie, Cassie—"

"What is it?" Cassandra asked.

"Are you all right? Pray, do not have another spell of the vapors."

"I'm all right. But it's so difficult for me to believe that a dream can actually come true."

Sister Martha thought for a moment, measuring her words. She felt it prudent that she again warn the gel that things were not always what they seemed. If she could only do that, her guilt would not weigh so heavily.

She started with a little laugh and said, "Dear, marriage is difficult, and there's a certain amount of disillusionment on an innocent's part. Pray, do not be too fanciful in your hopes."

That was the best she could do and not tell Cassandra the whole of it, Sister Martha reasoned. Silently she beseeched God for a miracle for the precious gel, and she prayed for forgiveness for her lies. It was not her intention to deceive.

"I know what Mama told me," Cassandra said. "But I am not like her. I shall welcome His Lordship's kisses and *that other* which I know he will want to do. It was just that Papa was so everlastingly mean to Mama that she turned away when he wanted to touch her. I often heard them in their room at night, quarreling fiercely. Loud slaps would follow, and then I could hear Mama sobbing while the bedsprings creaked. But Lord Ranleigh is a kind man, not like Papa at all."

"I pray that is so," Sister Martha said, and later, when they were on their way into town in an old, timeworn

26

chaise, with Sister Martha handling the ribbons, Cassandra reached out to pat her hand. "You worry overly much, Sister. Things will be just wonderful."

Sister Martha felt the love and concern, the pat carried. She did not answer. Scolding herself for being such a worry cat, she asked herself if it was not her duty to do the best she could by her children.

Well, this is the best I can do for my Cassie, and as far as Lord Ranleigh is concerned, I have not a feather of concern. He is getting a bargain.

As the chestnut mare stepped lively and the chaise bounced over the hard-packed dirt road, Sister Martha thought about the children she had reared. While they were small, they were not much worry so long as she could feed and clothe them. And the upper orders around had been most generous, but that was not so now.

She did not know the reason, except that times seemed harder, or—and she thought this most likely, since the flamboyant Prince Regent had come to rule in the King's place—the nobility were so caught up in their own hedonistic world that hungry children were at the bottom of their list of concerns.

This was not so with Lord Ranleigh. He had been most kind.

Sister Martha's thoughts lingered for a moment on Ellen Terry. Ellen was so troubled, and so restless. *What will happen to the child?* Sister Martha asked herself.

After a while she put her worry about Ellen aside and began thinking of the dress she would stitch for Cassandra. Dwelling on that made her happy. How she wished she could employ a modiste, but why ponder on something that could not be helped? Simply, there was no money for a modiste.

It was not far from the orphanage in to town. Along the narrow, cobbled street, on the right-hand side of Berrington Street, there was a draper's shop. She pulled the horse to a stop and handed the ribbons to a waiting boy. She gave him a shilling, for one look at his ragged breeches and his hungry-lean face told her that he needed the coin much more than she, and she was momentarily tempted to ask him to come home with her and share what she could give.

Smiling broadly, he gave a half bow and said, "Thanks, Sister."

"You're welcome, son. We won't be long inside. If you will have the chaise back here in half an hour, I shall be pleased."

Sister Martha looked after him until he was out of sight, and then she went inside the shop, Cassandra at her side.

At the sound of the door opening and closing, a dour, platter-faced gel dressed all the crack in a pretty sprigged muslin day dress suddenly appeared. Her gaze immediately focused on Cassandra's dress, which Sister Martha had lengthened by adding a band of faded, mismatched fabric around its hem.

"Good . . . good morning, Sister. I'm Stella. Is there *something* I can do for you?"

"Oh, there most certainly is something you can do for me," Sister Martha replied with asperity. "I wish to purchase cloth for a wedding gown."

An infuriating laugh spilled from Stella's throat. Sister Martha was incensed. "I said, I wish to purchase cloth for a wedding dress. I prefer simple elegance, if you take my meaning."

"Oh, I do. I do. The dress is for whom, you or your daughter? She seems hardly old enough to wed—"

"Never you mind that. Show me the cloth, or shall I ask for Madame Tristan?"

In the whole of Sister Martha's long life, she had never spoken to Madame Tristan, but this young snit of a gel would never know it.

Lifting her small chin, she stared straight into the

haughty Stella's eyes, silently and flagrantly daring her to refuse to help her. She quickly concluded that the gel could only be jealous of Cassandra's beauty.

"Follow me," Stella said. Purposefully, she whipped around and strode to a bolt of delicate white silk.

Cassandra could hardly hide her amusement. More than once she had witnessed an example of Sister Martha's indomitable will. What a wonderful teacher! Knowing that the cost of silk would swallow much of the good Sister's meager budget, she stepped forward and said, "I do not wish to be married in silk." She went to another table, which held bolts of cheaper cloth in many colors, and began fingering the fabric. "I prefer this soft sarcenet—"

"For a wedding dress! To whom are you becoming leg shackled? Someone's groom?"

Before Sister Martha could give her a silencing look, Cassandra, lifting her chin ever so slightly, said, "To Lord Ranleigh of Ranleigh Hall."

She heard Sister Martha's groan.

Stella did not try to hide her amusement. She gave a snickering laugh. "Oh, no doubt. And I am marrying the Prince Regent, who already has one wife he does not want."

Sister Martha said without pause, "I beg your forgiveness—"

Cassandra hushed her. "I'll wager ten yards of your finest cloth—the silk you just tried to sell us—that the next time I favor your shop with my presence I will be Countess of Ranleigh."

This brought more laughter from Stella, and when it abated sufficiently she wiped tears from her eyes and said with obvious glee, "But I must needs know your name and where you live, else you will never return. Then how could I collect your debt?"

" 'Tis Cassandra Edwards, and I live at Sister Martha's orphanage. But you needn't bother to come to collect. I shall be living at Ranleigh Hall and, if you are still employed here, I will return to collect *your* debt, after I am Countess of Ranleigh."

"Do not worry about my being here. My mam owns the shop."

Sister Martha smiled as she pridefully listened to the exchange. A new sense of peace came over her. Obviously she had worried about Cassandra needlessly, for her Cassie had adroitly proven herself a woman to be reckoned with in dealing with Stella, and without losing the decorum of a proper lady.

"Shall we purchase three yards, perhaps four of this lovely sarcenet?" Cassandra asked.

The sarcenet was a creamy white. Sister Martha, opening her reticule, lifted her lorgnette to her eyes and counted the coins.

"Make it four yards and a half," she said to Stella. To herself, she murmured, "I shall make it long enough to cover her ugly shoes."

Oh, how she wished she could buy slippers with roses on the toes; when Stella had taken away the bolt of cloth to cut the required yardage, Sister Martha, tears clouding her eyes, said as much to Cassandra.

A lilt was in Cassandra's laughter. "To marry Lord Ranleigh, I would go to the church barefoot."

At the door, she turned back. "I shall return for my ten yards of silk."

"That will be when hell freezes over," Stella called to her, laughing a loud, boisterous laugh. "You must needs get wed to Lord Ranleigh. Getting leg shackled to someone else don't signify."

"Lord Ranleigh it will be," Cassandra countered.

The door closed behind them, and they were once again on the narrow street. Sister Martha scolded Cassandra good-naturedly. "You'll have tongues wagging."

"But not as much as when I really am Countess of Ranleigh."

Sister Martha knew that this was so. Lifting her lorgnette, she looked at her watch and saw that it was not yet time for the boy to return the mare and chaise. "Let's walk a ways," she said.

They walked slowly. Cassandra offered her arm, and Sister Martha took it, lest she stumble over the cobbles. Sun sparked the plain-fronted store windows, and they gazed leisurely at the goods for sale. When they came to a store displaying boots and slippers they stopped, and Sister Martha watched as Cassandra bent to rest her forehead on the glass, gazing intently at a pair of pink slippers with tiny heels and rosebuds on their toes.

When Cassandra turned to Sister Martha, she was smiling.

"What are you thinking?" Sister Martha asked.

"Just admiring the pink slippers."

Sister Martha pried further. "I know that something is going through your mind. That smug smile is very revealing."

The smile evolved into laughter. "I promise that someday I will tell you."

Just then the boy brought the mare and the chaise to the front of the draper's store, and the two women made their way to it. "I did what ye asked," the little boy said as he let down the step.

"That you did, son," Sister Martha answered.

Laboriously, she climbed up and took the ribbons, and then she reached out and gave the boy a gentle pat on the head. "I wish I could give you more."

He bowed with a flourish and the big smile again appeared on his lean face. " 'Twas my pleasure, Sister."

She bade him a warm goodbye as she cracked the whip over the mare's back, and they were quickly on their way back to the orphanage. Cassandra sat beside Sister Martha, the roll of sarcenet on her lap. The chaise bounced over the road and they talked about the dress they would make.

"I will cut and you can stitch," Sister Martha said.

While in the store, in a tattered copy of *Belle Assemblee,* she had seen a pattern that would be perfectly beautiful on Cassandra's slender, curvaceous body. It was very fetching, and she could imagine Lord Ranleigh's dark eyes focusing on the deep décolletage when he saw for the first time his bride-to-be. She felt her face flush with embarrassment at the wicked thought. But she was not so old, she told herself, that she had forgotten that desire and physical attraction were very important in falling in love. Oh, how she wanted His Lordship to love and cherish her Cassie.

How could he not?

She turned and looked at Cassandra.

She looks like a countess, or mayhap a queen, with her braided hair wound around her head like a crown.

"I don't stitch very fast," Cassandra said. "Mayhap it will take longer than a week to be ready for Lord Ranleigh."

"We shall work at night, after the children are put to bed. Ellen will help."

"I doubt that she will," said Cassandra. "In truth, I am hesitant to tell her of my good fortune. She is so unhappy. When I awoke this morning she was already gone, most likely working in the garden. She likes to be alone."

"I realize that's so, and I wish I could help. But my hands are tied, even though my heart breaks for her. In five years, she will be your age."

"I fear she will not be at the orphanage that long, Sister."

"She's of an age that she can leave anytime she chooses."

Cassandra started to tell Sister Martha about the man in the circus who had said he knew Ellen's mother, but she did not want to add to the good woman's worries, since there was nothing she could do about it in any case.

They fell into silence, and Cassandra looked at the lush countryside. They were skirting Ranleigh land, and only the hillock on which she had sat—her hillock—kept Ranleigh Hall from her view.

So deep in thought was Cassandra that Sister Martha's voice startled her, and what the woman said startled her even more.

"Cassie, I am getting old."

Cassandra protested immediately. "You are not so old, Sister. Your heart is still full of love." She paused for a moment before adding, "I don't suppose one's heart ever grows old, just tired. And I can understand that."

" 'Tis something else. In my dotage I hold my children too close. . . . I'm very reluctant to give them their wings; I'm very reluctant to let you go."

Cassandra reached out to squeeze her bony hand. "I shall always be close by should you need me, and I will visit you often."

Ahead, the white clapboard house that had for so many years been a haven for abandoned children loomed into view, tall, almost top heavy with its thatched roof. Gray shutters hung drunkenly askew, and windows were covered with boards, the glass gone, broken or claimed by age and rotting frames that could no longer hold it. Cassandra quickly changed the subject. "After I am Countess of Ranleigh, I shall return home and tell you what I was thinking when I saw those beautiful pink slippers."

Two big tears clung to Sister Martha's wrinkled cheeks, while a faint smile curved her thin lips. Her deep pain was obvious to Cassandra, and she wanted so much to hug the good woman. But then both of them would be crying, she reasoned, and kept quiet.

"You will always be my beautiful fair-haired gel, Cassie. I hope that someday you will own a trunk full of slippers with roses on the toes."

And she prayed that this would be so. She bit her lip and shook her head—if only Lord Ranleigh wanted a wife instead of a nursemaid for his sickly heir.

My Cassie deserves better.

As the chaise turned into the gate at the orphanage, Sister Martha murmured under her breath, "I pray that I've done the right thing."

And then she added, "Please, Lord . . ."

Three

Cassandra did not want the children at the orphanage to know that she would soon be married to Lord Ranleigh of Ranleigh Hall. Not until he really came for her. Even the youngest of the children stood in awe of the rambling edifice two kilometers away, with its peaked roofs and long, narrow windows framed by dark stone. Cassandra did, however, in a very private moment, tell Ellen.

It was the night after the trip to the draper's shop. The attic was in darkness; only the night creaks of the old house invaded the quietness, and an occasional cricket, which had sought the warmth of the house, could be heard chirping in its comfort.

Taking a deep breath, Cassandra inquired, "Ellen . . . are you asleep?"

"No. I'm waiting for you to tell me why you and Sister Martha went into town this day. I felt that you were being very secretive, doing something you did not want to share with me."

"We were," Cassandra answered truthfully. "But only because I feared you would be upset when you heard my wonderful news."

Cassandra heard the covers being thrown back and Ellen's bare feet hitting the floor. Then a lucifer was dragged against the windowsill. A circle of yellow light held Ellen's stunning face like a picture frame. Her blue eyes were alight with curiosity. "What wonderful news, Cassandra? You must needs tell me. I'll die if you don't."

Cassandra laughed. The worst was over. "I'm going to be married, Ellen."

"Married!" the fifteen-year-old shrieked. "Who to? Oh, Cassandra, please tell me before I burst."

"To Lord Ranleigh of Ranleigh Hall."

The silence was deafening. And then the comfortable cricket let forth a litany of chirps, the sound in the quietness as loud as sharp cracks of thunder.

After a long moment that seemed an eternity to Cassandra, Ellen set down the candle and asked, "Why would you lie to me, Cassandra Edwards? I thought I was your friend."

Cassandra bounded to the floor and embraced Ellen. "You are my friend, and besides Sister Martha you are the only one who knows. Except Lord Ranleigh, of course.

"You are teasing me," Ellen accused.

Cassandra went to the stack of drawers and took out a tattered Bible, a gift from her mother when she was six years old. "I swear on the Good Book that I am telling the truth. If you will sit down, I will tell you the whole of it."

And she did.

Ellen's blue eyes, set beneath heavy dark brows, stared incredulously into Cassandra's face.

"Doesn't that sound like a story out of a book?" Cassandra asked when she was through.

Ellen continued to stare.

At first Cassandra thought the shock of the incredible story had rendered her speechless. She reached out to touch Ellen and felt her recoil. Discernible anger had turned her beautiful blue eyes black.

36

"Don't be upset that I am leaving," Cassandra said. "Ranleigh Hall is just over the hill. I will come back often."

"I'm not upset because you are leaving."

"Then what is it, Ellen?"

More silence. To fill the void, Cassandra told her about meeting a man who claimed to be Lord Ranleigh's brother.

"Where?" Ellen asked.

"On the hillock overlooking Ranleigh Hall. He suggested that I meet him there. Of course I would not consent to such a meeting, and when I returned home Sister Martha had the wonderful news that I would marry Lord Ranleigh."

Cassandra realized she was chattering to give Ellen time to get over her pout, but Ellen did not seem inclined to do that and Cassandra asked, "Ellen why can't you be happy for me?"

Ellen's countenance darkened even more. "Why did Sister Martha not match Lord Ranleigh with me? After all, 'tis a marriage of convenience. It might as well have been me. I'm much prettier, and more versed on how to please the mighty Lord Ranleigh."

Cassandra's mouth dropped open, and a long moment passed before she could speak. Finally, she asked, "What do you mean, you are more versed on how to please His Lordship?"

"Because I am worldly. You're the daughter of a vicar. You're too good. A man likes a little forwardness in a woman. Mistresses are uninhibited. That is why so many of the nobility keep one . . . even more than one."

The anger in Ellen's voice was blatant. Still, Cassandra could only naively believe that it was the hurt inside Ellen that made her angry at someone's good fortune. Later, when she spoke to Sister Martha about it, she assured her that Ellen's resentment was temporary, that she would, given time, come around and be happy for her.

"I'm not so sure," Sister Martha said.

They were in the sewing room, where she had for years mended clothes for her children. This day, it was different—she was making a wedding gown, her first—and she hummed as she spread the paper pattern onto the sarcenet. She had worked into the night, making from memory a pattern of the gown she had seen in *La Belle Assemblee.*

Now she turned to Cassandra and measured her slender waist, her hips, and then her bosom.

Cassandra told her about Ellen's remarks about pleasing Lord Ranleigh. "Is that so?" she asked.

Sister Martha thought for a moment. Where Ellen's breasts were large and full, bulging even above her neckline, Cassandra's stood out in peaks and only hinted at fullness.

A spinster herself, Sister Martha had no idea which bosom would please a man more, and she was a little embarrassed at thinking on it.

There is one thing I am sure of, she mused silently: *Cassandra is more beautiful inside. But what does it matter? If all Lord Ranleigh is interested in is a loving mother for his heir, his new wife could be as ugly as a mud fence. His Lordship had said that beauty was not a requirement.*

The rambling thoughts were a detriment to the job ahead, and Sister Martha pushed them from her mind. Her Cassie would fare well, she assured herself, resuming her humming as her scissors snipped away at the sarcenet, while saying, "You're very adept at embroidery, Cassandra. Since we don't have lace with which to trim the dress, let's embroidery the sleeves, and mayhap around the hem. Happy things, like flowers and humming birds. And butterflies. All in white, of course, since this is a wedding dress."

Cassandra, sitting on a stool at the end of the worktable, took a sleeve and began working. She found her-self laughing with pure joy. This could not be happen-ing to her. A week seemed such a short time. "We truly will have to sew into the night."

Cassandra did not mind the work, for she knew that she would sleep very little, so rampant were her thoughts and anticipations. If only she had seen Lord Ranleigh. She could not help wondering what he looked like, how many summers he'd had, and if his real smile even re-motely resembled the smile she had so often conjured up in her dreams. *That* smile would melt any gel's heart.

She set upon Sister Martha to tell her more. "Tell me more about Lord Ranleigh, Sister. Has he been here at the orphanage when I was not here? Before I meet with him, I so much want something to go on besides the pictures I have drawn in my mind."

She stitched away on the small sleeve, her fingers flying.

"His Lordship has been here only once," Sister Martha said, adding, "Most usually I went to Ranleigh Hall when I asked for help in feeding and clothing my children."

"Tell me—"

"He's a splendid dresser. I noticed that right away. No doubt his clothes are from London's finest tailors. He is a tall man, with broad shoulders. He seems to exude strength. His stride, when he walks across the room, is very purposeful, with no wasted motion. I saw him as all business."

"Is . . . is he handsome?" Cassandra asked, and then again, "Tell me about his smile."

"He seldom smiles, and he's handsome in a rugged sort of way. His eyes are very dark, very penetrating . . . very cold. I remember a feeling came over me that something in his life had hurt him terribly, and that it showed in those eyes. I cannot imagine what it was."

A pause, and then, "I remembering thinking at the

time that he had everything a man could desire. He's Lord of Ranleigh Hall, which is awesome. I was very, very impressed."

"Mayhap he's grieving for his late wife," said Cassandra. "I've heard she was quite beautiful."

"I saw him *before* she died, and he was the same. No, Cassie, now that I think deeper on it, there was definitely something bothering His Lordship. Even when he smiled, the pain was there, in his eyes."

In Kenmere, Lord Ranleigh's London town house in Belgrade Square, His Lordship rolled away from his mistress's naked body, which was wet with perspiration, and sighed with pleasure. He was spent. "Elsa, you are superb," he told her as he pushed himself up and sat on the side of the bed, reaching for his breeches.

Sharp nails scraped his back. Not meant, he knew, to hurt, but to seduce. "Not again," he said firmly.

"What is wrong? Are you losing your manhood? Am I no longer pretty enough?"

He laughed. "It won't work, Elsa. I am going to the club. Your carriage is waiting out front."

Bounding out of bed, she flung herself at him, swearing in Spanish.

He caught and held her flailing arms in a firm grip. "Calm yourself, Elsa. You know your temper tantrums will not work with me."

Elsa Cordley was half Spanish, half English. Her mother carried the Spanish blood. Lord Ranleigh smiled. His mistress had inherited her mother's temper, and her beauty.

"You're a jackanapes, Ranleigh," Elsa said. "If you were not such a cold-hearted bastard, you would marry me, now that she's dead. I would gladly warm your bed every night—"

Lord Ranleigh felt his jaws clench. He pushed her

from him. "There's never even been a hint from me that marriage was in the offing. I have no desire to be leg shackled to any gel."

This was true, he told himself. He would marry Sister Martha's charge because it was convenient for him to do so. He saw no other way. And, in truth, he mused, if it were not for his strong libido, he would not be here with Elsa.

After dressing quickly, in a coat of blue superfine, fawn breeches, a perfectly folded, pristine white cravat, and highly polished top boots, he went to the door and turned back to give the naked woman a half smile. Her flowing black hair falling over firm, protruding breasts made a provocative picture. Her eyes were as black as a raven's wing after a fierce rain, and her high cheekbones and pouting mouth were infinitely alluring, enough to turn any man's head.

Thank God my head is only turned when I need a woman to bed, he thought.

"I hate you, Ranleigh. I will make you pay for leaving me like this," Elsa said, her black eyes blazing. She scooped back a handful of hair and thrust her breasts even more forward. The nipples were hard and erect.

"Don't tease, Elsa. And don't threaten me. And, I would thank you to keep your voice down, lest the servants hear. My solicitor will send the voucher for your expenses, as usual."

He started to tell her about his coming wedding—that it would be a marriage in name only, and that it would not affect her in any way—but thought better of it. He liked her fiery temperament; it added to her charm. But he did not want to push her too far. Today he was not in the mood for it.

Quietly, he closed the door, and his quick steps took him down the winding stairs and out into the street, where a high-sprung coach-and-four waited at the curb to take him to White's. After a bout in bed he went to

41

the gentlemen's club for companionship. Although he furnished his mistresses with fine homes, he never went to them.

They came to Kenmere. He liked it that way.

Four

It was on the eve of Cassandra's wedding day that Ellen disappeared. Cassandra had not seen her since before noon, and she was not at the supper table. By now the children knew that Cassandra would be leaving on the morrow to live at Ranleigh Hall. Excitement abounded, and it seemed no one noticed Ellen's absence. Cassandra was happy for that, for she had learned in her short twenty years that children could be very sensitive to what was happening around them. Many worried as much as grown-ups. To alleviate Sister Martha's anxiety, Cassandra said that she was sure Ellen would turn up later, but she did not believe it.

Cassandra thought that Ellen was gone from the orphanage for good, most likely never to return. But to Sister Martha, she said, reassuringly: "You know Ellen, Sister. She can take care of herself."

"She's of age to leave if she wants to. I believe her restlessness has gotten the better of her. I doubt that we will ever see her again. Poor child."

The pain in her voice was evident. Even though Ellen had been difficult from the moment she'd been left at the orphanage, as Sister Martha had recently confided, the old woman loved her. Ellen was one of her children.

Cassandra understood, for she, too, loved the gel who

at one moment was like a loving sister, and then chameleonlike, become angry and jealous of Cassandra's good fortune.

Even after having given up hope, Cassandra, in her attic room, listened for Ellen's footsteps on the stairs. Any moment now the creaking attic door might open and she would be there.

Cassandra shut out the silence and listened, but Ellen did not return. Finally, in her prayers, Cassandra asked that God keep the wayward gel from harm. That was all she could do, and she extinguished the candle and welcomed the darkness. She was tired. During the past week the stitching of the wedding gown had gone on far into the night, until Cassandra's eyes were beyond seeing.

Now, lying on the narrow cot, she stared at the invisible ceiling. Since the last missive saying he would come for her on the twelfth of May, there had been no word from Lord Ranleigh, and at church on Sunday the banns had not been read.

Sleep would not come, and anticipation of being wed to Lord Ranleigh of Ranleigh Hall made Cassandra's heart pound in the back of her throat. Beyond doubt she would be the happiest gel alive should she truly marry His Lordship.

The restlessness finally drove her from her bed to check the time. Holding the clock to the tiny window over Ellen's cot and lifting the curtain, she saw that it was well past midnight. She raised the window and leaned out, looking to the hillock that separated the orphanage from Ranleigh Hall. Night sounds assaulted her ears: crickets chirping, night frogs croaking, owls hooting. In the distance, moonlight danced on the trees, and a soft wind rustled the leaves.

The wind was cool on Cassandra's face. Her thoughts returned to Ellen. Where could the gel be?

Returning to her bed and to the utter darkness of

the attic, Cassandra allowed herself to escape totally into her wonderful fantasies. A blurred image of Lord Ranleigh's face, holding a loving smile and eyes soft with love, swung constant before her; he held her close, his hands moving over her body. A flush of warmth, and another feeling she did not recognize, moved swiftly through her, causing her to toss and turn.

Thus, Cassandra spent her wedding eve, and finally she slept, until the bell above her head clanged so loudly she almost tumbled out of bed. She could imagine Cook in the kitchen, yanking hard on the rope and mumbling to herself that it was time for the gel to come help with breakfast. So she dressed hurriedly and went belowstairs.

"Did Ellen come home?" Cook asked. The plump woman with the protruding stomach sounded hard and uncaring, but Cassandra knew better. Cook's heart was as big as a bushel basket, else why would she be at the orphanage, working for a pittance?

"No," Cassandra answered. "I doubt that she will ever see the orphanage again."

"Mayhap gone off to look for that worthless mother. But I must say, her timing was not very good, this being your wedding day and all."

"I think she chose this time because she wanted to take attention away from my wedding day."

Cook smiled at her. "That would be like Ellen. Well, today is *that* day, is it not?"

"It is, Cook, and I'm so excited. I had trouble sleeping."

Cook talked as she rolled out fat biscuits and placed them in a pan. "Every gel does. Your whole life will be changing. Ye'll be answering to a husband."

She bent her head to Cassandra conspiratorially. "Mind that you do your duty by him."

Cassandra was filling eleven glasses with milk, and a cup with coffee for Sister Martha. "Duty? I'm quite looking forward to *that* part. I don't consider it a duty at all.

Cook clucked and her face flushed, as if she were terribly embarrassed. "Never let him know you feel that way. He'll think you a loose woman and compare you with one of them fashionable impures."

Sister Martha came to help with breakfast, putting chipped plates on the table and making sure a napkin was beside each plate, and Cassandra lost her chance to ask what constituted a "fashionable impure." She had never heard of one.

"Did you sleep well?" Cassandra asked Sister Martha.

"No, and when I did, I dreamt about Ellen. That gel . . ."

Cassandra hugged her and patted her shoulder consolingly. "Worrying won't help, Sister. Ellen is wise beyond her years; she will fare well. She wanted to leave. I saw the signs and spoke with her . . ." She paused for a moment. "I don't think anyone could have stopped her."

"Mayhap not," Sister Martha said resignedly as she dipped porridge into bowls.

"None for me," Cassandra said. "I couldn't eat a bite."

And so it went on the morning of Cassandra's wedding day. With the children seated on each side of the long, narrow table, Sister Martha announced that classes would be suspended until afternoon; early-morning chores would be done quickly, and then everyone was to dress in their Sunday best and wait for the arrival of Lord Ranleigh.

There had never been such an occasion at the orphanage, she told them, when one of their own would be marrying nobility, and she most certainly thought they should share in Cassandra's good fortune.

"Besides," she said, "Cassandra wants you there to wish her well, and to tell her goodbye."

"I surely do, even though I'm only moving a hillock away."

"Goodbye, goodbye," Clara, one of the three-year-old twins, said, waving a fork in the air. Marla, the other twin, joined in, and soon all ten children were singing in unison, until Sister Martha quietened them. "Let's bow our heads and thank God for our blessings," she said, and every little head bowed.

Cassandra watched, thinking that she would surely choke, and when the short prayer had ended she excused herself and went to the attic, carrying two pails of hot water. After two more trips she stripped off her clothes and climbed into the tin tub.

Butterflies played hopscotch in her stomach, and she noticed for the first time that undoubtedly she had lost weight. She was as flat as a pancake.

The hot water felt wonderful. She hummed as she scrubbed until her skin was red. Her eyes sought out the clock while her heart counted the minutes. *He* had said he would come before noon. *That* could be any time.

She giggled and wondered what he would say should Sister Martha announce to him, with that certain tilt to her head, *"Her Ladyship* is indisposed, due to lingering too long in her bath."

Most likely he would say good-naturedly that he would take a chair and wait, that Her Ladyship—of course, she would not yet be titled, but that did not signify—certainly was entitled to her time in the tin tub.

At last she stood and let the water drip from her naked body before stepping out onto the homemade rag rug. She rubbed herself briskly with a towel, after which she donned white cotton pantalettes. Hearing footsteps, she turned and saw Sister Martha in the semi-darkness.

"I wish there was more light up here." Her breathing was labored from the climb.

Through the one tiny window, a slice of sunlight cut the room in half; shadows played on the cots and on the rag rug.

Cassandra scolded, "You should not have climbed those stairs, Sister. I had in mind bringing my wedding gown belowstairs and asking you to help me dress."

"Yes . . . yes, I did want to help."

Cassandra looked at the beautiful gown, spread out on Ellen's cot. The embroidery on the tiny puffed sleeves and around the hem, moving upwards a good twelve inches, was the most magnificent she had ever done, and the tiny stitches by Sister Martha were a work of art.

Cassandra swiped at her damp eyes. And then she gathered up the gown and her brush and comb. "Come on, Sister, let's go where there's more light."

They went belowstairs to Sister Martha's small sitting room, which adjoined her bedchamber. When Cassandra had first come to the orphanage she had slept on a cot beside Sister Martha's bed. Since then she had learned that every child, until he or she became accustomed to the new surroundings, slept close to Sister Martha, so that he or she could feel her comforting hand reach out in the darkness to pat a shoulder or a small head, to quieten heart-wrenching sobs.

This day, Cassandra stood before a full-length looking glass while Sister Martha smoothed and straightened and fussed. With tears in her eyes and a lump in her throat, Cassandra stared unbelievingly at her reflection. An ugly duckling had turned into a beautiful, long-necked swan. She did not think this vainly; never before had she felt beautiful. She grabbed Sister Martha and hugged her. No longer could she hold back the tears; they streamed from her eyes. Not even the thought of her dead mother's absence could dampen her happiness, although she wished for her. She refused to think of her father the vicar. If he were here, he

48

would damn her to hell because a tiny part of her white bosom showed above the neckline of the lovely dress.

"You truly are beautiful," Sister Martha said, her voice low and choked. And then she laughed. " 'Tis a happy occasion, so let us not go maudlin.

It was still heavy on Sister Martha's conscience that she had not told Cassandra the whole of the agreement between herself and Lord Ranleigh: that Cassandra would be his Countess in name only. But who was she to judge? she asked herself. Mayhap Cassandra would be happy enough just being Lord Ranleigh's Countess. It would be a great improvement over being in service, a lady's maid or, even worse, emptying chamber pots.

Cassandra turned round and round in front of the looking glass. "I promise not to have another maudlin day as long as I live."

"Sit in the chair and let me brush your hair," Sister Martha said, and Cassandra did as she was told. She could brush her own hair, but the old woman wanted to do it for her, and for a long time they did not speak. The brush moved slowly, until layers of gold hair fell past Cassandra's shoulders. And then the old woman dressed it in a most extraordinary way, with some curls piled high on the back of Cassandra's head and the remainder falling down her back, while loose strands curled from behind her ears and fell to rest on the white flesh above her décolletage.

"With your hair pulled back from your face, your wonderful gray eyes show to advantage," Sister Martha said, fussing some more. Finally, she put down the brush and comb.

"One can overdo."

"I'm pleased," Cassandra said. "And my wedding gown must be the most beautiful in all of England. Not even Prinny's bride, should he divorce his wife and marry another, would have a gown more beautiful.

49

Thank you, Sister, so very much for all you have done for me."

" 'Tis beautiful. And you are beautiful." Sister Martha's voice suddenly became firm. "But you just remember, Cassandra Edwards, beauty is as beauty does. Always be true to yourself."

"I will," Cassandra promised, and then she left the room and returned to the attic to fetch her shoes, returning after a moment and bringing with her a quilted satchel that held her worldly possessions, most especially her diary and her precious valentine.

Sitting in a chair, she put on the black shoes, lacing them to the top. Just then a loud knock on the door invaded the silence. "He's coming," someone said in a falsetto voice. "His Lordship's coming in a fine coach and four. And he has a driver."

Cassandra recognized the voice. It was Tim's, a twelve-year-old whose body and voice were fast changing to that of a young man. He had come to the orphanage when he was yet in leading strings.

"We're coming, Tim," she answered, feeling panic wash over her. Looking at Sister Martha imploringly, she asked, "What do we do now?"

Sister Martha laughed. "We go out and meet His Lordship. Stay calm. He won't bite you."

"I'm not so sure." Cassandra took up the satchel and a small reticule and started for the door. "I feel I might have a fit of the vapors."

Sister Martha took her by the arm and shook her firmly. "Now you listen to me, Cassie. You're no longer a child who lives in a dream world. From this day forward you are a woman, and a fine one. You will be married, and I expect you to apply yourself. Just remember that whatever comes, you are to handle it as if you had been brought up in the world of the rich and powerful. Never, never doubt yourself, and pray, do not let anyone make you feel you are less than what you are."

Before Cassandra could respond, the old woman said again, "A fine woman," and then she added, "You will soon be a Countess."

At that moment Cassandra was seized with a premonition that some unknown force was drawing her into a vortex of unconscionable happenings that she could not control, and she was more frightened than ever before in her life.

But the fear passed as quickly as it had come.

Sister Martha was still holding Cassandra's arms, the pressure being the measure of the seriousness of her words. This was the closest she had ever come to scolding Cassandra, and it was as if she had poured liquid metal into her veins.

Squaring her shoulders and lifting her chin, Cassandra said, "I take your meaning, Sister."

A pensive moment passed, and then Sister Martha went on: "Remember, Cassie, adversity introduces one to oneself. And there will be adversity, setbacks that you, as a young gel, cannot now comprehend. But don't give up. Make your dreams come true. What has happened to you in the past, what you have endured, will strengthen you, if you will use the lessons purposefully."

"I'll remember," Cassandra promised, taken aback.

Then, as if she had said all she could say, the concerned look left Sister Martha's countenance, and she gave a pleasant smile.

Cassandra felt that she would burst. What a lucky gel she was! Already she was inexorably in love with her future husband, and had been for a long time. Suddenly her anxiety left her. Within the next few moments she would look into the face of the man who had this past year tramped through her mind, awake or asleep— her *dream man*.

Her imagination took her to London, where she was

descending a curving stairway. All the young bucks of the *ton* were at her feet, with one standing head and shoulders taller than the rest—Lord Ranleigh. He was arrogantly pushing the others aside and making his way to her to kiss her hand and smile into her face. He loved her as she loved him, and with no preliminaries, their eyes met and locked, and he declared his love.

The dream quickly faded, but Cassandra held it in her heart. She pinched herself. His Lordship was actually arriving at the orphanage on the day he had said he would come.

"Please, Sister," she said. "You go ahead and greet His Lordship. It would not do for him to think I am overly anxious.

The elegantly liveried coachman pulled the coach and four to an abrupt stop in front of Sister Martha's orphanage. Emerging from the depth of plush velvet squabs, wearing the ordinary clothes of the nobility, Lord Ranleigh sprang out onto the ground and with a sprightly gait made his way toward the dilapidated house with its thatched roof. He was appalled at the change since last he had been there.

Paint had peeled from the shutters and boards covered some of the windows. The porch roof dipped. He made a mental note to send a man over to make the repairs. Money was the answer, and that he had in plenty. He thought about the marriage agreement he'd made with Sister Martha. Had he not in the past made healthy contributions to her orphanage, he would not have had the gall to send the missive asking that one of her gels, one capable of loving a child, marry him in name only.

It was a nuisance, actually. His time could be better spent elsewhere, but he must needs get this matter taken care of.

His Lordship's quick steps took him to the ram-shackle porch. A board was missing. Careful not to step through the hole, he took the knocker and gave a loud rap, which brought Sister Martha, a smile a yard wide on her sunken, wrinkled face.

"Your Lordship, welcome," she said as she stepped back for his entry, after which she dipped into a courtly curtsy.

He took her hand and lifted her up, then bent and kissed it lightly. Out of the corner of his eye he saw more children than he had ever seen in one place in his life. They were standing lined in rows, as if they would at any moment begin the morning worship service with song. The hair on the boy's heads—and there were different sizes and ages—was plastered flat to their scalps, and the girls wore bows in their locks of different shades of color and length.

Where was his intended?

As if on cue, the children bowed in unison, saying, "Your Lordship.

Lord Ranleigh found himself smiling. Turning, he gave a bow; and then his eyes locked with huge gray ones in a face so beautiful his heart began to pound. His eyes quickly traversed her body: the tiny waist, slim, youthful hips, and breasts showing above the neck of her gown.

Long hair, the color of sunshine, curled on white bosom.

She was rather tall; and he liked his women tall.

Her neck was long and graceful, made more so by the upward tilt of her small chin. He liked long, grace-ful necks on women, and small chins.

It was a long moment before His Lordship realized that this must needs be Sister Martha's charge, to whom he was to become leg shackled. Then he immediately became angry. He'd told the good woman that he wanted a gel with passable looks who could and would love an ailing child. He had been tricked, and he voiced his displeasure firmly and concisely: "Sister Martha, may I have a private audience with you?"

"Certainly, Your Lordship."

She led the way to her small office and went to sit behind the battered desk. Somehow, the desk put her at advantage, even facing an earl. From there she was in control. Lord Ranleigh's frowning countenance puzzled her. She raised her lorgnette and looked at him quizzically.

"Is something wrong, Your Lordship? You did not give me time to present Cassandra Edwards. She's a fine woman—"

"I didn't ask for a woman; I asked for a gel, one who could care for my ailing son."

"Oh, my Cassie is more than capable of doing that. You should see the way she fawns over the children here. She is absolutely divine beyond bearing."

A terrible thought went through her mind. *Oh, if he refuses my Cassie, I cannot bear it.*

"She's a *femme fatale.*"

"A what? Your Lordship, you cannot mean it. Cassandra is as innocent as a babe in its mother's arms. It would never occur to her to be a—what did you call it?"

"A *femme fatale.* It means a woman who is so attractive to men she leaves them helpless to resist her."

Sister Martha took a deep breath and gave a little laugh. "I'm sure a strong, experienced man such as yourself can handle that aspect of your marriage, and I am equally sure that Cassie will never be forward with you. She's a very shy gel. A warm smile at breakfast will most likely be *all* you will get from her."

In some ways the years had hardened her, Sister Martha thought. She was well aware that that which she and His Lordship were speaking was not discussed among the upper orders; they only thought about it and did it—but talk of it? Never!

She watched as Lord Ranleigh seemed to sink deeper into his chair, his long legs crossed in front of him, showing muscular thighs. No doubt he was a hard worker, but she strongly suspected the muscles in those thighs were from boudoir antics, for which the nobility was so reputably famous.

Rising abruptly, she stood her full five-feet-two-inch height, a midget confronting a Goliath.

"If you wish to withdraw your offer, if it is not your desire to wed Cassandra Edwards—and remember, this began with your proposal for a comely gel—"

"To look after my son. So many nursemaids have come and gone."

"Then why are you complaining? Cassie is—"

"I know—perfect for the job."

For a moment Lord Ranleigh, now standing, stared at Sister Martha; and during that flash of time she saw sadness emanating from his dark, penetrating eyes. Then they turned hard again.

He said to her, "Sister Martha, my life is perfectly orchestrated. I have no plans to change it. Before I leave with your charge, would you please speak with her, explain her duties? I wager you did not show her my missives."

"Only the last one, where you said you would come for her on this day."

"I insist that you inform your charge—"

Sister Martha was incensed. "Her name is Cassandra, and I will do no such thing. You are a grown man, I believe thirty summers . . . if you want her position explained, then *you* do the explaining. If the time arises when it is necessary. But I doubt that will happen. I have told you that the gel is so innocent that most likely she believes birds mate by singing to each other."

Lord Ranleigh drew in a deep breath. He started to sit again but thought that it would gain him no advantage. He hated looking down at this sprite of a woman with a backbone of steel. It showed in her eyes. An argument with her was an argument lost before it began.

"I beg your forgiveness," he said sarcastically. "I should not have assumed that you would share my missive with this . . . this Cassandra. I'm usually more thorough in my dealings, but I have been so concerned about Jacob . . ."

"Well, do you or do you not want to marry my Cassie?"

"Are you sure . . . I do not wish my life complicated."

"I'm not sure of anything, except that you will have no worry about my Cassie seducing you. She's not that kind of gel. She will keep her distance."

And what if I seduce her? he thought, but he did not dare say it aloud in the presence of this stubborn woman.

"If things become difficult, I shall return her to you, Sister Martha. Then you will wish that you had explained my motive for marrying her."

"You do that, Your Lordship. Just bring her home. Now, we've kept the poor darling waiting long enough. What can she be thinking?"

Sister Martha led the way back out into the main parlor, and Lord Ranleigh followed. From what he could see, his intended had certainly not been thinking about what was going on in the tiny office, or worrying about whether or not she was acceptable. She was sitting on the floor with the gaggle of children gathered around her. They were gazing into her face intently as she was saying, "Bascom chased the rabbit into the trees . . ."

Lord Ranleigh did not know whether Bascom was man or dog, and he made a mental note to ask her later.

We can be friends, he thought, as the sound of footsteps caught Cassandra's attention. She jumped to her feet, and not too gracefully, and once again she stood before him, reminding him of some mythical Greek goddess.

His Lordship groaned inwardly.

"I present Cassandra Edwards to you, Lord Ranleigh," Sister Martha said, smiling proudly.

Cassandra dipped into a courtly curtsy. "Pleased to make your acquaintance, Your Lordship." She was smiling.

He took her hand and brushed it past his lips, and felt the fire that raced from the tips of his fingers to his heart, and then plunged deeper.

Damme, I should turn and run, like the rabbit.

But he didn't. Instead, he said, "We must needs be on our way. 'Tis some distance to Gretna Green."

"Gretna Green? Are we eloping?" Cassandra asked.

"In a fashion. I do not wish any fanfare."

Sister Martha spoke up. "That accounts for why the banns have not been read. I listened at church, and they have not been printed in the *Times.*"

"I asked for and received a special dispensation," His Lordship said. He turned and offered his arm to Cassandra.

She acted as if she had not seen the gesture. She was instantly hugging the children and telling them goodbye.

"I want all of you to be nice and mind Sister Martha. Tim, please read to the children at bedtime."

"But I can't read like you," he protested.

"Practice will make you better. And all of you do your reading and figures."

"We will," they said in varying voices, and she patted a small head and smiled. Her voice was low. "I know that you will."

And then, as Lord Ranleigh watched, she did the most amazing thing. Again, she sat on the floor, this time to remove her black, high-top shoes, exposing stockingless feet, a little leg, and well-turned ankles. She stood and handed the shoes to the tallest of the boys.

"Here, Tim, you keep these. I notice that yours have been sewn with wire. That will never do for a fine man like you."

Blushing, Tim thanked her profusely. She tousled his hair.

Sister Martha stepped closer. "Cassie, you . . . you can't be married in your bare feet."

Cassandra laughed and hugged the old woman. "Don't worry, Sister. I'm sure Lord Ranleigh will be most happy to stop in Wickham Market and purchase those pink slippers you and I were admiring . . ."

Five

Cassandra had never sat in such an elegant carriage. She sank back into the blue velvet squabs and gave a big sigh. It was a perfectly gorgeous day, blue skies and sunshine drawing the smell of spring from heather and new grass.

She looked at Lord Ranleigh sitting across from her. Why did he look so unhappy? Was not one supposed to be happy on one's wedding day? He was not at all like the handsome Lord Ranleigh who had for the past year occupied her thoughts and dreams. Not that this Lord Ranleigh was not handsome, she thought. He was immensely so, in an imposingly silent, brooding sort of way.

Hoping to lighten his mood, she smiled at him.

"I suppose that it would be beyond the pale of society for you to sit beside me . . . until after we are married," she said.

He didn't smile, nor did the hardness leave his eyes. He said in a firm voice, "Miss Edwards, I feel it is my duty to . . ."

He could not go on. The words choked him, and under his breath, he swore at Sister Martha. "The demme woman was supposed to tell this gel . . ."

"Your duty to do what, Your Lordship? I would not

stop you from doing your duty." She gave a little laugh. "In truth, I believe everyone should, and I most surely plan to be a dutiful wife—if that is worrying you."

"I assure you that it is not." He tried again. "I do not plan . . ." Again he stopped, and a long moment passed before he continued. "Jacob, my heir, is five years old, Miss Edwards. One of your duties—in fact, your *only* duty when you are married to me—is to oversee his care. He is very frail, and I have come to believe that it is partly because of the constant changing of nursemaids. They have come and gone, and none have taken to him. I've read where even an animal will die when if it is not shown affection from its mother. Of course, Jacob's mother is gone . . ."

"What about from Jacob's father? Do you not love your son? Do you pick up the child and hold him, and tell him that you love him?"

"Of course not. *That* is not done."

"I don't see why not, Your Lordship. Love is love, from whatever direction."

I do not love him. I can't.

Painfully, Lord Ranleigh recalled that the innocent child reminded him too harshly of his once perfect world, the world that had crumbled at his feet, until there was nothing left but stone-dead coldness in the center of his heart. He prayed silently that he would never be forced to reveal the whole of it. He would rather die.

To Cassandra, His Lordship said, "Jacob is my heir. I have vast estates, including Ranleigh Hall, and there's the title to consider. It is my duty to the Ranleigh estates that pushes me to see that Jacob survives. Your duty is—"

"I know, I know. To oversee his care, and to love him. That will be my pleasure. I love all children."

"I pray that is so."

The conversation lifted Lord Ranleigh's burden somewhat. In a subtle way, he had told her he expected nothing more than loving care for Jacob. Surely she had gotten the message. Or had she?

He looked at her and managed a small smile. "Now where are those pink slippers you wish for me to purchase?"

"In Dever's window. They are ever so pretty. They have very small heels, and a satin rosebud on each toe."

Lord Ranleigh lowered the window of the coach and called to the coachman, giving him office to go to Wickham's Market and stop at Dever's store.

They were approaching the edge of the village, and only a few moments passed before the coach and four came to an abrupt stop in front of the shop.

"I shall wait for you. Just tell Mr. Dever to add the cost of the slippers to my account."

"I will do no such thing," Cassandra said. "He would not believe me any more than Stella at the draper's shop believed that I would soon be marrying a member of the aristocracy. Mayhap after I am Countess of Ranleigh they will take notice, instead of laughing when I tell them I am married to the Lord of Ranleigh Hall."

Without waiting for the coachman to let down the step—he was entirely too slow for her—Cassandra bounded out of the carriage and reached back to take Lord Ranleigh's hand, tugging slightly and laughing. "Your Lordship, you must needs come with me."

Lord Ranleigh pushed himself up from the deep squabs and joined her on the cobbled street. It was easier to do her bidding than to argue with the stubborn miss, and once they had entered the store together he could not help but enjoy the enthusiasm with which Cassandra received the pink slippers.

She actually hugged them to her breast before putting them on, and her huge gray eyes sparkled with such life as he had never seen. Upon trying to speak, he discovered that a big lump had formed in his throat.

The poor gel had been deprived of all of life's finer things.

He pushed out the words, "You must needs hurry, Miss Edwards; our destination is a far distance and it is important that we be on our way."

"Destination, Your Lordship?" said Mr. Dever with the lift of a heavy brow. He was a pudgy pork of a man, dressed in a long-tailed coat and a white shirt with high collar points. He reminded Cassandra of her vicar father when he stood behooving the congregation to add to the coffers.

"We are going to Gretna Green to be married," Cassandra said nonchalantly. She stood and lifted her skirt so that she could gaze at the pink slippers. "They are ever so pretty. Thank you, Lord Ranleigh. You are most kind."

Lord Ranleigh grimaced. "Come, Miss Edwards, we must needs be on our way."

"Married?" the storekeeper said again, his eyes darting first to Lord Ranleigh and then to Cassandra in disbelief.

"Yes. I—"

Lord Ranleigh's long arm reached out and his big hand closed around Cassandra's slender arm, his fingers biting into the flesh. None too gently, he moved her toward the door, while saying, "Add the slippers to my account."

The door slammed behind them.

"Must you be so rough?" she asked.

"It seemed the only way to quiet you."

He practically pitched her into the carriage and then climbed in behind her, again sinking into the squabs opposite.

"Don't spare the cattle," he told the coachman, and instantly the carriage jerked and they were off and running, the horses' hooves pounding thunderously against the hard-packed road, pedestrians and animals scurrying to get out of their way.

Cassandra was more than a little angry. "What was the harm in telling the man we were going to Gretna Green to be married?"

"Miss Edwards, one does not tell one's business to strangers. Besides, we are eloping to Gretna Green, and eloping means that one does not tell *anyone.*"

Cassandra gave a mock bow from the waist, spreading her hands out with palms up. "I beg your forgiveness, Your Lordship."

When she raised her head she saw for the first time a genuine smile on Lord Ranleigh's face, his petulance gone. Excellent white teeth gleamed, and there were crinkles around his dark eyes, which seemed to have lost just a little of their hardness. Now *that* was more like the magnificent man of her dreams, and she laughed to show him that her anger had gone as quickly as it had come.

She was not one to hold a grudge—unless it was something really serious.

"I'm sorry if I hurt your arm," he said. "I would like for us to be friends."

"If you're begging my forgiveness, you have it." She grinned mischievously. "But next time, should there be a next time, which I don't recommend, I shall not be so nice."

Lord Ranleigh chuckled, and Cassandra liked that even better than his smile.

After that, they rode along in silence, passing small houses with beautiful gardens, large fields of growing crops, and, occasionally, a huge manor house grand in its presence. The sun was warm, but not hot, on the summer grass.

A long distance down the road, Lord Ranleigh gave orders that they stop at a posting inn for refreshments, and to change the horses.

Cassandra was careful not to even hint to the proprietor of the Red Edge Inn that they were on their way to Gretna Green to be married. Nonetheless, she saw raised eyebrows, for she was traveling without a lady companion, with Lord Ranleigh, whom everyone seemed to know.

But she was not about to explain; let them think she was a loose woman if their minds were bent in that direction.

Back in the carriage, they drove at breakneck speed until darkness was closing in around them, like a soft blanket. Still, they pushed on.

"Are we going to a fire?" Cassandra asked when Lord Ranleigh at last ordered the driver to stop and light the coach lanterns.

"It is necessary that we travel as far as possible tonight," he answered, "so that we will be in Gretna Green in time to be married on the morrow."

"What is so imperative about getting married tomorrow? Would not the next day suffice?"

"I do not want to compromise you. I don't want the gossipers sullying your good name."

"We should have brought Sister Martha."

Lord Ranleigh said, "No," so quickly that Cassandra thought on it for a long while. Why was he angry with Sister Martha?

So far, she thought, there had not been anything romantic about eloping. It seemed that at least His Lordship could hold her hand, or sit beside her so they could touch. How nice it would be if he stole a kiss and then apologized. She recalled that many times she had fantasized about his kisses and had felt her body flush warm all over. She did not speak her thoughts, and when she felt the carriage stopping she looked out to learn where they were, seeing at once that they were at a posting inn with two big red-and-black roosters sitting atop the roof, each looking as if he were about to spur the other to pieces.

"This is the Inn of the Fighting Cocks," Lord Ranleigh informed her, adding, "We will bed down here."

He bounded down to the ground and reached up a hand to help Cassandra.

"Bed down? Not together, not until we are married," she said, looking into his stern face.

"Of course not together, Miss Edwards. I *am* an honorable man."

"Oh, I know that. Sister Martha said you were of the first water."

As though she hadn't spoken, Lord Ranleigh said to the groom who met them, "Give the horses a good rubdown before putting them up for the night, Winns."

Then, taking Cassandra's arm, he maneuvered her toward the inn's door. She looked around. It did not appear to be a very nice place, not romantic at all.

Inside, they were met by a wizened little man with a bald head, off which candlelight reflected brightly.

"We are in need of two rooms," Lord Ranleigh told the bald man, "as far apart as can be managed."

The proprietor bowed from the waist. "Your desire is my command, Your Lordship. Follow me."

"Does everyone in England know you?" Cassandra asked in a loud whisper as they climbed the stairs.

Lord Ranleigh hushed her, then groaned audibly when she said, and not in a whisper. "I'm ravenous, Your Lordship. I will be ever so happy when we can sit down to a filling supper."

Mayhap he'll ask for champagne.

"I thought we would order food sent to the rooms."

"Oh, but that would break with propriety. Remember, we are not married yet. Tongues would wag for sure. No, I will not consent to that at all. In the dining room all will be proper."

"Are you always this bossy?" His Lordship muttered.

"I had meant that we would eat in our respective rooms."

Cassandra thought she had heard him correctly, but she was not sure. It sounded as if he had his teeth clenched together.

"What did you say?" she asked, turning back to look at him.

He didn't answer.

The stairs were dark, but not so dark that Cassandra could not see the stern look on His Lordship's countenance. She knew that meant for her to be quiet. A young boy was behind them, carrying their bags, hers the quilted satchel.

They went to Cassandra's room first, which was at the very head of the stairs. The bald-headed proprietor held the candle, and the bag-carrying boy, after setting her satchel down, turned the knob on the door, and then His Lordship turned on his heel and left, walking quickly down the long hall, the proprietor and boy close behind.

What a strange way for a man about to be married to act, Cassandra thought.

Left alone, she immediately began her toilette. First, her beautiful dress came off. It was not soiled; how could it be when she'd ridden all day in the closed carriage. Thank goodness it was not a steamy summer day. Had she known they were not going straight to a church to be married, she would not have worn her wedding dress.

Cassandra knew that this was not true. She had no other dress in which to meet His Lordship. She opened the window and flapped the dress in the cool breeze, and then she lay it on the narrow bed and pressed out the wrinkles with her hands.

She thought about Sister Martha and the work that had gone into the dress, the sacrifice entailed to purchase even the sarcenet, and for a moment she was prone to let tears cloud her eyes. And she would have had she not been anxious to meet His Lordship for supper in a very few minutes.

Standing naked, she washed herself with the water in the tin wash pan and envisioned him sitting across the table from her, candles burning alongside a bottle of champagne, which he would open with aplomb, laughing when it foamed out to wet the white tablecloth. She had never seen anything like that, but she had read about the way champagne foamed when it was uncorked. She had never tasted wine, but she was a woman now. Sister Martha had said so.

His Lordship would fill their crystal glasses and they would drink to their wonderful future.

And it was not beyond the pale to wish that he had ordered flowers for the table.

She would like that. She said aloud, "He wants me to love his heir, as if *that* would be a sacrifice."

After the washing she rubbed her damp body vigorously with an age-yellowed towel. The cold air from the window blew against her tingling skin. She pushed her long hair back from her neck and shivered when the wind touched the damp flesh there.

The open window let in the night sounds; an owl hooted, and then from out of the darkness came an answer. Then silence, until a frog croaked into the quietness. The moon was pretty in the dark sky.

Quickly, she donned her pantalettes and her white wedding dress. She brushed her hair, careful not to disturb the curls on the back of her head, and then descended the stairs, lighted by a single candle in a wall sconce.

Lord Ranleigh sat at a table in the far corner of the dining room, also dimly lighted. He rose when she approached the table and asked crossly, "What kept you, Miss Edwards? All the other diners have eaten and gone."

67

"That's wonderful. We shall have the dining room all to ourselves." She looked at the plain plank table, a far cry from what she had envisioned while dressing.

"Do you suppose we can have a bottle of wine?"

"No," His Lordship said, frowning ferociously as he regained his seat.

She smiled at him. "Very well. We shall save that until *after* we are married."

He leaned across the table. "Miss Edwards, must I remind you that our contract for marriage requires only that you nurse my heir back to health. You are not required to be romantic. In truth, I deplore such—"

An avalanche of memories assaulted him, of romantic meals by candlelight, of words spoken only in whispers, of . . .

His mind stopped there, for he willed it to do so. He looked at Cassandra and groaned inwardly. This was not working as he had planned, not at all. It was Sister Martha's fault.

A waiter, wearing a white cap and black kerseymere knee breeches, came to ask to take their order.

"We do not normally serve this late, but since 'tis Your Lordship, I am only too happy to be at your command."

Lord Ranleigh ordered for both of them, pigeon pie and any vegetables they might have left.

The waiter gave a half bow and left.

Cassandra settled back against the hard back of her chair and looked across the table at her future husband. She spoke with intensity. "Lord Ranleigh, I do not know why you are unhappy, but I do not expect to be married more than once, and I would like for it to be a happy time. I'm weary of your frowns, so I'm perfectly willing for you to return me to Sister Martha before any damage has been done."

Obviously shaken, he said quickly, "I am not unhappy, Miss Edwards. 'Tis only that I have things on my mind.

I beg your forgiveness. I do not wish to return you to Sister Martha."

He was quiet after that, and Cassandra decided that if it could not be a romantic evening, then it would be an informative one.

"Tell me about Ranleigh Hall," she said, attempting to be pleasant. "Since it will be my home—"

"Ranleigh Hall is big and busy. There are many servants, but you need not bother with them. Isabelle, the Dowager Countess, my mother, will be in full charge of the household, answering to me, of course."

"What is she like?"

"She spends a lot of time in bed."

"And she runs a huge household from her bed? I've never—"

Lord Ranleigh ignored Cassandra's remark; he did, however, go on to say, "I must needs warn you that the dowager was very fond of my first wife. She will not like it at all that I have remarried."

"Oh, but I would never try to replace your first Countess. I will have my own place. Sister Martha said—"

"Pray, do not mention that name—"

Cassandra gave him a quizzical look.

"I felt it my duty to warn you about the dowager."

There was something about his voice that sent chills up and down Cassandra's spine. She could not discern if it was dislike for the Dowager Countess, or admiration for her, that his voice revealed. Nor could she gather his feelings for his deceased wife.

She decided to let it go, thinking she would learn soon enough. "Your brother—"

The response was quick, like a whiplash. "Wade is a scoundrel. I glory in the time he spends away from Ranleigh."

Cassandra forced a little laugh. "Is there any member of your household of whom you are fond . . . except Jacob?"

Immediately, His Lordship's voice became soft, as did the look in his dark eyes. "Cynthia, my sister. She has seen six and ten summers. She's a bright ray of sunshine at the Hall. You will love her, too. I hope you will be friends."

"Oh, I shall be friends with her," Cassandra said, and then she told him about her love for Ellen and how concerned she had been about her since she had left the orphanage.

He was still shaking his head and clucking at Ellen's foolishness when the waiter brought their food, and after that there was not much talking. But later, in her room, when she was getting ready for bed, a terrible feeling of unease again invaded her being, and she knew that somehow the feeling was related to Lord Ranleigh's brother.

She recalled vividly her meeting with Wade when sitting on the hillock. She had been engulfed with the feeling that something sinister lurked behind his cold blue eyes.

A long time passed, and still the uneasy feeling clung to her, like a heavy mantle resting on her shoulders. The chill came again to traverse her spine.

She rose from the edge of the narrow bed, folded the thin blanket back, crawled into bed, and pulled it over her. Lying on her back, she stared into the darkness. The room was not unlike the attic in which she'd slept at Sister Martha's orphanage; both had low ceilings. Sleep came at last, and it was not His Lordship who danced through her dreams, but his brother Wade, his cold blue eyes mocking her. She awoke with a start.

After a moment the dream left her mind. As dreams so often do, she told herself, as her thoughts returned to her future husband, and to Sister Martha, who had warned her not to give up.

"And I won't," Cassandra said aloud, vowing silently

70

that somehow she must needs rid Lord Ranleigh of his perpetual frown.

Down the hall, the powerful Lord Ranleigh, who was always in charge of his life, sat on the edge of his bed, frowning.

"What a farrago," he declared, vowing that, if it killed him, today he would tell Miss Edwards that their marriage was in name only.

As His Lordship sat there, pondering, he thought about her asking that they have wine with supper. He would wager that she had never tasted the stuff. Her innocence was beautiful . . . or would be—if he were looking for a wife.

Six

"Why are we stopping here?" Cassandra asked.

Having left the Inn of the Fighting Cocks before first light, they had driven hell for leather and were now in Gretna Green, which was located on the southern border of Scotland, the favorite place for all Englanders who wished to elope. Cassandra did not understand the great rush, and she was even more puzzled by their stopping in front of a blacksmith shop.

Inside a ramshackle shack, with an open front and a dirt floor, was a burly man standing close to a tin barrel placed at an angle. As Cassandra watched, he withdrew a piece of iron, red from the heat, placed it on a work bench, and started pounding on it with what looked like a huge hammer. He barely looked up when the coach and four ground to a stop. She asked again why they were stopping *there*.

"In Gretna Green one gets leg shackled by a blacksmith," Lord Ranleigh answered. He hopped down onto the ground and reached back to help Cassandra.

"Well, this *one* does not," she answered quickly. She ignored the outstretched hand, while tilting her chin and setting her jaw in an indomitable line characteristic of Sister Martha.

Lord Ranleigh's brow shot up considerably. "I don't take your meaning, Miss Edwards."

" 'Tis simple. It would be sacrilegious to be married by anyone other than a vicar. A marriage should be blessed—"

"If that had been my intent, we would have gone to a vicar in Wickham Market. Here, there's nothing to it. The smithy simply announces us leg shackled."

"I hate that word."

"What word?"

"Leg shackled." Cassandra refused to look at His Lordship's hand, which hung suspended in midair.

"That's two words," he said.

"One word, two words, it's the same, and it is *my* intent to be married by a vicar, and to have our vows blessed by his praying over us. Lord knows marriage is difficult enough and without the Higher Power's blessing, I fear what it would be." She paused to look Lord Ranleigh straight in the eye, and without so much as a blush, she added, "I would not feel right being your wife in the biblical sense if our marriage was not blessed."

Lord Ranleigh dropped his hand to his side and swore audibly. It was Sister Martha's fault. She should have informed the gel. Well, there was nothing to it; he would have to tell her himself that they were not getting leg shackled in the biblical sense.

"Miss Edwards, our . . ." Dark eyes locked with gray eyes, and what His Lordship saw told him that when he so informed the stubborn miss of his intent, the hurried trip to Gretna Green would have been in vain. The glint in those gray eyes, and the upward tilt of her chin, was the exact same as Sister Martha's when her mind was set. This was the outside of enough. He recalled the Sister's words when he told her that if Miss Edwards became too difficult he would return her to the orphanage. She had stubbornly said, "You do just that, Your Lordship, return her to me."

73

Now, groaning inwardly, he told himself that when he had learned Cassandra was the daughter of a vicar, he should have looked elsewhere for someone to care for his heir. He looked at his watch, and at the sky. It was getting late and the sky was overcast, as if it might rain. He decided to bluff. Mayhap he had read her wrong, for surely she was not as stubborn as Sister Martha. He could not be that unfortunate. Giving her a conciliatory smile, he said, "Mayhap I should return you to the orphanage."

"Mayhap you should, Your Lordship, for I have no notion of getting married without God's blessing. I would not feel married."

She looked inside the shack. The smithy was still working on whatever he had been working on when they arrived.

Lord Ranleigh frowned ferociously, shouted to the driver, "Find a church, and make haste." He climbed back into the carriage and plopped himself down onto the bench opposite Cassandra. "I should have known . . . your father being a vicar—"

"Oh, but that has nothing to do with the way I feel, Lord Ranleigh. I did not believe my father a man of God, though I pray that I was wrong. I have my own convictions."

I can see that you do, he thought with total disgust.

Aloud, he said, "And just where did you get those convictions, Miss Edwards? From Sister Martha?"

"Some, but mostly from Mama. Though I did not understand her completely—she was so subservient to Papa—I did learn from her that one should ask God's blessing on whatever endeavor one undertakes, especially something as serious as marriage."

"I see," His Lordship said musingly. He looked across at her and thought again that it was unfortunate for him that she was so uncommonly beautiful. Warmth and sincerity seemingly exuded from her. The carriage was filled with it. She smiled at him, catching him off guard. He swore again.

He determined that it was because she was so innocent in the ways of the world. Later, when she learned the whole of it, she would be different, he told himself. He studied her face; even the pugnacious tilt of her chin added to her appeal. Today, her hair was no longer in curls on the back of her head, but fell in folds to her shoulders, the ends curling forward and resting on the white bosom pushed above the neckline of her white dress, which, with its intricate embroidery, was as fresh as if she had not worn it the day before.

Suddenly, guilt overtook His Lordship, and his anger turned inward. Bringing an innocent to Ranleigh Hall was beyond redemption. The Lord should rain hellfire and brimstone down upon him and all he possessed.

Fighting to shake the feeling, which he considered a moment of weakness, Lord Ranleigh settled back against the squabs and thought about Elsa, his beautiful, fiery mistress, and longed for her with all his being.

He would be safe with her.

It began to rain.

" 'Tis a bad omen when it rains on one's wedding day," Cassandra said. "There's only one thing worse."

Lord Ranleigh found himself smiling. Her countenance was masked in innocent belief. "And what is that?" he asked.

"If a black cat should cross the road in front of the carriage carrying the bride and groom. If that should happen, the bride must needs turn her hat inside out and wear it that way through the wedding ceremony.

His Lordship threw his head back and laughed. When the laughter subsided he asked, "Do you really believe that?"

" 'Tis so, and I'd appreciate your not laughing when I tell you something of importance."

"I apologize. I shall will that a black cat *not* cross our

75

path, for you are not wearing a hat. We would be in deep trouble, a terrible carriage accident perhaps—"

Cassandra sat forward. "Don't say that!" Tears clouded her big gray eyes, and Lord Ranleigh was at once sorry for trying to force levity. He had forgotten that she had been orphaned by a carriage accident. Reaching out, he took her hand and held it for a brief moment, squeezing and then releasing it. "I'm sorry. I am a cloddish simpleton when it comes to the feelings of others. Sister Martha told me about your losing your Mama and Papa—"

"I don't wish to speak of it. This is my wedding day, a happy occasion."

Cassandra's words brought His Lordship back to his intention of marrying a gel in name only, a loving, kind gel who would care for the Ranleigh heir.

He prayed: *God forgive me, I cannot love the child.* A great sadness overtook him, and he sat in silence while the carriage rolled over rutted streets.

At last the driver pulled the horses to a stop in front of a church, a small stone building grayed by mold and age. The steeple had been freshly painted a shining white.

The church sat back in a copse and was surrounded by grave stones, some old, Cassandra noticed, others seemingly only recently placed.

Not waiting for the driver to alight and let down the step, Lord Ranleigh opened the carriage door and got out, then let the step down himself. Just then the bell in the steeple clanged loudly, resounding rhythmically in the deep, dark silence of the woods. The sound seemed to hang in the damp air. The rain had subsided, with the exception of a drop now and then.

Cassandra took His Lordship's extended hand and stepped down, careful not to encounter a puddle and ruin her pink slippers. "Thank you," she said, smiling at her soon-to-be husband. Her heart was light, and she

76

knew without doubt that no gel had ever known such happiness. When she saw a man wearing a black robe hurrying toward them she was certain that God would bless this union.

The vicar was a small man, and his robe covered him from head to toe. He spoke in a kind voice, with a north-England accent.

"Welcome," he said, bowing slightly from the waist. And then he took Cassandra's hand and bowed over it. "You are a lovely bride, m'lady; happiness shows in your face."

"We wish to be married as quickly as possible, with as few words as possible," Lord Ranleigh said.

Scowling, he took the special license from his pocket and thrust it at the vicar, along with a five-pound note. Money should buy him haste.

This, however, did not happen.

"Come inside," the vicar said. "I shall get the missus for a witness. She saw you coming, and just knowing there was going to be a wedding, went to ring the bell. She will play the pianoforte. Music is fitting for a proper wedding."

"A witness is not necessary, and heaven forbid mournful music," exclaimed Lord Ranleigh.

As if His Lordship hadn't spoken, the vicar left, the long black robe flapping around his ankles, and he stayed so long that Lord Ranleigh thought he had absconded with his five-pound note. He returned, however, with a plump woman in tow.

She wore an apron, which she unhurriedly removed, folding it meticulously and placing it on the altar rail.

"I'm sorry for the delay," she said, plopping herself in front of the pianoforte. As her hands moved adroitly over the keys, a thin, high, slow procession of notes assailed Lord Ranleigh's ears. The purity of them brought unexpected tears to his eyes, and he swore under his breath. He remembered another time, another church, another bride. His heart had been in *that* marriage.

Now, he waited impatiently, and after an interminably long time the music stopped and the vicar stood before them, an ancient-looking black Bible in his hand. He opened the Good Book, cleared his throat, and the reading of the vows began, loud and solemn. Lord Ranleigh was encouraged when Cassandra promised to obey her husband. Of course, he was making promises which he had no notion of keeping, especially the one promising to keep himself only to his wife. How ridiculous! If that were so, if all men who made the vow kept themselves only to their wives, what would become of the courtesans of the world?

"Kneel before me," the vicar said, and Cassandra pulled on Lord Ranleigh's arm until he was on his knees beside her.

"Bow your head," she whispered, and His Lordship did so.

Then began the loud supplication to God to bless this union, to bring to it many children, which these two people kneeling before him promised to bring up in a righteous path.

Out of the corner of his eye, Lord Ranleigh saw Cassandra's lips moving. Quickly, he jerked his head back to the reverent position and closed his eyes, as hers were.

His voice rising to the rafters, the vicar implored God to bless this fine couple's home.

It was then that the guilt he had experienced earlier returned to engulf Lord Ranleigh. The secrets of Ranleigh Hall poured upward from his unconscious, and he acknowledged that Cassandra Edwards, the innocent orphan, deserved better than that which he had to offer.

If only he could change the past . . . if he, himself, could change. But *that* was impossible; the past was immutable. Hard, though it was, he had learned from it.

His Lordship returned his attention to the vicar's voice as it droned on above his head, and then his own lips, without provocation, started moving, echoing the words.

Ranleigh Hall needed God's blessing.

And I must needs talk with Miss Edwards—the Countess of Ranleigh—about her duties at Ranleigh Hall. And I must needs tell her what Sister Martha should have told her, that our marriage is to be in name only.

Vowing, for the tenth time, that he would, at the first opportunity, do this, Lord Ranleigh felt considerably better.

Making the vow was quite easy, His Lordship thought, but doing that which he had promised was considerably harder.

Finally, the vicar pronounced them man and wife and implored His Lordship to kiss his bride, which Lord Ranleigh did by brushing his lips across Cassandra's cheek.

For appearance's sake, he told himself, and then he offered her his arm and they walked out into sunshine.

"A good omen," Cassandra said.

Sunlight filtered through the trees, and the damp leaves glistened, while shadows danced around the bride and groom's feet. "Thank you for bringing me to this beautiful little church. I feel truly married," Cassandra said.

Lord Ranleigh started to answer but was just then interrupted by the vicar's plump wife, telling them goodbye. He thanked her for the beautiful music, smiled at her, then hurried to the carriage, Cassandra's arm still hooked with his.

"And God's blessing on you," the woman called.

Cassandra looked back. The woman was waving. Her husband stood by her side, Bible in his hand. Laughing, Cassandra waved and threw them a kiss. She wished she had a wedding bouquet to toss. Lord Ranleigh helped her up into the waiting carriage.

He did not immediately get in, but stood on the ground while looking at his watch. He was frowning. Cassandra, hearing a muffled "Demmet," asked, "What's wrong, Your Lordship?"

"We will never make it back to the Inn of the Fighting Cocks before nightfall."

"What's so important about returning to *that* place? I don't mean to sound complaining, but I thought my room miserly, more like a servant's room."

"It was the only accommodation left at the late hour we arrived. Since rooms are hard to come by, I reserved the same for tonight, and had we been married by the smithy, as was my desire, we would be well on our way there now."

Cassandra did not respond. There was nothing for her to worry about. She would not be going back to that awful room; she would be sharing Lord Ranleigh's room, and she was sure it would be a great improvement over the one she had slept in.

Having heard that men often got carried away and wanted to rush *things* before the vows were read, she thought it very noble of Lord Ranleigh to have her placed so far from him on the night before they were married. She really should have had a chaperone, but since she hadn't, he had taken it upon himself to protect her. She gave him a loving smile, and wanted to pinch herself for her good fortune. Sinking back against the squabs, she waited for him to join her. Now that they were married, he would sit beside her.

Instead of getting into the carriage as Cassandra expected, Lord Ranleigh walked to the front of it to confer with Mills, the driver. As she watched, words she could not hear were exchanged, after which Mills's head moved in agreement.

Lord Ranleigh came back and climbed into the carriage, sitting opposite Cassandra. He took from his waistcoat pocket a box of snuff, whiffed deeply, then said nonchalantly, "Mills thinks mayhap we can reach the Inn of the Fighting Cocks by midnight, with only a short respite for food and to let the horses rest."

Cassandra, as a dutiful wife—which she intended to be in all ways—settled back to wait and see what would happen next. It had been a strange wedding day, she thought, as the carriage pulled away from the little church in the woods.

At their last short stop the carriage lanterns had been lit, and now, ahead, Cassandra saw in the moonlight the two red-and-black cocks atop the inn, fighting ferociously. It was well past midnight, but she felt refreshed, having taken a long nap.

When she had awakened her head had been resting in Lord Ranleigh's lap, her bare arms covered with his coat. As soon as she stirred, he had explained that he feared she was cold and that her neck was going to break with her sleeping sitting up. So he had wrapped her in his coat and then rested her head in his lap to prevent this from happening.

After the lengthy explanation, His Lordship had moved back to the opposite side of the carriage.

As if I might bite, Cassandra thought.

"I appreciate that ever so much," she said, giving him a sweet smile. He scowled at her. What an enigma the man was. She racked her brain for a reason for his acting in this strange manner and finally decided that the poor man was just painfully shy.

But if that was the case, she reasoned, his shyness belied his ruggedly masculine build. Corded broad shoulders stretched his shirt to the splitting point, and his skintight breeches revealed sleek, muscled thighs. When he was frowning, as he was now, his face showed brooding strength and gave the appearance of more than the thirty years Sister Martha had said he claimed.

His dark eyes were razor-sharp and alert, hiding the hurt that was so often in evidence.

Now, his gaze was focused on the far-off darkness, averting any contact with her own. How she wished she knew this man who was her husband. But there simply could be no other answer, she decided; he was actually too shy to sit by her, or to touch her. And them properly married. Poor darling. She supposed it took one a long time to know one's husband. Who would have ever thought the powerful Lord of Ranleigh Hall shy? Her daydreams had not had him so.

"I quite enjoyed your sitting beside me. You must needs not be shy with me," she said as she pulled his coat closer around her. It felt so pleasantly warm, almost as if he were holding her. She sniffed the masculine scent of the coat.

"I explained my reason for being on *your* side of the carriage," he said, feeling anything but shy. He was plotting and planning on how to explain to this fetching gel that the wedding vows they had taken did not signify.

That was going to be difficult with desire running rampant through his veins. He *felt* like a rutting bridegroom, and he swore at himself for his weakness. Why had things not gone as he planned?

Lord Ranleigh vowed that when he again saw the good Sister—and he doubted that he ever should, so angry was he at her—that he would gladly wring her neck. He felt genuinely sorry for Miss Edwards. The poor gel did not even own a pelisse.

But that could be easily remedied with his money. As soon as they reached Ranleigh Hall, he would send for a modiste.

The sudden stop of the carriage rescued His Lordship from his unpleasant ruminations. The inn was dark, with not a glimmer of light anywhere. Moonlight shimmered on the roof, and on the fighting cocks.

His Lordship bounded down to the ground, and a loud banging of the iron knocker finally brought the proprietor to the door. He wore a white nightcap, a flimsy robe that stopped at his knees, and red house slippers. He stood in a pool of yellow light from the half-burned candle he held.

"It's Ranleigh," His Lordship said. "You were to keep rooms for us.

"But not this late, m'lord."

Lord Ranleigh's voice boomed through the quiet night. "You mean to tell me you have let the rooms I reserved? I suppose you've let my horses—"

"Not so, m'lord. Yer horses are in the stables, rested and ready to go on the morrow, and the rooms ye slept in are available, but the room the gel used was let not more than an hour ago. After I'd given up on ye. The poor, tired man didn't have the blunt for yer rooms, which I try to save for the nobility, so I let him have the room saved for the gel. I bound that I was only doing me duty. Ye can hardly blame a man."

"I suppose not," Lord Ranleigh said, not too worried. His quarters had consisted of two rooms, which would this night suit perfectly. Even though the hour was extremely late and he was dreadfully sleepy, he would take the time to explain the agreement to Miss Edwards, and after that there would be no problem. She would sleep in one room, and he in the other. They *were* legally married, so it would not be breaking with propriety, and there would be no question of his compromising her reputation.

It was a capital idea, an excellent time to do that which he had been dreading.

Fate was working in his favor, His Lordship decided, as he turned and went back to the carriage. After letting the step down he reached up and offered her a hand, which she took, gracefully stepping down onto the ground. "Your room is not available. You must needs share my rooms," His Lordship said.

Cassandra gave a little laugh. "I certainly hope that be the case. Does not a wife share her husband's room on their wedding night?"

"That is not necessarily so. Often there are extenuating circumstances."

"Well, I can think of none this night." Cassandra's heart went out to him. She could not understand his shyness about personal matters, but she told herself that she had only known him since yesterday, when he had come to the orphanage to claim her.

Her fanciful dreams did not count, she now realized.

Inside the inn, the proprietor shuffled across the stone floor and started up the stairs, holding the candle high.

Cassandra and Lord Ranleigh followed close behind him, carrying their own bags.

There was no footman at this time of night, the proprietor said, and when he had opened the door to the suite of rooms he'd saved for Lord Ranleigh he turned and disappeared back down the stairs as if he was afraid they would ask for food, or some other foolish necessity. Cassandra was glad that they had eaten a light supper at the last inn where they had stopped to rest the horses.

Seemingly nonplussed, Lord Ranleigh dragged a lucifer across the stone fireplace and lit a candle, casting the room in shadows and light.

Cassandra set down her bag and looked around. A well-worn rug of varying colors covered the plank floor. Faded velvet trappings framed the bed and the windows. Two large chairs, covered in the same fabric, flanked the fireplace. An iron kettle, steam slowly spilling from its spout, hung over smoldering coals.

"I'm happy to see hot water for washing," Cassandra said.

"Would you like tea? There's a pot waiting for hot water to be added. Normally, I would have my valet . . ."

On a table near the fireplace, cups and saucers and a teapot waited for their use. But Cassandra was more interested in a bath than having tea at this hour of the night.

"I prefer washing, then bed," she said. She was slightly embarrassed. She looked at Lord Ranleigh and thought he seemed gray, as if the blood had drained from his face.

"Are you all right, husband?" she asked.

"I'm most certainly all right, and pray, do not call me husband."

"And why not? You are my husband; I would like it if you called me wife."

No answer; just another scowl.

As Cassandra watched, her husband walked to peer into the adjoining room, saying after a moment, "I shall repair to this room and give you privacy."

Suddenly overcome by modesty, Cassandra thought that a capital idea. "I appreciate your thoughtfulness, m'lord."

His voice was crisp. "Do not call me m'lord. It is much too formal."

"Then what shall I call you? Ranleigh?"

"I prefer that. Or Lord Ranleigh, if you must."

Cassandra laughed lightly. "Just Ranleigh would not suit at all. I shall call you Lord Ranleigh, and I prefer you call me Cassandra, or Cassie. That's what Sister Martha calls me." When anger flushed Lord Ranleigh's countenance, she asked, "Why are you angry with Sister?"

"She did not live up to our agreement," he answered quickly, disappearing into the other room before Cassandra could question him further. Over his shoulder, he added, "I prefer to call you Lady Ranleigh, and I bid you good night. On the morrow, we must needs have a long talk."

"Stuff," she said, half under her breath, as she stared at the closed door. She wished she knew more about men and their temperament. She could not go by her dead Papa's actions, so that left her with no knowledge at all. What did His Lordship mean when he said that on the morrow they must needs have a long talk? About what? Her duties at Ranleigh Hall?

It all seemed so strange, not like a honeymoon at all. And why would she have specific duties at Ranleigh Hall? And why had he closed the door between them on their wedding night?

"I may have windmills in my head, but no man does that on his wedding night," she said aloud.

She took the cloth off the hearth and wrapped it around the bail of the kettle. Then she carried it to the washstand and poured the steaming water into a chipped porcelain basin, after which she added cold water from an urn until the temperature was pleasant to her touch.

Stripped naked, she scrubbed her entire body with a pleasant-smelling soap that she was sure was meant only for the nobility.

"That's me," she said, hardly believing her words and laughing aloud as she rubbed her skin with a dry towel.

It felt wonderful, and she was not tired at all. Poor Lord Ranleigh; he had appeared exhausted when he left the room. She looked at the clock on the mantel. Twenty minutes had passed; time enough for him to take a quick snooze. A plan quickly materialized.

Remembering her mother's utter dislike for her wifely "duty," Cassandra decided then and there that she would not be like that at all—she would make it easy for her husband to claim his marital rights.

She brushed her hair the required one hundred strokes, quickly donned a thin cotton gown—she wished it was trimmed in French lace—opened the door and went into his room. Her intention was to wake him and tell him she was not scared at all, as her Mama had said every gel should be.

But His Lordship was sleeping so peacefully she decided to crawl up into the high bed and lie beside him until he awoke and discovered her there.

The sweet, fresh smell assaulted Lord Ranleigh's nostrils. He sniffed, then sleep again claimed his exhausted mind. Warm flesh against his surely was a dream.

But a slender arm was flung across his naked body. He opened his right eye, then his left one.

Raising himself onto his elbow, he saw in the moonlight that the narrow window allowed into the room a beautiful face with tousled hair serving as a halo.

He had died and gone to heaven, and then he exclaimed, "Oh, dear God."

Unbearable longing filled him.

She was asleep, for her eyes were closed, and her breasts, beneath a transparent gown that showed brown nipples, rose and fell with pure, even breaths.

God's earth, this is my wife.

His Lordship's first inclination was to bound out of bed and run. But it was too late. She was awake.

"Ranleigh—"

His name was no more than a sigh against his throat, her warm body pressed against his.

No man could resist this, he thought, and caution went out the window. His own heavy breathing was loud in the silent room.

Shifting his weight, he was at once on his knees and pulling her gown up to reveal her nakedness. He prayed that she would awaken and not be frightened. She was, after all, a young gel.

But guilt had no place in His Lordship's emotions as he placed himself, naked, above her.

She stirred and moaned as his lips sought hers, burning, demanding, delicious, and then she was kissing him back and twining her arms around his neck.

"Are you awake?" he asked.

"Enough to know that you are my husband, and that I welcome you."

He thought he heard a sob; the kiss deepened until there was nothing except the two of them, loving each other, his burning lips on hers, moving to her throat where he felt the pounding of her heart against his lips.

"I am not afraid," she said in a low voice.

"Are you aware that there might be some pain?" he asked tenderly. "But it will only last for a moment. I promise to be careful."

And he was, as he listened for the whimper that did not come. Relieved, he allowed the searing passion to take him to the core of her. He heard a slight gasp and knew that he had taken her maidenhead. He paused, while his lips kissed her closed eyes, her tear-wet cheeks, her parted lips, and when he felt her relax he began again the gentle assault that bound two people together, shutting out the world, making them one.

"Oh, God," he whispered again.

Time gave itself unbegrudgingly to the silent and moonlit room. He felt her sharp nails bite into his shoulders, sweet delicious pain, as her body arched to meet his thrusts, time and time again, until in the spiraling rapture there were no thoughts or words, just raging ecstasy that took them beyond time, beyond themselves, so beautiful that Lord Ranleigh wished he would never return.

Seven

The coach and four topped Cassandra's hillock by midafternoon the next day. Below sat Ranleigh Hall, powerful, imposing, and still the most beautiful place Cassandra had ever seen. Flowers bloomed profusely in the gardens; waves beat against the rocks, filling the air with spray and the booming sounds of the sea. Cassandra sucked in her breath: She was coming home.

She was no longer a nubile gel wondering what *it* was all about. "She was a woman, a wife, a Countess. Life should be perfect, but it wasn't.

Last night her husband had been a wonderful lover, but at dawn when she awakened he was already out of bed, dressed, and gone, and when he returned to the room he seemed unhappy and spoke shortly to her, asking her to please hurry so they could be on their way.

So they had left the inn at first light, and brooding silence had been their companion ever since. It was as if last night had never happened. Upon entering the carriage, he gained the squab across from her and thereafter kept his gaze on the countryside, speaking only when she spoke to him, and then grudgingly.

Mayhap I will learn to understand him, she mused, praying that she would. She looked at him, studied the darkness in his eyes, the sadness, and realized that she

89

loved him too much to be angry with him. Then her gaze moved over his tall, muscular body, splendidly dressed, as if he was going to meet with the Prince Regent or some other dignitary. Fawn breeches stretched over his long legs, and an impeccably tailored coat showed his broad shoulders to advantage. Most likely the coat was from a fine tailor in London, for it looked as if no expense had been spared. She wore the dress that Sister Martha had lengthened with a band of faded cloth. He had not seemed to notice, and it was not until now that she found herself feeling dowdy.

'Tis because I will soon be among the strangers at Ranleigh Hall. As Countess of Ranleigh, I should be properly clad.

Letting down the window, she shifted her thoughts to the hillock from which they were descending. It was spring, and the trees were gloriously dressed, thrushes warbled, and bees hummed drunkenly as they gathered nectar to make their honey. Fields of spring crops stretched to the far hills, dappled gray and green by scudding clouds.

"They are expecting us, are they not?" she asked.

"No. My family seldom knows what I am doing," was His Lordship's quick answer, and then he added, "I saw no reason to tell them I was fetching a bride to Ranleigh Hall."

Cassandra could only shake her head in puzzlement. What an enigma he was. For a moment their eyes met, and then he looked away. If only she could read his mind.

How I pity her, he thought, and anger at himself roiled up from the depths of his soul. How unfair he had been to the innocent gel. And him a man of the world. He had broken all rules of honor. Miss Edwards . . . Lady Ranleigh could never be his wife. He did not want a wife; yet he had taken her without reservations. He cursed his libido. Only once before in his life had he shown weakness in that regard, and he had paid dearly

90

for his mistake. What a sweet gel, so naively innocent, his bride was. Bride! He choked on the word as his eyes traversed her youthful, budding body, clad in that awful dress, even with the extension still too short, from under which protruded incongruously the pink slippers with satin rosebuds on their toes.

His Lordship regretted infinitely that he had not stopped and purchased a gown for her to wear to Ranleigh Hall, but his mind had been selfishly on himself and the predicament in which he had gotten himself. He asked himself why he not been able to explain the agreement to her. He'd had the perfect opportunity when she had laughingly told him that she had come to his bed because she was determined to be a better wife than her dear dead Mama had been.

Again, he cursed sister Martha. The good Sister had failed in her duty completely, and he vowed that as soon as they reached the Hall he would explain to Cassandra that only for appearance's sake would they behave as if they were man and wife. He would tell her that what happened last night would not happen again.

But he found himself regretting that terribly. Never had he felt such fulfillment as he had with her.

It was waking and finding a stranger in my bed, he told himself, knowing it was not true.

As if he were saying goodbye to those wonderful shared moments, he let his mind relive the ecstasy, and his body became warm, his pulse beginning to pound.

For necessity's sake, he soon thrust the thoughts away and decided vehemently that he must needs not delay his journey to London to visit Elsa, his Spanish wildcat he kept for the express purpose of satisfying his raging libido.

He said to Cassandra, "When I next visit London I will send a modiste to Ranleigh. You must needs have suitable gowns—"

"Stuff! That will not be necessary. I shall go to London with you and visit a modiste there. Why have her come to me when I am perfectly able to travel?"

His Lordship gave a coaxing smile. "You don't understand. It will be your *duty* to care for Jacob . . . at Ranleigh."

"Balderdash," Cassandra said with alacrity. "I shall take Jacob with me. He will enjoy seeing the sights of London. As will I. I've never been there. Jacob's nursemaid will accompany us."

"Jacob is unable to travel, and a nurse for him is out of the question. One after another have come to the Hall, but they have left. *You* will be his nurse."

The conversation ended there, for the carriage suddenly pulled to a stop in front of Ranleigh Hall's huge lichen-framed doors, and a liveried footman was instantly letting down the step.

"Thank you, William," Lord Ranleigh said. He bounded to the ground, then reached back and helped Cassandra to alight.

"I beg your forgiveness, m'lord," William said. "I do not mean to sound forward, but 'tis good you are here. Young Jacob is on a dreadful tear."

"How is his health?" Lord Ranleigh asked anxiously.

"The same. Cook said his cough kept her awake into the night."

"Good Lord, is Cook tending him?"

"I'm afraid so. The last gel yer mater hired despaired of him and left in the wee morning hours of this day. Yes, m'lord, 'tis good yer home."

"Thank you, William," Lord Ranleigh said dismissing him.

They went inside the Hall, where they were met by a butler who, Cassandra noticed, looked at her as if she were hired help.

And, indeed, that is what he thought, she soon learned. After bowing to Lord Ranleigh the butler said, " 'Tis good you have brought someone to care for the young master." Turning to Cassandra, he welcomed her with, "I hope you will find it in your heart to stay, ma'am."

Cassandra was very much aware of his gaze moving over her wind-tousled hair, then down to appraise her dress. She almost laughed. Indeed, she did look like a servant. "I intend to stay," she told him. "I am Lady Ranleigh. His Lordship and I were married only yesterday in Gretna Green. But not in a smithy's shop. Our marriage was blessed by a vicar."

She proffered a hand, which the butler ignored. Embarrassed beyond bearing, she dropped it to her side.

Tilting his head back, the butler looked quizzically over his hooked nose up into Lord Ranleigh's face, obviously disbelieving Cassandra.

Lord Ranleigh said curtly, "Mansford, may I present my wife, Cassandra, Countess of Ranleigh."

The butler's face flushed a purple red, his words became largely incomprehensible. "Y . . . your wife. A new Countess! Saints save us. I thought there would never be another, so dear was your first one."

Cassandra quickly looked to see Lord Ranleigh's reaction. His dark eyes were blacker than midnight. The hardness of his voice when he spoke left no doubt of his anger, which sliced the air like a well-honed razor.

"Any reference to my first Countess is forbidden in Ranleigh Hall. Her name is not to be mentioned. I believe you, and the rest of the staff, have been apprised of that fact. If you cannot abide by the rules of the Hall, then I suggest you leave your post immediately."

The butler bowed twice, as if he were a puppet and had no control over what he was doing, each time almost stumbling over himself.

"I b . . . b . . . beg your forgiveness, M'Lord. I got carried away, so shocked was I. I . . . I do beg your forgiveness."

With that, he turned quickly and bowed to Cassandra,

somehow managing to sputter, "Lady Ranleigh, a thousand welcomes," and he departed with great speed, his long black coat flapping against his short legs.

Poor man, Cassandra thought, watching after him. Lord Ranleigh had left him no quarter. And it was strange indeed that Lord Ranleigh's recently dead wife's name could not be mentioned in the Hall.

Before making an inquiry about such an odd rule she sought his face and immediately decided against doing so. It would most likely be her head he would be biting off.

With determined cheerfulness, she said, "I'm so anxious to see Ranleigh Hall."

Lord Ranleigh did not answer.

"Oh, pooh," she said in disgust, and she quickly decided not to let His Lordship's obvious unhappy mood keep her from enjoying her first glimpse of the wondrous Ranleigh Hall. How she had longed to see it.

As her eyes moved furtively, her heart sang. Never had she seen anything so wonderfully grand. Even her dreams had not done the cavernous hall justice, for it reached at least two hundred feet in length, and bronze statues, with outstretched arms holding hundreds of lighted candles, furnished glowing light.

Chairs and ancestral portraits lined the walls. And to each side there were great tall doors that Cassandra could only assume opened into receiving rooms. She had seen sketches of Windsor Castle and was reminded of the rooms there.

Lost in her perusal, she looked up. From the two-story, curved-domed ceiling, which was decorated with dancing cherubs of gold and pink, and flying angels with halos, huge crystal chandeliers cast down circles of light to dance on a sparkling black-and-white marble floor.

They moved on. In the center of the hall, a round table held a huge bowl of fresh flowers, and at the far end, twin stairs led to a second-story balustraded balcony.

"The main part of the house was built in 1607," said Lord Ranleigh. "This floor was stone. Only in recent years was it replaced by marble and used for dancing." And then he added, "The chandeliers were also added then."

She said, "Oh! I was not aware that balls were held at Ranleigh Hall. When I watched"—she had told him of sitting on the hillock and staring down at his home—"it always seemed so ghostly quiet, almost deserted—"

"That is only recently. Before that, people came from everywhere for dancing, and then there were the hunts. I rather enjoyed those."

No man ever felt such pain, Cassandra mused as she listened to his words. Losing his first countess must have robbed him of his soul. Jealousy reared its ugly head, but she told herself that what was past was past. She only wished her husband could feel that way again. Then, a few steps farther on, she saw something that chilled her blood.

Cassandra did not have to be told that the portrait, which hung over a marble fireplace large enough to roast a full-grown cow, was of the first Countess. Laughing, piercing emerald-green eyes looked down on Cassandra. She had heard of the late Countess's alabaster skin and emerald eyes, but she had not been prepared for this.

A beam of light engulfed the lifelike portrait, as Cassandra, mesmerized, stood and stared at the sensuous, half-parted lips that seemed about to speak. One could feel the gusts of wind that lifted her rich auburn hair, sending it flying back from a heart-shaped face.

And the same wind pushed her transparent white gown against her flawless body, showing two perfectly pointed breasts with brown nipples.

Pragmatic and not one to equivocate, Cassandra

asked, "Must I live with *that*? Why did you not remove it when you knew I would be coming? There was plenty of time."

When there was no answer Cassandra continued, "Does *she* still rule Ranleigh Hall?"

Lord Ranleigh said as if he was speaking to himself, "I want the portrait there. I never want to forget . . ."

The deadness in his voice sent another chill up and down Cassandra's spine, and her anger flared, making her face feel hot and damp. He should not have married her until his grieving had past.

Mayhap it will never be over.

That thought sent Cassandra's heart into another tail-spin, to the very deepest cavern of her being.

They walked on until they reached the stairs, which they ascended to the second floor. There, Cassandra learned what it was really like to be made to feel unwelcome.

Lord Ranleigh's remark, "Might as well get this over with," warned her, but not entirely.

A knock on the door with a brass knocker brought a hopeful "Enter," which they did, passing through a very elaborate sitting room before reaching the bedchamber.

The Dowager Countess was propped up in bed against copious pillows, her white hair perfectly coiffed, her fat neck covered with rows of ruffled lace. The sleeves—huge puffs tied at intervals between shoulders and wrists with ribbons—covered her plump arms. The dressing gown was white, as was everything else on the bed, except a plate of chocolate bonbons that rested well within arm's reach. Cassandra waited for her greeting, which did not come.

Instead, the dowager, her eyes focused on Lord Ranleigh, said, "When I heard the knock I hoped you were Wade. He's been gone ever so long this time."

Cassandra saw Lord Ranleigh grimace.

"A bad penny always turns up, Isabelle; you can count on it," he said derisively.

"Your brother is not a bad penny. He loves his Mummy—"

"Yes, a grown man loves his Mummy. And his Mummy spoils him rotten."

Cassandra stood on first one foot and then the other. What was she supposed to do while these two squabbled over a brother who had been gone ever so long? Closing out the sound of the dowager's quarrelsome voice and Lord Ranleigh's stern one, she occupied herself by looking around the opulent room, which was literally wrapped in white silk—the bed trappings, the chairs that flanked the fireplace, even the fainting couch.

Yards and yards of the same white silk covered the windows. The carpet that covered the wood floor was also white.

The marble fireplace was black, and even before she raised her eyes, Cassandra knew that over it hung the first Countess's portrait. When she raised her eyes it was there, an exact replica of the one in the great hall, only smaller, staring down at her with those green eyes.

Cassandra turned away, biting her lip and fighting back sudden tears that threatened to reveal the churning that was going on inside her. The woman was everywhere.

She turned back to the bed in time to see the Dowager Countess plop a chocolate bonbon in her mouth. After chewing hungrily and swallowing she turned a cold gaze in Cassandra's direction, letting her sharp eyes take in the faded dress and its equally faded extension, and then move to look at Lord Ranleigh.

The tone of her voice was nasty. "Did you bring a new nursemaid from London? How long do you think *she* will last with the little monster?"

Lord Ranleigh's answer came quickly. "This is Cassandra, Countess of Ranleigh. We were married yesterday in Gretna Green."

97

Bits of bonbon, mixed with saliva, sprayed out onto the white gown, the coverlet, the pillows, and coughing and choking followed.

Cassandra wanted to grab the woman and pound her in the back. A stern look from His Lordship stopped her.

When the coughing subsided the dowager fainted dead away.

Lord Ranleigh tugged the bellpull and presently, as if she had had an ear to the door, a maid appeared, a vial of vinaigrette in her hand.

Moments went by, while the vial was waved rhythmically before the fainting woman's fat face, until she slapped at the maid's hand, knocking the vinaigrette to the floor.

Looking at Lord Ranleigh, the dowager said with extreme strength and feeling, "How dare you try to replace dear Sylvia with one of the lower orders? Someone not quality-born?"

Before Lord Ranleigh could reply, she added, "Your brother should be Lord of Ranleigh Hall. He would never dream of doing such a thing."

The stone-dead silence was palpable. It shook the room.

Cassandra felt herself stiffen, while her chin went automatically into its indomitable set. Looking up at Lord Ranleigh, she saw corded muscles on his neck fighting for control. He spoke in a light tone, undergirded with steel.

"I beg you not to embarrass Lady Ranleigh."

"Balderdash! A lady indeed!"

Then and there Cassandra decided to take a stand, else she would be at this woman's mercy for the rest of her life.

Sister Martha should have told her of this rude woman.

Cassandra stepped back and sank into a deep curtsy. "M'lady, I do not plan to replace the late Countess of Ranleigh. I intend to make my own place in your son's life . . . and at Ranleigh Hall."

She waited for the Dowager Countess of Ranleigh to speak, but her face was now turned to the wall

"Demme to hell," Lord Ranleigh said.

Whirling around, he grabbed Cassandra's arm and practically dragged her from the room, flinging back over his shoulder as they left, "Isabelle, come to the library within the hour. We *will* have an understanding about this. Jacob's life is at stake."

Cassandra did not know whether to cry or to laugh. She did neither.

As she followed her husband, she wondered what den of lions he would take her to next.

She did not have long to wait, for quickly they climbed the stairs to the third floor, where he opened the door without knocking.

There, in an austere room hardly better than the one Cassandra had occupied at Sister Martha's orphanage, a little boy sat at a wooden table methodically dissecting a wooden horse. Already its head had been removed from its body, and he was diligently working on the right foreleg.

A harried man, whom Cassandra assumed must be an instructor of some sort, for he held a book in his hand, sat on a nearby stool.

As Cassandra and Lord Ranleigh stood unobtrusively in the doorway, the black-suited man pleaded, "Jacob, we must needs do your lesson."

"Demme to hell," the little boy said, ignoring the man's pleading.

Cassandra listened in disbelief. The swearing, no doubt, was brought on because the tool he was using to kill off the poor horse had slipped, hurting him; his thumb went into his mouth and he sat there sucking on it.

Out of the corner of his eye, he watched the intruders, pretending to ignore them.

Cassandra knew exactly what to do with rude little boys who practiced bad manners toward their elders, most especially boys who used vile language.

Cassandra waited, and observed.

Jacob gave the appearance of a girl; ringlets of sand-colored hair touched his shoulders, and the white blouse he wore had big puffy sleeves and a bow at its neck. A skirt, not breeches, covered his legs, and he wore soft slippers on his feet.

"Jacob," Lord Ranleigh said, stepping into the room, "you really should be doing your lessons."

Not a *hello*, or *I'm glad to see you*, and Jacob made it plain that he was not glad to see his Papa either. "Don't lecture me, Your Lordship. I am not in the mood to study." Inclining his head toward the man in the black suit, Jacob continued in a commanding voice, "Tell him to go away."

"You may be excused," Lord Ranleigh said, and the man left.

It was obvious to Cassandra that Lord Ranleigh did not know his son's tutor's name, just as it was obvious that His Lordship did not know what to do with his son.

Jacob again became preoccupied with destroying the wooden horse, hitting it forcefully again and again with the iron tool.

"This demme horse—"

Lord Ranleigh said, "Jacob, this is—"

"I know. Another nurse."

For the first time Cassandra received the full attention of Ranleigh Hall's heir. He spat out at her, "Have you not heard what happens to nursemaids at Ranleigh Hall? They leave because they cannot stand me. I'm a terror." He laughed then, a thin, cynical laugh too old

100

for his five years. "The old dowager calls me a monster."

Cassandra gave him a smile, for in his tiny voice she heard a cry for help. She went to kneel beside him. "Poor horse. Let's let him have his head back."

Jacob was instantly on his feet. Reaching down with both hands, he lifted the horse's head and, had Cassandra not grabbed his arms and held them, he would have hit her on the top of the head with it. The intent was clear in his eyes.

Holding his arms, Cassandra realized the frailty of the five-year-old. His arms were like sticks in her grasp. Close up, his face was thin and gaunt, his blue eyes faded, sunken into the thin face.

"I am not a nurse," she said to him in a kind voice. "I'm your new Stepmama. Yesterday, I married your Papa, and this day I came to Ranleigh Hall to live—"

"And this day you may leave," Jacob said. "I don't need a Stepmama anymore than I need a nurse.

He still held the horse's head. Lord Ranleigh stepped forward, but Cassandra shook her head and, with her eyes, begged that he defer to her. Which he did, stepping back.

She took the horse's head and placed it on the table the tutor had been attempting to use as a desk.

"I will not leave, Jacob," she said. "Ranleigh Hall is now my home, so you may stop your ugly antics. Tomorrow, I shall work on your schedule, after I've had considerable time to think on why you are playing the bad boy."

"Demme your schedule. I won't—"

Cassandra smiled. "You will. And from this day forward every time you use a nasty word, your mouth will be washed out with foul-tasting soap."

She looked at Lord Ranleigh, wanting to say to him that if he had been using nasty words in front of his son he would be expected to stop. But she held her tongue, and rising, tugged the bellpull for someone to come. Soon thereafter Cook waddled into the room and took charge of the incorrigible heir to Ranleigh Hall.

When Cassandra bent to kiss him goodbye he slapped her away and said, "And don't come back,"

"I shall be back, Jacob," Cassandra answered pleasantly. "Next time I will read you a story."

Outside, in the wide hallway, Cassandra scolded, "The least you could have done was touch the boy. You *are* his father."

"That is not done."

"Stuff. If it's not done, then it should be."

"That is why I asked Sister Martha to recommend one of her charges for me to marry. I felt that mayhaps an orphan would be kind to the boy, give him the love he has never had. I was right. Just now, you were perfectly wonderful in dealing with him. I've always feared to be stern, his health being so poor. Besides, 'tis a woman's place to tend the boy."

And then he added, "I pray that you will stay. That is why I married you."

Eight

That is why I asked Sister Martha to recommend one of her charges for me to marry. I felt that mayhap an orphan would be kind to the boy. I pray that you will stay. That is why I married you . . .

Lord Ranleigh's words pounded Cassandra's brain. How naive she had been to think a man of the nobility would choose her, an orphan without a decent day dress to her name, to be his wife.

That only happened in fanciful dreams.

After leaving the pitiful little boy, Jacob, her husband—and this description brought a bitter taste to Cassandra's mouth—had taken her to *their* chambers, then left to go to the library for the audience with the dowager.

Cassandra could not imagine what more could be said between the two. The old woman had made it plain that she felt Ranleigh Hall disgraced beyond measure by Cassandra's entrance through its hallowed, lichen-framed doors.

"But of course there's more to be said," Cassandra said aloud. "He will tell her that I am to be Jacob's nursemaid, nothing more."

She went to look out the window and studied the angry sea, felt its fury mingle with hers as it sloshed against the rocks. Last night's closeness to His Lordship briefly passed through her mind; the warmth, the ecstasy momentarily returned.

She had felt so loved.

Not a bawler, Cassandra refused to cry. She could not help it if tears threatened. But she refused to let the wonderful feeling of being loved by her husband linger long in her thoughts, for this was the real world, not the world she had created on her hillock. She was no longer a young gel filled with impossible dreams.

Why does the disappointment hurt so much?

She turned back into the room and went to dig into her satchel, which a servant had placed in there, and found the lace-trimmed valentine she had so happily drawn while sitting on the hillock. She held it to her breast and wished she were that young gel again, that she was back at the orphanage, dreaming dreams that could not possibly come true.

The tears made their way to her cheeks. She felt as if she had been run over by a coach and four; the big wheels were crushing the life from her. Her own breath resounded in her ears, coming in ragged spurts.

Not once in her ruminations did Cassandra think to blame Sister Martha for her predicament. The aging mother of many had simply done what she thought best for one of her charges. And mayhap the good Sister had not been told that she, Cassandra, was coming to Ranleigh Hall to serve as a nurse for a neglected little boy, the heir to Ranleigh Hall, the entailed Ranleigh estates, the earldom. A little boy who wanted to destroy everything in sight.

Mayhap it was Lord Ranleigh's secret—until he told the Dowager.

Cassandra let her eyes once again peruse the elegant drawing room which, according to Lord Ranleigh, was a minute part of the quarters she was to share with him. Upon leaving the sparse room in which Jacob took his lessons, His Lordship had brought her here, striding through a wide corridor, twisting and turning down long halls, until they finally arrived at the far northeastern corner of the manor, on the second floor.

"There's a beautiful view of the sea," he had said when they entered, and he had gone on to explain that everyone who lived at Ranleigh Hall had his or her own apartment, complete with a small galley in which servants could heat food should it grow cold on the way from the main kitchen.

"Breakfast is served in the smaller morning room," he had said.

Here, where she was to live, she felt miles away from the Great Hall, and most especially away from Jacob. Already she had developed an affinity for the little boy, and she would not object to being his nurse, if that was not the *only* reason she had been brought to Ranleigh Hall.

Then she deliberately conjured up hope. Mayhap she had concluded too quickly His Lordship's intent; mayhap he would come tonight to her bed, as was expected of a husband, and they could be man and wife in the biblical sense as they had been on their wedding night, and he would make her feel loved again. Mayhap he did love her, or, as time went by, would come to do so.

She held fast to the thought that he had brought her to his apartment when he could have lodged her in a mean room next to Jacob's. He must be a good man, kind and gentle, the man of whom she had dreamed. As she stood there, thinking thus, letting hope replace her despair, the tears dried on her cheeks.

I have loved him for such a long time, even before I met him. I will believe the best of my husband.

As she stood surrounded in such luxury as she had never known, she said aloud, "I bound that *he* will come to my bed . . ."

His raging passion, of which she had received a liberal dose on their wedding night, would bring him.

105

Whatever had emboldened her to go to his bed? A hot flush of embarrassment swept her face and neck, and then her whole body felt warm from it. She grimaced at her naïveté in thinking he was too shy to even hold her hand when they were traveling in the carriage. In her mind's eye she could see his grim mouth and his square-set jaw as he sat back against the squabs opposite her. She had wondered then what were his thoughts.

A long time passed, until it dawned on Cassandra that the extensive mulling was only an indulgence to keep from looking at the portrait of Lady Ranleigh that dominated the beautiful room.

As they had entered the drawing room through the big double doors, she had caught a glimpse, as if drawn to do so, into a large mirror hanging on the wall opposite the fireplace, seeing a startling reflection of the late Sylvia Ranleigh.

In this portrait she wore a gown of emerald green satin, with an extremely low décolletage, above which white flesh bulged in abundance.

After the first glance Cassandra had averted her eyes from the portrait. Even so, the Countess's green eyes watched her every step. How could she live with that?

Cassandra forced her thoughts to the room in which she stood. She looked around at her new and strange surroundings. Crimson silk trimmed in gold fringe hung in swags and folds from tall, narrow windows. Gold ropes with tassels held back the silk, letting in light from the dying sun. Sofas and chairs were covered with the same bright crimson.

The room was cozy, she decided. Between the windows, the high white walls held beautiful paintings of undulating blue-black water, with seagulls flying above, their wings outstretched. One showed her hillock, carpeted in blue bells; in another, brown stone rookeries defied mile-high blasts from an angry sea. Obviously not painted by a grand master, but done exceptionally well, she thought as she began pacing.

Every nerve in her body was unstrung as she fought to keep her eyes from the portrait of the woman who had before her shared this room with Lord Ranleigh.

She had not ventured into the other rooms of the apartment, but she had no doubt that every room held such a likeness of the late Countess, probably even the small kitchen of which Lord Ranleigh had spoken.

Hearing a faint knock on the door, Cassandra, promising herself to think on what to do with the portraits later—for she could not possibly live with them—went to the door and opened it, expecting the maid Lord Ranleigh had said he would send to tend her. It was not the maid.

"Hall-o," a rather tall gel of slender build said.

Corn-silk hair fell around her shoulders, and her smile was meant to bring light to the darkest soul. Cassandra knew her immediately, and she tried to remember what Lord Ranleigh had said about his sister Cynthia. It was something about her being the only bright light at Ranleigh Hall.

Cassandra was glad to see her, to see anyone who wore a welcoming smile. She stared at her. Obviously she had been riding. Her habit was exquisite, purple and red velvet, and she wore riding boots.

"I am Cynthia," the gel said. "And you are my brother's new wife, the orphan who has given Mummy the vapors." A laugh followed; and then she asked, "May I come in?"

"Of course you may," Cassandra said, embarrassed that she had stood and stared so long. She added by way of apology, "I'm so happy to see you, Cynthia."

Cassandra held out her hand, and Cynthia clasped it warmly and held it a long time before letting it go. Cassandra stepped back and opened the door wider.

Cynthia swept into the room and went to sit on one of the crimson sofas, pulling her legs under her.

Cassandra lowered herself into a nearby chair.

"I came to tell you not to let Mummy bother you," Cynthia said.

"Is she ill?" Cassandra asked quickly.

That smile again. "Only when it is to her advantage. She's been that way since I was born. She never wanted me, especially since I was a woods' colt."

"What on earth is a woods' colt?"

A giggle. "A babe born on the wrong side of the blanket. Her husband, the fifth Earl of Bedford, had been dead ten months, but the records were altered to show that he died in April instead of May.

Cassandra laughed, then accused, "You're funning me."

"No, I'm not."

"Did the dowager tell you?"

"Of course not, goose. What woman admits to committing adultery? The nobility thinks it great sport to keep everyone guessing. You will learn that the blue bloods and the aristocracy behave abominably. Just think of Prinny and his many bits of muslin."

"That doesn't mean that your mother—"

"I have ways of finding out things about Ranleigh Hall and its occupants no one else is privy to. Why, my great, great, great-grandfather kept four mistresses at one time, right here at Ranleigh Hall." Another giggle. "He must have been a randy old man. He was seventy at the time, if I remember correctly."

Sighing theatrically, Cynthia turned and stretched supine on the sofa.

It was obvious to Cassandra that her new sister-in-law adored gossip. But Cassandra wanted to know more about the present occupants of Ranleigh Hall.

She asked again, "What ails the dowager?"

"You mean because she takes to her bed and stuffs

108

herself with chocolate candy? Sometimes she refuses to walk and has the servants carry her belowstairs in a sedan chair. Pure fiction."

"What is wrong with her this time? I mean, what is bothering her? Obviously, she did not know that Lord Ranleigh would be marrying one of Sister Martha's orphans, but it could not have been that. She was already in bed when we arrived."

"Oh, she's upset because Wade has been gone a fortnight. He's a charming rakehell, but he's her favorite." Her eyes twinkled. "Watch him; he will be after you."

Cassandra ignored this last remark. "The dowager made it plain that she favored her younger son and spoke rather crossly to Lord Ranleigh."

"Don't let that fool you. Your husband is the Lord of Ranleigh Hall. He'll only let Mummy go so far. If I were you, I would not cross him."

Cassandra wanted to ask about the dowager's devotion to the late Countess, but feared that she should not.

She did, however, broach the subject cautiously with, "Lord Ranleigh's first wife . . . were you fond of her?"

Deafening silence quivered in the room, and Cynthia's countenance suddenly changed.

Cassandra would have unsaid the words if she could have, but it was too late, and there was nothing for her to do but wait as the silence became longer.

At last, Cynthia, frowning, said succinctly, "The secrets of Ranleigh Hall are best left secret. I have told you one, no, two, counting the one about randy great, great, great-grandfather. That is enough." With that, she bounded to her feet, as if to go.

Cassandra desperately wanted her to stay, and said so. "I'm sorry I pried. If you will stay, I promise not to mention the first Countess again."

Cynthia sat back down. A winsome smile replaced the frown as she eyed Cassandra's dress. Shaking her head, she said, "I bound something has to be done."

"You mean about my dress? I know 'tis terrible, but it was the best Sister Martha could do. She has so many little ones to feed and clothe. Lord Ranleigh said he would send a modiste when next he goes to London, but I suggested that I accompany him into Town."

"That will take too long. I shall return shortly with one of my gowns. We're not too different in size."

Before Cassandra could object, Cynthia left, and in no time at all, or so it seemed to Cassandra, was back, carrying over her arm not one but two handsome gowns.

"This is my favorite, and it will match your eyes. I like dresses to match my eyes. Don't you?"

"I've never thought about it," Cassandra answered truthfully.

Pushing back a chair, Cynthia spread a dove-gray silk gown, with a bright-red ribbon at the high waist, on the colorful carpet. It appeared to Cassandra that hardly any material had been left to cover one's bosom, and the tiny puffed sleeves would barely cup one's upper arms.

" 'Tis lovely," she said over a lump in her throat.

"Then let's put it on. We must needs hurry, else Lord Ranleigh will find you half dressed." Another giggle spilled out into the room. "Of course, that would not matter since you are married."

"Should we not go to a dressing room?"

"No time."

The happy mood was infectious, and Cassandra found her spirits rising. She quickly stepped out of the faded, ugly dress and donned the gray silk. This time when she looked in the mirror she saw herself, not the reflection of Lord Ranleigh's first Countess.

"Try these on," Cynthia said, producing a pair of gray kid slippers, squealing with delight when they fit Cassandra's feet perfectly. "One must always match slip-

110

pers and gowns," she said, smoothing the skirt, plucking at the sleeves, straightening the puffs.

Until at last, giving her biggest smile yet, Cynthia declared, "Don't you look grand?"

Cassandra could have hugged her, for, indeed, she did look grand. And she felt grand. This lovely, lively gel had expunged all unhappy thoughts from her mind, and Cassandra would not dwell on them again. She was Lord Ranleigh's wife, and he would treat her so. He had not meant it when he'd said he had married her because she, being an orphan, would make a suitable nurse to his heir. It was simple; she had misunderstood.

"I do not need, nor do I want a wife," Lord Ranleigh was saying. "As I've said before, that which happened last night must not happen again."

"And why not?" Cassandra wanted to know. "Was I not pleasing to you? Is it not expected in a marriage?"

Lord Ranleigh groaned and held his head in his hands. Having just returned from the audience with the dowager, he was sitting on the sofa just recently occupied by his sister. Could this gel not understand what being "married in name only" meant?

He tried again: "In a normal marriage, yes, but ours is a marriage of convenience. You cannot say that you were better off at the orphanage than you are here."

He inclined his head to the opulent room, then went on. "And I am very pleased with the way you handled Jacob. I believe you will have him well in no time, with your kind ways."

Cassandra was so angry she could not speak, but her heart cried out in a silent, hurting way: *I don't want your fine furnishings, your riches, nor your beautiful gowns; I want to be loved.*

Lord Ranleigh continued, "You will be richly rewarded for your services. But you will be my wife in name only. But I do not want our arrangement to become common knowledge for the gossipmongers to chew on over tea."

"You mean that the dowager is not to know?"

"Most especially Isabelle. For appearance's sake, you and I are a happily married couple. And I expect that shall be so. We will be friends. As Countess of Ranleigh, you will have anything money can buy. Your spending will not be curtailed. In return, you will care for Jacob—"

"And pretend to be happy," Cassandra spat out, standing, for she could not bear to sit.

One would think that he was offering me the fox on a silver platter, after the hunt.

She wanted to slap the worried look from his face. And well he should be worried. How could anyone bargain over something as sacred as marriage? She kept her lips determinedly sealed. *Do not promise anything until you have thought this through,* she cautioned herself silently, glad that at last it was her mind and not her heart that was offering guidance.

How silly she had been to hope.

"Many marriages of this sort succeed. With the *ton* it is the thing," Lord Ranleigh said placatingly. "If you choose, and can do it discreetly, you may take a lover. . . ."

Cassandra's big gray eyes narrowed to slits, and her gaze never left his face; yet she did not speak, because she knew for sure she would choke on her words. How dare he suggest she break her wedding vows?

Lord Ranleigh became suddenly defensive. He was frowning and looking straight into Cassandra's face. "Demmet, you needed a way out of that awful orphanage and I needed a loving nurse for Jacob."

Cassandra continued staring, without so much as a blink. Let him talk to his heart's content, she would not reveal her inclinations to him now, maybe never. She set her chin in its stubborn line, as she had seen Sister Martha do so often.

Lord Ranleigh sighed audibly and slapped his palms against his knees, then stood.

Cassandra wanted him to leave, and she allowed herself only a small flinch when he said as he gained the door, "Demmet, rid yourself of that gown. 'Tis indecent, with half your bosom showing."

Nine

Cassandra had no notion of removing Cynthia's lovely gown. Hurt to the core, she waited until the door closed behind her husband-in-name-only; and then for a long while she stood remarkably still and stared at herself in the tall looking glass, thinking about the wonderful wardrobe she would order when she went to London. Before that sojourn she would return to Wickham Market and collect her debt from Stella, and mayhap order day, carriage, and riding dresses, all with low décolletage. A more fashionable modiste in London would be hired, one who would make her dozens of the transparent gowns she had heard the upper orders were wearing. Lord Ranleigh would . . .

It was no use. The wonderful, crazy thoughts of revenge did not diminish the pain, and she could no longer fight the tears that scalded her cheeks. Giving way to heart-wrenching sobs, she crumpled onto the floor and rested her head on the sofa. The unwanted tears dampened the crimson silk, causing a dark circle to spread out from her face. Between sobs, she planned to return to the orphanage and help Sister Martha with her children. Anything was better than this. Then she thought of little Jacob, his thin arms, his gaunt face, his haunting eyes.

Cassandra's thoughts turned entirely away from herself. She would go to Jacob. After all, she had been brought to Ranleigh Hall to be his nurse. Rising slowly, she dried her tears and tugged the bellpull. When a maid appeared she ordered water brought so that she could wash her face.

The maid's eyebrows shot up questioningly at her summons.

"Stop staring," Cassandra told her crossly, adding, "I am Countess of Ranleigh—"

"Yes, mum, I've been told."

"Then, when you answer my summons you are to act accordingly."

"Ye mean bob?"

"Yes, bob. And not condescendingly. Now, go prepare water for washing, and if the water is cold, bring it hot from the kitchen."

"Thet's a footman's job, to carry the tankards. I ken start a fire in the kitchen hearth up here," retorted the maid, her black bombazine rustling as she moved across the room.

"That will take too long."

Cassandra had forgotten that Lord Ranleigh had said their quarters had a small galley, and she suddenly remembered that she had not the slightest notion as to where it was located. But it was not the poor maid's fault, Cassandra reasoned, suddenly stricken with guilt. It was not her nature to be cruel to anyone. Undoubtedly, the maid had been told that the new Countess of Ranleigh was an impostor trying to replace Lord Ranleigh's precious first Countess.

"Stuff!" Cassandra said; "just pour the water, cold or not."

She followed the maid through a very pretty bedchamber, decorated in pale peach with touches of the same crimson that filled the drawing room and then into a large dressing room lined with floor-to-ceiling, gold-framed looking glasses. This did not surprise Cassandra. The looking glasses no doubt had been a necessity, so that the first Countess could admire herself from every angle, every hour of the day.

Another wall held a chiffonnier. Swinging open the door, she found it full of beautiful gowns. The smell of lavender rushed out to hit her in the face, and suddenly Cassandra felt that should she look up she would see the sainted Countess flitting just below the high ceiling, wings spread, and with scepter in hand, ready to strike Cassandra dead should she touch one of the fabulous gowns. A shiver passed through Cassandra. She did not like living with a ghost.

"Remove these at once," she said to the maid, and watched her cower, her hands covering her open mouth, her dark eyes glaring with fright.

"Mum . . . I mean Yer Ladyship, I kent do that."

"And why not? The woman has been dead three years now. Cassandra stood pensively for a moment. "I certainly hope His Lordship does not expect me to wear his late wife's clothing."

"I don't know what His Lordship thinks, yer Ladyship. He's a strange one, if I must say so meself. Who woulda thought he'd bring another to take *her* place."

Cassandra could see that this cowardly maid would most likely expire if she touched one of the garments.

"Never mind. I will have them removed when I engage a lady's maid—"

"Engage a lady's maid! The Dowager would not like that. She said I was to be yer lady's maid."

"I shall choose my own lady's maid. You may go now. I will pour my own water."

The maid leapt to attention, grabbed the pitcher, and splashed water into the basin.

"Thank you," Cassandra said. "Now you may go, and never mind coming back until I call you. I am accustomed to dressing myself."

116

"I hear yer from the orphanage—"

"That's right." Cassandra bent and splashed water over her face; and when she turned, the maid stood with a towel from the rack in her hand, which she stuck forward.

"Here, Yer Ladyship?"

Cassandra took the towel and began rubbing her face. Never had she felt anything so wonderful against her skin. "What is your name?" Cassandra asked when she was through drying.

"Millie, Yer Ladyship."

Cassandra forced a smile and returned the towel to the rack herself, saying, "Millie, I would like to be alone. When you return belowstairs, please inform the person to whom you are responsible to let you have your old job back. I plan to engage my own servants. No offense to you, but I think that best."

The last thing Cassandra wanted was sniffling servants who romanticized in a worshipful manner about the deceased Countess. Why couldn't they let the poor woman rest in peace?

"I don't want to lose me place, Yer Ladyship."

Cassandra gave the trembling maid a soft pat on the shoulder. "I will explain to the dowager that you would make a wonderful lady's maid for someone else, but that I prefer to choose my own."

Bobbing twice, Millie left, and Cassandra walked deeper into the quarters she was to share with Lord Ranleigh. Between their bedchambers was yet another sitting room, though this one was not as large as the crimson receiving room. There was a very elegant dining room—with yet another portrait of the late Countess. And there was a smaller dining room. No doubt for breakfast if he chose not to go downstairs.

Eleven rooms so far, Cassandra counted, all elegantly furnished. She returned to the Lord Ranleigh's bedchamber. A huge bed with dark-red velvet hangings seemed to fill the room.

There were comfortable chairs and a deep sofa situated around the black marble fireplace, in which a fire smoldered, emitting warmth against the sharp air that seeped in from the sea.

Red velvet framed the windows that afforded a splendid view of the blue-black water. As she watched, breakers climbed high into the air and fell loudly onto the rocky shore.

Cassandra walked on, Cynthia's gray slippers sinking deep into thick Persian carpet. She left the quarters and went out into the hall. Turning, she came upon several rooms that seemingly held no purpose. White cloths covered·a few pieces of furniture.

The musky odor attested that the quarters had not been used for quite some time. She went immediately and opened a window to let in fresh air and, looking down, discovered that she had turned the corner, for she could no longer see the sea.

Below was a beautiful rose garden, and beyond that, in the distance, the hillock on which she used to sit and dream. Her chest tightened painfully.

As she explored farther the empty rooms, the dark third-story rooms Jacob occupied came to mind, and she wondered why the boy was so exiled when these lovely rooms were available. Without thinking, she decided to move him, and she hurriedly made her way to the third floor, making mental notes of the many halls and passages so that she could find her way back.

At Jacob's door she knocked lightly then entered without being given leave to do so. Passing through the schoolroom, she found Cook sitting in a chair, rocking, while Jacob slept on a nearby cot.

Cassandra saw at a glance that he wore the same clothes he had been wearing when she saw him earlier; the sheets on the narrow bed were yellow, as if they had not been washed since last Christmas. She walked over and studied the boy's face, so beautiful in repose.

Cook scrambled to her feet. "This is a surprise, mum."

"I came to check on Jacob, and I am not mum. I am Lady Ranleigh."

"I beg yer forgiveness, Yer . . . Yer Ladyship. It will take a while to get used to another—"

"Balderdash! The other you speak of has been gone three years."

"I know . . . Yer Ladyship, but she was so dear. I fear that Ranleigh Hall will forever mourn her passing."

Cassandra was forced to remind herself that her anger was directed at Lord Ranleigh, not at the servants. Mayhap they had reason to worship the sainted woman. That they worshiped her was the painful part. She asked of Cook, "Does Jacob usually take a nap at this time of day?"

"Oh, this is not a nap. He's in fer the night."

"Dressed like that! And how many hours of sleep does he require? Surely he cannot sleep until morning."

"Not without help, mum . . . Yer Ladyship. The doctor says I am to give him a spoon of laudanum, and if he awakens in the night, I am to give him more. He needs his rest."

Cassandra was appalled. "Has the child been outside today? What exercise did the doctor order along with the sleeping potion?"

"None. His constitution is weak. Outside, he can hardly breathe.

Little wonder, being kept cooped up in these dark rooms.

Cassandra quickly decided that Cook was not the person to whom she should address her complaints. And she would not, this day, disturb Jacob from his drugged sleep. About that, she would address Lord Ranleigh, and at once.

Turning away from Cook, she quit the dingy rooms

and, walking as if the Hall were on fire, made her way back to her quarters. She shook her head in disgust; her husband must have windmills in his attic, and she would tell him so. But he was not there when she arrived, and she was forced to turn her thoughts to another matter, that of ridding the quarters of the first Countess's portraits.

His Lordship must needs go to the great hall if he wished to lay alms at his dear Countess's feet, but she, Cassandra, would not live one day in quarters where those green eyes watched her every move. She stared into those eyes; then her gaze moved to study the lips, which were no longer sensuous, but curled into a cat's possessive snarl. Grabbing the bellpull, she yanked it heartily, and when Millie appeared she asked that two footmen be sent.

"Whatever for?" the maid asked.

"To remove the dead Countess's portraits."

Millie appeared to be about to swoon, and Cassandra scolded, "Scoot, and be quick about it. I shall wait outside the door until they are removed."

Millie left without ceremony, and it was not long until four footmen, not two as Cassandra had requested, appeared, each looking as startled as poor Millie had been.

"Remove the late Countess's portraits," she said, "and be quick about it."

They stared at her in stone-dead silence, and she told them again, "Remove the portraits."

The tallest of the liveried footmen, giving the appearance of being in charge, stepped forward. "Mum, what shall we do with them? The Master would not wish—"

"I don't care what you do with them, but remove them from my sight." She paused to draw a deep breath. "And I don't care what His Lordship wishes. From this moment forward, when you address me it will be as Your Ladyship, or Lady Ranleigh, not mum."

The four bowed, mumbling in unison, "Yes, Yer Ladyship."

The footmen set about doing Cassandra's bidding. She watched as they carried one portrait away, then the other.

Left alone, Cassandra let her gaze move slowly upward. Above the black marble mantel the space was as empty as yesterday's dreams. She wondered what His Lordship would say when he learned she'd had the portraits removed, and felt her spine stiffen.

A soft knock interrupted Cassandra's ruminations, and when she bid the knocker "Enter," the door opened and Cynthia again stood there, smiling, words spilling from her mouth.

"I can't believe what you have done in the short time you've been here." And then she laughed, a short, tinkling laugh that matched the sparkle in her eyes. "The dowager is beside herself. She summons you to tea—"

"Where? In her awesome bedchamber?"

Cynthia said, "The dowager ordered a chair, and four footmen carried her belowstairs to the large receiving room off the great hall." She gave a cheerful giggle, and then said, "When she is not begging for attention she can climb those stairs two at a time. It's only when Wade is away that she becomes so helpless.

"Tea is always served there at five o'clock in the afternoon, but today, because of my brother's bringing you here, it will be later. Supper will be at eight in the main dining room adjoining, but you don't have to come. A servant will serve you in your quarters. I usually go to see what I can learn."

"But tea is a demand performance?" Cassandra said in a questioning manner. Stepping back, she invited Cynthia to come into the crimson room.

"And do tell me more about Ranleigh Hall's secrets."

The young girl stepped inside the room, closed the

door behind her, and then stood leaning against it. She still wore her riding habit.

"I think not," she said. "It will be much more fun to watch as you learn the secrets all by yourself."

"It would be much simpler if you would tell me. Then I would be prepared."

"You could never be prepared," Cynthia said. "Not in a hundred years." Another lilting laugh. "No, not a hundred years for you. By the way you've attacked the Hall this day, you will know all there is to know in no time at all. Now, I think we must needs go downstairs and drink tea with the dowager."

Cassandra sighed deeply, hating the thought. "If I must—"

"You must. But I will be there with you. Remember, I am on your side."

Cassandra thanked Cynthia. She liked the young gel tremendously, and felt comfort from her presence.

As they descended to the great hall, Cassandra inquired, "What happened in the library when His Lordship met with the dowager?"

"He told her that she was to treat you with respect, that you were now Countess of Ranleigh. My brother moves quietly, but his word is law around the Hall. So most likely the dowager will be outwardly docile, while she seethes inside. And she will plot against you, so watch out."

Cassandra turned to look at Cynthia. "How do *you* know what transpired in the library?"

The infectious smile broadened. "I had an ear to the door. I learned that early on . . . from the servants."

Soon—too soon for Cassandra—they were in the withdrawing room off the great hall. Sitting deep in a large chair was the dowager. When Cassandra and Cynthia entered she raised her lorgnette to her eye and turned to stare directly at Cassandra. Sitting near the fire was the tea table, draped in a fine white linen cloth.

"Welcome, Lady Ranleigh," the dowager said in a conciliatory manner.

Cassandra gave a perfectly respectable curtsy, and lied through her teeth. "I am pleased to be here."

"Tea will be served shortly," said the dowager. "In the meantime, mayhap you can tell me why the late Countess's portraits were so offensive to you that you took it upon yourself to have them removed."

When Cassandra did not answer immediately, the dowager went on, "Of course, as Lord Ranleigh said, you are the Countess now, and free to do as you wish . . . without my guidance. I do pray that he will not be upset with you."

"I appreciate your concern," Cassandra countered, then quickly added, "If I am to share His Lordship's quarters, I want things pleasing to look upon, and the late Countess's portraits reminded me of a cat about to strike. I shall find a painting to cover the faded places they left behind."

The dowager coughed, as if she had just swallowed her tongue. "Reminded you of a cat? How could you—"

"Let's not discuss the matter further, Countess. They have been removed and that is that."

Just then, a maid rustled into the room, bringing a pot of steaming tea and a plate of scones, leaving as quickly and as silently as she had come. The dowager pushed forward, poured, and handed Cassandra a fine china cup with steam curling up from the hot liquid.

Trying not to let her hand shake—for she had never touched anything so fine as the translucent cup and saucer—Cassandra sipped gracefully and watched through the steam the dowager, whom she thought, when not sprawled on a bed, was quite attractive in a pale sort of way. If Cynthia had not warned her, she would have believed the woman entirely helpless. She played the role of an invalid well.

There was something Cassandra wanted settled, so

she dove right in. "On the morrow, I will go into Wickham Market and engage a lady's maid for myself and a nursemaid for Jacob."

This time, the dowager did not just appear to be choking on her words; she coughed and sputtered, and her cup clattered against her saucer. When she could speak her voice showed no sign of delicacy. "I forbid it . . . ."

Cynthia, who had been silently observing, spoke quickly. "Mummy, remember brother's words—"

"What do you know about your brother's words? Our audience was in private."

Cynthia's laughter broke the awful solemnity. "You know that I listen at doors, Mummy I think it's wonderful fun."

" 'Tis beneath your station."

"I have no station. I'm just here, and I think it incumbent upon yourself to observe Lord Ranleigh's orders."

Cassandra's heart lightened. In this big, awesome manor house, she truly had a friend. She smiled at Cynthia, and the subject died then and there. Cassandra contemplated speaking of Jacob's living conditions but thought better of it. No doubt only objections would be voiced by the dowager, and it really was up to His Lordship to forbid her to put her plan into action.

And mayhap she would just do it, as she had had the portraits removed. Let him order her to leave. She would go, and he would have a sickly heir on his hands, with no nurse, and no hope of getting one to stay in this strange household.

As Cassandra sat sipping her tea, she visualized Lord Ranleigh's brooding eyes ablaze with anger when she moved his heir practically on top of him. "It is not to be thought on," he would say. Cassandra had learned that the nobility did not rear their children; someone else did.

Nonetheless, her resolve grew, for she recalled vividly

how Sister Martha had healed many a child with an abundance of love. In her mind, she could feel the hand that reached out in the dark of the night to give her shoulder a gentle squeeze, to quieten the sobs.

She also painfully remembered the cold hardness that had masked His Lordship's face when he had looked at Jacob, and she asked herself how a man could dislike his own son so much.

Most likely that was one of Ranleigh Hall's best-kept secrets, Cassandra thought. Returning her cup to the tea tray, she asked the dowager to excuse her and went upstairs to await the setdown from His Lordship.

Ten

"I want to go to your quarters with you," Cynthia said when teatime was over and Cassandra had started back to her quarters.

"Whatever for?" Cassandra asked. She was extremely tired. It had been a long day, and her mind was in a whirl.

"To see if Brother beats you." Cynthia was smiling. She danced along, keeping tune with Cassandra's hurried steps. The long, curving stairs were behind them.

"He will not beat me, so stop fantasizing. He is not a cruel man. Besides, what have I done to deserve a beating?"

"Removed *her* portraits."

"Most likely he will send me back to the orphanage," Cassandra said in all sincerity. She supposed that secretly, should she admit it, she wanted him to return her to Sister Martha. Living at Ranleigh Hall had been a young gel's dream; she was no longer a young gel.

"He won't send you away," Cynthia said.

"How would you know that?"

"Because he's desperate for someone to take over the care of Jacob."

"And I would like to know why. He can hardly abide the child. It shows in his eyes when he looks at him;

126

and he didn't even touch the boy, after having been absent from him for a number of days."

Cassandra quickly regretted what she had said. She should not be discussing the matter with this gel. She looked at Cynthia, who, for once, had a serious look on her face.

"Jacob is heir to Ranleigh, and heirs are protected at all cost. Brother loves Ranleigh above all things. But no rule says that one must needs be fond of one's heir."

"Ranleigh could have another heir."

"But he won't."

"How do you know that?"

"After Sylvia . . . never. I know my brother."

Cassandra lifted a questioning brow. "Some more of Ranleigh Hall's secrets, which only *you* know?"

They had come to the big double doors of His Lordship's quarters, and now Cassandra's, as well, and she said, "Cynthia, I do not wish company at this time. There are things I need to discuss with His Lordship in private."

"Will you tell me later?"

"No."

"But what if he beats you?"

"You're only funning, of course. But I promise to run down the hall screaming if he lifts a hand to me." Cassandra was smiling, and then a thought came to her. "Did he beat the first Countess?"

"No, not that he shouldn't have."

And then Cynthia was walking away, as if, should she linger, her secrets would be pried from her. Cassandra had noticed that when the gel wanted to dismiss a subject her infectious smile disappeared and her face became a blank mask. Now she was walking away without a word.

Cassandra called after her, "Thank you for being my friend at tea," and then she went inside her quarters, thankful to be alone. She sat on the sofa in the crimson receiving room, where, when His Lordship came, she could see his face when he noted the portrait of his precious Sylvia was missing. She braced herself for the setdown she knew was coming.

But it did not come. Straightaway she noticed that he was in a gay mood when he entered. It was obvious that he had been riding, for the legs of his buckskin breeches were dusty. He wore a spencer of impeccable tailoring, but no riding coat. He even smiled at Cassandra.

"I've been riding over the fields," he said by way of greeting. "They are in fine shape. The rains have come at the right time this year, and I'm looking forward to lucrative crops."

Cassandra saw something she had not seen before: caring. His penetrating, cold eyes were animated, and his austere demeanor showed genuine feeling. There *was* something the mighty man loved—the land. Just as Cynthia had said.

"Do you have an overseer?" she asked.

"Yes, a good one. He understands the importance of not robbing the soil by planting the same crop year after year in the same spot. Rotation is the secret. And he keeps good tenants."

He stood facing her across the room, his hands behind his back, his legs slightly apart. He talked more about the fields, and when Cassandra showed interest he suggested that she ride out with him in the near future, saying that he thought it would be good for her to meet the tenants. It would be her job to make sure the women were happy, and if they needed extra things she could see that they were forthcoming.

"That is, if you have time away from Jacob." A pause, and then, "Sylvia was good with the tenants, but she carried it too far. She spent entirely too much time away from the Hall, and away from Jacob."

Cassandra did not answer. She did not wish to discuss

the goodness of his first Countess, nor her faults, if she had any. She watched his eyes, to see if they observed the vacant spot over the black marble mantel. Finally, he went to sit in a deep chair, crossing his long legs in front of him.

Still, he had not noticed.

Unable to stand it any longer, she blurted out, "Do you not notice anything different about the room?"

"Should I?" He pushed forward in his chair and let his eyes peruse the room, and when his gaze fell upon the vacant spot above the mantel, his eyebrows arched fiercely and his dark eyes turned cold, penetrating, dark as midnight.

Only his voice held its composure as he asked, "What happened to her portrait?"

"I had it removed, and the one in the withdrawing room as well. I will not have those green eyes staring—"

"I wish you hadn't," he said flatly. "I need to see those eyes, lest I forget."

Had he beaten Cassandra, the pain would not have been more severe. The last thread of hope gave way to reality. "Shall I have them returned?"

"No, no. I pass the one in the great hall every day—"

An awful silence settled on the room, a mantle woven of a dark mist that light could not penetrate. Cassandra turned and looked out at the sea, at the great blue-black waves that no longer shimmered in the sunlight. She felt as if the waves were pounding her heart. Tears clouded her eyes, but pride kept them from falling.

"I visited Jacob again," she said.

"How was he?" The words were spoken with concern but not with caring.

"Cook had given him laudanum, and he was asleep long before bedtime."

"I suspect it was to quieten him. He is such a hellion."

" 'Tis unhealthy, the laudanum, and I plan to speak

to the doctor about it. In truth, I shall forbid the use of the sleeping draught, even if Jacob keeps the Hall awake all night with his tantrums. There must be a reason—"

"He's had too many nurses. He needs someone—someone like you—to love him. That is why I spoke with Sister—"

"I know. You've made it painfully clear that you married me to love your heir, and I do not wish to hear more about it."

So the subject was changed, and evening turned into night, without the moon, without light. A servant was sent for to set a fire in the grate and to light the candles, and Lord Ranleigh ordered supper brought to the dining room.

"You do not mind dining here with me, do you?" he asked.

Cassandra shook her head. For an instant her gray eyes met his dark ones, but he jerked his gaze away, as if, should he let his gaze linger, she would see everything, heart, soul, his very being. They ate the meal together, almost in silence. After dismissing the servant, a tall, gangly footman, they repaired to the center withdrawing room, and there Lord Ranleigh was solicitous of Cassandra's feelings, kind and informative.

The room was cozy and pleasant; a fire crackled in the grate, and through the windows Cassandra could see the moon, a perfect silver orb, which had appeared while they were eating and climbed up into a blue sky to illuminate the black sea.

Conversation became lively; politics of the day were discussed, as well as the Prince Regent's last spending spree, his wife's latest lover, the plight of little Princess Caroline, and Lord Byron's latest love affair.

Cassandra was well read; it was no trouble for her to carry her end of the conversation and she did, and enjoyed the camaraderie immensely. It kept her mind from the portraits, her terrible disappointment in her marriage, and her love for Lord Ranleigh, a love not returned.

Problems at Ranleigh Hall, the dowager, brother Wade, were not mentioned, and Cassandra felt this was intentional. They spoke of the latest styles, and Lord Ranleigh once again told her that he would send a modiste from London when next he went there.

"Which will be soon," he said.

He's forgotten that I intend to travel to London with him, Cassandra thought. But not wanting to disturb the ambiance of the room, she did not remind him. She would handle that when the occasion arose.

It was obvious to Cassandra that Lord Ranleigh was enjoying playing the part of a happy bridegroom, and soon it was time to repair to bed. Surely he would not leave her alone on their second night of marriage.

"I hope you find your bedchamber comfortable, and that you have a pleasant rest. I'm aware of how tired you must be."

"Oh, but I'm not," Cassandra said, then wanted to bite her tongue.

Lord Ranleigh stood looking down at her, his gaze focused on her white bosom, showing above the plunging décolletage of Cynthia's gown.

"When your new wardrobe is made have the necklines made to cover more of your . . . body."

"You mean my bosom?"

"Yes." With that, he whipped around and strode from the room. Cassandra watched him go, his broad shoulders determinedly squared, his stride purposeful. The door closed behind him with a small slam.

For a long while she sat and stared after him, wanting him to come back and hold her, to comfort her in this strange place.

What had happened to her dreams? Where had her youth gone?

131

She recalled the valentine she had drawn, sitting on the hillock and dreaming of living at Ranleigh Hall as Lord Ranleigh's bride, with servants bowing to her, and she wearing beautiful gowns befitting a Countess. How young she had felt, and so alive. If only she could forget.

She shook the memory away and, rising from her chair, snuffed the candles and quit the room. Once again she went to retrieve the valentine heart from her quilted satchel, this time to rip it in two, as if an arrow had shot through it, leaving it beyond repair.

In Lord Ranleigh's bedchamber, His Lordship decided to ready himself for bed without light from a candle. Moonlight cut a swath across the rich, red carpet. He did not need his valet; he wanted to be alone. Hot blood rushed through his veins like heated wine, and his head felt light.

Swearing under his breath, he removed his clothes, stretched his long, naked body out on the high bed, and lay staring out at the moon, which seemed to mock him.

Sleep was far from His Lordship's thoughts. The round, silver moon suddenly became blurred, and visions of tawny blond hair framing a face lovely beyond belief danced before his eyes, hair falling gloriously down her back, her gray eyes searching his questioningly.

For years devoid of all emotion except anger, Lord Ranleigh did not understand these feelings. He understood passion too well, but this was deeper than that which he felt for his mistress. There, passion spent itself and then it was over, and he was free again.

He asked himself what he wanted from this orphan he'd brought to his home to care for his heir, and the answer came without conscious thought: He was a lonely man. When at Ranleigh Hall he craved adult companionship, with no emotional attachment. Cassandra was erudite and pleasant to talk with. He had enjoyed their conversation at supper immensely.

If only this other would not torment him . . .

He turned his back to the mocking moon and stared unseeingly at the dark wall. He let himself slip back to the yesteryears. If only he could obliterate them from his mind. No, he did not want to forget; he *wanted* to remember. He must needs remember, and he must needs never love again.

The pain was too great.

Eleven

The next morning Cassandra rose at first light and ordered breakfast brought to her chambers. She did not have time to go downstairs to eat, and she did not particularly relish facing the dowager at such an early hour. Something more important was on her mind. She had several times awakened during the night, worried about little Jacob. Before going into Wickham Market to hire a lady's maid for herself and a nurse for Jacob, she must get the little boy out of those dark rooms and away from Cook and the doses of laudanum.

And a bath certainly would not hurt.

So deep was Cassandra's concern, she forgot that he had tried to hit her over the head with the toy horse he had dissected.

Millie brought the food on a silver tray; scrambled eggs, bacon, porridge, round biscuits, marmalade, and honey. And a steaming pot of coffee. Cassandra had never seen so much food this early in the morning in her entire life. She exclaimed to the maid, "Millie, did you think you were feeding a farmhand? I could never eat all this."

"Cook said ye needed to eat if ye was going to handle the little monster."

"I hope she doesn't call him that to his face."

"Oh, but she does. I've heard her."

"Well, you can tell her for me that from this day forward such words will not be used in front of Jacob. He is not a monster, just a neglected little boy."

"Ye had better tell her yerself. Cook is temperamental. The least little thing sets her off and she threatens to leave Ranleigh Hall at next day's first light."

"And I suppose everyone panics. Do they not think there are other cooks to be had?"

Taking up a heavy silver fork, Cassandra dove it into the food and started eating. The delicious smells filled her nostrils and set her taste buds watering.

Forcing herself to eat slowly, she said between bites, "You may go, Millie. And never mind telling Cook anything. I will take care of it myself."

Millie bobbed and sauntered toward the door. "I weren't going to. Nobody tells Cook anything."

With that, she bobbed again, then left, and Cassandra continued eating. She was amazed how quickly each dish of food vanished, and how quickly she reached for the next one. Careful not to burn her tongue, she gulped coffee from the beautiful china cup, while thoughts rambled through her mind, thoughts of Lord Ranleigh, who seemed to always be right there for her to think upon. She was still at a loss as to why he had taken such extreme measures to bring her from the orphanage to Ranleigh Hall to work as a nursemaid for Jacob.

If he had come to the orphanage and asked to hire a nurse, no doubt Sister Martha would have gladly put Cassandra's name at the top of the list. After all, she had seen twenty summers and had had experience with children.

Then, if she threatened to leave, he could have sought marriage to her, with the clear understanding that the leg shackling would be in name only.

That way. I would not have insisted on saying the vows in God's House.

It seemed to Cassandra that to be as smart a man as Lord Ranleigh appeared to be, he was quite foolish in the area of romance, and she supposed that it had been Sylvia who had made him that way by dying and breaking his heart.

"I'm his hostage," she said aloud, "and I would return to Sister Martha if it were not for Jacob."

She laughed then, knowing that that was not true at all. It was her love for her husband that was keeping her at Ranleigh Hall. Foolish it was, she admitted, but she could not help what her heart felt. It was her heart he was holding hostage.

Cassandra's logic told her that there was something terrible behind Lord Ranleigh's anger, something she did not know. Mayhap she would never know.

No, that was not right. She would pry it out of Cynthia.

She cocked an ear and listened for movement from his bedchamber. There was none. Most likely he was still asleep. Beyond the window, streaks of white light were just now breaking through the gray mist rising up from the sea. She looked down; every plate was wiped clean. She could not believe she had eaten so much. She drank the last of the coffee and rang for Millie to come back for the tray, which the maid did quickly, sauntering in and bobbing, as if she was still asleep.

"Yes, m'lady. I'm at yer service."

Cassandra smiled at her. "Thank you, Millie. Please take the tray, and have a footman deliver a tankard of hot water to the third floor."

Millie started to protest, but Cassandra gave her a setdown look, and the maid fell silent. Cassandra went on: "And have maids remove the white covers from the vacant apartment next door. I want the furniture dusted and the rooms aired."

136

Millie's eyebrows arched high above her small dark eyes. "Whatever for?"

"Never mind what for," Cassandra answered quickly. "Just go and do as you are told. And I forbid you to run to the dowager to report my instructions. My husband," she enunciated the words very plainly, "has given me free rein over the Hall. I may do as I please."

This was not exactly true; he had given her free rein to spend his money as she saw fit, thought Cassandra, but she would never get anywhere with her plan if she did not bluff.

"Yes, m'lady."

Millie bobbed so fast she almost lost her balance. Awkwardly straightening herself, she scrambled out of the room, carrying the tray and shaking her head.

Cassandra went about finishing her toilette. She donned the dress Sister Martha had lengthened with a faded piece of print around its hem. It had been freshly laundered. Cynthia's dresses were much too pretty to wear while doing chores, especially bathing Jacob. She brushed her hair until it shone like mellow sunshine, tied it back with a riband, and straightaway left for the third floor, opening the door without knocking.

Jacob sat at a low table, frowning down into a bowl of porridge, and said, "Take this slop and feed it to the pigs."

Cook was standing over him, her arms crossed on her ample bosom. Her voice was harsh. "Yer to eat it. Doctor's orders."

Cassandra stopped short. "What did the doctor order?"

"Porridge," Cook said authoritatively, without so much as a glance at Cassandra, who thought of her own healthy breakfast and how wonderful she felt after having eaten her fill.

"Why just porridge?"

"His stomach is weak. He must needs eat soft food."

"Balderdash! I shall speak to the doctor. Bring a soft-boiled egg with buttered biscuits, and plenty of jam."

"Lord Ranleigh will rue the day he brought ye here. Ye'll kill the boy."

When Cassandra, who was still holding the porridge, lifted the bowl and sniffed, Cook, incensed, grabbed it from her hands and slammed out of the room, black bombazine swishing after her. More snorts came from the hall, and the sound of heavy footsteps.

Just then two liveried footmen appeared, one carrying a tankard of water from which steam curled from the top, and the other a tin tub. Jacob's blue eyes widened. "And what are you going to do with that?"

The first footman set the tub down and the second emptied the tankard of water into it. As if the five-year-old had not spoken, and as if the new Countess was not present, they bowed to the room and turned and marched from it.

Cassandra's thanks bounced off their backs. She turned to Jacob. "Before Cook returns with a decent breakfast for you, you will have a bath . . . and fresh clothes."

She looked at him pityingly.

"I only have a bath once a week, and fresh clothes twice a week," Jacob said.

"That was before I came."

"I told you to leave."

"Well, I didn't. I am married to your father; Ranleigh Hall is my home, and you are my charge."

"I'm nobody's charge. Ain't anybody told you nothing? I'm a monster."

"Stuff! You are no such thing. You are a five-year-old who gets attention by being naughty. Well, that will stop. From this day forward you will get all the attention you need without being mean."

After adding cold water to the tub from the pitcher on the washstand, she bent down and tried to draw the

138

little boy to her for a hug but was met with a hard pinch to her cheek. A big smile showed his small teeth.

"At least you can smile about pinching me," Cassandra said, nonplussed. Holding him firmly, she began stripping his clothes from his frail body, and, even though he kicked and squealed, she soon had him in the tub and was scrubbing away. On the rack above the tin wash basin she found a white cloth and a worn towel, and by the basin was a bar of Jappa soap. Just what she needed.

"A footman is supposed to do this," Jacob said. "A gel does not look on a man's private parts."

"I'm not a gel. I'm your Stepmother, and you do not have anything I have not seen many like. At the orphanage I bathed little boys much dirtier than you. But they were appreciative. They had been sleeping alongside roads, and were half starved. You are a very lucky boy."

"Go back to the orphanage," Jacob ordered, and he started to pinch her again. Forewarned, Cassandra grabbed his hand and held it until the fight went out of him. She watched as tears clouded his eyes.

He said, "Why don't you pinch me back? That's what the other nurses did, and then they left. I ran them off."

Even though she was tempted to scold him, Cassandra said kindly, "I promise you that I won't leave. And today, you are going to move down to the second floor where I can watch over you, and where there is more light. A new nurse will be hired, and I warn you ahead of time, she will not leave just because you are naughty. You must needs learn that life will be much more pleasant if you behave like a little gentleman. I'm sure you know that you will someday inherit your Papa's title, as well as the Ranleigh estates."

"Why?" he asked.

"Why not? You are his heir."

139

Jacob turned to look at Cassandra, his face solemn. "Then why does he not love me?"

She was taken aback. The little boy had a perceptive mind. It had been painfully clear to her when she witnessed Lord Ranleigh's meeting with his son that what the boy spoke was true. She was silent for a moment, at first thinking she would assure the boy that he was loved by Lord Ranleigh, but somehow she knew Jacob would see through her lie.

Finally, she said, "Mayhap you are wrong, Jacob. Lord Ranleigh has a lot on his mind. Let's give him a chance by being nice to him. I wager things will change. Papas always love their sons, but sometimes it is difficult for them to show it."

"I don't want to be nice to him. He's a mean Papa. Besides, how can I be nice to him when he acts like he can't stand to touch me?"

Did His Lordship blame the boy for his beloved's death? Cassandra did not know the answer. She wondered if she was in over her head with this very observant five-year-old. As she rubbed his elbows—for they were covered with dead brown skin, from having not been washed—she prayed silently for guidance.

She soaped his sand-colored curls and poured water over them, while saying, "When next you see your Papa, run to him and hug his legs. Let him know that you love him and mayhap he will love you back. Love begets love, Jacob."

"I won't be nice to him," Jacob threatened, then became silent while Cassandra scrubbed. She stopped and gave him a kiss on his cherub cheek and smiled at him.

That was the best she could do. When she felt that he was reasonably clean she wrapped him in the ragged towel, lifted him from the tub, and held him to her breast. Tears clouded her eyes. Wheezing came from deep in his lungs, and she knew then that the little boy was sick beyond her help. A shiver danced across her

140

shoulders as suddenly a terrible premonition took hold of her, and, at that moment, she knew that, despite Lord Ranleigh's desperate desire for him to live, and regardless of how much she loved him, he would die.

The tears pushed their way onto her cheeks.

She swiped at them and sniffed, and said, "As long as we both shall live, Jacob, I will love you, and it doesn't matter what you do, or how mean you are to me. I will never leave you."

And she meant it with all her heart.

"I will not have it," the irate Lord Ranleigh said from between clenched teeth.

They were in the crimson room, Cassandra sitting, His Lordship pacing the floor. His dress was casual elegance. He had been out since long before dawn, he had told Cassandra, overseeing the dredging of a drainage ditch in the south field.

"What's done is done," she said. "I don't understand how you could have left your son in those dark, stuffy rooms and expected him to be healthy. Little wonder he has been called a monster."

"You should have asked my permission to move him. Another place would have been found. Ranleigh Hall has well over a hundred rooms."

"And you should have told me that you were marrying me to care for your son. Well, since you have made it painfully clear that that is my position at Ranleigh Hall, then I shall do what I see fit. I want Jacob close by, not to aggravate you, which it obviously does, but to make him feel a part of the family. I want him to feel loved." Her voice grew to a high pitch. "I want you to love him."

"That's impossible," His Lordship blurted out, his face a hard mask, his dark eyes deeply brooding. He stared at Cassandra and she stared back at him, incredulous. He was tall and imposing, but she would not back down. Nor would she fight with him. Somehow she would reach this hard-crusted man and make him realize how much his son needed his love.

And mayhap he will know how much I need his love.

So angry was she at the moment that she doubted that he knew what love meant, and she wondered if he had ever really loved the wife for whom he mourned, so fierce was his countenance. Or had he loved her so much that all tender emotion was now drained from him, buried with her?

Cassandra thought to tell him of her premonition that the boy would die. But she quickly reasoned that Lord Ranleigh would turn colder than ever and give up all effort to save his heir. He might even order her back to the orphanage. If that should happen, she would take Jacob with her.

"Would you like for me to return to the orphanage and take Jacob with me?" she asked. "I'm sure he would thrive there, where he would be made to feel wanted."

Lord Ranleigh's answer came quickly. "No. You will not return to the orphanage. You are my wife—"

"If I am to stay at Ranleigh Hall and take care of Jacob, he will live in proximity, as one of the family. I don't care what the upper orders do with their children; I expect you to treat Jacob with some measure of love. If you cannot find it in your heart to feel that love, then pretend," Cassandra challenged him.

Her voice was firm as Lord Ranleigh stared down at her. She stood, to better her advantage, and when the argument seemingly ended, for Lord Ranleigh was suddenly silent, she walked toward the door. "Please, come with me to visit Jacob in his new quarters. I cannot tarry long. I must go into Wickham Market and engage a nurse, and a maid for myself."

She opened the door and went out into the hall. Though he moved silently, she knew Lord Ranleigh was following her, and when, at the end of the long corridor she turned the corner, he stepped ahead of her and reached to open the door, saying, "This was once the nursery," he said.

"Why was he moved?"

"After the Countess died I requested that he be moved, but not to those dark attic rooms you speak of. I'm not a cruel man."

"Then why was he placed there? You are Lord of Ranleigh Hall."

"I suppose because he became so unruly. No one really wanted him near, and his placement was not discussed with me."

He paused for a moment, his hand still on the doorknob. "I should have objected, but I didn't. I kept thinking that we would find a nurse who would stay and everything would be all right."

Cassandra could not stop her words. "So you took drastic measures and married a nurse."

"Something like that," he said, his voice soft, his dark eyes studying her face.

Cassandra felt her face flush hot under the intense scrutiny. Stepping around his tall frame, she pushed the door open and there stood Cook, poking food at Jacob.

"Eat this, you little monster."

"Eat it yourself," Jacob demanded, and just as Cassandra and Lord Ranleigh stepped inside the door, he slapped at the spoon with a vengeance, sending a plop of mashed potatoes straight into His Lordship's left eye.

Swearing under his breath, Lord Ranleigh took a white linen handkerchief from his pocket and wiped his face, and Cassandra, as if nothing untoward had happened, went calmly to examine the food, again sending it away.

"Pigs would not eat this," she exclaimed. "Take it away and send some rich beef stew." She looked straight into the angry woman's face and spat out vehemently,

"Please note that I said send, not bring. Cook, I do not want to find you in Jacob's quarters again, and should I ever again hear of you calling him a monster—and I will surely learn of it—you will be banished from Ranleigh Hall."

Cook, having turned deathly pale, looked to Lord Ranleigh imploringly, but found no support.

"Do as the Countess says," he told her firmly, leaving her no quarter but to leave, which she did, hurriedly.

With the disappearance of Cook, Jacob jumped from his chair and ran to Lord Ranleigh, grabbing his leg and hugging it. "I'm sorry about the potatoes."

With a strained effort to be gentle, His Lordship disentangled himself, told Jacob that he must needs wash the potatoes from his face, then went to sit in a chair near the window to observe the room, which was pleasant enough, he thought. There was a table for studying, a bed with a yellow coverlet, and chairs and sofas. A cheerful fire burned in the fireplace.

Lord Ranleigh wanted nothing more than to escape from these familiar surroundings, to get away from Jacob, even Cassandra. He started to rise, but just then Cassandra picked up Jacob and plopped him onto His Lordship's lap, making escape impossible.

Then she handed him a wet cloth to use to clean Jacob's face, which His Lordship did.

"Papa, I can read," Jacob said. "Do you want to listen?"

"Of course he does," Cassandra said before His Lordship could answer. She picked up a tattered book and handed it to Jacob. "This is a good story."

Lord Ranleigh groaned under his breath. A shudder of revulsion passed through him. Beneath his clothes, the boy's frail body was nothing more than skin and bones. Suddenly the weight of guilt was heavy on him, and his voice turned gentle when he said, "First, Jacob, you must eat the beef stew, which will, I am sure, be here directly.''

"Then will you hear me read?"

Lord Ranleigh looked at Cassandra, who was staring directly into his eyes, daring him to refuse.

"Yes," His Lordship said, "after you have eaten I will listen to you read."

"Then I will eat every bite," Jacob said, and the room became loudly quiet.

She thought on the happening and was pleased with the progress, but she was also astute enough to know that one did not make one love someone.

After the stew had been brought and Jacob had eaten, he read a short story before Lord Ranleigh pushed him from his lap and excused himself, going, he said, to the stables.

Now, as Cassandra was preparing to go into town, she remembered she had no one with whom to leave Jacob, and she even considered taking him with her. Mayhap Cynthia would watch him while she was gone. Tugging the bellpull, she summoned Millie, who said Cynthia was out observing nature, most likely painting another picture.

That was the first that Cassandra had heard of Cynthia's painting. "Did she paint the nature scenes displayed in the Hall?"

"Yes, m'lady."

"And the late Countess's portraits?"

"No. Them wuz done by Thomas Lawrence, the famous portrait painter, so Cook said. Her Ladyship always had the best of everything."

"I suppose she did," Cassandra said, more to herself than to the maid. She had no choice but to ask Millie to watch Jacob until she returned.

"And do not let Cook near him. She dislikes the boy immensely. I can tell, and I am sure Jacob can as well. If you have to, lock the door."

Cassandra, ignoring the maid's frown, then told her to sit on the floor and play with Jacob if the boy so desired, adding, "Tomorrow I shall take him for a walk in the woods."

"Oh, no, m'lady. He gets sicker when he goes outside."

"Stuff! Fresh air will do him good."

Taking in hand her reticule and parasol, Cassandra quit the room, descended to the first floor, and left the Hall to go to the stables. Because she was not used to doing so, she had not ordered a carriage brought round. When necessary she could harness a horse with the best of grooms.

At the stables, she found the crested carriage hitched to four handsome bays, a coachman on the box, a footman on the back, and Lord Ranleigh sitting inside. He had added a cravat to his attire, and had pomaded his thick black hair. When she approached he smiled and jumped to the ground, and before a groom could let down the step, he had done so himself. Reaching for Cassandra's hand, he helped her into the carriage and climbed in to sit beside her.

Cassandra was amazed. The carriage started with a jerk, moving quickly up and over "her" hillock.

Why is he sitting beside me? He was so careful not to do so on our way to Gretna Green, and even on our way home, after we were married.

As if he could read her mind, His Lordship quickly explained that it was for appearance's sake.

Looking into his inscrutable face, Cassandra lifted a heavy eyebrow. "Appearance's sake? I was under the impression that you did not give a fig about what people thought."

"I don't for myself, but I do not want disparaging remarks made about you."

"Like what?"

"Like wondering why a titled man would marry a gel from Sister Martha's orphanage."

Cassandra gave a cynical little laugh. "You want them to think that you saw me on the hillock, drawing pictures of Ranleigh Hall, daydreaming like the foolish gel that I was, and that you were so smitten you could not resist me. Well, I shall tell them that you only wanted a nurse for your heir, and that you bribed Sister Martha to sell me to you."

"I did not bribe Sister Martha! And you would not dare say—"

"Oh, but I would."

Of course, she would not breathe the truth to a soul, for she was prideful in that way. In truth, she was happy to have Lord Ranleigh come along; they would surely be seen by Stella, the arrogant gel from Madame Tristan's shop.

Twelve

"What are you thinking?" Lord Ranleigh asked.

"That you are not the perfect man I envisioned you to be."

"What do you mean? I never pretended to be perfect—"

"I know, and you're not, but before I met you I would come to this hillock and gaze down on Ranleigh Hall and dream of living there . . . with you. You were perfect then. And I drew the most wonderful valentines."

She gave a little laugh. "I was just a foolish gel, and Valentine's Day seemed so romantic. Anyway, everything in the dreams was perfect, especially you."

Oh I should not have said that!

A riotous laugh filled the carriage. "Tell me where I have fallen short of perfection. I can't bear not to know."

Cassandra stared straight ahead, over the backs of the four bays, down the narrow, winding road. Hooves beating against the hard surface resounded in her ears. Chestnut trees bloomed profusely, and the stately oaks wore their green leaves gloriously. Wildflowers covered the countryside.

She marveled at their quiet beauty and wished her heart would be as quiet. At last she said, "It would be of no use to tell you." She looked at Lord Ranleigh. He was in a rare light mood. His big smile even reached his dark eyes.

"Oh, pray, do try," he said. "If I know my terrible shortcomings, I can strive to correct them."

His Lordship was funning. The last thing he wanted was to correct his ways. He had worked hard to push his anger to the bottom of his soul and build an impenetrable wall around his heart. No longer did his anger fester; it was just there, steady and calm, guarding his innermost self like a steel shield.

But there were two things his anger could not subdue: his libido and his love for Ranleigh Hall.

He did not want to stop caring about what happened to Ranleigh, but now, feeling hot blood moving through him like a raging river out of control, his loins aching, he prayed silently for the Lord to take his great passion from him.

But just for the moment, he was quick to remind the Lord. Just until he could visit Elsa. He squirmed on the plush squab and swore under his breath. This gel, with her innocence, was wrecking his resolve. Their thighs were touching, and he could feel the warmth of her body through their clothes. The bliss of their wedding night came to mind. It should never have happened. One did not taste and then not expect to crave. He had known better, knew better now, but the desire was there. He thought briefly to scoot himself over into the corner; instead he moved across to the opposite squab, all the while swearing at Sister Martha for sending Cassandra to him. The old woman should be hanged and quartered.

"Why did you move?" Cassandra asked. She wanted so much for Stella to see them riding together, in Lord Ranleigh's carriage, with the Ranleigh crest emblazoned on its panels.

"I refuse to ride beside anyone who does not think

149

I am perfect," His Lordship teased. "And most especially by someone who will not tell me my faults so that I might correct them."

"I don't think you could, even if you wanted to. And 'tis not important. No one is perfect."

He looked at her with incredulity. She wore a gray gown, with gray slippers to match. The gown's neck was low. Her hair was drawn back, making her look younger than her twenty years, and more fragile. The word made him smile.

Fragile! Cad's wallop, she was as tough as a Hussar's boot . . . but she had such an enormous ability to love, and she was filled with the compassion of Mother Mary. He had never known anyone like her.

"You are a perfect nurse," he said, smiling at her.

Cassandra could have slapped him. It was all well and good to be called a good nurse, but she wanted more than that from her marriage.

"Stuff! All I know about being a nurse is what I've learned at Sister Martha's, and what comes from in here." She placed her hand on her breast.

"If anyone can make Jacob well, you can," Lord Ranleigh said.

Without thinking, as if she were not in control of herself—and indeed, she wasn't or she would have kept silent—the words came out. "No one can. Jacob will die. I don't know what his problem is, but he is stricken with an incurable disease."

Lord Ranleigh sat forward on the squab, his face a hard mask, his eyes suddenly wet with anguish. "You must not say that. It is imperative that he live. Ranleigh will . . ."

He did not finish, and what he had said hardly registered with Cassandra. She did not argue. There was no need, and Lord Ranleigh was silent for a moment, staring at her.

150

Then he asked, "Why do you say that Jacob will not live?"

"I had a premonition of what will happen in the future, something that's in the hands of the gods. 'Tis a feeling that comes over me."

Lord Ranleigh leaned back and threw up his hands. "Pray, do not say that to anyone else. You will be accused of being a witch."

"Balderdash! Everyone has premonitions; they just don't pay attention to them."

"Then . . . this premonition, or feeling, could be a figment of your imagination?"

Cassandra could see that he was determined to disbelieve, and mayhap it was best that he didn't take her seriously, for, as she had reasoned before, as long as he believed Jacob would live, he would be kinder to his son.

She looked pityingly at His Lordship, then looked away, to the countryside, which was passing in a blur.

At last, Lord Ranleigh said, "I brought you to Ranleigh Hall to save him. You must needs—

"I will try, and I expect you to cooperate."

"How? What can I do?"

"I've told you this before, Your Lordship: by pretending to love him. He's a sharp little boy. I know that you don't love him, but you can pretend. And be good at it. He will recognize deception. He wants my approval, but he *needs* your love."

Lord Ranleigh did not say that it was impossible as he had done in the past, but he felt it. His happy mood had disappeared; his passion had subsided, and a stone moved into his chest, resting heavily, pulling him down into the depths of the black hole of despair.

He could hear his heart beat against the stone, but he said not a word as the carriage moved toward Wickham Market.

* * *

In Wickham Market, Cassandra went directly to an agency and inquired about the availability of nurse-maids. The woman behind the desk smiled, jumped up, and curtsied when Cassandra introduced herself.

"Lady Ranleigh, how may I serve you?"

"I desperately need an excellent nurse for a little boy," Cassandra repeated. "She must needs be kind, loving, and above all patient."

"Oh, I have the perfect nurse for a member of the nobility, Lady Ranleigh," purred the woman, who had a pleasant though wrinkled face. She was tall and thin, and wore a blue merino dress that buttoned to her chin. Her straight hair was pulled back and twisted into a knot on the back of her head.

"Never mind the boy's status in life," Cassandra said. "Understanding the child is of the utmost importance."

The woman opened a drawer and brought forth a sheaf of papers, and, lifting her lorgnette, studied each application with intensity, placing one after another aside.

Cassandra, sitting in a chair opposite the desk, waited.

Finally the woman's thin lips curled into a huge smile. "Ah, here's the one I've been looking for. The perfect nursemaid for your little boy."

Cassandra took the paper and studied it, then handed it back. "Entirely too young."

The woman's eyebrows shot upward. "Twenty-and-three too young! Countess, I am here to tell you that the young ones make better nurses."

"I want a grandmother, one whose children, and grandchildren, are too busy to pay her mind. May I see your discards?"

The woman shoved the stack of parchment sheets at Cassandra, who took them and leaned back into her chair. She studied them carefully, picking three that appealed to her. She handed them back to the woman. "I would like an audience with these applicants if they are available this afternoon."

"I'm afraid that's impossible. Mayhap I could have them here on the morrow."

"I don't want them *here*. I will call on them—"

"Whatever for? I've never—"

"I want to see if one can eat off the floor in their home."

Cassandra had heard Sister Martha say many times that a woman worth her salt would keep her floor as clean as she kept her tabletop.

The woman was shaking her head.

Cassandra stood. "I believe I saw another agency—"

"Oh, no. I would not have you go to that disreputable place. The stories I could tell you are beyond the pale. Pray, Countess, do sit down. I will send a man ahead to tell the nurses you are coming."

Cassandra remained standing. "That will not be necessary. Just give me directions to their homes and I will call on them unexpectedly. And the gel who is three-and-twenty as well."

"But you said she was too young."

"She is, for a nurse, but I am in need of a lady's maid."

"I fear she has no training for that."

"All the better. I will train her myself."

Disbelief shadowed the woman's thin face. She scrambled from her chair and grabbed a gray bonnet hanging from a nail that had been driven into the wall.

"I will accompany you. You cannot go out into the boondocks alone, not a member of the aristocracy. Footpads will be waiting to rob you."

"I do not plan to go alone."

"Then who—"

"My husband, Lord Ranleigh. Now, if you will give me the names and directions to their homes. . . ."

It was with obvious reluctance that the woman handed over the papers, which Cassandra deposited in her reticule. She thanked the woman and took her leave of the tiny office and the disbelieving lady, quickly heading to the coffeehouse where His Lordship had said he would visit while she tended to her business.

"Send the footman in for me," he had said.

That coffee reportedly was an excellent cure for the spleen and dropsy was the extent of Cassandra's knowledge of a coffeehouse; every village had at least one. And she understood that in London they flourished in every warren of narrow courts and alleys, especially around the Royal Exchange.

Supposedly business was transacted in these coffeehouses, and even auctions. She had never thought overmuch of such practices, nor had she bothered to learn that women were not allowed inside these sacred places that accommodated men only. Unless one was a pretty waitress who served the men coffee for a penny, and mayhap, if she were lucky, a smile.

Walking briskly, she was soon in front of Tidworth's, but the footman who had accompanied them into town was not to be seen. She looked around for a long moment, then innocently opened the door and went in to fetch His Lordship, squinting her eyes to locate him in the darkness.

The windowless place was no more than a hole in the wall. Even so, men sat in little groups, lifting their cups, some talking quietly, others laughing riotously. She suspected those of telling bawdy jokes. She had heard that men did that when they were out of earshot of ladies of quality.

She had stood in the doorway no longer than a minute when Lord Ranleigh was by her side, taking her arm in a firm grip.

"You are not to come in here. 'Tis for men only." He practically pushed her out into the street.

"Don't gels like coffee?" she asked, smiling.

"Not in coffeehouses. They are a place where men strike business deals."

And tell bawdy jokes.

She started to ask him how, with it being so dark inside, one could know with whom one was making a business deal. However, she refrained from doing so. Far more important was finding a nurse for Jacob.

Standing on the street, His Lordship looking down at her and her looking up into his stern face, she explained her plan to go to the homes of the applicants to view the premises before considering them for the job.

Lord Ranleigh frowned but did not put up an argument. In the short time he had been married to Sister Martha's charge he had learned to read the indomitable set of her shoulders. Her small chin looked as if it had been carved from stone.

He sent a lad to tell the driver to bring the carriage, and just then the footman sauntered up and unobtrusively leaned against the building, as if he had been there all along.

Watching the footman from the corner of his eye, Lord Ranleigh decided not to berate him. No doubt the young lad had a favorite lightskirt he had visited. Lord Ranleigh could certainly understand that. Looking at Cassandra, he wanted to take her in his arms and kiss away that stubborn look, and make her smile.

And ravish her.

He berated himself for such thoughts. Cassandra was certainly no lightskirt. He had never seen a gel so full of business. Before the driver could bring the carriage to a full stop she was tugging at the door. He stepped up, gently moved her aside, then waited for the footman to open the door and let down the step.

Cassandra was taken aback with herself. Would she never learn to act like a lady of quality?

"'Tis that I am in a hurry to find a nurse," she explained, and Lord Ranleigh smiled as he helped her up into the carriage, then got in himself and sat on the opposite squab. Leaning his head out the window, he gave the driver office to be off.

As the carriage moved out, Cassandra saw Stella standing in front of the draper's shop, watching intently, her hands shading her eyes. As they passed, Cassandra lifted her hand in greeting, then, turning to Lord Ranleigh, gave him her happiest smile, for Stella's benefit.

If only Lord Ranleigh were sitting beside me.

"Stuff," she said, "I forgot to give the driver directions to these women's houses, and he's headed back to Ranleigh." She opened her reticule, retrieved the four sheets of parchment, and handed them to Lord Ranleigh. "I'm sorry. I must have windmills in my head."

"I should have thought of that myself. I, too, had other things on my mind."

He signaled the driver to stop and got out, and when he returned to the carriage he sat beside Cassandra. This pleased her, especially when the driver made a turn and drove back down the street, again passing the draper's shop.

She saw Stella whip around, then disappear into the shop.

"Will you accompany me to the draper's shop to order some gowns?" Cassandra asked. "And to collect a debt?"

"What debt?"

Cassandra told him about her visit to the shop, about the arrogance of Stella, and then about their wager. "She owes me ten yards of silk."

"We'll collect right now," Lord Ranleigh said. His hand went immediately to the door latch. "I'll tell—"

Cassandra tugged at his sleeve. "No. 'Tis not important, at least not as important as finding a nurse for

Jacob. I cannot be with him every minute, and, to be perfectly honest, I do not trust Cook."

This surprised Cassandra, but the words had just come out. So they must have been in her unconscious all along, she decided. Mulling it over, she was still unable to put her finger on the reason for her thinking.

"Don't trust Cook?" Lord Ranleigh said, raising an eyebrow. Cassandra did not want to talk about it, not until she had had time to sort it out in her mind. "I don't like her calling him a monster, and the food she puts before him is hardly edible."

"Cook has been at Ranleigh Hall a long time—"

"Mayhap too long, but that is fine with me, as long as she stays away from Jacob."

Cassandra's mind was in sixes and sevens about the sudden feeling that Cook was trying to harm Jacob. Where did such thoughts come from?

She tried to scoff at the notion.

What a farrago of nonsense, she said to herself, but the feeling did not go away, not even when the crested carriage turned onto a deeply rutted road that led to the first applicant's home.

"I'll wait for you," His Lordship said when the driver pulled the bays to an abrupt halt. The now alert footman bounded down and let down the step.

Cassandra gave Lord Ranleigh a solid look. "Oh, no. I must have you with me. What I don't hear, you will hear; what I don't see, you will see. You can let me know your thinking by using those dark eyes of yours, mayhap looking up to the ceiling for no, or turning to look out the window. For yes, just look steady at me."

Lord Ranleigh shook his head, not in agreement, but in wonder. There was little doubt that the new Countess would not miss anything, and he was certain that she would be very adept at choosing a proper nurse without his assistance. He ran his hand through his dark hair.

He could not believe that he, an Earl, was out in the country interviewing nurses.

Quite below his station.

Nonetheless, he hopped down to the ground and reached a big hand back to help Cassandra. Seconds later, he was following her into the house. And within minutes, after having been met by a woman of about forty, Cassandra was walking briskly toward the waiting carriage, His Lordship using his longest stride to keep up with her.

He was scolding, "Cassandra, you did not stay long enough to learn anything about the woman. I was quite impressed."

"Did you not look at her hands?"

"Her hands? What do her hands have to do with being a nurse?. Most likely they were old hands, but you said you wanted a grandmother . . . she was clean—"

"Her fingernails had dirt under them."

The next applicant did not fare any better under Cassandra's scrutiny. Her flower garden needed weeding and her voice was entirely too strong, and when she spoke of children, her eyes did not soften. Nor did she smile. Any grandmother worth her salt would show emotion when she spoke of her grandchildren.

"Maybe they are little hellions," Lord Ranleigh argued.

"I suppose one could call Jacob a little hellion—he tried to crack my head with his horse. But that's no excuse not to love him."

Lord Ranleigh did not take Cassandra's reasoning, and he was infinitely glad when the last applicant, Mrs. Brodwick, passed her scrutiny with flying colors.

"You will do fine," Cassandra said, "but I warn you, your patience will be tested." To Lord Ranleigh, Cassandra said, "She reminds me of Sister Martha."

Lord Ranleigh saw no resemblance whatsoever. Where Sister Martha was rather tall, Mrs. Brodwick was a petite woman, with slightly rounded shoulders, a wrinkled face, and blue eyes that smiled when she talked.

Mayhap Cassandra saw something he did not see. The way she had studied Mrs. Brodwick, most likely she was looking inside her soul. He quickly observed that outwardly Mrs. Brodwick was spit-and-polish clean from head to toe; her garden had been freshly weeded and one could eat off her clean floor.

"I think you've made a wise choice," he told Cassandra, and she beamed under his approval.

They waited while Mrs. Brodwick gathered a few things and put them in a cardboard box, and when they reached the carriage and Mrs. Brodwick made to climb up onto the back and ride with the footman Cassandra told her, "You may ride inside the carriage with Lord Ranleigh and me. We can tell you more about little Jacob. He's a fine boy. . . ."

The last stop was for the gel who was three-and-twenty. Cassandra looked at the paper with Dora Finnigan's name scrawled across the top. She liked the name. She said aloud, "Three-and-twenty is a good age."

"May I accompany you for this interview?" His Lordship asked. He was smiling.

Cassandra did not catch his humor. "It will not be necessary, and you might not want to hear what I have to say. That is, if she's acceptable and I decide to engage her services."

Lord Ranleigh's curiosity was piqued. "Such as?"

"I do not want a lady's maid who worships the first Countess, like Millie—and everyone else at Ranleigh Hall—seems to do. That's why I refused to use anyone already at the Hall. This Dora, if she is acceptable, will be loyal to me, and to little Jacob. She will not gossip—"

"All servants gossip about the upper orders. It is part of their wage—"

"I shall tell her that the first whisper of gossip that

passes her lips will be cause to dismiss her, without recommendation for another post. I shall tell her—"

Lord Ranleigh smiled. He could just imagine what Ranleigh Hall's new Countess would say to this next applicant. Most likely everything she had learned from Sister Martha would pour from her lips.

"She's remarkable," he said softly, looking fondly at Cassandra, his wife in name only.

And then he asked himself why he must needs keep reminding himself of something he could not change—even if he wanted to.

Thirteen

Cassandra liked Dora Finnigan at first sight. She was a big, raw-boned gel and not at all pretty, but she had a gentle look about her, and soft blue eyes. Her hair was almost a noncolor, somewhere between light brown and blond. She was taller than Cassandra, and much, much thinner, as if it had been a long time since she had had a square meal.

She wore a faded blue dress, freshly washed and ironed.

By way of greeting, Cassandra said, "I am the Countess of Ranleigh. I've come about engaging your services at Ranleigh Hall. The agency in town sent me."

Dora stepped back and, with a wave of her hand, invited Cassandra to enter the minuscule house. "My name's Dora Finnigan, as I suppose the woman at the agency told you. I've heard that the Hall has trouble keeping a nursemaid for the boy, but I'm willing to try. I have good references."

Cassandra's eyes perused the sparsely furnished room. The wood floor was damp from a recent scrubbing, and clean sheets covered the narrow bed pushed against the wall.

"Do you live here alone?" asked Cassandra.

"No. Papa lives here, but he's drunk as a wheelbarrow

most of the time." Her eyes became anxious, her voice almost pleading. "I need the work, m'lady. He expects me to make my own way, so he told me this morning. I will do you a good job, Lady Ranleigh. I won't let the boy run me off."

"I have engaged a nurse for Jacob. It's a lady's maid I'm needing."

Relief washed over Dora's broad face, and then the apprehension returned. "I've no training to be a lady's maid."

"Dora, do you understand loyalty? *That* is what I expect. If you should come to work at Ranleigh Hall, you will work for me, and me only. You will not gossip with other members of the staff; should you do so, you will be promptly dismissed. The *first* time it happens, not the second or third. Lord Ranleigh and I have our own apartment, away from the rest of the Hall, and I will not have our affairs bandied about among the servants."

Cassandra could not bear the servants, and then, of course, the dowager and all of Wickham Market, mayhap even London, knowing that she was Lord Ranleigh's wife in name only. She did have her pride. And for some inexplicable reason, Lord Ranleigh did not want the fact known. She made a mental note to ask him *why* this was so important to him.

"I will be loyal—"

"I believe you. You have an honest look about you."

Cassandra sat in a ladder-back chair with a sagging cane bottom and told Dora about the first Countess. "I've only been at Ranleigh Hall a short time, and I must tell you the first Countess's spirit fills the place. Her portraits show her to have been very beautiful. The servants worship her memory, and the Dowager Countess plainly told me that I would never take her place."

"Oh, but that's not a fair way. They must give you a chance," Dora exclaimed.

"I will make my own place. My only interest is the

care of little Jacob, and, of course, being a good wife to Lord Ranleigh."

If he would only allow me . . .

Dora's countenance took on a dreamy hue. "A lady's maid to the nobility! Do you think I can please you?"

"I know that you can. I am not entirely helpless. In truth, I can do for my self. That, however, is not the thing with the upper orders. More important, this is the only way to keep the dowager from foisting one of her favorites off on me, so she can carry back on-dits. I'm sure of it. Now, get your things. 'Tis getting late."

Cassandra did not tell Dora that she, too, was in training to become one of the upper orders.

When Dora opened the door to another room, near the size of the one Cassandra was sitting in, she could see a hearth with smoldering coals, over which hung a kettle with steam roiling up from its spout. There was a small, square wooden table and two chairs like the one she sat in. Lying on a narrow bed was a grizzled man who appeared to be in a drunken stupor. His face looked as if it had not been shaved for a year.

As Cassandra watched, Dora bent over the man and said, "Papa, supper is in the kettle."

He moved and spat out, "Git away."

And Dora did. Carrying a box tied with a string, she came back into the room with Cassandra. "I'm ready, m'lady." Her voice was low and choked, as if filled with pain the poor gel could not express.

Cassandra said in a kind voice, "Dora, you will make a wonderful lady's maid, and a loyal friend."

Dora gave a wan, silent smile and followed Cassandra to the carriage. She sat beside Mrs. Brodwick, each holding her box of clothes.

Cassandra sat beside Lord Ranleigh, and, after she had made introductions all around they rode in silence toward Ranleigh Hall. Only occasionally did Cassandra feel His Lordship's eyes turned on her. She did not

163

dare ask what he was thinking. If he disapproved of her choice of a nurse for Jacob and a lady's maid for herself, he could tell her later. She prayed that he would be agreeable. As they topped the hillock above the Hall, the sun was setting in the west, leaving behind a blue sky streaked with gold and red. They were much later than Cassandra had anticipated, and she was anxious about Jacob. As soon as the footman let down the step, she scrambled out of the carriage without waiting for His Lordship's help.

He gave her a stern look, as if to say, "Proper ladies wait to be waited on."

" 'Tis only that I'm in a hurry to see about Jacob," she said, and this seemed to appease him, for his face suddenly softened.

Will I never learn to be a lady of quality?

Aloud, she said, "Mrs. Brodwick, you will share Jacob's quarters, for I want him watched over carefully, and Dora, there's a bedchamber and sitting room on the second floor for you. You will take your meals belowstairs with the other help."

"Yes, m'lady," they both said in unison, bobbing as they did so. Turning to the footman, Cassandra asked that he show them to their quarters. "Just around the corner from mine and Lord Ranleigh's apartment."

The footman, after bowing and saying "Yes, m'lady," guided Mrs. Brodwick and Dora Finnigan toward a side door that led to the servants' staircase.

It was only when Lord Ranleigh was alone with Cassandra that he let his objections be heard, but not about Mrs. Brodwick and Dora. "Fustian, Cassandra, that is not the thing."

Cassandra raised an eyebrow and turned to look at him. Mansford, the very staid butler, was holding the huge doors open for them. He gave the customary greeting, looking at Cassandra when he bowed. She smiled at him, and when they were out of hearing distance she innocently asked of Lord Ranleigh, "Why is it not the thing, Your Lordship? Most of what I hear is that 'tis the thing with the ton."

"We have servants' quarters at Ranleigh Hall. 'Tis the rule—"

"Stuff. Rules are made to be broken. If you are concerned that Dora will learn we are married in name only, and will pass the word on, do not worry. I've already informed her that the first on-dit that passes her lips will leave me no choice but to disengage her . . . without references. She desperately needs the work."

Lord Ranleigh was silent after that. But Cassandra noticed an odd expression on his face, as if he were about to laugh.

They climbed the wide stairs from the great hall to the second floor. Unable to stand His Lordship's silence, Cassandra asked, "Well, do you not have a word?" And then she added, "I would be most pleased with your approval of Mrs. Brodwick, and of Dora, as well."

When the huge double doors to the crimson room closed behind them Lord Ranleigh broke into laughter. Cassandra, though puzzled, loved hearing him laugh. Lines crinkled around his dark eyes, and it changed his whole countenance, taking at least ten years from his thirty summers.

But she could not see what there was to laugh about. "Are you enjoying yourself at my expense?"

"I believe you think rules are made *only* to be broken. I've never seen a place turned to sixes and sevens as you have turned the Hall in such a short time. I shudder to think what Isabelle will say when she hears of your special arrangements for Mrs. Brodwick and the gel Dora. For you to move the boy was taking undue privileges, as far as she was concerned. And she told me that your moving Sylvia's portraits strained her patience beyond endurance."

"And what did you tell her?"

"That if the portraits bothered you, you had every right to have them removed, that you are now Countess of Ranleigh."

"Thank you for that, and most especially for not telling her that, in truth, I am Jacob's nurse."

When there was no remark forthcoming she asked, "Do you think the Dowager Countess will disengage me, as I threatened to do to Dora if she passed on gossip?"

"She would not dare. But mark my word, she will be furious."

She did not care how furious the dowager became. Cassandra was pleased with her small household within the huge Hall. Let the dowager reign over her own staff, and the many rooms they kept meticulously clean, and that remained empty and silent as death. She told Lord Ranleigh, "I'm going to see Jacob. Do you wish to come along?"

The quickness of his negative answer made Cassandra cringe, and his next words made her anger flare. "I do not wish to witness the little monster's behavior when he meets his new nurse."

Cassandra placed her hands on her hips and looked into his dark eyes. "I hope I never hear you call Jacob a monster again." Her voice rose an octave. "How could you? Your own son? His name is Jacob."

A muffled groan was His Lordship's answer. He turned away, but not before Cassandra saw the anguish that replaced the laughter of just moments before. She wanted to take his arm and shake him, make him explain his feelings, but there was no time; She must get to Jacob. She had almost forgotten how obstinate the little boy could be, and she feared that he might be giving Mrs. Brodwick his best efforts to make her leave.

She quit the room, and her steps took her quickly to Jacob's quarters, where she found Mrs. Brodwick sitting in a chair, while Jacob, sitting on the floor and playing with a toy soldier, berated her.

"You won't stay. Nurses hate me, and I hate them. Besides, you are ugly and old. I prefer my new Stepmother—"

"Jacob!" Cassandra scolded. She was instantly on her knees beside him, holding his arms in a firm grip. "You are not to talk to Mrs. Brodwick in such a manner. You are wasting your time and effort; she will not leave."

Jacob smiled at her. "I want you to be my nurse . . . if I must have one. I can take care of myself."

"Yes, as most five-year-olds can. Well, that may be true, but you are going to have a nurse. So it will behoove you to behave like a little gentleman. Right now I am very disappointed in you."

The stern little face crumpled, and tears clouded his sunken blue eyes. "I want you to be my nurse," he said again.

Cassandra hugged his frail body to her, resting his head of blond curls on her breast. "I am your Stepmother, and I need help in taking care of you—"

"You are *his* wife. You'll never have time for me."

Jacob's voice died in the silence, and Cassandra wanted to ask if Sylvia had not had time for him, but felt the question inappropriate for such a young, troubled boy. He would talk of his late mother only when, and if, he wanted to do so.

"I will always have time for you, Jacob," she said, kissing the top of his head. Then she scrambled to her feet and pulled the bellpull, and when Millie appeared she introduced her to Mrs. Brodwick and asked that she take the new nurse and Dora Finnigan, her new lady's maid, belowstairs for their evening meal.

"But, m'lady, who will feed little Jacob?" Mrs. Brodwick asked. "I thought I was to have my meals with him."

"Today Jacob will dine with his papa and me."

Millie interjected, "M'lady, 'tis not the thing. I've

167

never heard of members of the nobility dining with their children."

"Well, now you have. Scoot, and do as I say, and tell Cook to send sumptuous fare for three."

Millie began guiding Mrs. Brodwick and Dora out the door, but Cassandra asked that they wait. "Before you leave, Mrs. Brodwick, I believe Jacob owes you an apology for the mean things he said to you."

"Oh, he need not. I understand little boys—"

Cassandra hushed her by raising her hand. "Oh, but he must. A gentleman does not speak unkindly without cause, most especially to someone who plans to take care of him."

Jacob's little round face broke into a disarming smile. "Do I have to?"

Cassandra stood firm. "Yes."

He went to look up at Mrs. Brodwick. "I apologize, and I didn't mean it when I said you were ugly. You're just not as pretty as her." His eyes turned to Cassandra, and a huge smile covered his little face.

Mrs. Brodwick said in a kind voice, "I accept your apology, Jacob. We are going to get along just fine." She laughed. "And I promise to work on my looks."

The new nurse had her doubts, however, about how sorry Jacob was. She knew little boys, and she knew this one was special, and she wondered how he would act when Lady Ranleigh was not present. Obviously, the child was smitten with his very kind and beautiful stepmother.

When Cassandra returned to her apartment, Jacob in hand, she found Lord Ranleigh waiting in the withdrawing room between their bedchambers. He still wore his coat and cravat, and his highly polished boots gleamed in the dim candlelight.

168

In the grate a lively fire burned, dispelling the chill from the sea.

"I thought we would eat supper here—" He stopped when he saw Jacob holding tight to Cassandra's hand. She could almost feel His Lordship's sudden hostility.

"I think that's a capital idea," she said. "I brought Jacob to join us, Mrs. Brodwick still being a stranger to him."

Demmet. greet the boy—

As if he could read Cassandra's thoughts, Lord Ranleigh reached out a big hand and took Jacob's small one, shaking it as if he were a stranger he had just met. "Jacob, 'tis nice to see you again."

Cassandra shook her head. She supposed that was better than his berating her for bringing the boy. Her heart went out to Jacob, who was shaking his papa's hand and looking up into his face searchingly. Finally, their hands parted, and Lord Ranleigh turned and stared out the window, into the blue mist rising up from the sea.

Cassandra broke the silence. "I told Millie to send sumptuous fare for three—"

"Then I must needs freshen up. If the two of you will excuse me. . . ."

His voice was cold and hard, and Cassandra watched as he left the room, every ripple of his muscular thighs moving against his skintight breeches, his broad shoulders stretching the fine fabric of his coat. He had the magnetism of an animal, the king of the forest, powerful, holding himself just out of harm's way—but coming close enough to tempt those who needed his love so very much.

In his own bedchamber, Lord Ranleigh shed his coat and cravat, then rang for his valet, saying to him when he came, "Fustian, Nelson, the woman is addling my brain."

Nelson was a large man, and a little overweight, with a head that was fast becoming bare of its brown hair. Lord Ranleigh had never had the close relationship with him that most men of the nobility had with their valets. He had always kept his own counsel.

Now, Nelson looked at him askance. "That's what women do best, but what has your new Countess done, Your Lordship? She's beautiful enough—"

"Beauty has nothing to do with it."

Oh, but it has. Lord Ranleigh's mind argued. *She's driving you mad with it, and her kind way with Jacob is the final nail in your coffin.*

Nelson smiled. "I suspect that it has. Why are you fighting it? Make hot, passionate love to her and be done with it."

"You are insulting me, Nelson. I thought that should I confide in you, you, of all people, would understand."

"I do. I do. And I say, make hot passionate love to the woman and be done with it."

"I can't do that."

"Why not? You have a mistress."

"That's not love with Elsa."

The valet's eyebrows shot up. "Are you saying that you are in love with your wife?" A big laugh, and then, "That's unheard of. The nobility marry for convenience . . . but I fail to see what you gained by marrying an orphan; certainly not land, certainly not social standing. In truth, people are saying—"

"I don't give a demme what people are saying. I'm telling you that I cannot risk sleeping with Cassandra . . . I would certainly lose control of my feelings."

"As you once did?"

"Yes. And see where it got me."

"It got you a son to inherit Ranleigh."

170

"A hellion, you mean. I'm hoping Cassandra can tame him, and I think she can. She has a kind way."

Lord Ranleigh could not tell his valet that he'd married an orphan because she was reputed to be good with children, that, in truth, he'd married her to keep her from leaving when Jacob got to be too much for her. He thought of kind-faced Mrs. Brodwick and wondered how long she would stay.

But Cassandra would stay; she was his wife.

Lord Ranleigh found that he liked talking to his valet. Had he not done so he would surely have burst, but he feared he had revealed too much. "Nelson, what I said about not sleeping with Cassandra . . . pray do not tell anyone. It is an agreement between Her Ladyship and myself."

"My lips are sealed; I give you my promise."

Lord Ranleigh went to the sideboard and poured himself a double shot of brandy, then poured one for the valet, handing it to him and saying, "Sit down, Nelson, and I will tell you the whole of it."

Fourteen

Although it was a long while before Lord Ranleigh returned to the withdrawing room where Cassandra and Jacob waited, when he did enter she looked up at him and smiled. The food had been placed on the table in the dining room, and she had dismissed the footman who had brought it, telling him that they would serve themselves. She had kept Jacob occupied by telling him stories.

"Oh, there you are," she said.

"I apologize for being late, but Nelson and I became enthralled in discussion and I forgot the time."

Before Cassandra could reply, Jacob jumped up from his chair and ran and hugged His Lordship's leg. "Papa, my new stepmother has been telling me stories. I'm glad you didn't come sooner."

Lord Ranleigh picked up the boy and held him for a moment. Cassandra would have waited all night for that. Her spirits lifted. "Let's repair to the dining room. If the food is too cold, we shall ring for Millie to come and reheat it."

"I like cold food," Jacob said, a big smile showing his small white teeth.

"He has such a pretty face," Cassandra said under her breath. "He reminds me of someone . . ."

172

She could not help wishing that he resembled Lord Ranleigh, for despite her husband's fierce demeanor he was a very handsome man. Lord Ranleigh did not carry Jacob into the dining room, as Cassandra wished him to do. She scolded herself for asking too much too soon. For him to touch the boy at all was a vast improvement. When they were eating he showed Jacob how to hold his fork properly.

After they had finished eating Mrs. Brodwick came and took her charge away. Cassandra kissed him goodnight, but Lord Ranleigh turned away and stared out the window until Jacob and Mrs. Brodwick were gone. Then, turning to Cassandra, he said, "Jacob should not be made to wear gel's clothes. Sylvia . . ."

And then he stopped.

"Did she prefer the little gel look?"

"Yes."

"Well, I don't, and I'm glad that we agree on that. I had planned to purchase some things for him while we were in Wickham Market, but there was no time. We must go again, and I do want you to go with me to the draper's shop so that I can win my bet with Stella."

Lord Ranleigh chuckled: "I will do that. I do not like you wearing Cynthia's gowns. I am not a miserly person, and as I have told you, you may have anything money can buy."

Money can't buy your love.

Cassandra looked away lest he read her thoughts. The ambience of the room was one of quietness. Coals smoldered brightly in the fireplace and candles flickered in wall sconces, casting light and shadows on the colorful carpet. Romance filled the air. And love. But not from her husband. She longed with all her heart for His Lordship to pick her up and carry her to her bedchamber.

Or his bedchamber.

She could not stop the desire that filled her, and she

felt no guilt for it, for her feelings were for her husband, whom she had loved long before she knew him. It crossed her mind to again climb into his bed, but her pride quickly rejected that. Even the thought put her to the blush. She no longer had an excuse for such bold action; she no longer thought him too shy to come to her bed.

And she no longer had to act the dutiful wife, for Lord Ranleigh did not want a dutiful wife; he was too much in love with his first Countess to make love to the second one; that was the truth of it.

She looked at him, his dark brow pulled together in a frown. The sadness was still there. "I have some news," he said.

"What news?" she asked with foreboding. Would he tell her that he was leaving Ranleigh Hall for another of his properties? Would she have to suffer being at the Hall with the dowager, without him? Or worse yet, would he tell her that he was going to London to see the mistress of which Cynthia had hinted.

The frown on his brow deepened. "Wade is returning to the Hall. Isabelle has received a missive saying that he is in London and will arrive here within a fortnight. He anchors his ship a short way down the coast."

"Why does his returning bother you so much?" Cassandra asked. "Ranleigh Hall is his home, is it not?"

"Unfortunately, yes." A long, deep silence followed, and then, "My brother and I do not rub well together. 'Tis almost like Cain and Abel in the Bible. I thought it only prudent to warn you."

"I am pleased that you thought of my feelings, but I saw the rage on your countenance when the dowager spoke so fondly of Wade. Could it be sibling rivalry, m'lord? I hear it happens in the best of families."

"It is not sibling rivalry! He's a scoundrel, and I can only imagine what he will say and do when he meets

174

his new sister-in-law. That is the only reason I told you of his return—to warn you."

"Could you be jealous, Your Lordship?" she asked in a teasing way, trying to lighten his mood.

Her ploy did not work. Lord Ranleigh simply did not answer. He glared at her, his mouth set in a firm line.

Cassandra spoke into the quietness. "I've already met Wade, and you have nothing to worry about, if, indeed, you are concerned that he will turn my head."

Lord Ranleigh sat forward in his chair. "The devil take me. When—"

"Do you remember my telling you that I used to sit on the hillock above the Hall and dream of living here as your wife? 'Twas a young gel's foolish dream that came true. Well, almost."

"Tell me the whole of it," he demanded. "Did Wade meet you there? Was it planned?"

Laughing now, Cassandra said. "No, we did not plan anything. We met by chance. I was sitting there, happy in my dream world, and he was walking in the woods."

The look of unutterable hatred on Lord Ranleigh's face stopped Cassandra's laughter, and she added quickly, "He asked if I came there often, and he suggested that if I did, he would join me. Later, Sister Martha said there was nothing untoward in his actions—that I should expect men to notice me. Even so, his suggestion that we meet made me very angry."

"Why so?"

"He had ruined my dream world, for should I return to the hillock he would see me and think I had come to meet him. I could not bear that."

Cassandra did not understand the intensity with which Lord Ranleigh looked at her, the feelings his words revealed. "Keep your distance from him, Cassandra," he said, and after that he was silent for a long time. She, not knowing what to say, let the quietness envelope her. This . . . this feeling of His Lordship's went much deeper than jealousy. Or did it? Had he been jealous of Sylvia?

She did not ask.

At last, Lord Ranleigh rose. When he spoke his voice was deadly calm. "I must needs get some sleep. I'm sorry we spoke of Wade. I realize I cannot do so rationally."

"I will heed your warning and keep my distance, m'lord, but I do not see where he could possibly—"

"Enough has been said," declared Lord Ranleigh sharply, and then his voice turned soft. "Cassandra, I am glad you are at Ranleigh Hall. You are delightful company, well read, erudite. I enjoy a sharp mind. Until you came, I did not realize that I was terribly lonely." Bending over her, he gave her a short kiss on the forehead. "Goodnight, my dear. I hope you sleep well."

He did not wait for a response from Cassandra. He quit the room, and for a moment she entertained the notion of slamming the beautiful vase on the table beside her at the door he had closed between them. She practically ran to her own bedchamber, where she kicked at a chair. "The jackanapes," she said, "the conceited jackanapes."

Tears poured from her eyes in torrents, as much from anger as from the pain in her heart, which came, she acknowledged when she was spent, from wanting to be loved. Not physical love, even though that was wonderful with His Lordship, but from wanting to belong to someone, to share a life, to be a life partner. Sister Martha had loved her, as had her Mama, but woman was meant to have a mate.

And a man was meant to have a woman.

If only she could know what was in her husband's thoughts, she mused. If only she knew more about the world of the upper orders. She felt as a child who had married a man of the world.

Her best defense was anger, which she directed at

herself. She was not sleepy. Instead of climbing up on the high bed, which looked not luxurious, but lonely, she stood before the floor-to-ceiling looking glass and said mockingly, "Cassandra, I do like cozing with you. I like a sharp mind." Her gaze examined the reflection of her slender figure, her small waist, her round bosom.

What's wrong with me? Why does he not want me?

"Just don't be so prideful," she scolded.

The pain was still there.

She went to the chiffonnier and pulled down the quilted satchel and took from it the lace valentine she had ripped in half. She wanted so much to be on her hillock, alone in her own little world, a world filled with dreams of her own making.

"That's foolish," she said, jumping up. "I must needs think of Jacob."

So she put the torn valentine back into the satchel, donned her night dress, and climbed into bed. Sleep came at last, along with dreams of the powerful Lord Ranleigh, her husband. He was holding her as he had held her on their wedding night.

"Sister Martha, why did you not tell me the whole of it? I would never have married Lord Ranleigh under such circumstances. One does not marry to become a nursemaid."

"I know that, child, and that's the reason I did not tell you. I had hoped—"

"I know. You had hoped that Lord Ranleigh would develop a *tendre* for me, and that I would be accepted into the upper orders. Well, it didn't happen. He loves to coze with me—he's said as much—and he's pleased with little Jacob's progress. But I want more than that from marriage. I want children of my own. I want to be loved."

For several days now, Cassandra had lived with an

overwhelming desire to see Sister Martha. It would be wonderful to be with her, to feel close to someone, to be away from the dowager and her coldness.

So, today, after dressing quickly, she had gone downstairs to eat breakfast, hoping that Lord Ranleigh would be present so she might tell him she planned to take Jacob to the orphanage.

Lord Ranleigh was nowhere to be found. Cynthia was there, and the dowager, poking food into her mouth while loudly extolling her second son's virtues and saying that her happiness had known no bounds when she learned he was at last returning to Ranleigh Hall.

"I almost wept with joy when his missive came," she said.

Cassandra looked over at Cynthia, who was silently rolling her eyes toward the ceiling. Cassandra could not help but smile, but when there was a break in the dowager's effusiveness, she announced that she planned to take Jacob to see the children at the orphanage.

Between bites, objections poured from the dowager: Jacob was too frail; the upper orders did not fraternize with the lower ones. To which Cassandra replied that until she had married Lord Ranleigh she had been one of the lower orders.

Without giving her time for further argument, Cassandra placed her serviette on the table and rose quickly from her chair, saying as she did so, "I beg to be excused. I must needs tell Mrs. Brodwick to dress Jacob for the ride to the orphanage."

Now, she and Sister Martha were in the kitchen, talking over cups of chocolate, a rare treat. Tim had taken Jacob under his wing, promising Cassandra that he would see that nothing happened to the heir of Ranleigh Hall.

"Mayhap you have not given His Lordship enough time," Sister Martha was saying. "I'm certain—"

"It will not happen," Cassandra declared vehemently.

"And after all that has been said, should he come to me to claim his marital rights, I would know that it was the animal lust of which he reeks. It would not be love. He's made that too perfectly clear. Also clear is that he is still in love with *her.*"

Sister Martha gave a serious cluck, and as they talked on, Cassandra told her of having the first Countess's portraits removed from the walls.

"On the day he brought me to the Hall." She could not help but smile at her brashness.

"Oh, Child, what if he had brought you back to the orphanage, before you had a chance to prove yourself?"

"Looking back, I think mayhap I was hoping he would do just that. I am not a woman of the world, Sister Martha; I know very little of his world. I did not think of the consequences. I was so angry . . . and hurt at the way I'd been treated by the dowager, who, upon first sight of me, told me I would never take dear Sylvia's place.

"Even the servants were near as outspoken about her, and His Lordship himself acted as if I had some dread disease that he might catch if he so much as touched me."

"I would suggest that you go slow and feel your way," Sister Martha replied. "I am not yet ready to concede that I was wrong. You are a beautiful gel, Cassandra, sweet, compassionate, and more than willing to be a good wife—"

"And I have a terrible temper."

"Only when provoked beyond endurance."

Cassandra languidly sipped her hot chocolate; she spoke of Jacob's health and her concern for the little boy, but, lest she worry Sister Martha overmuch, she did not tell her of her premonition that Jacob would die.

"When I hold him close I hear a wheezing in his chest, and this is constant. It's his lungs."

"Take him to Dr. Fred Morton in London, Cassandra. He's a wonderful doctor for children. If Jacob can be helped, Fred can help him."

Cassandra thanked Sister Martha, and, taking a piece of paper from her reticule, wrote down the London address. They spoke of other things: the children, and the orphanage in general. Cook had been feeling poorly. Cassandra spoke of Cynthia: "She's delightful. His Lordship adores her."

Cassandra was pleased to hear that Tim read to the other children before helping to tuck them into bed.

Much time passed, all too quickly. Cassandra jumped to her feet and declared that she must needs return to the Hall.

"Come again . . . soon. I miss you," Sister Martha said.

Hearing the break in her aging voice, Cassandra gave her a big hug and promised to return as soon as possible. "I miss you, too, Sister Martha."

When Cassandra was at the door Sister Martha spoke again. "Cassie . . . Lady Ranleigh, when you go to London, will you inquire about Ellen? I worry so about her."

"Of course I will. But I do not anticipate going soon; there's so much yet to be done at Ranleigh Hall. His Lordship has suggested that I purchase gowns from Madame Tristan in Wickham Market, which should suffice for now, until he can send a modiste from London. And Jacob needs new clothes."

"Cassie," Sister Martha said softly, "go to London for your new gowns. As the Countess of Ranleigh, you must take your rightful place with the *ton*, beside your husband. Pray, do not lose yourself in being a nursemaid. That was not my intent."

"I will think on it," Cassandra said as she gathered up Jacob, who declared he'd had a wonderful time and wanted to come and live with Tim and the others.

After considerable goodbyes, they left the orphanage in the crested carriage. Cassandra, looking back, did not see a rundown clapboard building, but a mansion filled with love and wonderful caring. Suddenly she wanted to run back to it and don some dress donated by a stranger, to read to the children, to help Cook prepare their breakfast. And then she looked down at Jacob. God must have sent her to Ranleigh Hall to love the little lonely boy. She reached for him and pulled him up onto her lap, pointing out the different wildflowers along the way, telling him also the names of the trees and the animals they saw. He laughed when a squirrel ran up a tree. "I wish I had a puppy," he said, and Cassandra promised him one.

They topped the hillock—Cassandra's hillock—and she caught her breath as she gazed down at Ranleigh Hall. The place was as gloriously lovely as it had been the first time she had laid eyes on it, peaked roofs reaching for the sky, chimney pots emitting gray-blue smoke, narrow windows set in dark-brown stone, round towers at each end, blooming flowers and neatly trimmed trees, and acres of manicured lawn.

A lump suddenly filled her throat, and for some inexplicable reason she thought about Wade Ranleigh and his calling the Hall a mountain of stone.

He would return soon to that mountain of stone. She wondered what his coming would bring. Conflict, for certain. A shudder traversed her spine.

"What's wrong, Stepmother?" Jacob asked, and she assured him that nothing was wrong.

The carriage descended into the valley, and soon they were at the stables. A groom met them, and let down the step, and another held the horses' heads while Cassandra and Jacob alighted. She saw Lord Ranleigh walking across the stable yards, his determined stride bringing him closer to her and Jacob.

He was smiling. "I understand you went to visit Sister

Martha. Did you tell her that I am quite put out with her?"

"I told her that *I* was quite put out with her for not telling me the whole of it."

She quickly changed the subject, for she did not want to have such a discussion in front of Jacob. "I went to breakfast, wanting to ask your permission to take Jacob with me, but you were nowhere to be seen."

"I had a meeting with my steward. But it was not necessary for you to seek my approval. Jacob seems to be faring well under your care. Until you came, it was bandied about that the fresh air was harmful to his health."

Jacob quickly spoke up. "I liked playing with Tim and the other children. I want to live there."

"I'm afraid that's impossible, but you may visit any time Her Ladyship wishes to take you," Lord Ranleigh said. He turned his attention to Cassandra. "I have told Clifton, the steward, to send someone to Sister Martha's to make necessary repairs. On your next visit you will find improvements."

Cassandra thanked him, and he said, " 'Tis little price to pay. She did choose a good nurse for Jacob. Now, I'm famished. Do you think we could have a repast together, mayhap in the small dining room in our quarters? I love looking at the sea while I eat; 'tis so peaceful."

In Cassandra's view, there was nothing peaceful about the sea this day. High waves beat against the rocks, sending out loud, angry booms, while sending a misty spray into the air.

The three walked leisurely to the big house, where Mrs. Brodwick met them, taking Jacob away with her. "You'll be needing a nap after you eat," she told him, laughing. And for once, Jacob did not argue. In truth, he looked tired out, and Cassandra wondered if she had overtaxed him. She kissed him and told him she would come to see him after his nap. Then she and His Lordship continued on to their quarters.

In the smaller dining room the windows were open, letting in the sound of the thrashing waves. Lord Ranleigh went and closed them, and then he rang for a servant and ordered food.

He still held his good mood, Cassandra noticed with relief. It did not seem to bother him that his buckskin breeches and highly polished riding boots were dusty. An impeccably tailored riding coat stretched across his broad shoulders, which Cassandra admired greatly. She wore the faded blue day dress with the faded band to make it longer. A riband, not a white rag, held her blond hair back from her face.

She felt His Lordship's gaze moving over her as, in a voice just short of scolding, he said, "I will not have you dressing like that. You are now my Countess—"

"Stuff. Who's to see me? I doubt those at the orphanage would know me dressed other than I am."

"I see you. And soon Wade will be here, and I do not wish to invite disparaging remarks about the way you dress."

Cassandra could not help saying, "I saw *her* gowns. They were beautiful. Made by Madame Franchot in London, and some, so I understand from Cynthia, were designed and made in Paris, by Madame LaRuette."

Lord Ranleigh's stare was like a steel beam piercing Cassandra's soul. His good mood had suddenly left him, and absolute fury suffused his face. She would have taken the words back if she could, but they were irretrievably out of her mouth.

Will I never learn?

"I've asked you not to speak of her," he said; and then he turned his back and silently stared through the window at the sea.

Millie brought their tea, scones, and jellies, and, because Lord Ranleigh was present, small sandwiches of

183

roast beef. She placed it on the table. And still Lord Ranleigh stared.

Cassandra felt unutterably alone, so far away was he. After Millie had bobbed and left, she said to him, "You remarked that the sea brought you peace. How can you feel that way? When it is so angry most of the time—"

" 'Tis not angry. It's exerting its energy, fulfilling its purpose."

"And you identify with that. What is *your* purpose in life, Your Lordship?"

His words made Cassandra sorry she had asked. "To make Ranleigh the best that it can be, and to see that the estates, and the earldom, never passes into the wrong hands."

How Cassandra wished he had said, "To be happy. To start life anew . . . with you." Changing the subject, she asked, "Do you plan to go to London soon? I shall go with you and order new gowns—"

His answer was quick and firm. "I will be leaving a fortnight hence . . . alone."

As if he expected no argument from Cassandra, he left the window and came to sit at the table, eating as if he was ravenous, but with very good manners. When he had finished they talked; cozing, as he would call it. The brooding left his eyes, and he smiled when Cassandra spoke about telling Jacob about the trees, and about the squirrels and rabbits that had skittered away from the carriage.

"I promised him a puppy," she told him, and was pleased when he said, "That's a capital idea. I shall look around for one."

Again his thoughts were elsewhere, and Cassandra could not help but wonder if he was thinking of his trip to London, alone.

Well, whether or no, she was going to London with him, as Sister Martha had advised. It would not be easy, she mused. Already she had learned that he was not a man from whom one could demand a favor. So she must needs think of a way to win his approval.

Sitting across the table from Cassandra, Lord Ranleigh was lost in a stormy sea of desire, confusion, and yearning. Pure agony gripped him. He must needs get to Elsa, he thought, unable to tear his gaze away from Cassandra. This gel was making him addle-brained. Even in that demme dress she looked fetching.

He looked deep into her big gray eyes, framed with long dark lashes, and wondered what she was thinking, knowing that he would only have to ask to find out, she was so honest and forthright. He thought of his own dark secrets and wished he could cast them from his memory. When he did, momentarily, his thoughts came right back to Cassandra. Bloody hell! What a coil!

He wanted to take her to London and buy out Bond Street, dress her in the fashion she deserved. He would, this minute, love to take her in his arms and hold her tightly against him . . . undress her and make exquisite love to her. A shudder racked his muscular body as he envisioned her curves fitted to his throbbing desire, her arms twined around his neck, her sweet mouth open to his searing kisses, as on their wedding night. He swore vehemently under his breath. Had that not happened, this unrelenting desire would not be tearing him apart.

That does not signify, he told himself.

He had no notion of acting upon his desires; he was a strong man, with a will of iron. Rising from the table, he turned his back to his wife, lest she see the swelling of his manhood. Quickly, he walked to the fireplace and leaned against the mantel, still turned so that she could not see. He ran his fingers through his dark hair, looking at the gilt clock on the mantel, counting the ticks.

Gradually, his hot blood cooled, and he managed to speak, saying in a kind voice, "The *next* time I go into town you may accompany me, Cassandra. This time I have much business to attend to and could not give you sufficient attention. I want to present you to the *ton* in proper fashion."

Sister Martha's insistence that she take her rightful place by her husband when he went to London came to Cassandra's mind, and she was quick to say, "I feel strongly that Jacob should see another doctor. He appears to have improved; at least he is happy, and I've stopped the laudanum, but the wheezing in his chest is very much present. Sister Martha gave me the name of a physician in London."

"Next time—"

"No, Lord Ranleigh. It is of the utmost importance that we take Jacob to another doctor now. Should he develop a cold, it could become very serious."

This was the truth of it. She was not above finagling, but she would not use Jacob's health to get her way about going into London with her husband. She *was* quite anxious to visit the doctor Sister Martha recommended.

When Lord Ranleigh was not quick with his response she went on, "I will not interfere with your transacting business, and after *we* have seen the doctor about Jacob I shall visit modistes and order gowns . . . so that on our next visit into town I will be prepared for presentation to the *ton*."

For good measure, she quickly added, "And I shall be properly dressed when your brother returns to the Hall."

Fifteen

London. How she had in the past longed to go there, and now she was going. She rang for her maid. "Dora, you must needs help me get ready for my first visit to London."

"Oh, m'lady, 'tis so grand. Imagine, going to London! It will be a honeymoon for you and His Lordship."

"His Lordship has a lot of business to attend to . . ."

Cassandra had found Dora quite efficient as a lady's maid, and a good friend, as well. She felt no compunction in confiding in her, with the exception of telling her that she was Countess of Ranleigh in name only. Each night she readied herself for bed, telling Dora that if she needed help Lord Ranleigh would oblige. Truth was, he took himself off like a fox being chased by hounds when it came time for bed, no matter how pleasant their time together had been that day.

"When is this visit to London?" Dora asked.

"A fortnight hence, but it will take that time."

Dora laughed. "The bustle you are in, you'll be ready by last light this day, m'lady." She was busily brushing and braiding Cassandra's hair, and then she wound it around her head.

"Like a crown," Dora said. "Or a halo of unfiltered sunshine."

Cassandra gave a huge smile. "Certainly not a halo. Lord Ranleigh would be the first to vouch for that. He did not want to take me with him to London, saying he had too much business to transact. But I insisted. And little Jacob will be going, too."

"Will you be needing a lady's maid?" Dora asked shyly.

"Of course, and I would have no one but you, Dora."

A big smile spread across Dora's broad face. Her words became measured. "A wife should accompany her husband to Town. If for no other reason than to keep him from harm's way."

"What do you mean, harm's way?"

"Well, they tell me there're light skirts everywhere in London, just waiting to prey on men. And there's the sociable impures."

"What's a sociable impure?"

"The ladies kept by the sociable pures, the nobility." Dora's soft blue eyes opened wide, unbelieving. Her lady's innocence was incredible. She stared into the looking glass at Cassandra's reflection, and expounded further, "Why, they tell me that at five o'clock those women ride in handsome carriages in Hyde Park, as bold as you please, and with no shame. At the theater they sit in elegant boxes. Dressed to the first stare, too. Of course the blunt for all this finery is furnished by a protector, you know . . . the nobility, in exchange for their favors. If you get my meaning."

A moment of fear clutched Cassandra's throat. Was her husband going to London to see his sociable impure? She had suspected as much, but now Dora was putting words to her fear. He *had* been adamant about going alone, until she told him that Sister Martha had recommended they take Jacob to Dr. Morton.

Had not Cynthia told her that men of the upper orders did not marry for love, but for convenience, to produce an heir? And almost always they kept their mistresses. And she had even said that after an heir was born it was perfectly acceptable for the wife to take a lover.

How utterly disgusting.

"Dora, you're pulling my hair. Be done with it. I must get busy. Go fetch Cynthia."

"Did I say something wrong, m'lady?"

"No. It's just that I am forced to ask Cynthia about borrowing more gowns. There's no time to order gowns in Wickham Market. Besides, I plan to order ever so many while I'm in London."

Dora bobbed and left Cassandra alone.

That was why he insisted on being married by a smithy. So he wouldn't feel guilt. The next time he wants to coze I will ask him if he keeps an impure.

Hot blood suffused her face; her heart pounded painfully against her rib cage. She said aloud, "Stuff; I'm letting my imagination run away with me." She splashed water on her face to cool it, then dried it with a soft towel. Then another thought assaulted her heart. If His Lordship was so much in love with his first Countess that he could not make love to her, Cassandra, how could he do *it* with one of those sociable impures? Becoming more confused by the minute, she was glad when she heard voices and recognized one as Cynthia's. Dora had not wasted time in bringing her. Appearing almost instantly in the dressing room, the maid said, "She's here, m'lady."

After telling Dora that she would not need her until later, Cassandra quit the room and went to greet Cynthia in the crimson room, giving her a kiss on the cheek. "I'm always asking favors of you, Cynthia, but I am in great distress."

Cynthia sauntered to the sofa by the window and sat down. She was elegantly turned out in an emerald green riding habit, except for her feet, which were bare. Dust around the skirt's hem indicated that she had been riding, or painting. Pulling her long legs up in a very unladylike position and squirming until she got comfortable, Cynthia said, "I hear that you are accompanying Brother into London. That can't be true; he would never allow—"

" 'Tis true, and I cannot go with these gowns I've been wearing. They are well and good for the country, but I feel I should be a mite more stylish in Town."

"I don't think you should go."

"Whyever not?"

Cynthia stared at Cassandra and shook her head incredulously. "You don't know very much about men, do you?"

"I'm afraid I don't, but I don't take your meaning."

"Brother is going to see Elsa—"

"Who's Elsa? You can't mean—"

"I do."

Cassandra felt her face grow hot. "How do you know this? How do you know her name? Cynthia, you are funning me."

"I'm not funning, and the only reason I am telling you is to keep you from being hurt when you learn, which you will if you go into Town. You might even see them together. He's been known to ride in the park with her."

Cynthia's voice became slightly scolding. "Cassandra, I told you before that men of the upper orders are scoundrels. Their wives are supposed to look the other way when they dally with their mistresses."

Cassandra felt that her knees were going to give way under her. This was the whole of it; Cynthia would not lie. She sat in a chair and drew a deep breath, after which she raised a thick, dark eyebrow and asked, "Who told you about the ways of the upper orders? I'm sure not the dowager—"

Cynthia spoke without hesitation. "Sylvia, Brother's first Countess."

"Of course. How could I be so addle-brained? My husband's first Countess *was* of the upper orders, and wise to the world." Cassandra was embarrassed by her naïveté. An orphanage was not the best place in which to learn of the ways of the world, she mused, nor was a vicarage, with a father who preached hellfire and damnation and accused her of unfit thoughts if she even smiled.

She waited a long while before she asked Cynthia the question uppermost in her mind, dreading the answer. "Who told you about Elsa?"

"A servant, but I can't tell you which one. Brother would have his head."

"Do you think I would confront Lord Ranleigh about his sociable impure?"

"Yes."

"Why? Am I such a slow top?"

"Because you can't help yourself. Right now you are about to burst, wanting to run to him, hoping he will say 'tisn't so."

Cassandra's answer was quick. "I would not ask him. I would never beg, nor would I demand he keep himself only to me, even though he promised before God that he would."

A little laugh came from Cynthia. "You will get used to the ways of the nobility—"

"Never," Cassandra answered with extreme feeling, and, weary of the subject, she sought to speak of something else. "You did not say that I could borrow more of your gowns."

Cynthia jumped to her feet. "Of course you may, pea goose. You may wear anything of mine that you wish. I don't know why the dowager insists on ordering so many gowns, as well as other things, for me. I think she dreams that somewhere out in the woods, when I'm painting, one of Sir Arthur's knights will be reincarnated and whisk me off, leaving Ranleigh Hall to her and her precious Wade."

"What about Lord Ranleigh? He's certainly a big presence at Ranleigh Hall."

"I think she prays he will die."

"Cynthia, you have windmills in your head."

Hurt showed in Cynthia's blue eyes, and in her face, masked with a smile. "Someday you will get my meaning, just as you did when I told you about Elsa."

"Please! I never want to hear that name again."

"Cassandra, you are not dense; you just refuse to believe. This is not Sister Martha's orphanage."

Cassandra's only answer was a further tightening of her jaw. She had heard quite enough about the ways of the upper orders, and more than enough about Elsa. It was the outside of enough when it had been told to her in abstract, but to connect Lord Ranleigh with a name—she could not bear it.

Cynthia jumped to her feet and grabbed Cassandra's hand. "Come on; you will be pleased at what I have to offer in the way of beautiful gowns. I'm so glad we are the same size."

And Cassandra was pleased, as well as amazed.

In Cynthia's apartment, which was in the opposite wing of the Hall, she pulled from a huge chiffonnier gowns, day dresses, walking dresses, pelisses, even ball gowns, that had never been worn.

"Why?"

"No one knows why the dowager does anything. Every season she orders new gowns from London. A very good modiste there has my size, which, unfortunately, hasn't changed since I was thirteen."

"Would you object to my engaging the same modiste? I would caution her not to copy any of your gowns."

"Her name is Madame Lenora, and her shop is on Bond Street. And I do not object if she does copy my gowns, which she wouldn't. She claims to be too creative for such a thing."

"Cynthia, come to London with us. I've heard that women ride out on morning calls; we could do that together, and mayhap go to the theater."

"You will have your hands full keeping up with Lord Ranleigh without being bothered with me. Besides, I prefer to paint."

They did not talk much after that, just exclaimed over how beautiful each gown was when Cassandra slipped it over her head. Twisting and turning in front of the looking glass, she felt tears brim her eyes. In her dreams on the hillock she had never worn such finery. One gown in particular pleased her beyond bearing, a cranberry silk with tiny buttons up the back, a plunging décolletage, and a high waist that made her bosom appear larger than it was. Hugging Cynthia, she said, "Oh, you are such a wonderful sister-in-law. How can I ever thank you?"

"Don't. It would make me feel humble. Now, happiness is all I feel when I look at you, even if you are a little dense about the impures and the like." Smiling, she said, "I'm funning, of course. There's nothing dense about you, Countess. You're innocent, and that's not a sin." She stood back, cocked her head to one side, and exclaimed, "The cranberry is perfect on you; it makes your gray eyes sultry, even seductive, and your hair the color of corn silk. You are a beautiful gel, Cassandra."

"I'm not—"

"That's why you are so beautiful. Sylvia was beautiful, but so vain that it ruined it all." And then she added, "It was the death of her."

Cassandra was too busy slipping out of one gown and into another to ask Cynthia what she meant.

Choosing her favorites from the stack of gowns piled on the bed, Cassandra, when she was through, was ever so pleased. She rang for a footman to carry them back to her apartment, telling him, "Be careful that you do not crush the cranberry silk."

Cassandra did not know why she felt the way she did; there was no answer for it, but somewhere inside her she knew the beautiful cranberry silk gown had a special place in her life. All her life these premonitions had come over her, and she would immediately forget them until something happened to remind her. Turning to Cynthia, she thanked her again, hugged her, and then left, trailing behind the footman. Her heart sang, and she did not know why, for by rights she should have been worried about a certain sociable impure named Elsa.

In Kenmere, Lord Ranleigh's London town house, he sat in his handsome library, leaning back in a red leather chair, his booted feet resting atop a huge Jacobean desk. He had been thus for an hour, pondering how his well-orchestrated plans had landed him in the mess in which he found himself. His only need in coming to London was to see Elsa.

His lordship's dark eyes stared at his first Countess's portrait, hanging above the black marble mantel. For a long moment he held those beautiful green eyes with his own. He studied the catlike smile, and the bulging white flesh of her bosom, flesh that once had set his passions aflame.

He whipped around his chair so that the portrait would be to his back. Today he did not need to be reminded of the past. In his hand he held a piece of parchment. It was from *that* which he needed to escape. The gel would be the death of him.

With great determination, he focused his thoughts on the finery that surrounded him, the red velvet drapes that reached the high scrolled ceiling, the beautiful carved wood bookcases that held numerous leather-bound books, the fire that crackled in the fireplace; and then his gaze returned to the piece of parchment.

Frowning ferociously, he looked again at Cassandra's flowing script: "First priority is taking Jacob to see Dr. Morton; second, visit a modiste's shop and select a handsome wardrobe for me. Not knowledgeable of the latest styles, I need your help, Your Lordship, desperately; third, we must needs locate Ellen for Sister Martha. You remember my telling you of the gel who ran away from the orphanage, worrying Sister Martha to death, do you not?"

Lord Ranleigh stopped there, for that was enough to keep him busy for days. When was he to see Elsa?

Just then a scratching on the door claimed his attention.

"Enter," he said, quickly removing his feet from the desk and straightening in his chair. His cravat was askew, and he straightened that.

Nelson, his valet, who looked more like a pugilist than he did a servant, entered and set a great silver tray, loaded with hot biscuits, scrambled eggs, ham, and an assortment of jams, on the desk in front of His Lordship. From a Wedgwood pot he poured steaming coffee. After which he handed His Lordship the morning *Gazette*.

"Will that be all?" Nelson asked anxiously.

"Thank you, that will be all, Nelson," Lord Ranleigh said. "Until further notice."

The valet was relieved. Earlier, he had shaved His Lordship and laid out his clothes, changing them at least thrice. Since becoming leg shackled, His Lordship had become quite particular.

"Seeing Elsa, I suppose," the valet had inquired.

This had brought a glare from Lord Ranleigh, and the valet had taken himself off to fetch breakfast.

Now, breakfast served, he left as quickly as he had

earlier, for His Lordship's humor had not improved a whit.

Left alone, Lord Ranleigh sipped his coffee, holding the cup with one hand while he unrolled the morning *Gazette* with the other. It was awkward, and he wished he had waited until he had eaten.

Suddenly, his eyes bulged, for there before him in bold print was all the news about his visiting London. He jerked himself up, swore, "The devil take me," and spewed coffee all over himself, the paper, and his breeches. His blood pounded in the top of his head, and he said again, "The devil take me."

What a coil!

Elsa would read this for sure . . . and she would be knocking on the front door within an hour, her anger riled, her black eyes flashing.

Forcing himself to settle down, he read the article carefully and found a modicum of comfort in that it did not mention his recent marriage.

That comfort, however, was short-lived when he'd had time to think on it, and he infinitely regretted that in the past he had not gone to Elsa, instead of having her come to him. He set his cup down and covered his eyes with his hand.

"What a coil!"

He should have foreseen this, he told himself. It was not unusual for his visit to London to be noted in the paper. He should have slipped in town in darkness, unnoticed.

But how could he, with Cassandra by his side, and another carriage trailing, carrying a lady's maid, a nurse, and Jacob?

He had for a while thought there would be a third carriage, and there would have been had not the boxes of gowns Cassandra had borrowed from Cynthia been stuffed into the boots of both carriages.

"Gowns no doubt cut to her navel," he said as he

196

jumped to his feet, nearly upending the leather chair that had been holding him, and yanked the bellpull not once, but twice, hard.

A sheepish footman appeared almost immediately. "M'lord, you rang?"

"Tell Lady Ranleigh I wish to see her immediately, here in the library."

Cassandra came and stood in the doorway, silently staring at the portrait of Lord Ranleigh's first Countess.

"Well, why don't you come in? Are you afraid I will bite you?"

"I hear you are in a terrible humor." Cassandra stood like a statue, and just as silent.

Demme the woman. Why did she have to be so appealing?

She wore a morning dress of fine lilac cambric; her hair hung loose to touch her shoulders, and her gray eyes were anything but smiling. He watched her throat flutter, the only movement connected with her stonelike countenance.

Feeling his own breathing alter, he said again, *sotto voce,* "Demme that woman . . . that gel."

"I'm sorry, Your Lordship, but you must needs remove that portrait if you wish me to enter your splendid library. I refuse to be in her presence—"

"Gad's wallop! You are not in her presence. She is long dead—"

"But you still stare at her portrait and wish she were alive. That is well and good, but do not subject me to your longing. I feel as if at any moment she will float out of the frame and come to flog me for being here with *her* husband."

He laughed, and felt better. "That is ridiculous."

"Will you remove it or not? I must not waste time. I am quite busy. Jacob needs my attention."

This was not true at all. Mrs. Brodwick had taken Jacob to the mews to see the horses, and Ranleigh's Town carriages, but it seemed that the only way to get

197

her husband's attention was to throw in something about Jacob.

He pushed his chair back and quickly crossed the room. Wrapping his long finger around her small wrist, he tugged at her in a good-natured way. He even managed a smile. "Sylvia is not going to float down out of the frame and flog you. I shall have the portrait removed later, if that will make you happy."

His Lordship did not know why he had said that. It was not his goal to make any woman happy, unless it served his purpose of keeping his heir alive. Still, when he felt a warmth and a fast beating from Cassandra's wrist his own blood started pumping faster, and he dropped her arm as if it were hot.

It was just as well, he thought, for she showed no sign of entering the room. Her heels were dug into the soft carpet as if they were encased in stone. He went to the mantel and, with great effort, turned the portrait to the wall.

"Does that make you happy, Lady Ranleigh? If so, mayhap we can discuss this list of things you have written down that will occupy my time while I am in London. I warned you that I had business to transact."

Cassandra stepped into the room. "What could be more important than a visit to the doctor with your son?"

"Jacob seems to be doing quite nicely. I saw him walking with Mrs. Brodwick in the woods, and he has gained weight since you came to Ranleigh Hall—"

"And he is now taking riding lessons from Elmo, but the wheezing in his chest is still there, mayhap not as often, but there, nonetheless. I feel strongly that he should see a physician who specializes in children's diseases. The doctor in Wickham Market is a quack. Can you imagine giving a child laudanum just because he misbehaves? I even got the notion that Cook was trying to kill Jacob."

Lord Ranleigh's countenance darkened, as if he had rather not be reminded of Jacob's behavior before she came to Ranleigh Hall. Cassandra looked at him. He should feel guilt. He had been a horrible father. Her gray eyes locked with his dark eyes.

He said, "Let's deal with the present. Can you not take Jacob to see this new doctor?"

"Dr. Fred Morton."

"Dora and Mrs. Brodwick will accompany you . . . while I take care of business."

"And what if 'tis the doctor's wont to talk with you, Jacob's father, about a special treatment? I'm only his stepmother; in truth, a surrogate nursemaid, if my memory serves me correctly."

By now, Cassandra had claimed a leather chair, which practically swallowed her. She clasped her hands demurely in her lap, lifted her chin just slightly, and waited for His Lordship's next argument. If Cynthia could be believed, his important business was to see this Elsa, and she could not see how *that* could be more important than accompanying his son to a physician. She was sorry; she could not look the other way while her husband dallied with his mistress. It might well be the way of the *ton*, but it was not her way.

When it appeared that Lord Ranleigh was at a loss for words, though she doubted it, she continued, "I'm sure Dr. Morton would be insulted if a member of the nobility did not come to inquire of his son's well being. 'Tis the thing—"

" 'Tis not the thing. A man has business other than raising a recalcitrant boy, and if he were not my heir—"

"But he is. And his bad behavior was brought on by neglect; yours, as well as others."

Lord Ranleigh could not believe he was sitting here arguing with this chit. How dare she cross him? Did she not know a woman's place?

But he did not say these things, for he was sure his

new wife would have a sharp answer. There was nothing to it; he would visit the doctor . . . and then visit Elsa Having decided it, he moved on to the next item or the list.

"About visiting the modiste with you—"

"Yes," Cassandra said quickly.

She watched as he rose from his chair and strode across the room to stand before a tall bookcase. Reaching high over his head, he retrieved a large leather bound book, taking from it a key. He then went to a safe that rested in a corner of the room and opened its door, revealing a stack of notes the like of which Cassandra had never even dreamed. Leaning forward in her chair, she gasped audibly.

Lord Ranleigh stepped back, as if to afford a better look. "As I told you, there's no limit to the blunt a your disposal. I want you to go to the best modiste in Bond Street, and order gowns to your dear heart's de light."

He paused, and then, tentatively, said, "However, have no notion of accompanying you in such a venture Dora can—"

"But, Your Lordship, Dora knows less about Bond Street than I do, and even less about the latest fashions You must needs go."

Lord Ranleigh glared at her ferociously; she smiled at him, and he wondered what next was on the gel's sharp mind.

Sixteen

Why will he not look at me when he is talking?

Cassandra stared at the good doctor as he prosed on about Jacob's health: "As all children, Jacob only needs proper nourishment, love, and affection, and I would not leave out discipline."

He looked away, and Cassandra willed him to look at her, or at Lord Ranleigh, who seemed not to notice the doctor's discomfiture. He had examined Jacob thoroughly, and now Jacob and Mrs. Brodwick were waiting in the carriage while he handed down his prognosis.

Cassandra was waiting for him to tell the whole of it.

He was a small man, with graying hair and sharp blue eyes. A pince-nez hung from the lapel of his dark frock-tailed coat. Occasionally he lifted the pince-nez to his eyes and read from a large book on the desk in front of him.

Cassandra and Lord Ranleigh were standing; he, anxious to leave, she probing deeper: "Dr. Morton, what about the constant wheezing in his chest?" she asked.

"Do not fret overmuch, Lady Ranleigh. The Lord's Will will be done. I'm sure Sister Martha taught you that."

Earlier, Cassandra had told him that she had lived at

201

the orphanage, and that Sister Martha had spoken of his expertise with children. He had smiled, and, for a while, reminisced about going to Sister Martha's and treating her children when all of her home remedies had failed.

"Never lost a one," he said, his eyes still focused on something other than Cassandra. From a black satchel he took a bottle of clear brown liquid and handed it to Cassandra. "Give this to Jacob when the wheezing gets bad; it will clear the phlegm from his throat."

There was nothing for it but to leave, Cassandra conceded. Lord Ranleigh's hand was on the doorknob, and he was saying, "Thank you, Dr. Morton, for seeing Jacob on such short notice. I take the good news with extreme relief." He looked at Cassandra and smiled fondly. "I fear the Countess is overly protective of the boy. Now, mayhap she can relax."

They took their leave, but on the way to the carriage Cassandra reprimanded His Lordship thoroughly. "You were too quick to believe. The man is not telling the whole of it."

Lord Ranleigh stopped and took her arm. "Why are you bent on believing the worst about Jacob's health? I own that he was in a bad way when you came. But he is better now, so let it be. I thought that all along, but I gave in to your insistence to stop your nattering." His voices was almost scolding. "You are a very stubborn chit, Lady Ranleigh. Sometimes you overstep your bounds."

Without giving Cassandra a chance to reply, he dropped her arm and walked on. She followed, sputtering to herself that the doctor was withholding something from them. And then she reminded herself that what prompted that belief was the premonition she had had, the feeling that had suddenly come over her. No one really believed in portents, except those who had them. Of course Lord Ranleigh did not believe her.

"You're most likely right," she said. "I pray so."

Cassandra was amazed at how fond, in the few weeks she had been at Ranleigh Hall, she had become of the little boy. How her heart had ached for him when first they met. She shuddered, remembering the laudanum-induced sleep, just because he misbehaved. And he did misbehave, she thought, remembering his attempt to whack her with his toy horse.

Looking at the elegant crested carriage, she saw that Jacob and Mrs. Brodwick were laughing together.

When they reached the carriage a footman let down the step and Lord Ranleigh helped Cassandra inside, then sprang up to sit beside her, giving the driver office to go. As the carriage rolled slowly over the cobbled streets, he said to Jacob, "The doctor gives a good report, Jacob. Now, mayhap Lady Ranleigh will stop fretting. A lot of nourishing food and the wonderful care you are getting will put more weight on your bones, and you will be as strong as a pugilist."

His Lordship directed a smile at Cassandra, but the smile quickly faded when Jacob asked, "Will you take me to see a bout, Your Lordship?"

"I think that's a capital idea, Jacob," Cassandra cut in. "And while the two of you are so occupied, I will shop for clothes for you."

Lord Ranleigh could see what was coming—the time he had allotted for his visit to Elsa was again being taken. He was quick to say to Cassandra, "I thought you were reluctant to visit Bond Street without me as your escort."

"I shall take Dora and Mrs. Brodwick. But when I visit the modiste, I will need your attendance. She might try to sell me gowns that are much too revealing."

Lord Ranleigh recognized a threat when he heard one. He could not believe what was happening. There was nothing to it; he would have to help the Countess select gowns, else she would do exactly as she had threatened. And she might possibly go so far as to purchase one of those transparent gowns, which, he understood, were all the rage with the *ton*. He did not want his wife exposing herself in such a manner. Feeling the seemingly ever-present delicious pain in his loins, he determinedly changed the direction of his thoughts.

He loved to watch the bouts, but not with a five-year-old whom he could hardly bear. But then he was suddenly aware that the feeling of repulsion when he touched Jacob had greatly diminished. Unable to explain it, he shook his head. He even found sympathy for the boy, and guilt rode him for having neglected his care.

But he had not been aware of the poor care until Cassandra came to Ranleigh Hall. He only knew that every nurse left; and he knew nothing of children and what caused bad behavior. He looked at Cassandra, seeing her kindness, which spilled from her huge gray eyes when she looked at the boy. It would not hurt to devote an afternoon to the boy, taking him to see the boxing.

Another thought came to him, and he immediately acted upon it. Leaning his head out of the carriage window, he told the driver to take them through Regent's Park, and past Carlton House.

A crack of the whip and a turn of the carriage was the driver's answer. Lord Ranleigh said to Jacob, "The Prince Regent lives in Carlton House when he is in London. You must needs familiarize yourself with Town, Jacob. When you inherit the earldom you will spend much time here."

"May we stop at Gunther's for a sweet? Mrs. Brodwick read to me about the sweetmaker."

"After we've seen the Park and Carlton House," Lord Ranleigh promised, and he did not object, or draw back, when Jacob moved to sit beside him.

In truth, the ride was so pleasant that His Lordship's

concern that Elsa would come knocking on Kenmere's door slipped totally from his mind, and he found that he was surprisingly content riding through the park with the Countess, Jacob, and Jacob's nurse.

Seventeen

Cassandra was taken aback when she visited the many shops on Bond and Oxford streets. The approach to Lord Ranleigh's London home had brought them through the mean streets of the east side, where children begged and strewn garbage was being ravaged by dogs traveling in packs, thus impeding the movement of the carriage. But once the crested carriage tooled off the deeply rutted dirt streets onto cobbles, they had moved at a faster pace, and upon entering London's west side, Mayfair, where the upper orders lived, gas lights lined the streets, and with every mile the shops became more elaborate, the churches more impressive, the houses more palatial.

When Cassandra first viewed Kenmere, Lord Ranleigh's London town house in Belgrade Square, she thought she would faint dead away. The four-story edifice equaled Ranleigh Hall in splendor, if not in size.

From chimney pots smoke swirled slowly upward to meet a velvet-blue sky, and when the carriage came to a stop, two huge doors swung open, forming a gaping aperture through which more splendor could be viewed.

Now, with Lord Ranleigh and Jacob at the bouts, and the gels on their shopping spree, Mrs. Brodwick acted as guide to the shoppers. She had worked in London before her marriage, and now she felt quite important, pointing out the specialty of each shop on Bond and Oxford streets.

Inside the shops, Cassandra was treated with the greatest respect when she introduced herself as Lady Ranleigh, so different than when she had told Stella at the draper's shop in Wickham Market of her impending marriage to the Earl. But now Cassandra was dressed differently. She wore a blue walking dress and carried a matching parasol, thanks to Cynthia.

In Old Bond Street, Weston, the tailor who sewed Lord Ranleigh's impeccably fitted clothes, was so anxious for Cassandra's business, he bowed low to her and promised magnanimously: "I will come to Kenmere for measurements. The clothes will be stitched right away, then delivered to His Lordship's home."

In view of that, Cassandra limited her purchases to a few garments she found on the racks in children's shops; knee breeches, shirts, silk stockings, and patent low cuts. Since Lord Ranleigh had instructed her that it was considered bad form for members of the upper orders to ask the price of *anything*, she conformed to that notion, although it was not her nature. Then, remembering the huge stack of pound notes in Lord Ranleigh's safe, she stopped her worrying and quit the shop, after which they went to Bertin's and purchased scented roses for the three of them. "Wear them in your hair when your best beau comes to pay his addresses," she said, giggling along with Mrs. Brodwick and Dora.

Cassandra could not remember when she had had such a grand time. They returned to the carriage and took a vote on where to go next. It was still early afternoon.

Mrs. Brodwick wanted to return to Gunther's, and it was unanimously decided that they would go there for one of Mr. Gunther's famous apricot tarts.

"Dora, you're going to think you have died and gone

to heaven when you put your mouth to one of Gunther's apricot tarts," the nursemaid said, and when Dora's broad face broke into a huge smile Mrs. Brodwick expounded profusely about their earlier trip through Regent's Park.

"And we even passed Carlton House. It was a high good time we were having, after the good doctor pronounced nothing wrong with Jacob's health. His Lordship took great pleasure in pointing out the sights. He even laughed on occasion."

Cassandra instructed the driver to take them to Gunther's, in Berkeley Square. A footman helped her into the carriage, which moved grandly for everyone to see. Her eyes were wide as they traveled down the cobbled streets.

Women strolled leisurely, their abigails walking three steps behind them. Once or twice, Cassandra leaned forward and stared.

Since the women did not dart in and out of shops, she could see no purpose in their being on the street, except to show off their finery and to smile and speak to gentlemen they met. Curled feathers dressed their hats, and their walking dresses were fit for an extravaganza. Without exception, their parasols matched their gowns.

As they rode along, Cassandra wondered if one could be Ellen. Mayhap the gel had landed a husband of the upper orders who could afford to dress her in high fashion. She prayed that it was so. Would that not be something to tell Sister Martha?

Cassandra found herself looking for Elsa, until she realized her good mood had left her. Straightening, she told herself that she would not know the light skirt if she saw her. No doubt she was very, very beautiful, and dressed as fine as any woman she had seen on the streets—with Lord Ranleigh's blunt.

Tears instantly flooded Cassandra's eyes, and she

willed them away. Today her husband was with his son, watching a boxing match, and on the morrow, she and Lord Ranleigh would visit a modiste. He had promised, and she believed him a man of his word.

Earlier, when they were driving with Jacob through the park, she had extracted a promise that he would take her to Hyde Park to experience the five-o'clock squeeze she had been told about.

Mayhap if I can keep His Lordship otherwise occupied, he will not have time to visit Elsa.

The thought absolutely astounded Cassandra. She was not in any way a conniving person. *Until now,* she thought, and then she told herself that women in love acted strangely if that love was threatened. She wanted . . .

I must needs be rational and not get carried away, she scolded herself. She had not realized that her sorrow was so apparent until Dora bent forward and asked her if anything was the matter.

Cassandra blinked away her tears. " 'Tis a beautiful day, and the apricot tart at Gunther's will bring a wonderful completion to our outing."

Upon arriving back at Kenmere—after a hurried but successful visit to Gunther's—Cassandra was surprised to see tethered to an iron post four handsome bays, hitched to a superbly appointed carriage attended by a powdered footman in gorgeous green-and-gold livery. Sitting on the box was a coachman wearing a coat of many layers, a three-corner hat perched atop his snow-white wig.

She strained to see inside the conveyance. Finding it empty, she left her own carriage and hurried to lift the knocker on the huge door, which was opened quickly by the butler. His face was ashen.

He stepped back and bowed to her. "Welcome home, m'lady. There's a caller in the receiving room."

"Who—"

"Miss Elsa, m'lady, Miss Elsa Cordley. She's awaiting Lord Ranleigh."

"Oh, is she now?" Cassandra would have addressed the butler by name, but she had not had time to learn it. "What is your name?" she asked. "I can't call you Butler, now can I?"

She looked him up and down; anything to delay thinking about the visitor in the receiving room.

The butler's long-tailed coat fit him perfectly; his cravat, snowy white, touched his chin, which he held stiffly at an authoritative angle. He was not overly tall, but nor was he short. His sharp, aristocratic nose, smooth dark hair, and twinkling eyes gave the appearance of a man who was sure of his position in the household. She liked him.

"His Lordship calls me Worth," he said, and then with a smile added, "My true name's Tiddleworth, but I would not dare let the other servants know that. They would snicker behind my back."

"I promise not to tell, and if I hear anyone snickering behind your back I shall have them dismissed. Or I shall say that the name is a very prominent one. I recall reading about a famous general by that name."

The butler beamed. "Thank you, m'lady. I think His Lordship has found himself a jewel. By your authority I will ask that woman to leave."

"No, no, don't do that. I will receive her, but only after I have freshened up a bit."

She went directly to her suite on the second floor, as elaborate as her rooms at Ranleigh Hall. And, as at Ranleigh Hall, they adjoined those of His Lordship.

Dora was waiting for her. "Seeing that you had a caller, I thought you might need me."

"I do." Cassandra went to the washbasin and splashed cold water onto her face, for it was flushed hot with anger. How dare that light skirt come here! Even before she had dried herself, Cassandra asked Dora to bring the cranberry silk. She could only imagine the finery Miss Cordley would be sporting.

"And wind my hair into a halo."

"Yes, m'lady," Dora answered, and with great speed she did as she was told. Cassandra was amazed that, with her height and broad frame, she could move so quickly.

The blue walking dress worn for shopping was replaced by the cranberry silk, freshly ironed and smelling of lavender. She slipped it over her head and smoothed the skirt, and after Dora had laboriously buttoned the tiny buttons down the back she wound Cassandra's sun-streaked hair atop her head. Cassandra could only pray that today it would prove to be her halo.

"How do I look?" she asked, turning in front of the floor-to-ceiling looking glass. She caught her breath; never had she seen a gown so beautiful. Now she even gave credit to her own body's curves, which, she was forced to acknowledge, enhanced the gown's fitted waist and low-cut, revealing neckline.

Dora gave a deep sigh. "You are the most beautiful Countess in the whole of England, and as regal as a queen."

Cassandra could not help but laugh. "I hope that I don't resemble the Prince Regent's poor wife. I would look like a painted barn, if what they say is true."

Taking a bit of pale rouge, she dabbed lightly at her high cheekbones. Her almond-shaped gray eyes shone with the same anger that had flushed her face. "I'm ready," she said, more to herself than to Dora.

The maid gazed at her admiringly, and her eyebrows arched upward when Cassandra said, "I only hope I am not too late."

The words came out before Dora could stop them. "Too late for what, m'lady?"

"I wish to see the caller before His Lordship returns.

Would you have tea sent to the receiving room? And please make haste."

With puzzlement showing on her face, Dora bobbed and quit the room, and Cassandra walked swiftly out into the hall and down the curving stairs to the first floor, where she swept grandly across the great hall and entered the receiving room in which her husband's paramour waited.

Eighteen

Cassandra was not prepared for the striking woman who sat poised elegantly in the rose-colored beigere chair, as if she was accustomed to the grandeur the room afforded: draperies, royal blue silk reaching from the gold-scrolled ceiling to puddle on the floor, long sofas and deep chairs the same blue silk, and carpets of varying shades of blue, rose, and gold covered the floor, fit for any palace in England. Ancestral portraits graced silk walls.

Cassandra stared boldly into the woman's dark eyes, as black as wet coal and blazing like the fire that burned in the black marble fireplace. Her dress was plum in color, with yards and yards of French lace; no doubt, Cassandra thought, paid for by Lord Ranleigh. Elsa Cordley did not look like a light skirt off the street. In truth, there was something exotic about her. Her skin was very delicately tinged a light bronze; her hair, as black as her eyes, hung in disarray down her back, and black ringlets framed a very, very beautiful face.

Cassandra felt her heart pumping blood so fast that she thought her veins would burst. Her heart ached; she wanted to turn and run. But she remained fast.

Walking closer to the woman, she offered a hand. "I'm the Countess of Ranleigh."

213

With the infinite grace of a long, sleek cat, the courtesan rose from her chair and began a deep, courtly curtsy. She never recovered. At the very instant the words left Cassandra's mouth, Miss Cordley crumpled to the floor, to lie in her heap of finery.

Like a sack of new potatoes, Cassandra thought, before calling, "Someone come quickly. The woman has fainted."

No one came, and remembering her position, Cassandra ran to pull the bellpull, yanking it with great fervor.

A footman appeared almost instantly. "You summoned, m'lady?"

"Yes. I must needs get this . . . this woman on her feet and gone from Kenmere before Lord Ranleigh returns."

She tuned her ears to the sound of huge doors opening or, worse, purposeful footsteps striding across the room behind her.

"Yes, m'lady." When the footman started into another bow Cassandra scolded, "There's no time for that. Did you not hear me when I said make haste?"

He turned and left, and just then a low moan floated up from the floor. Cassandra knelt and, taking the woman's shoulders, shook her, while saying, "Wake up. Whatever made you faint?"

"Lord Ranleigh . . . he . . . he can't be married . . ."

The words were weak and garbled. "If 'tis so, I will kill him," said the courtesan, who, Cassandra noted, did not look quite so glamorous with anger twisting her face.

" 'Tis so. His Lordship and I were married in Gretna Green a few weeks ago. By a man of the cloth, which means our vows will be held sacred."

At least mine will.

There was another distraught moan.

Then the footman returned to hand to Cassandra a

vinaigrette, which she waved under Miss Cordley's nose. But not for long. Coughing and sputtering, the courtesan grabbed the small vial, drew back her arm, and slammed it across the room. It hit the silk-covered wall with a huge bang. Quickly, she was on her feet and making toward Cassandra, who stepped back and looked round for some avenue of escape.

"I shall gladly kill you and eat your liver for breakfast," Elsa Cordley threatened as the footman placed himself in front of Cassandra, taking a small and ineffective fist to the chest before he could reach out and restrain the flailing arms.

She tried to kick him in his most private parts, but he warded that off by lifting a knee and by pushing her back into the chair from which she, only moments before, had risen.

"Would you have me carry her to her conveyance?" the footman asked. His face was flushed red, and he looked as if he would enjoy smacking her.

Cassandra could imagine him forcibly carrying the angry woman to the waiting carriage, while she kicked and screamed, the servants watching.

"No. Just hold her there for a moment. When she calms down mayhap I can speak rationally with her."

"Never," Miss Cordley screeched. She pushed herself forward, only to be restrained by the footman's big hand. "I'll never be rational about Lord Ranleigh. He loves me, and I love him with all my heart and soul. I can't live without him. So why should he marry *you?*"

She looked at Cassandra venomously, and when Cassandra stood her ground and stared back at her, trying her best to appear unruffled, the courtesan went on in a loud voice, "Had His Lordship wanted to be leg shackled, he would have done so with me."

Then the unexpected happened. Elsa Cordley fell back into her chair, covered her face with her hands, and began to weep.

215

Sympathy replaced Cassandra's anger; but not so much so that she let down her guard. And no more would she have done so if a tiger were threatening to leap at her throat. She asked herself if she should dismiss the footman, who had heard too much already, or let him stay to protect her. She quickly decided to dismiss him, and said to the footman, "Teddy, you may leave now."

"But Lady Ranleigh, you might be in danger should I leave."

Cassandra forced a confident smile to her lips. "I bound that Miss Cordley is in shock, but she is calmer now and will listen to what I have to say."

"I am not calmer. I will not listen to your lies."

After the footman left Cassandra stood and stared at Elsa Cordley, wondering what more she could say that hadn't been said already. There was no time to think.

She began: "I know how you must feel, Miss Cordley. His Lordship has done you a terrible wrong by not informing you of his marriage. You have every right to be angry. But what is done is done, and I must needs think of some way to make it right for you."

"How could you make it right?" Elsa Cordley asked, her lips curling scornfully.

"Outside of Lord Ranleigh being your lover, what else will you miss about him?"

"His protection, of course."

Cassandra stopped, and, looking at the woman, lifted a quizzical brow. "His protection? I don't take your meaning."

"Are you such a slow top? I'll miss the blunt; you know, that stuff with which one pays one's servants, buys gowns—"

Cassandra immediately pounced on the solution. She would give her husband's mistress the stack of pound notes from his safe. *That* should satisfy her.

"I will be most fair with you, Miss Cordley. To compensate you for Lord Ranleigh's unfair treatment of you, I shall afford you enough blunt to take care of your most extravagant needs until you have obtained another . . . protector."

Cassandra hated the word. Imagine her husband being called the protector of a light skirt. He should be horse-whipped.

"Where would you get blunt like that? 'Tis a well-known fact that the aristocracy don't allow wives access to funds." She looked at Cassandra, still disbelieving her. "If, indeed, you are Lord Ranleigh's wife."

"I am. And if you will wait here, I shall return with so much blunt, you won't believe it."

A slow smile softened Miss Cordley's face, and Cassandra knew she had hit the right cord. Blunt. Now if only she could get the stuff and get Miss Cordley out of the house before Lord Ranleigh and Jacob returned. As she left the room, she forced her quick steps not to appear hurried, but as soon as she reached the great hall she literally ran the length of it and up the winding stairs, swearing under her breath at the many steps. She held the skirt of her cranberry silk gown halfway to her knees to prevent tripping—very unladylike, but necessary.

Inside the handsome library, she stood and stared at the many leather-bound books, her heart pounding at such a rate that she could not think which book His Lordship had hidden the key to the safe.

All the demme books looked alike.

Finally, she spied it, the third book from the wall, on the third shelf from the ceiling. Not that the spine was different from the others, but she had carefully observed Lord Ranleigh taking the book down, then replacing it in the exact spot from which he had taken it.

Now, she couldn't reach it.

There was nothing to it but to stand on a leather-tooled table. Standing unsteadily on the chair, she climbed on to the table and took down the book, and in an instant, the key was in her hand, and she reached inside the safe to procure the stack of notes. She felt no guilt. Had not Lord Ranleigh said that there was no limit to the amount of money available to her . . . as long as she did not expect to be his wife.

Cassandra took the full stack. Then, taking a few bills off the top, she put them back into the safe. That woman did not need so much. With her beauty she would be promptly snapped up by another man of means.

But Sister Martha could use some help.

The decision was easy. She would give the remainder of the pounds to the orphanage. Retrieving what she had put back into the safe, she pushed the notes under the cushion of the leather-tooled chair, leaving the key on the table. No need to lock an empty safe. Hurriedly then, she pushed the chair back to its proper position and quit the room.

If only she would not encounter Lord Ranleigh downstairs.

Luck was with her.

Elsa Cordley looked up anxiously when Cassandra re-entered the receiving room, and, with delicate, grasping hands reached out to take the pounds from Cassandra. Seeing the large amount, her black eyes looked as if they would explode inside her head.

Cassandra was relieved. The woman was not so much in love with Lord Ranleigh as she was with the "protection" he had afforded.

"I hope this will somehow compensate you for your loss of my husband," she said as she gently guided the courtesan toward the door.

"I will try to make do," Miss Cordley said, sighing deeply and smiling benignly.

"I'm certain you will do just that . . . with your

beauty. And I must needs remind you, Miss Cordley, that the huge amount I gave you is payment in full for your services. I'm certain you would not want to stir Lord Ranleigh's temper by asking for more." Before an answer was forthcoming, Cassandra closed the door behind the departing woman, then ran to a window to look out, feeling great relief when the handsome carriage tooled into the growing darkness and out of sight.

Lord Ranleigh was nowhere to be seen.

Cassandra turned back into the room, and it was then that the enormity of what she had done hit her. A great shudder passed over her. Lord Ranleigh would surely kill her, or at best, have her flogged when he knew. She looked at the tea service and the round biscuits, which had not been touched, now as cold as the dreams she'd dreamed on her hillock overlooking Ranleigh Hall.

"It cannot be helped," she said aloud. She would do the same thing over again, and suffer the consequences when the time came. She left the room and walked slowly to the end of the great hall. She had started up the winding stairs when she heard the door open behind her. Turning, she saw Lord Ranleigh and Jacob entering. Her eyes went to Jacob. He had a new haircut; not too short, but enough off that he did not look like a girl. "You look wonderful," she said to him.

He tore his hand from his father's and ran to Cassandra. She sat on a step and opened her arms to receive him, ruffling his blond curls and hugging him tightly. "Did you have a good time, Jacob?"

"Yes, indeed. But now I'm ever so glad to see you. Next time you will come so you can see all the things Papa showed me." He looked up at Lord Ranleigh. "Tell her, Papa, where you took me. And show her her gift."

Lord Ranleigh took a seat beside Cassandra and began, "After the bouts we went to St. Paul's Cathedral,

219

where, in Paul's Walk, there is a market, a meeting place for all kinds of people. I thought, since Jacob would someday inherit the Ranleigh earldom, he should be exposed to that part of London. It will not be good for him to grow up in the country and not know the needs of people less fortunate. People were clamoring all over themselves, some to sell their wares, others to strike a bargain, some to steal."

"We shopped for a gift for you, and Jacob chose this necklace." He pulled from his waistcoat pocket a circle of thin gold, holding a heart-shaped locket. Taking Cassandra's hand, he cupped her palm and placed the necklace in it. "He said it would be your valentine, but I guess he couldn't wait."

"An early valentine is wonderful," Cassandra said in a choked voice. Her hand was shaking, for she remembered her own lace valentine, now torn in two. She opened the locket. One side held a miniature of a young boy, the other side a likeness of a young girl, mayhap two years younger.

She wondered if they were sweethearts, or if they were someone's children, a brother and a sister.

"I'll treasure it forever," she told Jacob, looking down and finding that he was half asleep. Long lashes rested on his cherub cheeks.

"I hope I didn't tire him out," His Lordship said.

Rising to his full height, he reached down to take Jacob, and together, he and Cassandra ascended the stairs, Jacob cradled in his long arms.

They went directly to Cassandra's quarters, where she rang for Mrs. Brodwick. The nurse came quickly and took Jacob from Lord Ranleigh. "I will let him rest a bit, and then I shall feed him a good meal before putting him to bed for the night. Tomorrow he will be rested and ready to go again."

"Wait," Cassandra said when the woman started to leave.

220

She went to her reticule and retrieved the bottle of brown liquid the doctor had given her and handed it to Mrs. Brodwick.

"If he should start coughing, give him a small dose of this. And send for me."

"Yes, m'lady," Mrs. Brodwick said, leaving without fanfare.

Cassandra and Lord Ranleigh were alone.

He quickly turned away from her and went to look at the courtyard below and at the stables beyond. "Tomorrow, I must needs tend to business—"

Most likely a visit to Miss Cordley, Cassandra thought, as she tried to shut out the vision of the woman's beautiful face, and another vision even more painful, that of her husband holding his mistress in his arms.

Another thought was as devastating: Should His Lordship discover that Cassandra had given away all his blunt, there would be no tomorrow. Of that she was certain.

"Tomorrow, mayhap you can accompany me to the modiste, and later we can ride in Hyde Park, with all the other nobility I've read about. I'm most anxious to see their finery." She smiled at him. "I'll wager that none of your friends know that you are married."

A small groan escaped Lord Ranleigh's throat. He turned away from the window with the full intent of saying to Cassandra that he had told her his purpose in coming to London had been business, that she had no right to interfere, that it was his wont on his next trip into Town to fetch her and introduce her to the *ton*. But not *this* trip. He would tell her that it had been she who had insisted upon coming this time, under the pretext of Jacob's needing to see a specialist.

He had suspected it and the doctor had proved him right: Jacob was not seriously ill, as his new wife claimed.

None of these things spilled forth; he could not force

221

them from his mouth, for when he looked at Cassandra, so innocent, so beautiful, words failed him. He stared at her, unblinking, until at last he said, "Would you have supper with me? Afterwards, mayhap we could coze for a spell."

"I bound I need to wash my face and hands, and mayhap change into a fresh gown. This one seems a little tired—"

"Oh, no, please do not change. 'Tis the first of Cynthia's gowns that does you justice." A short pause, and then, "I suppose it is all right for a husband to say that his wife looks fetching in a certain garment, that it does justice to her wonderfully shaped body—"

"It is perfectly all right. And I will not change if you desire that I not. But I will freshen my face a bit, and wash my hands." She looked into a tall looking glass that hung on the wall. "I'll call Dora to dress my hair."

"That seems a lot of trouble just to be eating with your husband." He gave a little laugh. "I understand that oftentimes a gel lets herself go after she's caught the man of her choice."

"Oh, but I did not catch you. You came to Sister Martha's looking for me." She could not help adding, "Not necessarily for me, but for a nurse for Jacob. A permanent nurse."

" 'Tis true, and Sister Martha made a good choice, even though at first I thought you a mite too fetching, that you might tempt me in a way I could not control. But I've grown used to that aspect and feel safe in spending time with you without endangering our relationship."

"You mean that of being married in name only?"

"Yes. That is what I mean. 'Tis for the best. As I have explained, closeness brings the danger of emotional involvement, and I bound that that will never again happen to me. One does not knowingly rush toward pain."

"I know," Cassandra snapped. "You've many times apprised me of your feelings. Now, if you will leave, I will summon my maid."

His Lordship went, saying he would go to his own quarters, and within the hour they would meet in the second-floor dining room.

Cassandra waited until his footsteps died in the hallway; when she heard a door open and close she removed her slippers and ran as fast as she could down the long hallway to His Lordship's library, where she grabbed the pounds from under the cushion and crammed them into the bosom of her gown. Should Lord Ranleigh stop by the library on his way to the dining room and see the lopsided cushion, and then the blunt beneath it, their coze at supper would not be pleasant. At the last minute she thought to hide the key. Then, stealthily, she made her way back to her own quarters and then summoned Dora.

Cassandra looked at the clock on the mantel. There was still time for a bath; not in the tub, mayhap, but a quick wash with water from the porcelain basin would suffice.

"Have a footman fetch hot water," she said when Dora entered, her dark eyes big and questioning.

"You washed only this morning, Countess." A big smile spread across her broad face. "Would you be having a cozy little supper with your husband?"

"Yes."

My husband in name only.

Dora left, and soon a footman brought the hot water in a brass-bound tankard and, after filling the ewer, sat it on the floor of Cassandra's dressing room, leaving quickly after that.

"Would you unbutton me, Dora?" Cassandra asked, turning her back to the gel.

The maid did so, and Cassandra held the gown in front so that it would not slip from her body and spill the pounds onto the floor. She thought to change to a fresh frock but decided against it. It would not hurt to appease His Lordship and wear the cranberry, as he had requested.

She asked of Dora: "Would you please wait in the next room until I call you?"

"Yes, m'lady."

When she was alone Cassandra removed her clothes down to the bare skin. She took the pounds she'd stuffed into her bosom and hid them in the satchel with her precious valentine and her diary, which, she reminded herself, she had grossly neglected of late. She set about finishing her toilette, splashing her face with water and letting it run down onto her naked body. With a soft washcloth she scrubbed herself until her skin tingled and began to turn red. She then splashed herself with lavender water from a bottle that had been placed on her dressing table.

It felt wonderfully refreshing, and she wondered if she would ever become accustomed to such luxury.

From a large chiffonnier, she took fresh pantalettes and slipped them on, calling to Dora, "You can come back now, Dora."

When she started to slip into the cranberry silk the maid objected. "You should be having a fresh gown." She went to fetch one.

"His Lordship asked that I wear this one," Cassandra said, and she saw Dora's eyebrows quirk upward and a knowing smile spread across her face.

Knowing the maid's thinking, Cassandra did nothing to disprove it; after all, did she not want the maid—and every other servant—to think she was on loving terms with her husband.

When the buttons were again fastened down the back, to well below her waist, Dora loosened Cassandra's yellow hair and brushed it until it shone, and then she rebraided it and wound it around her head, forming a golden crown.

"A bit of rouge for your cheeks," she said, and then, "A bit of gloss for your lips."

When the maid was through Cassandra stared at herself in the looking glass. Pleased with the way she looked, she dismissed Dora, telling her that she would not need her until morning. She made her way to the dining room on the second floor, in another wing of the elaborate town house.

As she walked, she reflected on her treatment of Miss Cordley; she had not been unkind and had dealt with the truth as she saw it. No decent married man—and Lord Ranleigh *was* decent and he *was* married—would keep a mistress. So, in truth, she had done His Lordship a wonderful favor by getting rid of Elsa Cordley for him.

Coming to the dining room, Cassandra gasped. Such grandeur! The table was set with fine china, glistening crystal, silver epergne of fresh flowers, and tall flickering tapers. And there was a bottle of champagne and champagne flutes. She remembered another night when she so much wanted his Lordship to order champagne, in that awful Inn of the Fighting Cocks.

Now, Lord Ranleigh stood with his back to her. An open window let in an aromatic scent of honeysuckle and blooming roses. Cassandra sucked the sweet scent deep into her lungs, and her breath caught in her throat when Lord Ranleigh turned and smiled at her. He had changed to a blue velvet evening coat, underneath which he wore a white silk waistcoat embroidered with flowers and honey bees. He wore white silk stockings, showing the muscular build of his legs. His cravat was fresh and impeccably creased.

"You asked me not to change," she teased, "and now I see that you have fresh clothes, in which, I must say, you are most handsome."

This brought a chuckle from His Lordship, and Cassandra was pleased to see that he was in a fine mood. His hand touched her arm as he made to guide her to the table.

There was something overpowering about His Lordship's nearness. It sent shivers up and down her spine, while at the same time there was a contrasting warmth deep inside her. For a moment, she let herself believe that she truly was his wife, that he felt the same deep thrill by their touching as she had felt. It was a wonderful feeling.

"I'm pleased that you did not change, for that color is quite becoming on you. I wonder why Cynthia never wore the gown; but, of course, she is of a different coloring—"

The meal was served by a liveried footman wearing white gloves. He poured the champagne with great ceremony, letting Lord Ranleigh whiff and taste before nodding approval. And so it went. They ate the sumptuous meal of stewed kidneys, cold roast beef, an array of fresh vegetables, and finally, a delicious pudding made of currents topped with raisin sauce.

Lord and Lady Ranleigh sat for a long time afterwards; they drank delicate mulberry wine, and Cassandra told him that she had never before tasted anything stronger than water. The ambience of the room was romantic; the candles flickered, the fire sputtered.

It was obvious to Cassandra that they were in danger of spending the night at the table, so she took it upon herself to say that it was growing late and that tomorrow would be a busy day, with their shopping in the morning, and then the ride in Hyde Park in the late afternoon. "In view of all that is to be done on the morrow, do you not think we should repair to our quarters?"

"If we must," he answered, "but I hate to see the evening end. It has been most pleasant . . . and I've never seen you look lovelier. Have you changed since coming to Ranleigh Hall or am I imagining it to be so?"

" 'Tis the dress, I am sure," Cassandra answered, rising and accepting His Lordship's arm as they left the room. Strolling the long, wide halls, on the way back to Cassandra's quarters, her feet moved without effort. She had never felt so elegantly dressed, or so happy. Gone from her mind was the encounter with her husband's mistress. Mayhap he would never know the woman had come to Kenmere. She pushed the thought from her mind, telling herself that she would know what to do when he discovered that she had taken the large sum of money and given it to his courtesan.

She would explain *then*. But not now.

Thinking thus, Cassandra entirely forgot that the long row of buttons down the back of the cranberry silk gown had to be unbuttoned, and that she had dismissed her maid until morning.

Nineteen

Lord Ranleigh felt himself shudder. He looked at Cassandra, seeing not his wife but a woman whom he desired beyond reason.

And it was against propriety, against all that had been drummed into him from childhood. Being of the nobility, one did not take a woman without offering something in return, either money or one's heart. He had given this woman *carte blanche* to his funds; he could not give her his heart.

He tried to remove his thoughts, correct them to something noble, his duty to Ranleigh Hall, or his mistress, flaming, beautiful Elsa, whose beauty dimmed beside the woman who now walked beside him, her arm against his, scorching his flesh. From experience, he knew the capacity of her desire.

He was bound to fail in his resolve, he knew that, for his mind went right on wanting too touch her skin, take her in his arms, press her belly against his, feel the warmth that was bound to flame into incendiary heat.

Dear God, he prayed to no avail, for his veins pounded like the drums of His Majesty's marching band, and hot blood raced through his body, like a rampaging river lapping fiercely at its imprisoning banks. Any moment now the river would overflow its prison.

These were His Lordship's thoughts as his feet moved him closer and closer to the door of Cassandra's quarters, where, by all that was right, he should leave her. "Will Dora come to help you undress?" he asked.

"I dismissed her for the night," Cassandra answered, feeling embarrassed at her ineptitude. Again, she asked herself if she would ever learn to be a lady of quality.

Words came against Lord Ranleigh's will. "Then I shall help you. The buttons—"

"Oh, how could I have forgotten?"

This was true; she had not thought that she would need help in unbuttoning those tiny buttons that reached from her neck past her waist. In truth, she had not given the buttons a thought. She spoke quickly. "I shall sleep in my frock. I've done it before."

"That won't be necessary. If you do not wish to disturb Dora, and it is quite late, then I shall assist you. After all, I am your husband."

"In name only," Cassandra reminded him.

"And I shall honor that. I assure you that I will not be tempted beyond endurance. Our agreement will hold fast."

"That is your agreement, not mine."

They had arrived at the door of her quarters, and His Lordship reached to turn the knob. His hand trembled and his teeth clenched together, while his mind reminded him of his duty to Ranleigh Hall. That was first and foremost.

Inside the room, he struck a flint and lighted a candle, which flickered and danced until it caught. Light spread in a small yellow circle, leaving the room in shadows. Taking the candle in hand, he silently strode into Cassandra's bedchamber.

There, there was more light; a half-moon pushed silver bars across the huge bed, canopied with lavender silk. Tearing his gaze, and his thoughts, away, he placed the candle on a table and turned to Cassandra, who had followed him and was standing where moonlight struck her face and her hair, which was wound like a golden crown around her head. He had never seen anything, or anyone, quite so beautiful, so innocent. Her gray eyes looked up at him questioningly.

Silence fell again, and there seemed no acceptable way to fill it. "I will unbutton your gown," he said at last, "and then I shall leave."

Taking her by her shoulders and turning her back to him, he began. Slowly, methodically. Only his labored breathing could be heard in the loud silence that insisted upon hovering around them. He swore under his breath. His long fingers were like fists fumbling with the mutinous buttons.

Neither spoke. It was like a ritual, he thought, something that must be done quickly lest he lose his reasoning. He smelled the lavender on her skin. It wafted up to him, and when only half of the buttons had been loosened he heard himself groan at the sight of her bare skin. More than once his fingers felt its smoothness, a touch as brief as the flap of a hummingbird's wing.

He remembered their wedding night when she had come to his bed . . . because she had thought him too shy to approach her, that it was her duty as a wife to submit to him. He'd lost control. The memory engulfed him and danced before his eyes, in bed together, loving each other until heaven and earth came together timelessly. Her hair had been loose and flowing provocatively . . .

Now, without conscious planning or thought, his hands moved to unwind her braids, combing the long golden strands with his fingers until they fell loosely down her back, soft and fragrant, smelling of soap and fresh well water. He turned her to him and took her lips in a slow, seductive kiss, while his big hand curved around her nape, his fingers stroking her sensitive skin.

230

The heat, the wanting, was there, as he knew it would be.

"You are so beautiful, Cassandra," he said. " 'Tis your only fault."

Cassandra knew that she should respond with words, but she did not want to break the spell. She molded her body against his hard length and, reaching up, wound her arms around his neck and pulled his lips harder against her own. She tasted his tongue and gave him hers, and the passion between them grew until there was no turning back.

She knew when the moment came; desire filled the moonlit room, and when he picked her up and held her in his long, strong arms, her only words were to tell him her gown had not been entirely unbuttoned.

"Never mind the buttons, my love," he whispered.

"But how?"

She was whispering, too, and they both laughed. He placed her on the bed and turned her so the buttons would be exposed to him. As quickly as lightning streaking across the sky, his fingers set to work.

Then Cassandra heard the sound of cloth ripping, and almost instantly the cranberry silk gown was on the floor, along with her pantalettes, her silk stockings, and her pink slippers. She was naked before him and unashamed, for he was her husband.

Soon he was naked, too, and above her. The magic spell was still there, and passion possessed and guided them. She lay beneath him and he kissed her lips, nipped at her ears with his teeth, ran his tongue over the sensitive skin of her neck.

She heard herself moan with pleasure. Like the courting ritual of a graceful animal, she thought, feeling loved.

His breath was heavy in the air, and little moans of pleasure gurgled from her throat. He kissed her breasts, sucking the hard brown nipples until she begged him

231

to stop lest she explode. Only then did he rise and let his hardness dive deeper and deeper into her, in perfect rhythm, until her body quickened beyond bearing, and then it shuddered like rumbling thunder shaking the earth, and she reached total fulfillment in a spiraling world of ecstasy, where she stayed, passing into oblivion, not knowing her name or caring, and love for His Lordship poured from every ounce of her throbbing, trembling body. She held back nothing, giving herself totally to his love.

A great gasp came from him, and he went limp and lay silent on the bed, while outside the window a cricket chirped and a moth flitted softly against the glass pane.

Still, reality did not come to Cassandra. Her husband had transported her to another world, and she wanted to stay there, with him, forever and ever.

She purposely did not remember that their marriage was in name only, that the stalwart sixth Earl of Ranleigh had married her to save the heir to Ranleigh Hall.

This night, they were husband and wife in all that was Holy.

A spiritual coming together, she thought happily as, with great tenderness, he held her to him, stroking her. Then, twining his body around hers until not even a thin slip of paper could have been slipped between them, she heard a gentle snore and knew that he was asleep, and soon she drifted into that same world of nothingness, with not even a dream to disturb the memory of what had happened. Her last thought was that she wanted to hold on to their love forever.

They slept thus, until a silvery dawn broke the darkness and sunshine swept across the bed.

Lord Ranleigh awakened Cassandra with, "This should not have happened."

He bounded from the bed and dressed quickly. His

passion spent, he could think clearly now. Whatever had possessed him to succumb to his physical need? Then he reasoned that as long as it was physical need that was involved, he was safe. It was his emotions he must protect.

He should have visited Elsa yesterday instead of taking Jacob to the bouts.

He looked at Cassandra, her hair in disarray, the white coverlet pulled up under her chin, as if he had not seen her naked only a short time ago. He could still smell her fragrance of lavender and spring flowers.

"Why should it not have happened?" she asked.

"Demmet, you know very well what I am talking about. If you had not tempted me beyond bearing—"

A soft laugh interrupted His Lordship. "Mama said that one of the reasons a man marries is to have someone to blame his shortcomings on. You were the one who could not leave, the one whose passion was uncontrollable."

She paused for a moment; and then, her eyes searching his countenance for some assurance that what they had done was real to him, she asked, "You enjoyed our loving, did you not, Your Lordship?"

"Of course I enjoyed it. What man would not? But we broke our agreement, and for that I am very angry with you."

It was plain that he was not teasing, and Cassandra felt her mind, her body, her heart, plummet square into reality. His dark eyes held that brooding look Cassandra had come to hate. Why could he not be happy? She blamed his first Countess, for there was no other reason. It was obvious that guilt rode him, that he felt unfaithful to his dead wife. She could not help herself; something inside her exploded, and anger showed in her voice when she asked, "How can you be in love with a ghost? Can you not accept that she is gone?"

For a long moment he looked at her without speaking. Infinitely conscious of the loud silence between them, Cassandra stared at him as he stood there, like an oak tree, tall, strong, unbending, his eyes regaining that brooding look. Then, turning, he quit the room, closing the door firmly behind him.

Dear God, is he going to his library? If he did, he would find the empty safe. Hurt replaced her anger, for it seemed that nothing she did was right, except care for Ranleigh's heir.

Surely, upon finding his funds missing, His Lordship would return and demand to know what she had done with the many pounds, and she would have to tell him that she'd given them to his mistress. Or would she?

Mayhap she would deny knowledge of what he was talking about.

I will deny taking the money.

In her mind's eye, he was towering over her, his brooding eyes staring into hers, while he accused, "You alone knew where I hid the key."

Pushing herself up from the bed, she reached for the cranberry silk gown and saw that the last three buttons had been ripped off. She vaguely remembered the sound of ripping cloth. What would she tell Cynthia?

Knowing that her sister-in-law would not care—she had never worn the gown—Cassandra tossed the cranberry silk aside and rang for Dora to come help her dress. Today was today; she must needs forget last night. Tears clouded her vision, and she determinedly pushed them away. She thought of the beautiful lace valentine, now torn in two.

"Nothing has changed, nor will it ever," she said aloud, as Dora gave a soft knock, then entered the room.

Twenty

Cassandra blamed herself. If she had not deliberately kept His Lordship away from Elsa, and even worse, had not paid his courtesan off, he would not have lost control of his lustful feelings in the way he did. And she had been naive enough to think that mayhap he loved her. She had felt so loved when they were joined together as one. Her anger grew as she gained a chair and sat down, lest her knees buckle beneath her. She stared down at her bare feet, fighting tears, swearing under her breath, contemplating . . .

Mayhap she had connived to keep her husband away from his courtesan, but she would not accept his accusation that she had tempted him beyond bearing into making love to her. That simply was not true. The pain was excruciating. How foolish she had been to sit on the hillock and dream about being married to the Lord of Ranleigh Hall, to draw silly valentines, like a blubbering, lovesick idiot.

She bounded from the chair and dressed hurriedly, brushing her hair, braiding it, and tying it with ribands, and then she stormed from the room and went downstairs. Her last thought before entering the dining room was: *The mighty Lord of Ranleigh had best stay away from me.*

Lord Ranleigh was already seated at the table, his head bent over his plate. A footman stood by the sideboard, laden with food that sent out aromatic odors that ought to water her taste buds but did nothing of the kind.

"Do you wish to be served, m'lady?" the footman asked.

"I shall serve myself, but thank you anyway," Cassandra answered. She picked up a plate and stood and stared at the food; mutton, eggs, ham, hot biscuits, and an assortment of jellies. From the corner of her eye, she sought out her husband.

My husband!

The words left bitter bile in her throat, and she felt that she would be sick and throw up on the beautiful carpet on which she stood. Her stomach roiled in great waves of nausea, slamming against her throat. She swallowed and reached for a biscuit and some currant jelly.

As if he had just spied her, Lord Ranleigh was instantly standing beside her. "That will not sustain you for the day ahead," he said.

She looked up at him; he was smiling down at her.

"And what does that mean?" she asked, and not in a pleasant tone.

"I have sent a servant to Madame Lenora, Cynthia's modiste, to tell her that we shall visit her before eleven o'clock."

He hasn't found that I took all his money.

"What makes you think Madame Lenora will make room for our visit on such short notice? Mayhap she will be too busy."

Cassandra had lost all interest in a new wardrobe, and she no longer cared that Lord Ranleigh accompany her. And she would have told him so had she not wanted his help in locating Ellen for Sister Martha.

In his next breath Lord Ranleigh said, "I will not have Wade seeing you in our sister's gowns. He would surely know that things were not exactly as man and wife between us."

So that's it. She realized then that his brother's imminent return to Ranleigh Hall was never far from her husband's thoughts. She said again, "Mayhap the modiste will be too busy to see us. I'm sure she is swamped with orders from the nobility."

"She will see us. I asked that a whole wardrobe be made. No modiste could resist such an order."

She looked at him. It was amazing, for his demeanor had returned to that which it had been before their wondrous love of last night: solicitous, friendly, distant.

"What a farrago," she said quietly, not realizing she had spoken aloud. Lord Ranleigh asked her what she had said, and she answered quickly, "I was talking to myself."

Again, he smiled at her. "You seem preoccupied, Cassandra. I hope that what happened last night will not harm our friendship. I promise that it will not happen again."

Cassandra wanted to spit or slap his handsome face, or worse, kick his shins and break his well-shaped legs. How could any man shut out that which was so beautiful?

"I will meet you downstairs long within the hour," she said, and then she added, "I would appreciate your help in looking for Ellen Terry. I promised Sister Martha."

Without waiting for Lord Ranleigh to reply, Cassandra placed her plate on the table and, turning, practically ran from the room. She needed desperately to see Jacob, to feel his little arms around her neck, his damp kiss on her cheek. Pulling the hem of her blue morning dress to her knees—so against propriety for a lady of quality—she climbed the stairs with great speed, going directly to the nursery, where she found Mrs. Brodwick sitting by Jacob's bed.

"Is he ill?" Cassandra asked anxiously.

"No, but I suspect he became very tired on his outing with His Lordship. He slept like this all through the night."

Cassandra went to him and, bending down, listened to his breathing. The wheezing was there, and his little face was pale. Pushing back his golden curls, she kissed him on his damp forehead and felt tears push at her eyes.

Just in case Jacob was not fully asleep, Cassandra said, "Mrs. Brodwick, let's go to the other room, so that we will not disturb his sleep. 'Tis a relief to see him resting so quietly. I'm sure when he awakens he will be talking all about that wonderful outing with his Papa." She kissed the boy again. "His Lordship has grown so fond of Jacob. I believe he actually loves him. . . . Well, he always did, but just did not know how to show his affection."

"I'm sure that being around you has taught Lord Ranleigh that loving someone is nothing to be ashamed of, and that one should show affection. 'Tis a pity the nobility think they must needs be so stiff, and unemotional."

In the small room adjoining Jacob's bedchamber, Cassandra turned to Mrs. Brodwick. "Can you hear the wheezing? I fear Dr. Morton did not tell Lord Ranleigh the whole of it when he examined him. I felt it at the time."

Mrs. Brodwick's voice was low when she answered. "Yes, I can hear the labored breathing. Mayhap the good doctor was trying to spare you worry. Mayhap he thinks the boy will outgrow what is ailing him."

"That's nonsense. Or course I shall worry. I'm not a slow top. Why did he think I brought Jacob all the way to London . . . to be lied to about his condition?"

"Mayhap in time Jacob truly will outgrow the problem. Children have . . ."

238

"You don't believe that any more than I do," Cassandra said. She did not want to tell the nursemaid about her terrible premonition that Jacob would die, but she did want to alert her to the seriousness of his condition so that she would be constantly vigilant.

"What makes you so sure that he will not outgrow the weakness in his lungs?" Mrs. Brodwick asked.

"A mother always knows," Cassandra said, and she went on to caution Mrs. Brodwick to never fail to come to her, no matter the hour of day or night, if Jacob's condition worsened. "When we return to Ranleigh Hall I shall take him for walks to build up his strength. Already the good food you prepare for him has put weight on his small frame."

Without warning, Cassandra was crying. She could not help herself, and she did not pull away when Mrs. Brodwick put her arms around her and let her sob on her shoulder.

The good woman soothed, "There now, Countess, tears will not help, except to rid you of the tension you feel. Your body is as stiff as a board."

Cassandra straightened and dried her eyes with a lace-trimmed handkerchief pulled from her bosom. " 'Tis more than my concern for Jacob—"

"I know. 'Tis a shame. His Lordship should be horse-whipped."

Cassandra knew then that the old woman knew that which she, Cassandra, had tried so hard to keep secret. So much like Sister Martha. "How did you know?"

"Because I've lived so long, and because I've known rejection in my life."

They sat on a sofa and talked for a long time. "I love him so much," Cassandra said, and felt better for having said the words aloud. She told her about sitting on the hillock, staring down at beautiful Ranleigh Hall, about the wonderful dreams she had dreamed, and about the valentine heart she had drawn, then tore in two when she learned she had been brought to the Hall only to save the Ranleigh heir.

"Did you pitch the valentine away?" Mrs. Brodwick asked.

"Oh, no. I have it in a safe place."

Mrs. Brodwick smiled. "Then you have hopes that someday you can paste it back into one piece. If that were not so, you would have destroyed it completely."

Cassandra sat pensively. She knew that she should leave and get herself ready to go to the modiste with Lord Ranleigh. Still she sat, feeling comfort from the kind nurse's presence.

Mayhap she did still hope, mayhap her resolves of only a short time ago would somehow change. She shook her head. No, she would not hope, for the pain would be too great when she learned that wishing would not make it so. Had she not learned that already?

She heard restive hooves clopping on the cobbled courtyard below and, rising, went to the window to look out. It was a coach and four, the coach emblazoned with the Ranleigh crest. "I must go," she said. She cautioned Mrs. Brodwick again to watch Jacob carefully. "Come for me at any time."

"That I will do, and you are not to worry that I will share your secret with anyone, not even Dora. Although I believe the gel to be totally loyal."

"I'm certain of it," Cassandra said, and then she thanked the nurse for her kindness and left. She thought to go to her quarters and change into a more suitable dress but changed her mind. It mattered not that His Lordship thought her poorly dressed for the occasion, or that her hair would look better with the braids wound around her head.

Lord Ranleigh was waiting in the luxurious carriage. When Cassandra approached he gave her a smile that did not reach his brooding eyes. She had come to hate that look and saw no reason to return the gesture.

A footman helped her up, and she sat against a deep velvet squab opposite His Lordship. She did not want his thigh rubbing against hers. From now forward she would not allow fate to be tempted, she resolved again, just to make sure her heart took her meaning, and she promised herself that she would see that His Lordship kept his distance.

By way of greeting, Lord Ranleigh said pleasantly, "You left the dining room so quickly, I did not have a chance to tell you how lovely you look." Reaching across, he took her hand and kissed it, letting his warm lips linger much longer than was necessary. If, indeed, the kiss was necessary at all, Cassandra thought. And then, suddenly, she came to the realization that he was doing the proper thing just for show, to make the servants who were watching pant over his affection for his second Countess.

Jerking her hand away from his firm grasp, she accused, "Lord Ranleigh, you are a hypocrite."

Twenty-one

In another part of London, in a dark coffeehouse near Covent Garden, Lord Ranleigh's brother, Wade, sat across the table from a man dressed to the nines, arguing vehemently with him. He pushed a stack of notes in the man's direction.

" 'Tis not enough blunt. You're short by two thousand pounds."

"Your load was short by half. Don't take me for a slow top, Wade Ranleigh."

"Can I help it if a part of it was stolen before your men came for it? I delivered it to England's fair coast, and that is what our contract called for."

The man laughed without mirth. Contempt spewed from his hooded eyes. "What contract? Nothing's written."

Wade could feel his face growing hot; he cautioned himself to watch his temper, but that was, as usual, difficult to do. Answering the man's laughter with a small laugh of his own, he said in a forced, good-natured tone, "You know, Lord Burlington, we've never needed anything written. I trade on my word—"

Lord Burlington's eyes moved furtively, even though the windowless room was almost too dark for seeing, and was relieved when no one was in proximity of them.

"Demmet, you are to call me Samuel, and don't tell me more about your word. All of England knows what it's worth. The load was short. When my men went to get it half was missing, and that is that."

He shoved the stack of notes back across the table, rose from the rickety chair and, taking up his black cane, strode purposefully toward the door. Had he not been transacting business with a scoundrel, he would not have been caught dead in the place. Relief washed over him when the door closed behind him. On the street, with fresh air in his lungs, he walked with a strut, using the cane for effect. At the corner he waved for a chair. Two men stopped, and he climbed aboard. "Take me to White's, fellows."

When he was aloft he took from his waistcoat pocket an enamel snuffbox with a hummingbird painted on it, flipped the lid up with one hand, as he had seen the Prince Regent do, and breathed deeply. He was now in his element, one of *them*, the elite of the West End.

Still sitting at the table, Wade smiled. So what if his gamble had failed? "Nothing ventured, nothing gained," he said aloud. He had thought the old goat senile enough that the stolen-goods excuse would work. He folded the notes and put them in his coat pocket, carefully, so that they would not cause a bulge. Though short, it was a considerable amount, enough for a go at White's gaming tables and later a visit to his paramour.

That brought another smile. He did not have a paramour, as such. The woman of his choice at the moment was Lady Bessmore, who had a husband and two children. Stolen hours with the lady set his passion soaring. For years, since he had been in leading strings, he had been driven by a neurotic frenzy to dally with that which belonged to someone else, and his conquests had been many.

Wade Ranleigh was a handsome rakehell, and he knew it. He had sapphire blue eyes that could charm any woman he turned them toward. But those same eyes could turn mean, as well he knew. In truth, he knew his nature well, did not argue with it, and liked himself in spite of it.

He did not wish to immediately leave the disreputable coffeehouse. In his business, he spent more time in dark places than where there was light. He felt rather at home here. A pretty girl came to offer him another cup for a pence. She bent over him, exposing a delectable bosom. He grabbed her hand and squeezed it, felt nothing, and released it. She was too willing.

He took the coffee and gave her two shillings, one above the charge, just to see her smile and, after drinking the dark brew, reluctantly left the place and made his way slowly to the top of St. James's street, reaching White's in time for the noon meal.

Beau Brummel and his entourage sat in the bow window, passing judgment on fashionable London, as they did every day. Each wore a well-creased, snow-white cravat, to emulate Brummel, the so-called arbiter of the gentlemen of the *ton's* apparel, as well as the ladies'. When Wade entered they clapped, and Brummel made an indistinguishable remark, which, if heard, would have had him thrown out of the exclusive club.

Wade walked on; he was much too busy for the likes of the dandy. He went directly to the betting book, because from it he could learn everything that was going on in Town. Men foolishly bet on everything, from whose wife was rendezvousing with whom, or when some member would take a new wife, or if the expected child of the nobility would be a male and entitled to inherit his father's title and the entailed estate.

That he had been the second born had always stuck

painfully in Wade Ranleigh's craw, and this day, he wondered how his plan was working that would soon make him the seventh Earl of Ranleigh. He thought of his brother and was overcome with revulsion. How dare he cut his allowance from the estate to a pittance?

Reading the book, he was disappointed that nothing that interested him had been recorded since last he was there, a number of weeks ago. He started to turn away, but the last name on the page caught his eye, a wager between two very popular members, Lords Ormathwaite and Manchester, a wager that the marriage of the sixth Earl of Ranleigh to an orphan would last long enough to produce an heir to the title and the Ranleigh estates. There was even a bet on how long the present heir, five-year-old Jacob Ranleigh, would live.

"So 'tis common knowledge that the little monster is in very, very poor health," he said under his breath, already counting the months, mayhap days, when he would be in line to inherit. And then the sixth Earl of Ranleigh would have precious time to enjoy his "orphan." The plan was already set for his early demise.

That the heir's condition had worsened made Wade Ranleigh extremely happy, while, at the same time, he refused to believe that the mighty Lord of Ranleigh Hall had taken a second wife. Had not his first Countess taught him a lesson?

Wade turned away from the betting book and sought out an acquaintance who would know the truth of the prattle that had been written in the book. His heart was pounding in his throat. Under ragged breath, he ranted and raved and swore like one of His Majesty's sailors off the docks. "The double-crossing jackanapes . . . "

"What's wrong, Wade?"

The voice came from behind him, and he turned to find himself facing Lord Manchester, one of the bettors on his brother's marriage, and one of the *ton's* renowned gossipers. He was handsomely dressed in a dark coat and knee breeches. His valet had done a splendid job on his toilette, thought Wade. His face was cleanly shaven, although above his thin upper lip he sported a mustache, dark brown sprinkled with gray.

"What do you mean, what's wrong?" asked Wade.

"You look a little green around the gills."

Wade had never liked Lord Manchester, and now, looking at the gloating look on his face, he liked him less.

"Only a fish can look green around the gills," Wade answered flippantly, pretending levity.

Lord Manchester would not let go.

"Does your brother's getting leg shackled surprise you? I hear he went to Gretna Green. The news took London by storm, and all the hopeful Mamas of the *ton* are weeping in their laced-trimmed crying rags." And then, thoughtfully, "Lord Ranleigh must have had a reason."

Wade did not answer; His Lordship went on, obviously enjoying himself, and Wade would not deny him. "Of course, it has to be a disappointment to you, in line for the title and all."

"I don't take your meaning."

Another laugh. "Well, no doubt there will be another heir. I hear she's a ripe age, not much over fifteen summers, from her looks."

Wade balled a fist, while on his face a slow smile softened his countenance. He lied without effort. "I care not that my brother has taken himself another wife. Mayhap he will have better luck than he had with Sylvia. But one of Sister Martha's orphans! The gel would have to be an embarrassment to him, as well as to the rest of the Ranleighs."

"I hear she's a looker: tawny-gold hair, big gray eyes, and the sweetest smile. Of course, a man of the aristocracy usually does not marry one of the lower orders."

Wade looked at him through narrowed slits and asked

himself what the man wanted. What was his motive? Had he been waiting by the betting book to witness Wade's reaction upon reading the news? And then the thought occurred to him that mayhap Lord Manchester simply wanted to talk, to pass on-dits.

Mayhap something I need to know, thought Wade.

Slapping Lord Manchester on the back, he invited him to join him for the noontime meal, a sumptuous fare the club would be offering.

Lying came easily to Wade Ranleigh. He knew nothing of the noon fare; he had just this day arrived back in Town. A wicked storm had delayed the unloading of his ship.

" 'Twill be a pleasure to dine with you," Lord Manchester said, a look of delight on his craggy face.

Wade wanted to hit him.

They started to ascend to the second-floor dining room. Halfway up the grand stairs, Wade stopped to stare in the gilt-framed looking glass that hung on the opposite wall. He stood tall and straight, and his navy-blue superfine coat fit him perfectly. A lock of brown hair—which was never pomaded, but lay free and easy on his head—fell onto his forehead above sapphire-blue eyes. He was handsome and, of this, too, he was very much aware, thinking his knowing added to his charm.

It was not unusual for his sapphire blue eyes to spark with anger, and this day was no exception. How dare Lord Ranleigh wed . . .

He hoped no one noticed; *that* would start on-dits flying about London. He turned from the looking glass and, forcing a bounce to his steps, soon caught up with Lord Manchester. At the top of the stairs, meeting them head on, was Lord Burlington, his black cane in hand. He averted his eyes and didn't speak.

This did not bother Wade a whit. His mind was on worming from Manchester more about Lord Ranleigh's activities while Wade was away making blunt on which to live in the style he deserved.

As always when he entered the dining room, he was taken aback with its exclusive atmosphere, its ambience of grandeur, though Ranleigh Hall was just as grand. Knowing that those present were superior to the lower orders never failed to give him a thrill. He looked around. Men of means sat at tables covered with linen cloths, stopping just short of the floor. Gleaming crystal, highly polished silver, and fine bone china sat atop the cloths and glistened under the light of a huge chandelier hanging from the center of a very high ceiling.

As he walked, his Hessian boots, with a tassel dangling from their V-shaped front, sank into scrolled red and white carpet.

The maître d' seated them at a round table in the middle of the room. Wade would have preferred a window but did not voice a complaint. He ordered quickly, without thought of whether or not he would enjoy the food, and immediately began his crusade for information.

"As you were saying, Manchester, my brother married an orphan. What do you make of it? Do you think he's gone daft?"

Manchester's eyes were keen on Wade. He smiled that slow smile that irritated Wade endlessly. The smiling old goat had a gloating look . . .

"Not at all, Wade. I, for one—if she's as pretty as reported to me, and were I not already leg shackled— would take a go with her." He paused for a moment. "What's your interest? 'Tis a well-known fact that you and your brother don't rub well together—"

"You don't take my meaning! I'm thinking of the Ranleigh name."

This brought a roar of laughter from Manchester; and then, *"You* thinking of the Ranleigh name?"

Wade rose and pushed back his chair. "I refuse to

sit in your presence and be insulted. I thought you were my friend, and that you would tell me the whole of everything you know. I'm away from London so much, with my shipping business."

"Sit down, sit down. I meant no offense. Let's eat, if that slow waiter will bring our food, and I will share my collection of on-dits about London society with you."

Wade sat back down, took up his serviette and touched his damp brow, which felt as if it were on fire. "Only about my illustrious brother. I'm rushed for time. I've written my mother to expect me at Ranleigh Hall shortly. I just don't want to arrive there and not know what has taken place—"

"Plenty," Lord Manchester said.

A white-gloved waiter appeared with the food, a huge silver tray laden with two bowls of stew made from mutton, round biscuits piled high on a platter, and two bowls of clotted cream and strawberries. Steam curled from the spout of a silver coffeepot.

He transferred the food from the tray to the table, filled the china cups with coffee, bowed, and left.

"On with it, on with it," Wade said as he bent over the stew and started ladling it into his mouth. "Tell me the whole of it." His words became somewhat garbled as they passed over his food.

Lord Manchester leaned back in his chair, as if he was in no hurry to eat, as if he wanted to savor every minute he was making Wade wait. At last he said, "On-dits have it that Lord Ranleigh left Elsa high and dry."

"I don't take your meaning."

" 'Tis simple. He comes into town with his orphan, pays Elsa a substantial sum and tells her to take the high road."

"When?"

"Only yesterday. And I, myself, saw him at the bouts with his heir."

"Gad's wallop, it grows worse. He must needs be smitten with the gel, which means he plans children, most likely a whole line of males to . . ."

Wade stopped there. His intent was to worm information out of old Manchester, not inform Lord Manchester. But this did not bode well; it did not bode well at all. He asked, "What will poor Elsa do?"

Manchester laughed. "Already she has put the word out that she needs a new protector. Most likely she will be in the squeeze this day, looking, or rather letting the gentlemen of the *ton* look at her."

A thought struck Wade square between his sapphire blue eyes: Most likely, his brother would be riding in the five-o'clock squeeze, showing off his new bride. He rose quickly, this time with the full intention of leaving, and he did.

"Ranleigh, you're not leaving," said Manchester.

Wade did not answer. The old goat was of no further use to him. He made a quick exit, causing eyebrows to rise, but he did not care, and on the way down the elegant curving stairs, he only briefly glimpsed himself in the looking glass when he passed.

He took a large round watch from his waistcoat pocket and looked at the time. There was ample time before five o'clock to go to Tattersalls to acquire horses and a handsome carriage, and then to call on Miss Elsa Cordley, his brother's ex-courtesan.

Twenty-two

"What does your brother Wade have to do with my being dressed fabulously, or with our being happily married, which, of course, is a game you wish to play?" she asked.

Lord Ranleigh did not answer, and they rode on in silence.

At Madame Lorna's, he was helpful but not demanding. She chose silk, twill, stuff, satin, and printed muslin, thin, but not transparent, for her wardrobe. He encouraged her to choose whatever she liked, and he was most helpful in choosing the patterns, some from Paris. Not once did he object to the modiste's suggestion that a neckline should show a *little bosom*.

"Make several gowns of each fabric," he told the jubilant modiste. They turned to pelisses, and mantels. "Six each," he said, "and make half fur-lined. " 'Tis cold on the estate, us being so close to the sea."

Cassandra buried her face in the wonderful woolen fabric to hide the tears that threatened, and then she stood behind a screen to be measured. Lord Ranleigh paced the floor, and not once did she catch him looking in the direction of the screen.

"I hope the gowns are pleasing to your brother," Cassandra said when they left the shop.

"I've asked you to keep your distance from the scoundrel," Lord Ranleigh said, turning to glare at her.

"Oh, I intend to. But our paths will cross, and no doubt he will notice the fine way your wife is turned out."

She was being dreadfully unkind, she knew, and beneath her anger she was sorry for the pain that came to his brooding eyes when she spoke of Wade.

And she was glad that she had given Elsa all his blunt. No doubt he had blamed the poor woman every time he went to her to be serviced, saying it was her fault that he could not behave himself. Mistresses were a disgusting sort, she decided.

From the modiste's they went to a milliner shop and purchased hats and bonnets, and then to Oxford Street, to Botibol's, a plumassier, and bought ostrich feathers for a huge gypsy hat and flowers for the bonnets.

The gypsy hat was Cassandra's favorite. She asked if she could wear it. Lord Ranleigh laughed and said, "Of course you may. It matches well enough your gown."

Next, they visited a bootery, buying slippers and half boots in every color so there would be a pair to match each gown, and then they went to a shop on Regent Street, where night dresses, pantalettes, and silk stockings were purchased.

At the jewelers, Lord Ranleigh purchased a diamond necklace, pearls, and numerous bracelets, which Cassandra exclaimed over with a lump in her throat.

As angry and hurt as Cassandra was, she could not help but be happy about her good fortune. In truth, she admitted, she was a little drunk with the whole of it. Wait until she showed her new clothes and her jewelry, to Cynthia and to Sister Martha. She could almost hear Cynthia squeal with delight.

When Cassandra would pass a looking glass, and all the shops seemed to have at least one, she stole a look at her wonderful gypsy hat. Never had she seen such finery; never had so many pounds been spent on her. She tried to count the number of gowns and couldn't. It was almost disgraceful.

Then and there, Cassandra decided that when she returned to Ranleigh Hall she would go into Wickham Market and open an account at the draper's shop and have Sister Martha go there and order clothes for herself and for the children. Cassandra no longer needed the ten yards of silk from Stella, so that would go to Sister Martha for a church dress.

After all, there was no limit to Lord Ranleigh's means, so he had told her, and he had said that she could spend to her heart's content.

They were now on their way back to Kenmere. As the carriage jostled along over the cobbles, she asked of His Lordship, "When may we look for Ellen Terry, the gel who ran away from Sister Martha's? If you will do that for me, then I shall not bother you any more, and you can go about your business."

"I should think—"

Cassandra hushed him and looking him straight in the eyes, added, "Your Lordship, I want you to know that I release you from any vow that you made on your knees before the vicar. I realize it was I, not you, who wanted to be married in the church, and have our marriage blessed. The vows you made were made under duress, and I am sure God understands that."

Lord Ranleigh almost choked; he coughed and sputtered, "I don't take your meaning."

"I mean you are free to visit Elsa . . . if she will still have you."

Lord Ranleigh looked at her incredulously. Where did she learn of Elsa? And what did she mean if Elsa would still have him? "What do you know of Elsa?" he asked in a voice bordering on scolding. "Who—"

"Cynthia. And if she hadn't told me, I would have learned when your paramour came to Kenmere."

"What? Countess, what are you talking about?"

"I'd prefer that you not call me Countess. That's just for show, anyway. In your heart I'm Jacob's nurse."

"That don't signify at this moment. I asked you what you meant about Elsa coming to Kenmere."

"When you and Jacob were at the bouts, this . . . this woman came to see you . . . I suppose to offer her services. But don't fault her. She did not know until I told her that you were married. I felt so sorry for the poor thing."

She was not funning, of that Lord Ranleigh was sure. But she had to be, he told himself. This could not have happened. He leaned back against the squabs and looked away. "I pray this is a dream," he said, drawing a long breath.

"Well, 'tisn't. And Lord Ranleigh, you should be horsewhipped. You failed to tell her you were married, just as you failed to tell me that our marriage was to be in name only."

"That was Sister Martha's fault."

When Cassandra did not answer, but sat there with her chin set in that stubborn line he'd learned to expect when she was overset, he said in a pleading voice, "Te . . . tell me the whole of it."

"That's all. Except I paid her so that she would have money to pay her servants, and to buy food and beautiful gowns until she could get another protector."

He sat forward and glared at her. He felt blood rushing to his face, and could not stop it. He did not know whether to laugh, cry, or to be angry. Frowning ferociously, he blurted out, "You paid her? What with?"

"With the blunt you had in your safe. Remember, you told me that it was there for me to spend, and I believed Elsa's need to be a worthy cause." Again she said, "Your Lordship, you should be horsewhipped, doing the poor woman that way."

"Countess—"

"I asked you not to call me that. To be a countess, I would have to be married to you. I don't feel—"

"Don't change the subject."

"Sometimes you are a slow top, Your Lordship. I *told* you that after telling her of our wedding vows, which had been taken before God, and blessed by Him, I paid her for her future services, so that she would not go hungry until she found another protector. I thought I was doing you a favor, saving you the embarrassment of having to tell her. But this morning I saw that I was wrong, so I suggest that you go to her and explain that you *do* need her services; that, in truth, you are not married. That your marriage is a farce."

Lord Ranleigh could see that to argue with the gel would be an exercise in futility. And scolding would do no good. Her innocence of the ways of the world made it unlikely that he could explain his actions. So he said nothing, not for a long while.

He studied her gypsy hat, adorned with ostrich feathers, and the face beneath the hat; her gray eyes and her bosom that bulged enticingly above her gown. He thought of last night.

Passion roiled in his veins.

He said quickly, "I hope you like your new clothes."

"Oh, I do, ever so much. I've never seen such finery, and I thank you from the bottom of my heart. And I may as well tell you, Lord Ranleigh, that I plan to stay at Ranleigh Hall. There'll be no more thought of going back to Sister Martha's. I can do more good at the Hall, taking care of Jacob and using your blunt to help the orphanage."

An awful silence hung over the carriage, for Lord Ranleigh suddenly found himself speechless. He listened to the wheels moving over the cobbles and tried not to think. It was not until the carriage came to an abrupt halt in front of Kenmere that the silence was broken—and then by Cassandra when she said, "Lord Ranleigh, I plan to lock my door at night. I realize that at times you cannot control your rutting passion, so a locked door will ensure that never again will there be a need for you to say, 'This should not have happened.' "

Cassandra left the carriage in great haste and practically ran up the stairs and then to her quarters. There, she jerked from the chiffonnier the quilted satchel that held the precious valentine she had torn in two. She ripped it again, into four pieces, then discarded the pieces in a wicker basket near her bed, feeling a modicum of satisfaction. In the carriage he had not argued with her, or denied that he would visit Elsa, as she had stupidly hoped he would. When she told him that from now forward her door would be locked to him he merely leaned back, took a deep breath, and said, " 'Tis for the best."

It was then that all hope had died inside—for the second time.

" 'Tis not Elsa, but his first Countess," she said aloud, "for, without doubt, his soul died when she died."

Cassandra was no longer angry, nor did not cry. Her tears had been shed, and the air from the sea had dried them. "Never again will tears dampen my cheeks over a man who has made it perfectly clear that he feels nothing for me except lust. Elsa can take care of that."

"What on earth do you mean, m'lady?"

Cassandra whipped around to face Dora, her faithful lady's maid. "Dora! I thought I was alone. I feel foolish, caught talking to myself."

Dora bobbed. "I knocked, and when you did not answer I entered to see if there was something wrong. One of the servants said you had left the carriage quickly and had run to your quarters. You look distraught, m'lady. Is something wrong?"

"Nothing is wrong that you can help with, Dora, and I would like to be alone. I'll ring for you later."

"Yes, m'lady," said Dora, bobbing again before leaving.

Cassandra had caught the hurt look on the maid's face and was sorry, but she did not want to chance Dora's seeing the ripped valentine. And then the thought occurred to Cassandra that a servant would surely see the valentine if it was left in the wicker basket. Gossip and questions would fly among the household help: "Why would the Countess rip apart the valentine?" they would say. "Who had drawn it? Surely not Lord Ranleigh. Did the new Countess have an old lover she was trying to forget? That must needs be so, else why would a valentine be in her thoughts when summer was drawing to a close?"

After retrieving the pieces of her precious valentine she placed them between the pages in her diary. She could not remember when last she had written in the journal. It was only when something of great importance happened. This day, she felt consumed with feelings but totally impotent, for there was nothing she could do about the turn of events. You could not make one love someone when he or she was determined not to do so. And lust was not love.

Although she felt she should hurry to see Jacob, she took up a quill and wrote about the wonderful wardrobe her husband had purchased for her.

Then, in short, crisp words, she recorded the destroying of the lace valentine, and having given up hope that Lord Ranleigh would ever love her. She did not lament about the terrible blow to her heart, saying only that His Lordship's heart would always belong to his first Countess.

Having put her feelings on paper, Cassandra felt better, but drained and tired. She closed the small book and returned it to the quilted satchel. Now she must

257

needs go to Jacob. She smiled wanly. He would run to her, hug her, and call her his new Stepmother.

Later, Cassandra was back in her quarters, sitting in the beautiful receiving room with all its exquisite appointments. The visit to Jacob had been enjoyable; she had had a repast sent up, and they had eaten together. She had read to him, after which they went for a walk in the park near Kenmere. When they returned he was tired out and did not object to Mrs. Brodwick's putting him in bed for a nap, but not before he was bathed and his clothes had been changed.

Now Cassandra did not know what to do with her time. She had asked Lord Ranleigh to go with her to look for Ellen, but after her telling him she intended to lock the door between them, she was not sure of his intent. She rang for Dora and asked that the maid take a missive to His Lordship. It seemed rather silly to be writing a letter to one's husband, but she would *not* go to his quarters.

"But His Lordship's gone, m'lady," Dora said. "He left soon after your return, or so one of the upstairs maids said. She was watching from a window."

Of course, pea goose, he could not wait to go and reinstate Elsa, thought Cassandra. She said, "You may go, Dora."

The maid bobbed and left. Alone, Cassandra began pacing the floor. She let out an occasional swear word, but not loud enough for anyone to hear, and then she crossed herself to say to Him that she was sorry.

Soon a knock on the door claimed her attention. Upon opening it, she saw Lord Ranleigh standing there. He was immaculately and elegantly turned out, with a fresh white cravat that contrasted with his sunbronzed skin, and, although his eyes were not smiling, his sensuous lips were.

Cassandra stepped back, and he entered. "I'm happy *this* door is not locked to me."

Cassandra ignored the remark. *That* subject was closed. "I thought you were gone," she said. "Dora said—"

"I was, for a short while. I went to White's to gather news. I made inquiries about Ellen Terry but failed to find anyone who knew her. Then it occurred to me that she might be riding in the park in the five o'clock squeeze. Mayhap you and I should go. Having never seen her, I would not recognize her."

Cassandra thought this a capital idea and said so. "I shall be ever so grateful for your efforts, Your Lordship, even if we do not find her."

"Don't be so sure that we won't. Although you may not be happy with the news. Did you not say that she is startlingly beautiful?"

"Oh, she is that. The most beautiful gel I've ever seen."

"Mayhap some gentleman of the *ton* has claimed her."

"He is not a gentleman if he would claim an innocent gel, just because he has blunt and she is in dire need," Cassandra quickly answered.

Lord Ranleigh, looking down into her face, smiled and said, "Well, we are not going to find your friend here in this room. Do you wish to change—"

"Should I?"

"I think not. You are beautiful in that dress. Any dress, for that matter. I meant to tell you that this morning when we were shopping. And wear the big hat. You are adorable in it."

A smart black Tilbury, hitched to a glistening black horse, sporting a gold harness, waited in front of the town house. Lord Ranleigh helped Cassandra up and then climbed in to sit beside her, taking the ribbons from the groom.

At the corner he turned sharply, on one wheel. Cassandra could see that he was in a fine mood and decided that she would try not to mention his brother Wade's name. Holding on to her hat and laughing when the Tilbury righted itself, she felt grand.

She could not help it. It was the hat, she told herself.

They soon joined a great procession of grand carriages. Many fine horses, sporting the finest of bridles and saddles, some even trimmed in gold, trotted this way and that, with titled men, just as finely turned out, riding astride.

Women rode inside the carriages. Lord Ranleigh gave Cassandra their names and titles, and once he stopped to introduce her as his wife to Ladies Alvanley and Sefton.

"That's His Grace, the Duke of Beaufort, the aging quidnunc," he said when a man on an excellent bay rode alongside the Tilbury and indicated he wanted a word with His Lordship.

Lord Ranleigh pulled his horse to a stop and introduced Cassandra as Countess Ranleigh, after which His Grace said that he was ever so happy to meet His Lordship's new Countess, whom he had heard so much about. "M'lady, your beauty is the talk of the *ton.*"

Cassandra thanked him, and then he said to Lord Ranleigh, "I see your brother has returned to London."

Cassandra, upon hearing Wade's name, shivered. Surely Lord Ranleigh's fine mood would vanish. She turned her head to look at her husband and watched him turn pale, as if the devil had just passed over his grave. His brow furrowed into a deep frown, and his dark eyes turned the blackest black, as she had seen them do when his anger came to the forefront.

"Fustian; am I supposed to care?"

"Have you seen him?" His Grace asked.

Lord Ranleigh's answer was sharp. "No. London is a

big place; 'tis not likely that our paths will cross. He does not stay at Kenmere."

"Oh, that's common knowledge about Town. But he's here, in the park, so I understand, with a very beautiful gel riding beside him in a very beautiful carriage. Rented, I hear."

"Mayhap the gel is Ellen," Cassandra whispered for Lord Ranleigh's ears only, and when he did not immediately respond she leaned forward and addressed the Duke. "Your Grace, do you know the lady's name? Could it be Ellen Terry?"

"I know of no Ellen," said the Duke dismissively. A smug smile, and then he turned his gloating eyes on Lord Ranleigh.

"Your Lordship, the lady—and I use the term judiciously—is Miss Elsa Cordley."

Twenty-three

"Good day, Your Grace," said Lord Ranleigh.

Out of hearing, he let out a string of expletives, slapped the horse's back with the ribbons, and guided him out of the procession of carriages. The horse took off at a trot.

"Where are we going?" Cassandra asked.

"We came to look for your friend, not listen to gossip from an aging quidnunc. As we pass the carriages, you peer in and see if the startling beauty is in one of them. I must needs keep my hands on the ribbons."

Men riding horses scattered to give them space. Women in the carriages leaned out to look, some waving jeweled hands at His Lordship.

"I could see better if you would not go so fast," said Cassandra.

"I beg your forgiveness." He slowed the horse, but not to a walk. Cassandra took a deep breath and relaxed. She was enjoying herself tremendously, peering into the carriages, seeing the wonderful gowns and hats the women of quality wore.

A few even smiled at her. She smiled back, while at the same time wondering if they were being friendly or if they were smiling because Lord Ranleigh had married a gel from the lower orders. She was glad they did not know the whole of it.

"Smile," she told His Lordship. "Make them think you are happy."

Lord Ranleigh smiled, and was surprised to find that for some inexplicable reason he was happy; and he found himself truly caring whether or not Cassandra found the runaway.

That his brother Wade and his ex-paramour were together in the park did not bother Lord Ranleigh a whit. Let the scoundrel have his fun. He nodded to Lord Ashley as they passed, then leaned his head to Cassandra and told her conspiratorially, "He's a lousy gambler. He lost a bundle at White's last night. I hear he had to visit Clarges Street and mortgage his wife's jewelry."

"He doesn't seem bothered," Cassandra answered.

"A gentleman never lets it show when he's unhappy about losing at the gaming tables. 'Tis not the thing."

Cassandra was learning more and more about the lives of the upper orders, and the games they played, and she was not sure she would be happy living in that manner. It seemed so false and frivolous. She reminded herself that before she had become apprised of this she had dreamed of being one of them, of living at Ranleigh Hall as Lord Ranleigh's Countess.

But that was because I wanted to be his wife.

She glimpsed a head of glistening ebony hair and leaned almost out of the Tilbury, searching the woman's face, praying that she would look into Ellen's big blue eyes. Once or twice she thought she saw her, and each time she said to Lord Ranleigh, "Slow down; I believe the woman in the carriage we just passed is Ellen," only to be terribly disappointed when Lord Ranleigh stopped the Tilbury and the woman turned and returned her gaze.

None was as strikingly beautiful as Ellen.

Cassandra became disheartened. They had circled the

park, passing many fine carriages and, after Lord Ranleigh's splendid change of mood, had stopped and visited with a few of the occupants.

"This is my wife, the Countess of Ranleigh," he said more than once, and Cassandra thought she heard a touch of pride when he spoke. The gentlemen bowed their heads in acknowledgment, and the ladies of quality lifted their lorgnettes and gave her a once-over stare, and then reluctantly acknowledged her as the Countess of Ranleigh.

At last she saw them, Wade and Elsa, sitting close together in a flamboyant carriage, with a driver wearing a coat of many layers and sporting a three corner on the box.

"There they are," Cassandra cried, restraining herself to keep from pointing.

"Who? Not Ellen?

"No, pea goose, Wade and Elsa."

Cassandra looked at Lord Ranleigh and waited for the frown to appear on his dark brow, for his eyes to turn black with anger. She regretted infinitely that she had foolishly paid his paramour for her future services. Had she not, Elsa would not be here with Wade. She said, "It did not take her long to find another protector."

Lord Ranleigh gave a little laugh. He was not frowning, and his eyes crinkled when he laughed. He said, "Wade could never be anyone's protector. He spends money like it is water. On himself. He's rented the carriage and persuaded Elsa to come this day to prove to me that he's irresistible to women. He wants anything and everyone that belongs to me. That is the reason I have warned you to keep your distance from him. It would not be you he wanted, but to take something that belongs to me."

Cassandra did not answer. She wanted him to go on, to talk, to tell all that was buried inside him. But he became silent after that. He pulled the Tilbury alongside the carriage in which Wade and Elsa rode and nodded his head by way of greeting, and a smile played around his mouth when he said, "May I present my bride, Cassandra, Countess of Ranleigh." To Cassandra, he said, "My brother, Wade."

He then turned his eyes to Elsa. "I believe, Elsa, that the two of you have met. When you came to Kenmere and the Countess paid you a huge sum of money to keep you until you can find another protector."

Wade's answer was a charming laugh. "I have met your bride, Brother. We rendezvoused on the hillock above Ranleigh Hall—"

"That is a lie," Cassandra cried. "We did not rendezvous. I was there and you came upon me, scaring me out of my wits."

As if Cassandra had not spoken, Wade, fixing Lord Ranleigh with his penetrating blue eyes, pushed on. "She had in her hand a valentine she intended to give to you. Did you receive it? Is that how she won you and wormed her way into the Hall? All the way from Sister Martha's orphanage?"

Lord Ranleigh was quick to answer. "The Countess told me of the valentine, and of meeting you, Wade. And you are wrong, as usual. I went to the orphanage for a wife because I desired a woman with high moral standards and a kind and loving heart."

Dismissing Wade, he turned to his ex-paramour. "Elsa, if you have not found another protector when the blunt the Countess furnished you is gone, contact my man of business and he will provide a small pension—"

"A *small* pension!" Elsa screeched, and Cassandra was sure that had she had something handy, she would have thrown it at Lord Ranleigh.

"I deserve more than that, you jackanapes," Elsa

Cordley said. "Why did you not tell me you wanted a wife? I would have . . ."

The Tilbury pulled away, but not before Cassandra looked into Wade's blue eyes, studied his fair countenance, and saw something familiar . . . and something sinister. He truly was a scoundrel. To her surprise, Lord Ranleigh was chuckling.

"How can you laugh after being attacked in such a manner?" she asked.

"You really did me a favor, Cassandra, and I thank you. My time with Elsa had run its course. I . . ."

He did not finish. Cassandra wanted to know the whole of it but did not ask. It was not her concern, now that she had decided to lock the door between them and had told him so.

She asked herself if she had locked her heart against this stalwart, mysterious man beside her. Almost, but not quite, she mused, acknowledging that it would take time.

But I will not allow hope.

"Are you satisfied that Ellen is not in the park?" His Lordship asked. "I'm quite ready to return to Kenmere."

"And I, too," she answered. And then she asked, pain showing in her words, "Do you think Ellen is anywhere in London? Is she still alive?"

Lord Ranleigh took her hand and squeezed it gently. "On the morrow I will visit the East End. I pray that I won't find her there, but should I, you have the right to know." And then he added, "You have such a caring heart."

"I learned how to care from Sister Martha."

"I don't believe that for one moment. I'm sure she helped, but what you have is inborn. It comes from your soul, and I envy you the wonderful quality."

After that they rode to Kenmere in virtual silence. It was pleasant; wisps of fluffy gray clouds scudded across the sky. Dusk had begun to hover. They passed palatial homes with lighted windows, and English gardens. The air was sweet with the scent of honeysuckle, and of blooming roses. Morning glories were waiting till morning to bloom.

At Kenmere, candles flickered in the narrow windows across the imposing edifice. A groom came and held the horse's head while Lord Ranleigh helped Cassandra alight. She had in mind to go to her quarters and order supper and then visit Jacob and hear about what he had done after his nap. Mayhap she would read to him another story, or listen while he read to her.

That was not to be.

When she and Lord Ranleigh reached her door he asked if he might come in.

"Why?" she asked in all sincerity.

"I would miss our little visits should we discontinue them. You will allow me that much, will you not?"

Cassandra felt perfectly safe in acquiescing to His Lordship's request. She had told him, and she was sure that he would heed her desire, that her bedchamber was forbidden to him. "Come in," she said.

Inside the room, a fire burned in the grate, for the night air had suddenly become damp and quite cool. A window was open, and His Lordship went to close it. "Shall we order supper?" he asked, turning to smile at Cassandra. "It would be pleasant to eat before the fire. A table can be moved."

She felt a sharp lance of pain dance across her shoulders. Why did he have to look at her that way? Why did he not just go away? "Yes," she said, and almost before she spoke the table had been moved, fresh flowers placed at its center, and His Lordship was lighting two tapers.

But then something happened. A knock was heard and the door immediately burst open. It was Dora.

"Mrs. Brodwick wants you to come quickly. Little Jacob is making an awful sound when he tries to breathe."

The table was almost overturned with the haste in which Lord Ranleigh left the room, with Cassandra outdistancing him by three strides. Her heart was in her throat. Long before she reached Jacob's quarters, she could hear the sound: the croup. Many times she had heard it at Sister Martha's. She grabbed the boy and put her head to his chest, hearing a rattle.

"Get me a pan of boiling water with mint . . . and a sheet with which to make a tent." She looked imploringly at Lord Ranleigh, who was holding the little boy's hand. "Don't just stand there."

Lord Ranleigh, Dora, and Mrs. Brodwick all moved at once.

"Jacob, Jacob," she said. " 'Tis your new Stepmother. I will help you breathe. Relax, sweetheart." Intuitively, she pressed on his chest, then held him close to her, trying to breathe for him. He gave a slight cough. The rattle was worse; his body grew limp in her arms. "Bring the water and the sheet," she screamed.

" 'Tis here, m'lady. What—"

"Spread it over me, tent-fashion."

This they did.

"Now, put the water where the steam will come up into Jacob's face."

She bent forward, holding him over the steam, and it seemed like forever before the awful sound abated and his breathing became easier. Still, she stayed there, holding him, until steam no longer came from the pan.

"Hand me the brown liquid, Mrs. Brodwick," Cassandra said as she removed the sheet from over them, and the frightened nursemaid poured the liquid in a spoon and handed it to Cassandra.

Jacob opened his eyes, then his mouth, welcoming that which would bring him relief. After that Cassandra rocked him and sang to him, and he was soon asleep.

Looking around, Cassandra glimpsed Lord Ranleigh. This surprised her, for she had been sure that he had long ago repaired to his quarters. He stood there, watching her, an incredulous look on his face. Moving closer, he put his big hand on her shoulder consolingly, and then he took Jacob's hand and held it for a moment.

"He will be all right now," she said. "It was the croup, a common malady of young children. Why don't you repair to bed—"

"But you haven't eaten."

"I'm not hungry."

She said to Dora and Mrs. Brodwick, "Go to bed. I will stay with Jacob."

The maid and nurse left, and Cassandra spent the night in Jacob's room, holding him and praying that the little boy would not be taken from her. Lord Ranleigh refused to leave and sat beside her. She could feel his dark eyes on her; she could feel his concern for Jacob, not as his heir, but as a little boy who needed a father.

Time passed. Beyond the window, daylight stole the darkness, and first light streamed through the windows. Jacob stirred and opened his pale blue eyes.

"Why are you holding me?" he asked.

"Because you were ill, and I was worried about you."

He placed his head of golden curls back on Cassandra's breast and murmured sleepily, "You're a good new Stepmother."

Suddenly, then, from somewhere the truth hit Cassandra like a bolt; the answer to one of Ranleigh Hall's dark secrets was clear. From the start, Jacob's little face had reminded her of someone from her past. The image had stuck in her mind.

Now she knew that the memory was of the man she had seen briefly on her hillock, Wade Ranleigh. She sat in stunned silence, pondering, but not doubting, that the little boy she held in her arms, the child she had come to love so very much, was *not* the true heir to the earldom and to the Ranleigh entailed estates, but was, in truth, the scoundrel's son.

Twenty-four

The days following Jacob's bout with the croup were quiet at Kenmere. Cassandra did not like his color, and the wheezing was still in his chest, but each day she told herself that tomorrow his cheeks would regain their color, and that his sweet smile would return. She did not like London and wanted very much to leave . . . and they would, His Lordship said, when Jacob was stronger. And after he had found Ellen.

One day he told her, "Cassandra, I will find the gel Ellen for you," and Cassandra believed him, for the same determination was in his demeanor when he spoke that was so evident in his purposeful stride and in the fierceness that showed in his eyes.

Her new wardrobe was delivered to Kenmere, as Madame Lenora had promised, and Jacob's clothes were sent from Weston's. Each day she dressed him in different pantaloons, a new shirt, silk stockings, and low-cuts, and told him he was adorable. He would laugh and hug her and call her his Stepmother. They walked in the park, a little farther each day. She thought of returning to Dr. Morton for a consultation but decided against doing so. Most likely he would tell her not to be overset, that God's Will would be done.

While Cassandra was diligently watching over Jacob,

Lord Ranleigh was diligently looking for Ellen. Finding no news of her on the West End, he went to the East End and walked among the seething rubble of street vendors, crippled soldiers and sailors, and ballad singers. He looked into the faces of flower girls pushing carts and hawking, "Flowers fer sale. Take one to yer lady love, or keep it fer yerself."

Cassandra had described Ellen in such detail that Lord Ranleigh felt he knew her, but there were so many black-haired, blue-eyed gels. Once he stopped a flower gel and asked her if she had once lived at Sister Martha's orphanage. Her answer was a scowl. He bought flowers from her anyway and brought them home to Cassandra.

He visited theaters in Covent Garden and in Drury Lane, looking for Ellen's mother, finding no one who had heard of a Mrs. Terry, or of a Miss Ellen Terry. Or, for that matter, of Sister Martha's orphanage.

He went to the docks. Often times gels met the incoming ships to sell favors to the men who had been at sea for some time. He saw his brother's new ship, *The Sylvia*, but Wade Ranleigh was nowhere to be seen. Not that he wanted to see the scoundrel, Lord Ranleigh mused.

Faring no better in his search for Ellen Terry at the docks than he had at the theaters and the other places he had looked, Lord Ranleigh, that evening, said to Cassandra, "There's one more place."

"Where?" she asked, fast losing hope.

"The Cyprians' Ball."

Cassandra raised a brown eyebrow and, placing her hands on her hips, asked, "Your Lordship, pray, *what* is a Cyprians' Ball? You can't mean—" Her gray eyes were round with disbelief.

Lord Ranleigh could not help but laugh. His wife's innocence astounded him. They were in the small garden at the back of the house. He had just now found her there, picking roses. In one hand she held three beautiful red buds with long stems, in the other a pair of garden shears. The gown she wore was one of her new ones and one of his favorites, a blue, very soft, muslin-embellished with butterflies embroidered around the hem, and around the revealing neckline.

He drew a deep breath to slow his rapid heartbeat and, taking her arm, said, "Let's sit over here, and I shall tell you the whole of it about a Cyprians' Ball."

He led her to a bench under a tall oak tree. It was late and quiet. Late evening shadows danced on the ground, and the moon, a perfect silver orb, had started its ascent into a blue-black velvet sky sprinkled with twinkling silver stars. The scent of the roses and of nearby honeysuckle filled the air.

Lord Ranleigh found his voice choked when he tried to speak. His mind was not on a ball of any kind. He looked at Cassandra. She appeared ethereal and unsubstantially thin, as if the soft wind might blow her away. No doubt her concern for Jacob had taken its toll.

Her gray eyes appeared sad, and . . .

She spoke. "You were going to tell me about a Cyprians' Ball. I cannot imagine."

He laughed, embarrassed. Their wedding night rose up in a great smothering wave, reminding him that they were man and wife. Still, it was a new experience for him to go against propriety and speak of such things to a lady of quality.

"A Cyprians' Ball is held annually, at the Argyle rooms—"

"I have my new gowns; mayhap I could go."

"I'm afraid, dear one, that that is impossible—"

"Why?"

Her eyes were looking straight into his face, making him uncomfortable. " 'Tis not the thing," he said.

"Lord Ranleigh, I'm quite tired of hearing 'tis not the thing.' What is not the thing? What harm—"

273

"A Cyprians' Ball is for cyprians only, and you know what a cyprian is . . . you met Elsa. They come to the ball, dressed in finery, feathers in their hair, and wearing satin slippers on their feet, looking for a new protector among the nobility, or the first protector, if she has not had one before and has decided to become a kept woman. That is why I thought Ellen—"

"I've never heard of anything so disgraceful."

" 'Tis the way of the *ton.*"

"The more I learn of London's society the less I think of it, Your Lordship. Besides, I don't believe Ellen would frequent such a place—"

"If you do not wish me to go—"

"Oh, I didn't say that. Mayhap she would be there, but should you find her in such company, I warn you ahead of time, I will fib robustly to Sister Martha."

He smiled. "I believe that you would."

They were silent after that; he reached out and took her hand, feeling contentment wash over him, thinking that he could stay this way forever.

It was Cassandra who broke the silence. "You seem to know so much about cyprians, Your Lordship. Have you attended one of *their* balls?"

"Yes," he said in a low voice. "That is where I met Elsa."

Cassandra held her temper. Tears stung her eyes as she rose and went to finish her rose gathering, bending over a sprawling bush of huge red roses in full bloom. Before she could snip the first glorious rose, Lord Ranleigh had taken the garden shears from her hand and was snipping away. "Did you have in mind a dozen, or even more?"

"A dozen will be plenty. There're fresh flowers in my rooms. Dora is very thoughtful about that, but today I wanted to pick them myself."

"How thoughtless of me," he said, giving back to her the shears and taking the roses she held in her hand.

274

"You pick and I will hold them for you. Gather more than a dozen; my hands are large."

As long as the tears were stinging Cassandra's eyes, she bent over so that His Lordship could not see. Her heart ached. If only she did not love him so much. It was an absolutely awful feeling, loving a man who admitted he went to a Cyprians' Ball to find his pleasure. Were all men animals? She supposed so, if they wanted to mate with just any gel who was in season, and she supposed cyprians were in season all the time.

Her hands moved quickly from rose stem to rose stem, and the quietness was absolute, until Lord Ranleigh, laughing, said that his hands would not hold another rose.

"I got carried away, I guess," Cassandra said. She straightened and looked at him. "Let me help you."

"Oh, no. I made a bargain and I shall keep it. Take my arm and, like a gentleman, I will guide you back into the house. 'Tis quite dark."

That wasn't so at all, thought Cassandra. The moon was bright in the sky, giving plenty of light for one to see. Nonetheless, she took his arm and they went into the house and climbed to the second floor by way of the servant's stairway. At the door of her quarters she reached to take the roses. "Thank you, Your Lordship. I will put them in water."

"There's so many, I fear you need help."

As Cassandra watched he miraculously managed to transfer the bundle of roses into one arm without dropping a single one, and then, with his free hand, turn the doorknob. Leaning his tall frame against the heavily carved door, he pushed it open. He was smiling, and his dark, usually brooding, eyes, were alight with what appeared to be amusement.

She gave a little bob and said, "Thank you, kind sir. You are the perfect gentleman."

He entered without being asked.

275

Cassandra went to fill a large Wedgwood vase with water from the ewer, saying when she returned, "This should hold them."

So together they arranged the huge bundle of roses in the vase, and, after placing them on a round, ornate table by the window, stood back and admired their handiwork.

Moonlight was beginning to slant through the window and cast elongated shadows on the silk-covered walls, and on the rose petals, making them varying shades of red, like velvet whipped by the wind.

"We could most likely find employment arranging roses for the upper orders," she said, and they laughed some more. Cassandra thought how wonderful it felt.

But the good mood disappeared as fast as it came, and tension began to gather. It seemed to Cassandra that neither knew what to do or say, and she wondered why this should be so. *Everything* between them was settled. Her bedchamber door was no longer open to him. They were friends; that was all.

She was glad when he at last said, "Mayhap we should repair to the dining room. The servants most likely would like to be dismissed."

Cassandra wanted to stay in her own drawing room and smell the roses. She wanted him to hold her, to bury his face in her hair, loose and touching her shoulders. She scolded herself, but she could not help those feelings, which came against her will.

"You go ahead, Your Lordship. I think I shall order a small repast sent here." She forced a small laugh. "'Twould be a shame to leave the beautiful roses."

"Then I shall dine here with you . . . if you don't mind. As I've told you, I so enjoy cozing with you, and I did help you gather the roses."

Cassandra wanted him to go. Looking into those dark eyes she saw burning, unadulterated lust. She had come to know the look. And her own body was fast betraying her. She lashed out angrily, "I think not, Your Lordship. Tonight, I prefer to be alone."

As if she hadn't spoken, the next instant his long fingers were twined into her golden hair, his dark head bent over hers. Before she could turn her head he was kissing her passionately and holding her throbbing body to his great length. To her horror, she felt her lips tremble beneath his. Tears again pricked her eyes. She swore at herself, and at him, noiselessly, as she struggled against giving in to the passion that held them in its fierce grip.

Her strong will won. She pushed him away with as much force as she could muster, gave him a good solid kick to the shin, and then spat out at him, "Go to Elsa to satisfy your lust. Mayhap at the Cyprians' Ball you can reinstate her services."

He stared at her for a moment, and she had the satisfaction of seeing color suffuse his neck and creep upwards into his face before he turned on a booted heel and left.

Lord Ranleigh swore, for he carried with him the hard edge of his wife's voice. Words irrevocable in their expression, terrible in their finality. He felt a tightness in his chest and, as he walked the length of the long, silent hall, his thoughts were as confused as they had ever been.

Alone, in his excellent library, he sat for a long time and stared at the back of his late Countess's portrait. He did not need to turn it for, with explicit vision, he could recall every line in her beautiful face, every stray hair blowing in the wind . . . and, in a sudden twist of memory, he could see the double bed in their room at Ranleigh Hall, the white sheets crisp and inviting, her auburn hair tumbling over the pillows, her white naked body full and rich and warm . . .

And he could remember every lie she had ever told him.

Time passed, and his suffering became total. Why could she not have taken her lies with her to her grave? He slammed a fist against the top of the huge Jacobean desk, making it quiver. Why could he not find Ellen Terry so that he could return to Ranleigh Hall, where he could find peace in the land.

What a farrago this had turned out to be. Logic told him that he had handled his marriage to Cassandra poorly. He told himself that he was glad she had locked the door between them; and then he acknowledged that it was a lie, that the only peace he had found had been in her arms. She'd called it lust, but he was beginning to think it was much more than that.

"I will test it," he said to himself, vowing that he would avoid her as much as possible, seeking her out only to inquire about Jacob. She had been brought to the Hall to nurse the heir back to health, and she was doing an excellent job.

So the least he could do for her was to find her runaway friend, and abide by the rules she had set down.

Besides, he did not want his shin kicked again.

He felt his leg, where a knot the size of a hen egg had formed, throbbing with every heartbeat. As did his heart, which would never again be free to love. Burying his face in his hands, he let dry sobs shake his body, glad that he was alone.

The day of the Cyrpians' Ball, Lord Ranleigh, dressed to the nines, unobtrusively stood in a small alcove of the Argyle room and observed the effort the demi-reps had made to emulate the grandeur of the upper orders.

Huge chandeliers hung from the carved ceiling, as grand as at Almack's. At the room's far end a band sat on a dias, playing music for dancing. On the dance floor was a sea of plumed heads, dipping and swaying and smiling at their gentlemen partners. One could almost smell their burning sexuality. He thought of the first and only time he had come here, looking for something to fill his life but not his heart. He had met Elsa. In retrospect, the time he had spent with her had been empty and cold. He looked around to see if she had entered the ballroom since last he looked.

She wasn't there.

Nor was his brother.

He had met Elsa soon after Sylvia's death, after which he had learned the mean truths that had almost destroyed him. Even now, thinking on it, he felt drained of energy, emotionally exhausted. He recalled the old cliché that only the strong survive, and survive he had.

Now his eyes darted furtively from one beautiful woman to another, searching for black-as-midnight hair and startling blue eyes, a gel so beautiful that should he see her he would know her at once, so Cassandra had told him when she had first asked him to search for Ellen.

There were dozens of the sort out there, some dressed in the transparent muslin that was all the rage at the moment, others wearing the latest fashion from Paris, all showing cleavage. Nowhere in London would better-dressed women appear, or on the continent for that matter, even in Paris. He saw Harriette Wilson, the queen of the demi-reps. Her beauty was legendary.

Her bright auburn curls sparked the air around her. She had tiny hands and feet, a small waist, and a voluptuous bosom, which she displayed with obvious pleasure, and she was sought after by all the *ton*, even the Duke of Wellington and Beau Brummell, both present tonight.

Little wonder, His Lordship thought, that, if one could believe the on-dits, her protector, the Duke of Argyll, was excessively jealous of her. This night, the fashionably turned out Duke, wearing black tails and a stiffly starched white cravat, was by her side, behind her, in front of her, bending over her, and it appeared that she could not take a step without treading on his highly polished evening boots.

There were others whom Lord Ranleigh knew but chose to ignore. He stood in fear that his brother, Wade, would suddenly appear and cause him embarrassment.

As the men twirled ladies around the dance floor, His Lordship searched for Elsa, his former paramour, thinking he might have missed her. He found that it brought relief to think of her as his *former* paramour, and he smiled when he recalled Cassandra's feat of "paying her for future services." And then she had proceeded to convince him she had done him a favor.

As he stood and watched, Lord Ranleigh was surprised to find that he was missing his wife in name only. A long time passed, his thoughts remaining in that vein, until he realized that if his mission was to be successful, he must needs mix and mingle with the dancers, and begin asking questions.

This was not to his liking, and what he anticipated would happen did. More than one of the cyprians left their dance partners and came to dip into a curtsy before him, saying coyly, "Your Lordship."

His wealth was the drawing card, he told himself, and refused none of them. Not one had heard of the gel.

Men sidled up to him, and more than one asked, "Marriage to your orphan soured already?" His Lordship did not answer, and he scowled when the Duke of Wellington jabbed him in the ribs in passing and raised an eyebrow, silently sending his wicked thoughts.

The evening grew tediously long for Lord Ranleigh. After looking into every smiling face there he kept his eyes peeled on the door. Mayhap the striking beauty would enter late for effect. He held out little hope, however. He was beginning to believe that she had come to a mean end. He searched the room for Harriette Wilson, elbowed his way around the possessive Duke of Argyle, gave a splendid leg, and asked her to dance. Unlike every other gentlemen of the *ton,* he did not lust after the queen of the demi-reps. This night, he sought information. He sent her out, twirled her around, then brought her back to him.

After the third coming together he asked her if she had seen, or heard of, Ellen Terry, describing her in the same way Cassandra had described the runaway to him: "Her eyes are like a river of blue water, bottomless, restless," he said. "And her hair is as black as a raven's wing when wet."

Laughter came from the auburn-haired beauty. "That could describe any number of gels."

"Ellen was interested in the theater. Her mother was an actress—"

Miss Wilson smiled up at him, lifted a delicate brow, and asked, "Why did you not say so in the first place, Your Lordship?"

Lord Ranleigh felt his heart jump. He smelled success. "The devil take me. Do you know her?"

"No, I do not know your Ellen Terry, but I am well acquainted with her mother. Occasionally she does bit parts in the theater, but her main occupation is keeping Lord Cruikshank happy. I hear that just recently her daughter came to Town but was almost immediately shipped off to Paris."

"Tell me the whole of it," Lord Ranleigh pushed.

Harriette Wilson looked at him quizzically. "What's your interest? Grown tired of Miss Cordley?"

"This has nothing to do with Miss Cordley," His Lordship answered with alacrity, his voice slightly sharp. "My . . . wife, the Countess of Ranleigh, before our marriage lived at an orphanage where the gel Ellen lived. According to the Countess, Ellen wanted very much to see her mother, and when she heard she was in London she left the orphanage and came in search of her. The good woman at the orphanage, Sister Martha, is terribly concerned about her charge, who has only five and ten summers."

Their dancing had almost stopped. While they conversed, plumes of many colors bobbed around them, and tinkling laughter could be heard from the courtesans. Purposely. It was their job to please, and to make their partners laugh, Lord Ranleigh thought, becoming more uncomfortable by the minute.

"Then you truly are not here to shop?"

"No. No. That's not my intent at all. In truth, if I can only locate this recalcitrant Ellen, I shall straightaway return to Ranleigh Hall. I'm needed there—"

"She's in Paris, as I told you. Alexandria—that is the chit's mother—could not get her out of town fast enough, so on-dits have it. The gel was much too beautiful, and Alexandria feared she'd lose Lord—"

"What is she doing in Paris?"

"Supposedly studying for the theater. I'll wager some French Count has already seized her, if she's as beautiful as is reported." She paused, gave another little laugh, and asked again, "Are you sure you are not—"

"No, I'm not, and that is the truth of it. I'm only doing a favor for the Countess."

She raised an eyebrow a fraction, smiled, and inclined her head.

Cleverly done, and very seductive, thought Lord Ranleigh.

She asked, "Do I hear the sound of love in your voice, Your Lordship? You know 'tis not the thing to be in love with your wife. What would us gels do if *all* men married for love?"

Lord Ranleigh felt a sense of irritation, and he did not know why. His voice was short. "Mayhap you should marry and settle down."

"Oh, my, my, my! 'Twas not long ago that Elsa

Cordley was keeping your bed warm, and you thought it the thing. Are you now preaching the virtue of married bliss? How unutterably boring."

Lord Ranleigh did not respond.

Harriette Wilson's small feet began moving again. Lord Ranleigh's tall frame gladly moved with her, gracefully taking the lead to dance the sinful waltz. He wanted nothing more than to be done with her, with the Cyprians' Ball, with the search for Ellen.

When the music at last stopped he returned Miss Wilson to Lord Argyle's side, thanked her sincerely for the dance, and for her help with his inquiry. "Miss Wilson," he said, bowing to her; and then, turning to Lord Argyle, he thanked his lordship for allowing Miss Wilson to dance with him. His resolute steps then took him toward the door with great speed, before another courtesan could curtsy in front of him and ask him to dance.

"I wish you luck, Lord Ranleigh," Harriette Wilson called after him in her melodious voice.

He did not turn back to answer, and outside, he gave a boy a sovereign to fetch his conveyance, tonight the Tilbury pulled by a black horse.

Trotting along the street, under the bleakness of the summer sky, he was conscious of loneliness again. No longer did he belong to the world he had just left, and for some inexplicable reason he felt an outsider to Kenmere, a stranger to his wife. He was suddenly taken aback that he was now calling her his wife, not Jacob's new nurse.

He cracked the whip over the horse's back and told him to hurry along. Silently, he prayed that Cassandra would wait up for him so he could tell her what he had learned of Ellen and be done with it. Soon they would return to Ranleigh Hall, where there would be plenty to occupy his mind.

And then he thought of the inevitable meeting up with Wade.

He thought of seeing Isabelle again, of having to endure more of her histrionic scenes, her fawning over Wade. Only when he thought of his sister, Cynthia, did he feel a lightness of spirit. He stopped the Tilbury in front of Kenmere. A groom came and took the ribbons.

The house was dark, with the exception of the great hall. Light showed from the long, narrow windows on each side of the huge double doors, which he opened without the assistance of a butler. He heard her voice almost before he saw her sitting on the bottom step of the stairway. "I dismissed the butler for the night and told him to leave the doors unlocked."

" 'Tis later than I intended. I had almost given up hope when Harriette Wilson gave me some news." As he talked, he closed the distance between them, and when his gaze fell upon her he felt his breath catch in his throat. She looked like a child, sitting there on the stairsteps; fronds of tawny-blond hair framed her pretty face and fell onto her shoulders, as if she had been riding in the wind. Yet she was demure and proper, the way she held her hands in her lap. Her dress hardly covered her feet, which, to His Lordship's astonishment, were bare.

When Cassandra saw him looking at her bare feet she quickly covered them with the hem of her gown and said, "When I lived at the orphanage I went barefoot, and I find that on occasion I miss the freedom."

"If 'tis your wont, go barefoot."

She laughed, a sweet, golden sound that was pleasing to His Lordship's ears. She said, "Should I do that at Ranleigh Hall, the Dowager Countess would surely find fault, and she would be quick to remind me that your *first* Countess did not do anything so unladylike, that only the lower orders would think of behaving in such a manner."

Lord Ranleigh knew that this was true, and there was little he could do about it. Unless he put Cassandra in the position of reporting each offense to him, of being a tattletale. He would most certainly take action, but she would not like that. He said in all sincerity, "When Isabelle comes to know you she will love you." Cassandra doubted that. Dismissing the dowager from her mind, she inquired about Ellen. She could not believe that her mind had so totally strayed from the runaway.

"Did you see Ellen at that awful ball? I waited up to hear."

"No," he said, and he could hear a big sigh of relief come from Cassandra. He quickly added, "I learned that her mother does, indeed, live in London, under the protection of Lord Cruikshank. Occasionally, she does bit parts in the theater."

"Where's Ellen? Did she find her mother, that awful woman who abandoned her when she was only three?"

"They were together for awhile, but now Ellen is in Paris, studying to become an actress."

His Lordship thought it best he stop there. If he did not tell Cassandra the whole of it, then she would not be forced to lie to Sister Martha. Better that he be the sinner than the innocent before her.

"Well then, I can repair to bed. Thank you for the good news, and for your concerted effort to find Ellen for me. I've been so worried that she might have come to a bad end, and it would hurt Sister Martha something terrible, and me as well. I love Ellen, and I wish her the best. Mayhap she will come back someday, and I can tell her in person."

Lord Ranleigh felt his heart hurting his lungs as he drew a deep breath and tried to speak. Words wouldn't come, and he could only stand and listen to the silence, to the stillness in the great hall. By now Cassandra was standing and had started up the stairs.

She stopped to ask, "Your Lordship, did you see Miss Cordley? I hope she has found a protector by now, if that is her wont. And, as I told you, I'm perfectly willing that you reinstate her as your mistress. I no longer hold you to the vows you made before the vicar."

At last, His Lordship found his voice, barely. "No, I did not see Elsa. And Cassandra, it is not my wish to reinstate her as my mistress. I can't explain why . . . I just don't want to."

Twenty-five

"I think it a capital idea that I take you to the theater before returning to Ranleigh Hall," Lord Ranleigh said to Cassandra the next morning.

"Only last night you were talking of how anxious you were to return to the land."

Cassandra shook her head, thinking that she would never understand her husband. After the Cyprians' Ball he had walked with her to the door of her quarters, where they had stood and talked for a short while—she had refused to allow him entry into her drawing room— and he had spoken longingly of returning to Ranleigh Hall, saying it was therapeutic for him to see the crops grow and to converse with his steward. "And you can soon begin getting acquainted with the tenant farmers' wives. You seem the type—"

That was last night. Now, they were at the breakfast table, and he was saying, "I do want to return to Ranleigh as soon as possible, but I find that I would very much like to show you off to the *ton* before leaving."

He smiled at her and went on, "You've voiced displeasure with London society, and I fear that once we leave I will never persuade you to return. Should that happen, on-dits will fly that I'm hiding you out in the country, that I am ashamed of my orphan. When, in truth, I'm quite proud of you."

"Is that what they call me?"

"I'm afraid so. Last night at the ball several of the gentlemen asked me if I had tired of my orphan. It was quite natural that they think I was shopping for a replacement for Elsa."

Cassandra did not answer straight away. She chewed, swallowed, and thought. From the corner of her eye she looked at his handsome face, at his dark, brooding eyes. Her heart pounded, and she wanted to slap him. Why should he affect her this way? At last she said, "So you want to continue putting forth the illusion that we are happily married, that I am, in truth, your wife in every way."

"Yes—"

Cassandra stood abruptly, and had not His Lordship grabbed the back of her chair she would have overturned it. Anger washed over her. She must needs have windmills in her head. After this she would have breakfast sent to her room.

Making her way from the dining room—before tears wet her cheeks—she whipped around at the door and said, "I care not what the *ton* thinks. And I care not what your brother thinks. No doubt we will see plenty of him when we return to Ranleigh Hall, and mayhap I will tell him that you married me to save the Ranleigh heir, that you are so much in love with your first Countess that there's no room in your life for me." Anger held her in its grip, and she went on recklessly. "Mayhap he will want to be cozy with me."

She stopped before she said, "As he was with your first Countess."

"Cassandra, you wouldn't." Lord Ranleigh was instantly by her side, taking her arm. She jerked away and ran out into the hall, with him in close pursuit,

288

pleading with her to pray reconsider. "Blister it, Cassandra . . ."

Gaining her quarters, Cassandra practically fell inside and managed by sheer willpower to slam the door in His Lordship's face. Alone, flinging herself on the bed, she was free to cry, and she did, unashamedly, while calling His Lordship a jackanapes, a corinthian, a crim con, a fop, cork brained, and any other unworthy name she could think of. At the vicarage and at the orphanage she had not learned too many hateful words, and it did not matter, she learned, for calling His Lordship names did not help. Still, the tears flowed, subsiding only when she was spent and dry inside. Rising from the bed, she went to the porcelain wash basin and poured fresh water from the ewer and washed her face. She looked into the looking glass and instantly looked away, for she could not stand her ghastly appearance.

Her eyes were swollen and red, sunken, and the rest of her face was as white as a sheet.

And her stomach was suddenly queasy, as if she might lose her breakfast.

And it's not caused by what I just saw in the looking glass, she thought. She said aloud, " 'Tis morning sickness."

She covered her face with her hands and a groan escaped her throat. She was not wise in the field of birthing, but she had heard of the signs, the weeping, the melancholy. She was *enceinte;* she was going to be a mother. Quickly, she sought a place to sit, lest she faint and fall to the floor.

Twenty-six

The next day preparations began for the return to Ranleigh Hall. Cassandra awoke early, after having spent a restless night, still in shock about her discovery. She must have conceived on her wedding night. It was a wonderful dream come true. Even as a young gel, she had prayed for a baby of her own. She thought back over her life. It had been so easy to love other people's children, and now she was going to have a child of her own.

Of course, the ideal would be to have a loving father for her child, but that would make things too perfect. And life was not perfect, she told herself; then she said aloud, "I will let nothing make me unhappy," and began planning what she would do when her little girl arrived. Her body vibrated with excitement. She thought about Jacob and wondered if she would feel differently for her own child than she did for him, knowing the answer instantly. Jacob was her child.

Since coming to the realization that Jacob had been sired by Wade Ranleigh—and there was no doubt of this in her mind—Cassandra had thought a lot about Lord Ranleigh's relationship to the boy, his hostility toward Jacob, and wondered if he knew of his late wife's adultery. Surely not, she concluded, or why would he still be in love with her, and her long dead?

These thoughts had troubled Cassandra's sleep more than one night. Now, there was something else to consider. Should her child be a son, he, not Jacob, would be the true Ranleigh heir.

Cassandra had no trouble with that decision. Since birth, young Jacob had been told that he was heir to the earldom, and to the Ranleigh entailed estates. And that was that, she thought. As long as he lived, he would be the first son, the one who would inherit, according to England's law of primogenitor. Even if she had six sons, which was unlikely considering the way things were.

A thought rose sharply in Cassandra's mind: Because of the law, would someone want Jacob dead? She scolded herself for not having seen it earlier. But she had suspected, and quickly, acting on instinct, had forbidden Cook to come near the child.

And most likely saved his life.

A surge of dread moved over Cassandra, an unexplainable fright. She rang for Dora, wanting her to come and help her pack for the long journey. While waiting, she stood and stared out the second-story window, wishing that none of this was true, that she was wrong about Cook, and about Jacob's future, which, if her premonition could be considered, would be short-lived.

They had been returned to Ranleigh Hall a fortnight before Cassandra found the poison. She was in Jacob's old rooms. If asked why she had gone there, she would not have known the answer, except that she had been drawn there by some foreign force. And no one would believe that.

Before climbing the stairs to the third floor, she had gone to Jacob's new quarters and had found them empty. Going then in search of Cynthia, she found her in her apartment, loaded down with her easel and paints in preparation for going into the woods to paint.

"Have you seen Jacob and Mrs. Brodwick?" Cassandra asked.

"Mrs. Brodwick took him for a walk. She asked that I tell you," Cynthia said. "She would have told you herself except they had King Arthur."

King Arthur was the tiny puppy His Lordship had bought for Jacob before they left London.

"Jacob was holding on to the leash," Cynthia said, her eyes twinkling. "He was giggling so hard he could not talk, and King Arthur was dancing around him. 'Twas a sight: such a tiny dog, and Mrs. Brodwick dancing around, getting King Arthur to bark and jump all the more."

Cassandra could envision the scene. She said, smiling, "Such a powerful name to be given to such a small dog. But Jacob was adamant. He loves stories about King Arthur."

Now, standing in Jacob's old room and holding a minuscule vial of arsenic in her hand, Cassandra shuddered. Whoever had hidden the poison behind a loose board had not bothered to remove the label. She took it to the window and held it up; a good half of the white powder was gone. More than enough, she thought, to kill a child the size of Jacob, even if it had been given over a long, long period of time. She put it back and left. She must needs talk with someone whom she could trust.

Cassandra considered going directly to Sister Martha, but then thought better of it. The dear little old lady should not be worried about something she could do nothing about.

She would talk with Cynthia, Cassandra decided. Had not the gel said she knew Ranleigh's secrets?

As Cassandra turned and left the room, she said aloud, "What shall I tell her? That I have found a via of arsenic . . . and that I believe before I came to Ranleigh someone had been giving small doses of arsenic to Jacob. She will laugh at me, and say that most likely it has been used to kill rats and has been put in the wall so the boy could not find it."

Cassandra knew better.

She quietly descended the stairs and left the manor through a side door, going into the woods and toward the sea, coming to the craggy shore. The sun was a burst of red over the blue-black water, this day calm and fascinating in its austerity. She stood for a long moment and watched, willing herself to be calm. She had no idea in which way to turn to find Cynthia, whose painting consisted mostly of the sea, high waves angrily crashing onto the peaked cliffs of washed stones.

Shading her eyes with her hand, Cassandra peered to the right, and then to the left, and decided to go to the right, careful not to slip and fall. Her mind came to the precious baby growing inside her, and once again she was filled with unbelievable happiness. It was still her secret.

This made her smile, and she accused herself of becoming secretive, like the other residents of Ranleigh Hall.

She walked on . . . and on. "Cynthia," she called more than once. Then, rounding a bend, she saw anchored offshore and quite a distance out, a ship, and she remembered Lord Ranleigh telling her that Wade anchored his ships down from the Hall.

Since returning to Ranleigh Hall, Cassandra had diligently avoided Wade Ranleigh. Surprising to her, it had not been difficult, the place being so huge. Wade had eaten his meals with his doting mother, and when Cassandra did not eat with Jacob and Mrs. Brodwick, she had her meals sent to her bedchamber.

Lord Ranleigh ate in their quarters' dining room, alone. No longer did they come together in the evenings to coze. She knew not what he was thinking, or how the crops were doing, and just two days ago he had come to her and said he was going to another of the Ranleigh farms; he was needed there.

He had not said when he would return, and Cassandra found herself listening for his purposeful footsteps and tried in vain not to think about him. In a strange, unorthodox way, she was settling in at Ranleigh Hall. She had even called on the tenants' wives, as Lord Ranleigh had suggested.

Cassandra saw a figure moving toward her, and as it came closer she saw that it was Wade. At first she started to duck out of sight and wait for him to pass, and then she changed her mind. Mayhap the scoundrel would reveal something she desired to know. Hurriedly she planned: She would not appear curious . . . she would let him talk . . . she would listen . . .

She thought about Lord Ranleigh's insistence that she have her own gowns when Wade came to Ranleigh Hall and, looking down at the rather plain blue morning dress she wore, she was thankful for it.

Her hair was loose and flying and wrapping around her face. She pulled at a strand and tucked it behind her ear.

A gull drifted far overhead, its wings outstretched, its neck craning toward the sun.

A wave thudded against the rocks and exploded in a cloud of spray.

Cassandra breathed deeply and at last allowed herself to look at the tall figure presently upon her, smiling charmingly. Before she could prevent him from doing so he had taken her hand and, bending over, was kissing it with damp lips. Revulsion roiled inside her, and with forced calmness, she withdrew it from his grasp. "The orphan, my sister-in-law," he said disparagingly.

"The Countess of Ranleigh," said Cassandra, and she

watched as the color drained from Wade's face. Hatred glowed in his blue eyes.

Why is he so bothered? I have done nothing to him.

"I beg your forgiveness," he said. " 'Tis true. Now that you are married to the sixth Earl of Ranleigh you are the Countess. Quite a step up in the world, is it not?"

"Good day, sir," Cassandra said, stepping around him. With his hostile attitude, she would learn nothing from him. He grabbed her arm, and before he could order her to stay, she said, "Unhand me, Wade Ranleigh, or I shall box your ears."

Riotous laughter mixed with the sounds of lapping waves and the keening wail of the seagull. "You are a spirited one. I can see why Brother sought you out."

"He knew nothing of my spirit . . ."

Cassandra could have bitten off her tongue. It was none of Wade Ranleigh's business *why* Lord Ranleigh had married her. But it was too late, for Wade jumped onto her words like a starving hound grabbing a bone. He released her arm. His voice was soft, cajoling. "So you were strangers, you an orphan, he a member of the aristocracy. 'Tis strange, indeed."

"I see nothing strange about it."

"Nor I, now that I've gotten a better look at you. And dressed in finery! What did you do with the poor dress you wore when I found you mooning over Ranleigh Hall . . . drawing sweet valentines."

"I still have it, and I still wear it occasionally."

His searing gaze moved over her. There was a lazy, indolent, almost seductive, smile on his face. Cassandra felt as if he were undressing her and she could not stop him. Her face flushed hot with embarrassment.

"Well, Countess, I think my brother is a very fortunate man to have become leg shackled to you. Though 'tis a mystery. A man of the nobility most usually marries for convenience. Most often to join an estate to his already enormous holdings, and to have good lineage for his heir."

He paused, looked keenly at her, and went on, "Oh, so that's it. You are here for breeding purposes, in case the young monster dies. Is that it?"

" 'Tis none of your business how many children your brother and I have," Cassandra said, and then she asked, "Did his first Countess bring a large estate with her dowry?"

The laughter came again, making Cassandra cringe.

"Her outstanding beauty was her dowry. My brother lost his head over her. He was totally besotted. She married him for his title . . . and his wealth. Her passion was for me."

So that is why Lord Ranleigh bears such hatred for you.

Cassandra asked, "Does he know that Jacob is your son?"

Obviously nonplussed, Wade said, "I apprised him of the fact after her death, but he would have none of it. He would never believe his precious Countess unfaithful."

Wade's words hurt, and Cassandra did not know why they should. Already she knew of her husband's devotion to his first Countess. She looked at Wade and saw the same evil lurking behind his blue eyes, the same ominous force that had been there when first she met him on the hillock. The tight darkness of fear crept over her, and she began thinking of a way to get away from him without letting him know she was frightened.

She couldn't think. She needed to get away and think.

"I envy Brother. You are as beautiful as Sylvia, but in a different way." A pause, and then, "Those gray eyes could undo any red-blooded man. That leaves out Lord Ranleigh. He's too levelheaded to feel passion. I so hope that we might be friends." He reached out and touched her arm, then ran a warm palm down to her hand.

Shuddering, she slapped at his hand. "Being friends does not give you the privilege of touching me. I am your brother's wife."

"That didn't stop his first Countess. She was wild for me."

They were standing on a narrow outcropping of flat rocks. Below, the surf roiled white in a steady roar. Should he push her, the fall would not kill her, but it would harm her baby.

For a moment Cassandra contemplated asking Wade about the poison to see his reaction but thought better of it. She must stick to her plan. She quickly changed the subject. "I am looking for Cynthia. Have you seen her?"

"No, and I think you should turn around and go in the other direction. She never comes near my landing dock. It is off limits to anyone except myself. That's one concession big brother granted to his unworthy sibling. I have it posted."

Why?

But Cassandra did not ask. Instead, she said, " 'Tis not important that I find Cynthia. I think I shall cut through the woods and return to the Hall." As nonchalantly as possible, she bade him good day and moved away, walking slowly until she reached the protection of the woods, breathing a huge sigh of relief to be out of his presence, and out of his sight.

Her intention was not to return to the manor; it was more important than ever that she talk with Cynthia. She walked on, in the same direction she had been going when she met Wade. The roar of the sea was to her right. Thinking that Wade might be following her, she looked back over her shoulder, listening for footsteps. When she felt safe she called softly, "Cynthia, Cynthia," and was surprised to hear Cynthia answering through the trees, "Cassandra, I'm over here."

Cassandra went in the direction of the voice and saw

Cynthia near the edge of the woods, easel and paints in close proximity. Her arms were behind her back, the palms of her hands pillowing her hair. She turned her head and smiled as Cassandra approached.

"Did you grow tired of painting?" Cassandra asked. She looked at the partially finished painting of the sea flowing inland, into a cove hidden by overlapping trees growing on each side. A small boat, holding a man paddling with huge oars, was headed into the cove. The man and boat were so small that Cassandra had to look twice to see that the boat was loaded with cargo.

Cynthia sat up. "I didn't grow tired. I saw Wade walking along the shore and became distracted."

"Did he see you?"

"He waved but did not come by to talk. He's very distant."

He's also a liar, thought Cassandra. So anxious was she to speak with her sister-in-law about the poison she had found in Jacob's old rooms, she plunged right in. "Cynthia, I must speak with you in confidence."

Cynthia laughed. "Half the fun in knowing secrets is keeping them and knowing that you are privy to information others just guess about. So I promise to keep your secret." She patted the ground next to her. "Please sit. You look distraught."

"I am distraught." Cassandra sat, not caring if the ground stained her new gown. "I went to Jacob's old rooms and found a vial of arsenic hidden under a loose board. When I first came to Ranleigh Hall I suspected— and I don't know exactly why—that Cook was trying to do harm to Jacob. Now I believe that each day she was putting a minuscule amount of the poison in his food. Why would she want to harm a little boy?"

Cynthia was silent for a long while.

Cassandra began to feel foolish. All around her birds flitted from tree to tree, calling to one another, while crickets chirped and an owl hooted.

At last Cynthia spoke: "Do you remember my saying that you would learn Ranleigh's secrets on your own?"

"Yes . . . yes, but what does that have to do with someone trying to poison Jacob? Is that a secret you knew about? If so, Cynthia, it's time you confide in me."

"I did not know, but I believe it possible that Wade would do such a thing, or have it done. Who would inherit Ranleigh Hall, the title, the entailed estates, if Jacob should die?"

"Not Cook."

"Don't be a pea goose, Cassandra. If Cook was trying to harm Jacob, it was in conspiracy with Wade. And mayhap Isabelle. She hates the child."

"Oh, dear merciful God," Cassandra said, shivering, thinking that if they knew she was *enceinte,* that mayhap another heir would be born, her life and the life of her child would be in danger. "Pray tell me what you know, Cynthia."

"Arsenic killed Sylvia—"

"What? Who—"

"No one. She did it to herself. She was so in love with her beauty. People, most especially men, would comment on her beautiful white skin, and she would beam and smile with pleasure and fling that auburn hair back over her shoulder. Well, when she was too sick to live, she admitted to mixing arsenic with the powder she used on her face and her arms and shoulders, even her bosom, which was always showing. When it had penetrated her system she said, 'I never dreamed I was using enough to harm me.' Her beautiful green eyes sank back into her head, and she lost all that auburn hair. It was when she was dying that the servants began to worship her, and that was true about Mummy, too. Death did, ironically, bring the Countess the adoration she craved."

Cassandra was speechless with the enormity of what they were discussing.

Cynthia said, "Most likely the leftover arsenic was used to kill rats, which probably gnawed their way through the roof."

Cassandra wanted to believe that.

Cynthia jumped up. "Come on; I want to show you what I was painting. 'Tis no good trying to keep secrets from you, and besides, I quite enjoy talking with you about things."

"What are you saying, Cynthia?"

"Come and see my latest discovery."

Cassandra followed her, and soon she recognized the scene Cynthia had been painting: a cove sweeping back into the woods, except there was no loaded boat and man.

"The man in the boat is Wade, the cargo is barrels of rum from France," Cynthia said.

"Cynthia! You are funning. Wade is not a rumrunner."

"And why not? If he can conspire to kill his own child, if he can take his own brother's wife, he can be a rumrunner and think nothing of it. Wade enjoys living on the edge."

"He spoke of having the place posted. Should we go—"

"Definitely. I would have never learned Ranleigh's secrets had I been fainthearted." She stopped to giggle. "I even watched him making love to Sylvia. They had a special place—"

Cassandra said, panting, "Cynthia, I must stop for a minute. I'm out of breath."

Cynthia turned around and gave Cassandra a quizzical look. "You're not *enceinte*, are you."

Cassandra started laughing. Could nothing be kept from the gel? But she didn't care. She was ready to share her secret. "I'll tell you if you will promise not to tell anyone else."

"You've already told me," Cynthia said, squealing and jumping up and down and hugging Cassandra, reminiscent of her reaction to the new wardrobe Cassandra had brought from London.

"I think it's absolutely wonderful—"

"Promise you won't tell," Cassandra pleaded.

"Why not shout it from the top of Ranleigh Hall? Tell the world that Lord Ranleigh is to be a father, that his new Countess is *enceinte*?"

"That would not do, pea goose. Think of the consequences, Cynthia. If Wade could conspire to kill Jacob, his own son—though we do not know that for sure—he could conspire to do away with the tree that is to bear new fruit. Another heir would put him farther from the title and all the wealth that goes with it."

Cynthia was pensive. She put a protective arm around Cassandra and they walked on. "Mayhap we should turn back."

"What were you going to show me?"

"A cave at the end of the cove where Wade hides his rum."

"Do you think Lord Ranleigh knows?"

"Definitely not. He would call the officials. Illegal rum on Ranleigh land! Never, never, never . . ."

They turned back. Cassandra did not want to chance another encounter with Wade, most especially when she was viewing his contraband rum. They were soon back to where they had started, at Cynthia's painting place.

"No, you cannot carry the easel," Cynthia said when Cassandra offered to do so. "We must needs consider your condition."

Cassandra laughed. "I am not an invalid. Women have babies all the time."

"But this one is special, and I intend to take care of you."

Cassandra knew there was no point in arguing, so they walked back to the Hall in companionable silence. Her own thoughts ran deep. She wondered whether to tell Lord Ranleigh what she had learned about his hated brother.

For certain, she would not tell her husband about the baby, lest he think she was trying to again be his wife, and not in name only.

Twenty-seven

Cassandra did not know when Lord Ranleigh would return. Her morning sickness came often. With the retching, she could not keep her pregnancy from Dora, but when she asked the maid's help in guarding her secret, she vowed her loyalty, and Cassandra believed her. Dora brought her food and locked the doors when Cassandra was being sick.

When she felt well she often asked Jacob to join her, or she would go to his quarters to eat with him and Mrs. Brodwick. They took long walks and ate picnic lunches in the woods and romped with King Arthur. Always she asked Mrs. Brodwick to accompany them in case Wade tried to do them harm. For protection, she carried a small boot pistol she had found in Lord Ranleigh's bedchamber.

Jacob's riding lessons were going well, and again Cassandra kept a close watch, going riding with him and his instructor, never far away, her eyes alert.

Reading and ciphering had been resumed with a new tutor, with the understanding that the tutor, not Jacob, was in charge.

Outwardly, it was the perfect household, thought Cassandra, but she was lonely for Lord Ranleigh. She needed his presence, and she could not explain why.

She missed their evening chats and found herself thinking of something new she had read in the *Gazette*, or the *Times* that she wanted to share with him. This loneliness was there inside her, a constant thing, even though she had told him she would no longer be available to him when he wanted to coze. Her temper had gotten the better of her.

No, not her temper, she thought; the words had been driven from her mouth by the pain in her heart.

One day a missive came from Sister Martha, asking that Cassandra come to see her. Gathering Jacob up, together they hitched a horse—so that Jacob would have the experience—to the black Tilbury and off they went, King Arthur sitting on Jacob's lap, Mrs. Brodwick squeezed in beside him.

Passing over Cassandra's hillock, the woods were full of twittering birds, and Jacob said, "Look, Stepmother, at the beautiful bluebells."

They arrived at the orphanage before noon.

Cassandra knew immediately that the news from Sister Martha was happy. The moment they were seated in the small parlor, Tim having taken charge of Jacob and King Arthur and Mrs. Brodwick going to visit with Cook, Sister Martha proudly produced a letter from Ellen. "She sends you her regards, Cassie. Married to a fine Frenchman, she is, and I guess there could be no better news."

Cassandra took the letter and read it and smiled at Sister Martha. "Well, you did a fine job with the rebellious gel." And then she laughingly added, "I'll wager that Frenchman will have his hands full."

"Most likely so," said Sister Martha.

After that, they talked of other things, until at last Cassandra told her about the baby she was expecting. "The way I count it, she will come in February, most likely on Valentine's Day."

"A very special valentine," Sister Martha said, her

faded eyes damp with tears. She hugged Cassandra and told her how happy she was. "I knew I was right; I knew you would win the hard man with your loving ways. Do you think he will want a girl or another heir?"

Cassandra said quickly, "He has an heir, so I'm sure a girl will be just fine with him."

She could only pray that this was so.

"Well, I have some more good news," Sister Martha said. "When your husband was on his way to one of his other properties he stopped by to tell me that he had visited the draper shop in Wickham Market, where he opened an account for the orphanage and asked that the bills be sent to him. I almost fainted. No longer will my little gels go to church with pieced dresses, or without shoes that fit. I am to take the boys shopping at Mayberry's for their clothing . . . I'm sure you saw the repairs to the house. Well, Ranleigh men did them, and even built a new porch.

"And by the by, he told Miss Stella at the draper's shop that his wife, the former Cassandra Edwards from Sister Martha's orphanage, was to be given *carte blanche* for anything her heart desired.

"He didn't," said Cassandra.

"Oh, but he did. He told her she could give the ten yards of silk to me for my church dresses, that you no longer needed it." She stopped to laugh. "The haughty gel's eyes almost bulged out of her head, so His Lordship said."

She looked lovingly at Cassandra and said again, "I knew my Cassie's loving ways would win the hard man."

Cassandra did not have the heart to tell Sister Martha that she had *not* won the hard man. That was one secret she would never share. Nor did she tell the good Sister about someone trying to poison Jacob, or about the mean, conniving ways of Wade Ranleigh.

No, the good Sister deserved to be as happy as she

was at this moment, and Cassandra prayed that the happiness would last forever.

It was a bright sunny day when Lord Ranleigh returned to Ranleigh Hall. Cassandra had risen early; for once her stomach did not feel queazy and she ate the breakfast that Dora brought as if she was famished. She had begun a one-sided dialogue with her baby, telling it how much she loved her, or him, and that she did not care if *it* meant boy or girl. "But please be healthy," she said, patting her stomach.

Now, Cassandra, wearing a soft pink morning dress, was in the crimson room, feeling elegant indeed. Shafts of golden sunlight slanted across the colorful carpet; gray shadows danced on the walls. Through the open windows came the sound of waves pounding the rocky shore, and the scent of fresh air, clean and sweet.

Settled into one of the crimson chairs, she wrote in her diary, something she had done daily since returning to Ranleigh Hall. It was her sounding board and helped relieve the ache in her heart for Lord Ranleigh. She wrote about the baby, and about His Lordship, and about Jacob.

After closing the diary and placing it between her thigh and the chair cushion, she picked up a tiny white baby bonnet she had sewed yesterday and started embroidering butterflies and flowers and minuscule hummingbirds on its band. She heard footsteps, and then the creaking of the big doors opening. When she looked up her eyes were looking straight into her husband's handsome face. He was smiling, and Cassandra was so happy to see the smile. Too often he was grim, or solemn, or sad, and she must not forget angry. He was always angry.

For a moment she thought he would come to her, mayhap reach out and touch her by way of greeting.

306

but he stopped short of that and said, almost whispering, "Cassandra."

Hurriedly and stealthily, Cassandra wadded up the little bonnet and pushed it under her thigh with the diary; then, bringing her hands to rest demurely in her lap, she greeted him with, "Welcome home, Your Lordship." She looked him over.

He wore casual clothes: no cravat, no high collar points. His breeches hugged him tightly, showing his muscular legs. She sucked in her breath and dropped her gaze to her hands.

"Have you been all right since I left, Cassandra?" Lord Ranleigh asked. "I did not mean to stay so long, but details detained me." His voice grew anxious. "Was Wade bothersome? Did the dowager—"

Cassandra gave a little laugh. "No. Neither bothered me. I encountered Wade only once. It was not pleasant, and I avoided him after that."

"And Jacob?"

"He's more than fine, and so is King Arthur. I believe the dog has had a great healing power on Jacob. Thank you for getting it for him."

" 'Twas my pleasure," Lord Ranleigh said.

He was still standing, looking down at her with questioning eyes. It made her uncomfortable. She asked, "Did you want to address a certain subject, Your Lordship? I have some things—"

"Yes, yes," he said, as if returning from a trance. He went to sit on one of the deep crimson chairs and said no more. She studied his countenance and thought that he looked embarrassed. "What is it, m'lord?"

"I have made arrangements for Wade and the dowager to live away from Ranleigh Hall. That was my mission when I left here. My grandmother left me a large estate in Shropshire that is quite productive. It is not entailed, and I have deeded it over to Wade and Isabelle, with an adequate income for the dowager. I would not expect her to live in lesser style than she has done here at Ranleigh Hall. I cannot live under the same roof with the scoundrel, and you should not be subjected to Isabelle's histrionics."

Relief washed over Cassandra. "But Lord Ranleigh, my feelings should not be considered. I am here to watch over Jacob."

"You are here for more than that, Cassandra." A long pause, and then a deep breath. "I have fallen hopelessly in love with you. I can no longer deny my feelings."

She scoffed. "Do not mistake lust for love, and don't play games with me. Mayhap you should return to London to see Elsa."

"I know the difference between the two emotions of which you speak. You've taught me." His voice was firm and fierce.

So typical of him, Cassandra thought.

A silence fell upon the room, and she felt a shudder dance up and down her spine. She wanted to speak and couldn't, for she did not know what to say. Surely His Lordship could not be saying that he had stopped loving his late Countess. She looked up at the faded place over the mantel where her gorgeous likeness used to hang.

And then, in utter incredulity, she heard him saying, "What I felt for Sylvia was unadulterated passion, which I, at one time, mistakenly called love. I thought she was so beautiful, so alive in her flirtatious way, until everything turned to hatred inside me."

"How so? I can't believe this. I thought—"

"I knew what you thought; I let you go right on thinking that I loved her so much that I could not love you. That was never true, and I confessed as much to my valet when I found myself so desperately wanting to tell someone the whole of it. I should have been telling you. I kept her portraits to remind me to never love again, should I be tempted. And then you brazenly re-

308

moved them. Still, there was one in the great Hall. I looked at it every day, and remembered."

Cassandra had no words. She wanted to hear the whole of it, and finally it came. Lord Ranleigh said in his straightforward way, "I love you, Cassandra. I did not want to love you; I did not want to love anyone. My heart was too full of bitterness. I was a fool. I wasted precious time . . ."

A silent sob caught in Cassandra's throat, and familiar tears clouded her eyes. This could not be happening.

His Lordship gave a little smile, and went on. "I thought I was safe with a gel from the orphanage. I would have the best of two worlds: a nursemaid for Jacob, an erudite companion for myself . . . without emotional involvement."

As if he had run out of breath or he had said it all, he stopped, and Cassandra sat trying to understand. It was not easy to turn her thinking so easily. At last she asked, "What made you hate her? What did she do?"

"She gave birth to my brother's child."

Cassandra sat forward. "You *know* that Jacob is not your son, yet, you claim him for your heir?"

"I needed an heir. Even though I had not been in Sylvia's bed for ten months, I claimed Jacob as my heir, but not as my son, not in my heart. I almost hated him because of what he reminded me of. I'm terribly ashamed of that now. But I would never let Ranleigh lands fall into Wade's hands. I was desperate to save the boy when I wrote to Sister Martha for help."

He leaned back and stretched his long legs out in front of him. "Sister Martha did not know the whole of it, but I did tell her I wanted a wife in name only, that I needed a nurse for Jacob who would not leave. She failed to inform you . . ."

It all became clear to Cassandra, and she scolded, "You wanted someone to love Jacob; yet, your own hatred spilled over onto the innocent little boy. Because

309

of what his mother had done! I'm ashamed of you. You should be horsewhipped."

"I'm afraid 'tis so. I'm terribly ashamed of myself, and I am ever so grateful to you for showing me what love can do—that it can heal one's soul." A long pause, and then, "I'm speaking of my soul, Cassandra."

As if he could not bear the distance between them a moment longer, Lord Ranleigh was instantly on his knees beside Cassandra's chair. He took her hand and kissed the palm. "I will not blame you if you never forgive me, but I truly do love you, Countess."

"When did you start?" she asked pragmatically. She wanted to know if her baby had been conceived *before* he had started loving her, or if lust was his purpose for their first coupling. There was no question that she had loved him on their wedding night, and long before that.

Cassandra's question brought laughter from Lord Ranleigh. He answered with alacrity. "When you made me take you to the church so that our vows could be blessed by God."

He lifted her hand to his lips again, kissing it not once but thrice, while looking at her with adoration, and then he began rubbing her arm with slow, tender strokes. There was gentleness in his smile, and passion in his dark eyes.

Cassandra could not stand that. Her body had a way of betraying her. "Lord Ranleigh, if you will return to your chair, there are some things I wish to tell you."

Lord Ranleigh did as he was asked, though reluctantly, and she told him then about her belief that Cook was poisoning Jacob with the arsenic left from Sylvia's beauty treatment, mayhap in a conspiracy between the servant and Wade. "I am so convinced of this that I have started going with him everywhere, carrying the small boot pistol I found in your bedchamber."

"The devil take me," said Lord Ranleigh. "You would not shoot—"

"To protect Jacob I would."

Cassandra started to tell him about Wade's rumrunning but thought better of it. There would be a terrible confrontation, and mayhap one brother would kill the other. Wade would soon be leaving Ranleigh Hall, so let the officials deal with him. No one could do wrong forever and not get caught.

Cassandra told her husband everything else, except that she was *enceinte*. That could wait until the shock of his declaring his love for her had worn off. Surely he must be funning . . .

Lord Ranleigh spoke. "Of course, we cannot prove that what you believe about Cook and Wade are true, but Cook will leave the employ of Ranleigh Hall without references."

His eyes were on her; the steady, questioning gaze burned the space between them. His anxiety was evident, and when the ambience in the room grew heavy, she, feeling empathy for him, began to speak of the deep love she held for him, getting no more than two words out of her mouth when the door burst open and Jacob came running in, grabbing Lord Ranleigh's leg. "Papa, Papa, I'm so glad you are home. But I wanted my new Stepmother to come see what I have just drawn. You can come, too, Papa, now that you're here."

Lord Ranleigh patted the boy on the head, gave him a smile, and said, "Later, Jacob. As you said, I have just returned home and I have business with Wade and the dowager, and with Cook."

He stood and looked at Cassandra, as if waiting for assurance that he had not spoken of his love for her in vain, that he would not be forced to endure the familiar pain of rejection once again.

To her, it was a reprieve. Her heartbeat was thudding

311

in her ears. She said, "Your Lordship, when you are finished pray return. I will have an answer for you."

And then, getting up from her chair, she went with Jacob to his quarters, leaving her diary and the tiny baby bonnet behind on her chair.

Returning from viewing Jacob's artwork, of which Cynthia was his instructor, Cassandra rang for Dora, tugging the bellpull so hard that the bell could be heard clanging all the way down the hall.

"What is it, m'lady?" Dora asked, pushing the door open as she spoke. "Are you sick again? That baby—"

"No, Cassandra, I'm not sick again. I shall never be sick again, or unhappy, or sad, or doubtful. The world truly is a wonderful place." She was darting about, starting her toilette as if the house were on fire and she only had a moment to escape. Off came the pink morning dress, and she stood there in her pantalettes, wearing her pink slippers from Dever's. Bending over, she removed them.

Dora stood with her hands on her hips. "Tell me—"

"Lord Ranleigh loves me. He said so."

"Well, I think he should, being married to you and all."

"Oh, but you don't understand. He did not love me when . . ."

She stopped there, for it would take too long to explain to the gel, whose broad face was awash with disbelief. "I will tell you later, Dora. I'm much too busy now. Lord Ranleigh will return directly, and I must needs be ready."

"Ready for what? You looked perfectly all right in the lovely pink dress."

" 'Twas not striking enough." Cassandra went to the chiffonnier and pulled out the dress made of cranberry silk, the one from which Lord Ranleigh had ripped the buttons. Meticulously, and secretly, she had mended the fabric and reattached the buttons. She had offered to return it to Cynthia, but the generous gel had refused. Examining it now, Cassandra could not see the mending and was pleased. Dora took it and held it up for her to put it on.

"No," Cassandra said. "I must needs wash and use lavender water."

"But m'lady, you washed not two hours past."

"I want to wash again. Now, make haste and help me, or shall I call Mrs. Brodwick away from Jacob?"

Cassandra was laughing. She told Dora to go to the other room until she called her, and when she was alone she stripped naked and scrubbed as if she had been weeding the garden all morning long. She splashed herself with lavender water, savoring the memory of *that* other time. "But his Lordship would not . . . not in day's light."

She knew that he would, should the mood strike him.

Soon Dora was back in the room, dressing Cassandra's hair. When she began to braid it, Cassandra stayed her with her hand. "No, no, leave it loose."

"M'lady, I thought he liked your hair to crown your head."

"Only at times," Cassandra said.

So the maid brushed her tawny-blond hair until it shone like soft sunshine, then put a pinch of rouge to Cassandra's already bright cheeks and gloss on her lips. Standing back, she admired her handiwork with enthusiasm. "I've never seen you look so grand, Countess Ranleigh. Any man would have windmills in his attic not to love you."

Cassandra became pensive. "He said that he did."

"Well, believe him, and that's the best advice I can give you." Dora made for the door in a rustle of black bombazine. With her hand on the knob, she turned back and smiled at Cassandra. "I can't wait to hear the whole of it."

Cassandra laughed and promised that she would indeed tell the maid *why* she had been brought to Ranleigh Hall, under the guise of being the Countess of Ranleigh. With that, the maid left and Cassandra was alone. She went into the withdrawing room between hers and His Lordship's bedchambers and looked at the gilt clock on the mantel. Lord Ranleigh had been gone less than an hour, and heaven only knew when he would return. But she was willing to wait. She had waited a long time to say the words, "I love you, my husband."

And she wanted to hear again his glorious declaration of his love for her, so that it could sink into her heart, her soul, her mind. The anticipation was overpowering.

She went to sit in a chair flanking the fireplace, in which cold, dead coals lay. The room was deathly still, making the beating of her heart loud in the silence. With a trembling hand she reached to straighten her skirt. She felt a young gel waiting for her suitor, not a woman waiting for her husband.

Her thoughts turned to the baby she carried within her. She wanted to share the wonderful news with His Lordship but felt apprehensive. What if he immediately denied Jacob the right to inherit, saying that his *own* son was entitled to Ranleigh Hall? She could not forebear it. She told herself that it was not worth thinking on and cast it from her mind. She heard footsteps, determined, purposeful, and then the door opened and he stood there.

She stood and watched his eyes move over her, a smile on his face instead of a frown, his dark eyes alight and sparkling. It was a beautiful but serious face, she thought as she returned his smile, and when he opened his arms, she swept into them with no hesitation. She was home at last.

He held her tight against him, though very gently,

and it was with gentleness that he kissed her at first, and then the kiss became deeper, his arms stronger around her until they were molded together as one. She could feel his heart beating against hers. Heat from his body permeated her own, bringing familiar desire. He lifted his head and looked into her face. "Is this your answer, Countess? Do you forgive me for all my transgressions, even Elsa? Pray do, for I love you with all my heart."

"Yes, yes," she said, her voice barely above a whisper. "If you will promise to never, never seek out a courtesan again."

This brought a little laugh. "I promise. If my plan works, Ranleigh children will be running all over the Hall, most likely like Jacob, bounding into our quarters at the most inopportune times. Does that appeal to you, Countess?"

Now was the time, Cassandra knew. So, standing in his embrace, she told him that a Ranleigh was already on its way.

He looked at her, incredulous. "Our wedding night?"

"Yes, our wedding night. That is why I asked you *when* you began loving me. I wanted our child to be born out of love, not for the convenience of producing an heir." And then she was quick to add, "Ranleigh already has an heir."

"Yes, Jacob will always be the first born. He is my heir. Nothing will change that."

"Then we have no problems left to solve," Cassandra said, relief washing over her.

"Oh, but there is one other thing—" He reached into his impeccably tailored coat pocket and pulled out the pieces of Cassandra's precious valentine that she had drawn on the hillock.

"Will you help me put this back together? Make it whole?"

"Where did you—"

"Out of the diary you left in the chair. I did not read your diary, I swear, but I did pick it up, and these pieces scattered onto the floor. It seemed to be a drawing of Ranleigh Hall enclosed in lace. I also saw the sweet baby bonnet. I thought you were making it for the wife of one of the tenants who was *enceinte.*"

Cassandra told him the story of the valentine. "It was spring," she said, "and Valentine's Day was long past. So I planned to have it for next year. A valentine to myself." In a very quiet voice, she added, "I guess I never really gave up hope of your loving me, or I would not have kept the pieces."

He held her and kissed her, and she was in a dizzy mood of happiness. It seemed that she was in the center of a rainbow, with glorious reds and blues and yellows wrapping around her like a mantle, as together they sat on the floor and placed the pieces together, making it whole again, each line of the meticulously drawn lace meeting exactly.

Lord Ranleigh said, "We'll keep it forever, and each year on Valentine's Day, we will take it out and remember how very fragile love can be." His voice was choked and raspy as he went on, "Later, we will paste it, but not now."

"I love you, my husband," Cassandra said, and he picked her up in his strong arms, his purposeful stride taking them to the door to his bedchamber.

"Lord Ranleigh, we can't. 'Tis still light."

He laughed, a sweet, melodious sound to Cassandra's ears, and then he said, "We'll do it again tonight."

Cassandra snuggled her face against his warm neck and felt the pounding of his heart. Her own heart was absolutely out of control. She had no doubt that again the buttons would be ripped from the beautiful cranberry silk gown, and she had no doubt that they would be together when next year's valentine was long past yellowed with age.

Epilogue

Jacob lived five more years. When Cassandra confronted Dr. Morton, he told her that it was inevitable, that Jacob had been born with a weakness in his lungs. "Had I told you," he said, "you could not have enjoyed the time he had left, which went beyond the seven year life expectancy of the disease by three years." Looking at her fondly, he added, "Your love gave him that extra time."

The officials did not punish Wade for his rum-running. Fate did. A huge storm took his ship down, with Wade at the bow.

Isabelle, the Dowager Countess, reigned supreme over the estate in Shropshire. She never returned to Ranleigh Hall.

Time passed—happy years and fruitful. Three children were born to Lord and Countess Ranleigh: daughter, son, daughter, in that order; but Jacob was the first born, the Ranleigh heir, until the day he died.

Cassandra's precious valentine turned yellow, and became brittle; yet it never lost its place beside the bed shared by His Lordship and his Countess. Enclosed in a silver frame, under protective glass, the valentine became a symbol of their life, torn apart by past hurts, then put back together by love.

About the Author

Irene Loyd Black was born in Scottsboro, Alabama, and moved with her family to Oklahoma when she was five years old. She wrote her first play when she was eight, which she produced on the front lawn of her family's farm with the help of her brothers and sisters. Playing the Queen of England, Irene used her mother's sheet-covered chairs to make the throne, picked roses from the rose garden, and twined them together to make the crown.

An avid reader and history buff, she has traveled to England five times. Two of her books have made the Waldenbooks bestseller list. Irene lives in Oklahoma City with her husband, James Deatherage.